Welcome to Terragard!

WORLD OF TERRAGARD™
BOOK ONE

BY

D.S. TIERNEY

Cover Illustration by Raymond Minnaar
www.raymondminnaar.com

Terragard Map by Daniel Hasenbos
www.danielsmaps.com

Editing by Drew Tierney
Additional Editing by Adam Baulderstone

Dark Ages by D.S. Tierney
www.dstierney.com

ISBN: 978-0-578-58396-9

terragardtales@dstierney.com

For Robyn:
Of all the worlds I dream,
There is none better than the one I share with you.

Special Thanks to The Mechanics:
Jay, Ryan, Sanjay, Mike, Genevieve, Wayne and Chris

Note From the Author

How to Read The World of Terragard

Each novel in the World of Terragard series is written as a standalone story that you can pick up and read in any order. While there are crumbs and connective tissues sprinkled through each narrative, it is my goal that your enjoyment of this book only be deepened by, without relying on, events in other stories.

My suggested reading order is the order in which they were published, as denoted by the book numbering. Feel free to ignore this, as it is, after all, just a suggestion.

Thank you for joining me on this adventure, and the many more to come!

Cheers!
D.S. Tierney

Terragard
Ice Fields
The Papality
Upper Anghor
Tandana
Baltrude
Taryn
Greater Anghor
Dire Lands
Cattachat
Krypholos Ocean
Farelan Wood
Sentent Sea
Bar Church
Thousand Rivers
The Frontier
The Pipers
Gorsha
Empire of the Dhogs
Incursion Zone
Trindian Island
Thump
Crown of the Seven Kingdoms
Golganna
Krau Plains
The Tare
Soren'sa
The Keeps
Temen'sa
Rhysin
Last Zorn
Salaz
Orrish Isles
Parthia
Sangantide
The Sandy Kingdoms

It is understood that there have been three Dark Ages.

The first when the moon Nacinth shattered - rendering the world a wasteland. Birthing new races and lands, the world was rebuilt over a thousand years of turmoil.

The next when the Pale Lyzan King reigned and commanded scores of dragons to raze the cities of man. Even now, the Lyzan hold to a prophecy that their great Pale King will be reborn.

The final Dark Age...when Zorn conquered the world, he sought to bring unity and enlightenment through the sword. When he died, the false peace shattered, and the nations tore themselves apart.

I fear another such Dark Age would be the end of Terragard.

- Wizen Marliveaux, Magicai of the First Order
Annum 1347

1

"A poor thief is a poor thief."

- Blue Fingered Hobbe

Upper Anghor, Annum 1352

Grint wasn't a hero. It wasn't a concept he dwelled upon as he pulled his coat's thick, leather collar against the chill biting the back of his ears. Heroes did brain-addled things like saving people or going on long-winded quests. And their motives were always thick with steaming piles of altruism. That wasn't Grint. He was a thief, an exceptional one if you asked him, and a taker who enjoyed stealing coin as much as spending it. If he could just get the butterflies out of his gut, tonight would be a marvelous night for larceny.

Grint leaned against the inn's window. The splintered wood framing creaked against his weight as he wiped a sleeve across glass tarnished with soot. Firelight burned within, sliding its warm light across a face described as both rugged and handsome with a youthful appearance that dared one to guess his age. With a free hand, he rustled a mane of shaggy, red hair and scratched the stubble of a beard that never quite grew no matter how long he went between shaves.

"Wolves are active tonight," an old man said as he walked past. His torch flickered in the wind as he peered into the dark woods, listening.

"They sound scared," Grint said. Their yelps had been echoing through the trees since he stepped outside.

"Ayup," the old man said, still looking into the dark. "There're outhouses behind the inn. This is a respectable town."

"Ayup," Grint replied. Aping the old man's accent was an instinctual response, a bit of cheek that flavored most of how Grint interacted with the world. The old crow deserved it. He wasn't relieving himself. He came out hoping the mountain air would quell the thieves' gut and let him get back to his business. Hobbe always said he didn't care how good a thief someone was, they all got the thieves' gut. That was true to a point, but Grint was sure it was worse for him.

Besides, the spot gave him a good view of the card game he stepped out on. It was unusual to get up in the middle of a hand, but Grint needed the air and losing a few hands would help with appearances. Maybe one of them would slip up and peek at his cards. It wouldn't matter if they did. The first part of the job required them to accuse Grint of cheating. But ferreting out someone's proclivities was a great way to survive another day.

"Are you one of the logging boys?" the old man asked, satisfied that the wolves weren't coming into town to eat their livestock. There was a downturn to the man's mouth that Grint didn't appreciate. Was it a permanent feature or directed at him?

Kambar was one of a dozen small hamlets along the mountains of Upper Anghor. The fifty-odd families who lived here were self-sufficient and traded among themselves, seldom seeing anyone from the capital. As remote as they were, the towns maintained a few establishments for the logging companies that worked the steel oak forests saturating the mountain slopes. The loggers were under contract by Duchess Aerienne to farm the towering oaks which could rise as tall as two hundred feet. The trade of steel oak kept Upper Anghor independent from Greater Anghor to the south, but such political motivations were uninteresting to Grint. What intrigued him was the coin the loggers earned each month when they met their quotas.

"Have a good night," Grint ignored the question as he stepped onto the porch that ran along the front of the nameless inn. Two loose chains hung from the eaves and swayed in the breeze. The discarded sign, splintered and worn clean, leaned beneath a window. Grint hadn't bothered to inquire further to the name, knowing it would be an infuriating play on words: The Oak-Inn Shield or the Kambar Mount-Inn. *Blind madness*, he thought.

A small flame sparked to life, illuminating a thin man of a sallow complexion wearing a black, woolen arming cap. The suddenness of it made Grint flinch, pulling him from his thoughts.

"The Mother Moon is full," puffs of smoke rose from the pipe as the stranger spoke.

"Uh, and the night is...dark," Grint responded with a shrug. A disapproving clucking sound followed Grint through the doorway.

The tavern offered a warm embrace, most welcomed after the autumn chill. Embers danced from shifting logs within the dominating stone hearth. Dark flagstone walls, chipped from years of wear, cast odd shadows from the flicker of candles set in pockets. The rafters shook as a trio of musicians played a tune about a farmer becoming a king. Loggers and townsfolk alike laughed and clapped along, stomping their feet in appreciation. The smell of roasting chicken, ale and sweat sat thick upon the air. Grint smiled. Backwater, filthy taverns made him feel alive.

By the end of the night, I'll have every coin in this room. The queasy feeling faded as he imagined a pile of gold cupped in his hands. Thieves' gut was no match for succulent gold and savory silver. He'd spend that money or gamble it away because there was always another job. Marm always had interesting contracts if he meandered over to Tan Tan. Or the Barlabee Brothers down in Dook. *No chains on my ankles,* Grint sang in his head to the tune the band played.

"Another ale?" the svelte serving girl shouted over the noise.

Grint nodded, trying to recall her name. The buzz from a half-dozen ales made mundane details slippery, but Grint wasn't here to make friends. Not with the business planned. *Another ale can't hurt,* he thought as he cut his way through the crowd. The room was bursting with patrons, ten to twelve to a table, except for the solitary table in the back corner where a woman being called 'cold' and 'best not to bother' sat. She watched the room over steepled fingers and a flagon of wine. Her appraising stare focused on the card game, and that was what unnerved Grint. Was she a thief catcher? An adventurer on some Kry-damned quest? When the fighting started - and it would, that was how it always played out - would she join in?

The tavern's owner, Nigel, an aging man of medium build sat in front of the bar chatting with the logging captains as they drank flat ale from chipped, wooden tankards. Behind the bar was an array of shelves lined with cups, bowls, mugs, hunting trophies and an ugly, twelve-inch-tall statue of what appeared to be a woman with a triangular head and four snaking arms. What the artist wanted to convey eluded Grint, but he appreciated that it was carved it from jade.

"Took you long enough," Toothless said as Grint sat down at the table littered with coin, cards, dice, and mugs of ale. A fat brown cat curled around one of the table's legs, waiting for any mice daring enough to come sniffing around for crumbs swept off the table. The game was a popular variation of Fiddler's Fair called Cheat Me, and they had been at it for several hours.

"I was trying to give you a chance to steal back the coin I've fleeced you for," Grint answered with a winning smile. Elti, the only woman at the table, threw back her head with laughter. She had been reticent to say much about herself but had the look of a south sea pirate with cooked skin, tattoos, and a swath of shaved scalp on the right.

"You raised seven silvers while outside," Black Samuel sneered as he licked his lips. The fat-fingered oaf sat across from Grint, a pair of cards mashed against his mud-stained vest. Yet this slovenly appearance, with greasy, unkempt hair and bits of cheese tangled within his dark beard was purposeful. The stains were even and brushed on. The crumbs were impossible; Black Samuel hadn't touched a bite of cheese all day. That ill-temper he radiated was quite real, so Grint kept quips about a passing relationship with soap to himself.

Grint peeled up the corners of his dog-eared cards and looked at the three and seven cards in his hand. "Seven silvers, you say? That was very generous of me. Why don't we make it twenty though?"

As Grint shoved the small stack of silver coins into the pot, the priest beside Black Samuel whistled and folded his cards. "No faith, Valun?" Toothless asked.

"I have faith in wine," Valun said. The priest was a follower of Petra, Goddess of Harvests, a broad definition that included the harvest of wood. Valun had been traveling with the loggers, blessing their camp. Typical priests of Petra were drunkards who found worship at the bottom of a cup. Valun did not contradict the stereotype.

"If you want me to think you have twenty-four points in your hand, you're a pitiful liar," Black Samuel said, pointing a meaty finger at Grint.

"Why do they call you Black Samuel?" Grint asked before draining the last dregs from his mug. "Or did you call yourself that? Did you wake up one morning, see that shag of black hair and decide...black hair? 'Black Samuel!'"

"It's because his teeth are black," Elti said. The woman had her feet up on the table and was picking bits of chicken from her teeth with a two-pronged metal fork.

Grint leaned forward, squinting his steel-gray eyes. "Why yes, I see that now. I doubt I'll be able to look at anything else all night. How unfortunate."

"Enough about my teeth," Black Samuel said, keeping his mouth hidden.

"You bought no cards this hand," Marcus, the final player at the table said as he looked over at Grint. The kid was on the edge of manhood yet holding on to childlike awkwardness with his mannerisms and soft-spoken nature. Valun vouched for him, saying he was the fastest logger anyone had seen. With those skinny arms, Grint would make a Goblin's wager he wasn't.

"I bought too many," Marcus added as he folded.

"Just you and me now," Black Samuel said with a black-toothed smile.

"Are you going to run your mouth or ante up?" Grint asked. The serving girl swayed over and set a new mug beside Grint. *Anya? Artis? Andee?* Grint worked through a list of names, trying to remember hers. Instead of leaving, she leaned against him and ran her fingers through the tangles of his hair. The warmth from her body was pleasant.

Beads of sweat sprang to life on Black Samuel's forehead. As they trickled down, they gave his waxy complexion an awful sheen. Licking his lips was his tell for a winning hand and that tongue was wagging like a happy dog's tail. Yet there was doubt. To see Grint's cards he would have to go all in. He could bark at Grint all night but now had to back it up with coin.

"Would you hurry," Valun leaned against an elbow as he sipped his mulled wine. "I would like to play another hand tonight."

"You shut up," Black Samuel growled, but it lacked any conviction.

"Which cards are worth twelve points?" Grint leaned in to (*Arielle's?*) body and whispered the question so that everyone could hear. Elti and Valun snickered.

"The howling hounds," she replied, furrowing her brow, trying to connect how someone was winning at a game without knowing the rules.

"Oh," Grint said playing off her confusion and peeking down at his cards again - a three and a seven. "Can I take my bet back?" This elicited a few more laughs and even a wild bark from an onlooker at the next table.

"You're always so funny," Black Samuel said with no amusement. "Let's see how you laugh your way past two stars." He slapped his cards on the table and shoved a pile of coins forward. Both cards depicted bright stars with the number eleven inside.

"My cards don't laugh," Grint smiled. "They howl at the moons," and turned over two skeletal hounds barking at a night sky. The number twelve painted within Effulg while the shard of Nacinth stabbed towards her. The proportions were off, but those sorts of imperfections spoke to Grint. They were from his personal deck, swapped while everyone watched Black Samuel shovel his coin into the pot.

Valun whistled and Elti grunted as she took her feet off the table. Black Samuel stared at the two dogs with a vacant, dumb look, trying to work out what just happened. All the while his jaw opened and shut trying to form words, but none tumbled out. Grint raked the pitiful number of coins toward him, waiting for someone, anyone to call him out. So far, only young Marcus had the wherewithal to look confused as he glanced at the discard pile.

That's right, kid. Put it together, Grint thought. "I'd give you all a chance to win your coin back, but I doubt there's two coppers left in this town. Not that your, uh, quaint mountain village is poor," Grint finished with an apologetic glance at *Attila?*

A loud, cracking slam made the table shudder and the coins jump. A few pieces of copper continued spinning as Grint beheld the large, black-bladed knife jammed in the center of the table. Black Samuel took his hand off the hilt revealing intricate threads of black and silver wrapped in a crossing pattern.

"Onion-eyed pignuts!" Grint eyed the blade, noting that the length of the blade was on scale with a man's forearm. "Is that a knife or a sword?"

"I'm calling you a cheat!" Black Samuel's face darkened with each word. The music quieted as everyone watched the table, including the proprietor, who appeared displeased by the brewing conflict and large knife penetrating the table.

The clay mug had a rough texture, but the ale inside was smooth. Grint drank deep and sighed as he put the mug down, "Why is it that whenever someone loses coin, they call the winner a cheat? We've all lost our fair share of hands tonight. Calling me a cheat now is so...so..." Grint snapped his fingers, trying to remember one of the ten-coin words that Hobbe loved throwing around.

"Clitch," Toothless added, nodding with satisfaction at his answer.

"Yeah, clitch...wait, what? No, it's not clitch," Grint said shaking his head.

"What kind of word is clitch?" Elti asked as she looked around.

"No such word," Valun added.

"He means cliché," Nigel said as he tapped a massive, bloodstained cudgel against the knife's hilt.

"Right, cliché." Grint kept his eye on the cudgel.

"Don't know what neither of those words mean," Black Samuel's voice was a mumble as he retrieved the blade. Under the scrutiny of the owner, the divot left behind by the blade looked much larger than it was. A long moment stretched out as Nigel weighed the damage against the possibility of a full-fledged brawl. His bouncers, two large pieces of muscle named Tahr and Grag, who up to this point had been sitting behind the bar eating chicken legs and playing a game that involved slapping one another across the face, were making their way over.

"Maybe we wrap this game up," Nigel said as more of a command than a suggestion and shouldered the cudgel.

It was at this moment the serving girl picked up Grint's winning hand. "I didn't think our dogs were skeletons," she said. That small comment was enough to light a fire in Marcus's mind and he rummaged through the discards. When he found what he was looking for, he slammed it face up on the table: a twelve-point, gray fur hound, howling at Effulg with no sign of Nacinth.

"Cheater!" Black Samuel roared as he shook a fist in the air. Elti slid a spiked set of brass knockers over her knuckles as she stood.

"You have a good explanation for this?" Valun asked, his friendly demeanor vanishing.

"Let's not be hasty," Grint said. Holding his hands out to soothe the growing hostility, he let the pocketed three and seven cards fall from his sleeve. The slip of the cards looked accidental as intended. That was all part of the con.

Chaos erupted with everyone shouting, pointing fingers, and waving daggers. Black Samuel was past civility and flung the table aside. As it shattered against the flagstone wall, the brown cat hissed and darted off. Black Samuel was a good head taller than Grint and wider by a mile. As he advanced, Grint planted his feet and prepared to disarm that gorgeous blade from Samuel's hand. The fight was a necessary part. Getting stabbed to death was not.

The fracas ground to a halt as the two meatbags, Tahr and Grag, intervened. The first stepped in front of Black Samuel, shoving him back, while Grag wrapped a thick fist around each of Grint's arms. "You're going nowhere," his hot breath, smelling of eggs left to sit in the sun, enveloped Grint's face.

"Out of my way," Black Samuel yelled. "I plan to open that runt up and see how many more cards spill out."

"Not unless Nigel says." Tahr stood a head taller than Samuel and leveraged that size to quiet the gamblers.

"I have no desire to fight," Grint offered to anyone willing to listen.

"No?" Valun mocked. "Shouldn't have stolen from us then."

The loggers gathered around, cheering for blood, and chanting for a fight. None of them cared who had cheated as long as there was blood. Black Samuel was drinking in their adoration and strutting about, miming what he planned to do with his knife.

"How about we call it even and walk away?" Grint had no expectations anyone would accept the offer, otherwise he wouldn't have made it, but it played up appearances.

"They'll be walking away," Tahr waved a hand to the other players. "You?" his jowls swayed back and forth as he shook his head. Grag squeezed Grint's wrists, and he clenched his teeth to swallow the pain.

"There's still time to reconsider," Grint said trying to convey more bravado than his strained voice would carry. "I am very dangerous."

Black Samuel threw his head back and let out a booming laugh, echoed by the onlookers. As the rich sound subsided, he stepped forward, waving his knife back and forth in front of Grint's face. "You won't be doing nothing dangerous. Not with your arms in those vices."

A slow smile split Grint's face and the deep, mirthful malevolence within the expression gave Black Samuel pause. "He only has my arms," he said with a wink.

Black Samuel frowned as he worked out the puzzle, but Tahr solved it first and shouted, "Grab his kry-damned legs!"

Grint kicked, and the toe of his hard-soled walking boot connected with the hilt of the Black Samuel's dagger. The blade flew free and stuck in the rafters with a metallic twang that reverberated in the stunned silence. Black Samuel looked up, exposing himself to a second kick. The blow caught him beneath the jaw, and he stumbled into the crowd.

Planting his feet, Grint threw his head back into Grag's face. There were several indistinct groans over the meaty, cracking sound of the bouncer's nose shattering. Warm blood drenched the back of Grint's neck. Grag's hands fell away as he dropped to his knees, clutching the ruin of his face. Free from his fleshy restraints, Grint picked up a chair and put his back to the wall. Goose pimples rose along his arms as the chill from the stones bled through his coat. The crowd formed a semi-circle, caging him in and remaining out of reach. Grint jabbed the chair towards anyone who ventured too close, but it was a flimsy, pathetic deterrent that wouldn't last long if anyone rushed him.

"Enough," Nigel shouted, and the crowd parted to let him pass. Any concerns over property damage fled as he swung the cudgel round, smashing the chair into splinters. Grint imagined how ridiculous he must look standing there with only a shard of wood in his hands. The crowd's roar was appreciative and Grint prepared to duck the next swing, but Nigel changed course and punched the head of the cudgel into his gut. Grint choked for air that wouldn't come as stars, vast and brilliant, danced across his vision. Falling to his knees, his face was flush with fire as lances of pain radiated out from his stomach.

"I will kill that man," Black Samuel proclaimed, but the voice sounded disjointed and thick, like he was speaking with a mouth of honey.

"There will be no killing without my say," Nigel said, quieting the cries for blood. Five sweaty digits snaked their way through Grint's hair and yanked hard, directing his gaze. Their faces were close so that as Grint's vision returned, he could make out the imperfections in Nigel's green eyes and the deep pock marks hidden just beneath his gray beard.

"We have a right," Toothless whistled his r's, a sound that trailed off as Nigel turned an icy stare on him.

The innkeeper stood, pulling Grint to his feet alongside him. "We all have a right and we'll exact our toll this night as Petra demands!"

"That's blasphemy against Krypsie," Grint said, regaining his breath. It burned his throat to speak, but he couldn't help himself. "I'm telling the Papality."

Nigel pressed the end of the cudgel into Grint's neck and stared at him sideways. "Annabelle, dear, fetch me some rope."

"Annabelle," Grint snapped his fingers. "Her name is Annabelle," he continued under Nigel's cold gaze. "I was way off."

"Don't want him hung," Black Samuel growled.

"And he won't be," Nigel pointed the cudgel in Samuel's face, who quieted as he leaned away from the weapon. "We'll tie him to the rafters and take turns hitting him with Glory."

"You call your stick, Glory? That's adorable!" Grint laughed.

Refusing to respond, Nigel twisted Grint's hair as he dragged him towards one of the support posts. "Tahr, take the rope from her and toss it over those beams and help me with your brother."

Nigel loosened his grip as the crowd parted to let them pass. Grint leaned against a support post, his vision swimming, and marveled at the angry faces surrounding him. The whole tavern was taking part. Everyone except the cold woman who remained seated and watched the proceedings from beneath her hood. If she was a thief catcher, she was a piss-poor one.

"Stop being a baby," Nigel slapped Grag whose moaning had reached a dramatic level. "Annabelle, don't just stand there. Tie him up." The girl jumped at the sound of her name, her chin quivering in what might have been a shake of the head. "Don't worry now, he won't try nothing. Will you?"

"Wouldn't dare," Grint replied, bravado wafting off him in obnoxious waves. Just minutes ago, she was draping herself over his shoulder, but now hesitated to step close. Her hands shook as she wrapped the rope around his waist in slow methodical circles, treating him like an adder that could strike any moment. When she screwed up the courage to glance up, she found Grint smiling ear to ear.

"What?" her voice cracked.

"I had hoped we would tie each other up tonight." A few chuckles cut through the angry mutterings, which set Nigel off. Storming forward, he grabbed Grint by the hair and tore a clump out with his twisting.

"Stop that," Grint said, slapping at Nigel's arm.

"I wanted to give Grag the first crack at you, but I think it'll be Annabelle, considering your rudeness."

"Rudeness? That was foreplay! I feel sorry for the women in your life," Grint said, watching the innkeeper's eyes bulge and face turn red.

"Someone bring me a gag," he demanded through grit-ted teeth.

"Now you're getting it," Grint laughed.

"I'm tired of his flippancy!" Nigel looked around and found that the entire crowd had their backs to him as they watched the hearth. "Anyone?" A loud, thrumming wind was beating against the walls from without, and the fires in the hearth were dancing in time, spilling embers onto the cracked, wooden floor.

"What is that?" Elti asked. "That wail?"

"I don't hear no wail," Black Samuel sneered. He opened his mouth to insult the woman, but then the sound intensi-fied, and they all heard it. It was a scream or screech not un-like a child who fell from some great height.

"That's an unnatural sound," Valun said as it continued to intensify.

"Tahr, go look," Nigel commanded, but the bouncer didn't move. "Are you deaf? Go look."

"Not going out there with no banshee," Tahr said, his fat-ty jowls shaking in time with his head.

"No such thing as banshees," Toothless added. "That's a stirge!"

"That's not a stirge," Grint said. He had untied himself and was throwing the rope on the floor. "That's a dragon."

"No such thing as dragons," Marcus stammered.

"Yes, there are," Elti and Black Samuel said in unison. Judging by the number of paling faces in the crowd, more than not knew what they said to be true.

Torches blazed past the windows, back and forth they went as panicked shouts accompanied them. Nigel took a few hesitant steps toward the door, and Grint wondered if the man would have the stones to go out. The answer would remain a mystery as a townsman burst in, torch held high. It was the old man Grint encountered earlier and his mouth was working, but no words came out.

"Mason," the innkeeper called out. "What in the hells of Astapoor is going on out there?"

Mason looked around as if he was just now realizing where he was and shouted, "Dragon!"

An earth-shaking thud and a blood-curdling scream drowned out the old man's proclamation. Grint took a step back before the front wall of the tavern caved inward, burying old Mason amidst the stone and straw debris of the roof. A mammoth dragon head swung round, knocking loose any falling beams as it uttered an ear-shattering roar.

The dragon's head was the size of ten men and was the only part of the beast able to fit inside the tavern. Its long, serpentine neck stretched through the hole, obscuring a winged body larger than the inn itself. Its blood-red scales glistened in the firelight as a forked tongue flicked out, tasting the human fear. Golden eyes, alive with chaos, stared at the inhabitants who backed against the walls.

Nigel crept forward, hoping to pull Mason from the debris, but the movement caught the dragon's attention and it knocked them sideways with its monstrous head. They soared like leaves on the wind, crumpling to the floor after striking the wall. Grint could see the rise and fall of their chests. Alive, if not a little broken.

One brave fool brandished a broken table leg at the dragon. Its rebuttal was as swift as a bolt of lightning and before the man could move, two giant nostrils flared before his face. The dragon exhaled, blowing the man's hair back. A hysterical scream broke the nervous silence before the logger fainted. Bits of the thatch roof dislodged in great chunks as the tavern shook. Men and women dove for cover from the assailing shower. The dragon's roars were triumphant...and hungry.

The dragon quieted, its eyes coming to rest on Grint, who leaned an arm against the beam, coils of rope at his feet. Annabelle, hands over her face and cowering behind Grint's legs, screamed. It was a piercing sound that made Grint's eyes water, and the dragon shake its mammoth head. The beast roared again and Grint could smell slaughtered sheep on its breath.

"I don't want to die," Annabelle cried. It was a nice respite from the screaming, which returned once she finished speaking. Grint hoped she would faint soon.

Soft thuds, much like the sound of rain drops against thatch, rang out. First one, then three, and then a score in rapid succession. The townsfolk were shooting arrows as someone shouted orders. The folk of Kambar had dug out militia armor, unused for a decade, and mounted an offensive. It wasn't the brightest idea, but Grint had to tip the proverbial cap to them for not just rolling over in the face of danger. The dragon cocked its head and something like amusement passed through its eyes.

A large spear bounced off the dragon's neck, sufficient enough to garner the beast's full attention. More debris showered down as it pulled its head free. Grint could hear the screams of a dozen men fleeing. The dragon roared and spat fire, lighting the night as if the sun had risen and set again. There was nothing that anyone in the village could do to stop the beast. It would rage on until everything that remained smoldered in ash. Grint's knuckles popped as he flexed them. It was time.

Black Samuel's knife remained buried in the rafters. Shouldering past Elti, Grint leapt at the blade, his fingertips brushing against the hilt as he came away empty handed.

Black Samuel laid with his hands over his head just a foot away, so Grint stepped on top of him and tried again. This time his hand grasped the hilt of the dagger and his weight pulled it free. In all Terragard, there were perhaps a hundred knives that might surpass this one's perfection of weight, balance, and sheer beauty. How Black Samuel had come to own it was a true mystery.

"What are you doing?" Toothless asked, standing a few feet away, his trousers wet with urine. If Grint needed help, he wouldn't find it here.

Annabelle's shrill screaming rose above everything else, which was at least something Grint could remedy. Walking over, he lifted her chin and pulled her into a deep kiss. She tensed at first, shocked by the suddenness, but then returned it with fervor. When he stopped, she looked at him with desire and confusion, uncertain of how she should feel.

"Wish me luck," Grint said.

"With what?" she asked, terror and a scream building back up in her throat.

"This," he said with a wink as he sprinted towards the dragon. The creature was spitting fire above the homes as Grint reached the gaping maw that was the tavern's front door. An upended barrel rocked back and forth amid the wreckage and Grint used it to leap onto the dragon's flank.

Once there, the dragon roared and whipped its head about. Horn-like protrusions jutted between the scales, and Grint used them to climb out of reach of its razor-sharp teeth. With an angry screech, the dragon spread its wings and in one great beat, rose toward the stars. Grint looked down into the receding inn. Annabelle held an outstretched hand toward him - and abruptly fainted.

At least the screaming stopped.

2

"I've met the Dragon King and he asked me, 'Why shouldn't I let my dragons devour you?' I told him of my undying love for dragonkind. He guffawed, belched fire, and asked, 'Why?' Well, your kingship - dragons ate my last three wives!"

- Morro the Mad, the Wandering Jester

They had been referring to Eleanor as 'the cold woman' for the better part of the evening. It was not a distinction that bothered her. Nor was sitting in a low-lit corner of the tavern. The torch behind her was slowly dying, and she waved away the clueless pip of a girl who came to relight it. Eleanor enjoyed the darkness and deep shadows. Even with her hood pulled up a few drunken loggers thought to approach her, but something in her depthless brown eyes chased them off. Before long, word spread about the cold woman and attention tapered off. By the time the Cheat Me game was erupting into accusations of treachery, the only person who paid her any mind was the waif who refilled her wine whenever she held it aloft.

Trained in the art of seduction by paramours, Eleanor could wrap any man or woman in a web of pure infatuation. Were that her goal, any of these mud-thubbing loggers would murder their mothers for a mere glance or brush of her finger. Luckily for them - that was not what Count Danghier desired. The Master bestowed upon her the grand honor of this quest. Greater still would be the renown upon completing it, and the ascension of rank within the count's inner-circle. All other goals, entertaining as they may be, must fall aside.

The expedition began as many did with the count's necromancers divining answers from the spiritual plane. The art of scrying, while helpful, often became riddled with ambiguities as the threads of life altered from moment to moment. Pull too hard on one and others fell away. Through the myriad possibilities, they gleaned a starting point for her: Dirty Gull, a disreputable port city on the northern coast of Taryn. The main industry in Dirty Gull was the procurement of salt fish, where catching one of the monstrous, man-eating sea monsters required the proper lure. Three decades earlier, the city rioted against the practice of throwing condemned criminals into the ocean as bait. Since then, Dirty Gull had fallen into a state of perpetual corruption making it the perfect place to find a suitable thief. Upon her arrival the mission changed.

A shambling corpse crawled from the sewer with a message, "Cardiffe. Black hair."

On it went, the necromancers providing a sliver of detail each time. In Cardiffe, they spoke to her through the flames. In Hangham, the rats. Through smuggler dens and prison barges, from one dirty tavern to the next she followed the trail, uncovering the description of a thief named Black Samuel. The last missive directed her south toward Hyriad in Greater Anghor. It was happenstance she found him in a tavern with no name - in a town few knew existed.

Yet, Eleanor hesitated to approach the brawny, erstwhile scoundrel. There were a dozen ways to insinuate herself into the game, but she remained content to watch it unfold. There was much to learn about a person from how they played cards. How they reacted to highs and lows, their predilections, and their fears. As the night progressed, she became less inspired by the man long sought. He lacked subtlety, had a handful of tells, tried to bully every pot, and barked like a rabid dog. Worse, it wasn't an act. That was Black Samuel plain and true.

The quixotic nature of scrying came to mind. Had the necromancers pulled too many threads, changing the quarry? Eleanor went around the table, judging each player. The pirate woman had skill, but a general malaise overall. Petra's priest had yet to win a hand, and the gangly boy would get chewed up by the larger world. The local wasn't worth considering, but the red-haired man - well he interested Eleanor.

Before she approached, tempers flared, and drew the collected patrons into a maelstrom of madness. Her thief was a cheat, spilling cards from his sleeve with such graceful elegance it became impossible for her not to see the design behind it. There was skill in his fighting, even a modicum of grace, but he allowed the upper hand to slip from his grasp. What was there to gain? The question rankled her. Why draw their ire unless he had a partner mixed in? No one stepped up to help. As they tied him to the beam, she wondered if her judgement was askew. Perhaps he was just an inept cheater.

When the dragon crashed through the wall, all thoughts of cons and thieves fled from her mind. Eleanor reached under her cloak and grasped the hilt of a long dagger. It was a comforting gesture and nothing more. This blade would do little to the dragon aside from infuriating it. Eleanor's blood froze as the dragon swept its gaze across the room and those golden eyes met hers. Of all the myriad creatures in Terragard, dragons terrified her most.

Count Danghier sought to cure her of this fear by dropping her within the deep, craggy mountains north of the Krau Plains. According to the Magicai, the abyssal caverns stretched for miles, some touching the Sun in the Center. While the oppressive heat was too much for even the hardiest Stoneskin miners, dragons found it palatable and used the labyrinths as pupping grounds. In the texts, during certain solar cycles, the younglings would climb to the surface to temper their scales in the cold mountain air. Not every one of them survived the process. That was according to the Magicai. Eleanor wondered if any of them ever witnessed the event for themselves or if they just imposed their views as they believed.

It was enough that the count believed, so Eleanor traversed the mountains, searching every cave and cavern, sustaining herself on spring water and the occasional mountain goat. For three weeks she braved the harsh elements, relying on wits and a will to survive. On the twenty-second day, she took shelter in a cavernous maw, pungent with the stench of bat guano. Slipping on slick rocks she brought her hand down on a cluster of daydream mushrooms, mashing them between her fingers. The fungus was high in protein, but hallucinogenic. It had been two days since she had solid food, so the mushrooms were tempting, but best avoided. The sky rumbled and spit sleet out in chilling waves, driving Eleanor deeper to stay dry.

That was when she heard the first cry as young claws scratched their way up the tunnel. The dragon pup that appeared was already the size of a horse and given another three months it would be a mammoth with scales stronger than steel. Eleanor's only hope to slay one was to fell the beast before the tempering occurred. The blade trembled in her shaky hands as waves of nausea and terror threatened to choke her.

The dragon's scales shone deep black with speckles of white that reflected the gray afternoon light. It stumbled around the cave in a drunken stupor, blinking eyes unaccustomed to sunlight. As it neared, the pup stopped and flared its nostrils, smelling the stink of fear radiating off Eleanor. Focusing its pale-yellow eyes, the pup made a barking sound and nipped the air as it trotted closer.

With her back to the wall and cold sweat trickling salt into her eyes, Eleanor dug deep to find a moment of courage. Her blade was quick, shattering brittle scales and cutting through tender sinew. The dragon pup tried to rear away, but Eleanor ducked below and hacked again, this time removing the young beast's head. Without a brain, the body lumbered before falling on its side in a shuddering thud. The convulsions started moments later, followed by a thick, mucus-like froth that stank of sulfur and fountained into the air.

The head was heavy, forcing Eleanor to drag it through the dirt to the weathered leather bag the count provided. More barking pups ascended the tunnels and swarmed over the carcass of their fallen sibling. A deep, wailing roar followed, signaling the impending arrival of a parent and the need for a hasty departure. The ledges and rocks were slick with frozen sleet, and she lost her footing several times in a mad dash to get clear of the cave. The deep roar of a fully grown dragon echoed through the mountains before it took flight. Eleanor wedged herself between some rocks, letting a thin layer of sleet cover her as the beast soared in a wide circle.

The dragon was tenacious in trying to track her, and it took Eleanor a full month to climb out of the mountains and deliver the head. Her reward had been a pack of faithful hounds though it had always felt like a hollow victory. Killing the pup had not cured her of her fears and the proof of that was how she froze before the red scaled dragon's roar. In the deep recesses of her fear, she wondered if this was the same dragon from the cave. Dragons were intelligent despite their bestial appearance. Had it tracked her? No, that was just madness trying to creep into her mind.

The next moments transpired from the corner of her eye. Eleanor watched the red-haired man kiss the barmaid and sprint headlong towards certain death. It took him three heartbeats to run outside and leap on the monster's back. The beast screamed in defiance, rattling the woodwork and drowning out the screams. The rider remained unperturbed as the dragon beat its wings and shot skyward.

"Blood-soaked madman," the pirate woman said as she brushed debris off her coat. Eleanor agreed. Who sought to battle dragons? Even she had faced only a pup and then only at the behest of her master. This man leapt onto the back of a grown dragon with little regard for his own fate.

Stepping through the shattered doorway of the tavern, a bitter wind brushed Eleanor's cheek. Effulg's fullness made it easy to distinguish the dark shadow of the dragon against the stars as it soared and rolled to dislodge the passenger. Fire blooms lit the sky, but there was no view of the rider. He must still be on its back, or the dragon would have returned. Even without seeing him at work, the display was breathtaking.

Townsfolk stood on the muddy path they called a street and stared at the night with mouths ajar. Those who had been in their houses came out and joined the militia in viewing the spectacle. Dragons were elusive beasts, sometimes hiding from view for centuries. The simple folk of Kambar had not seen one in generations and dismissed the cautionary tales as fanciful. This tale was different. Its telling would pass down from generation to generation, growing in grandeur each time as stories did. In the stories to come, the dragon would grow to the size of a mountain and the gambler to the stature of a visiting king. A monument to this moment would dominate the town square and families would claim lineage with the king. A few generations further and a war would break out wiping the sweet hamlet of Kambar out of existence.

Eleanor didn't need a scryer to see the chain of events leading to that day in some distant century. For now, she stood amongst the denizens of Kambar while they made appreciative sounds as if watching an alchemist's sky-fire show. Even had she the desire to warn them of the poisonous seed they planted - they wouldn't listen. Half-hearted cheers rose and quickly fell as the heroics forced each person to confront the impotence of their own inaction.

The whispers grew as the battle lingered on, "How long can this continue?" "How can he survive?" And they spoke the worst in the quietest of breaths, "What if he loses?"

Inevitably, one would win out over the other. The hope that the rider would win ebbed and flowed with each looping twist or roar from the primal beast, but the townsfolk held on to their hope with steel gauntleted fingers. They knew failure meant their destruction. The militia had been ineffective and if the scaled monster returned, it would offer no quarter. Those who survived the onslaught would find their deaths delayed behind a short life of begging and starvation.

"Behold," an old woman cried out. The dragon roared once more breathing a pillar of fire three miles high. Then, like a candle being snuffed, the fire faded. The darkness left behind a ghostly image of the dragon with its wings spread wide. Until that too faded. Night blind, no one saw the beast or hero fall. The last remnant of the battle was a distant thud that trembled the earth. Eleanor judged it at two miles, maybe more. The mountains could play tricks with sound.

"Are they both dead?" A man wearing leather armor too small for his rotund belly asked, looking around for answers no one had.

"No one survives a fall like that," someone answered. The milling crowd kicked their feet and made disgusted sounds, not wanting to admit the truth of that statement. No man could fall from that height and survive.

"Unless..." Eleanor whispered.

"Unless what?" a woman asked, her brows raised as she sought answers. Eleanor turned and stared with cold regard. A strong woman with thick arms, perhaps a smith by trade. She swallowed hard and withered under Eleanor's gaze.

The idea born in Eleanor's mind was almost too preposterous to give credence to. Just as the cards spilled conveniently from the hero's sleeve - had this been a show? A mummer's farce on a grandiose stage? It was ludicrous!

No one could train a dragon - domesticate one. But what if? The town of Kambar survived - almost unscathed. The taller barns needed minor repairs, but other than the tavern, the dragon destroyed nothing. Even its flames missed anything of importance. Igniting only trees and hay bales.

A sound theory, but Eleanor let it go. She was unwilling to accept that a man who trained a dragon would stoop so low as waste it on cheating at cards instead of conquering kingdoms. That would be an egregious lack of vision.

With nothing more to see, she walked back into the tavern. The townsfolk began the chore of repairing their village as the loggers gathered their belongings to return to camp. A handful of the tavern's patrons remained, including the innkeeper and card players, all covered in dust and straw. The priest attempted to soothe everyone with useless benedictions that only the gangly boy seemed willing to hear. Eleanor wanted to hate them for their weakness, but how could she when she showed an equal measure of cowardice when faced with the dragon?

Her bag lay askew on the floor beside her seat, so she set it on the table to confirm the contents. With the red-haired hero gone, she didn't see another option outside of Black Samuel. It irked her to give the barbaric thief the glory of serving the count. Black Samuel was a feeble specimen and feared he would not have the subtlety to infiltrate Ballastrine's manor and gain what the master desired.

Perhaps she should leave Black Samuel here and continue south to Hyriad. Time had yet to run dry in the hourglass, and Hyriad was large enough that she could find a local seer to divine a new name. And if there wasn't anyone else, then she would do the job herself. The count could forgive if he got what he wanted. *The ends justified the means.*

Eleanor's shoulders sagged as she exhaled and pounded the flat of her fist against the table. The count allowed a certain amount of leeway in executing her duties - but diverting from the path he clearly set before her was self-delusion. Or worse, self-destruction. It would be Black Samuel she took with her and pray to the unholy dead that her ability to coach him along the way would prove enough.

A flash of movement beside the wrecked wall caught her eye, and she shifted her weight while opening her right shoulder. The knife in her hand hidden below the table. This gave her a clear view of the hooded man, hidden in the shadows outside the tavern. He did not look in her direction, instead his attention was on the street and the people busying themselves with repairs or putting out fires. His right hand hung by his side and working through a series of hand gestures that none in Terragard could decipher. The hounds knew to remain outside town and out of sight. By ignoring that command, Bowman faced grievous consequences and her wrath, but how angry could she be? Easily her favorite, Bowman knew well her fear of dragons and came to confirm her safety. Eleanor signed her own message, *I will rejoin you soon.* Just as quick as he appeared, Bowman vanished into the night.

"What was his name?" a logger asked, drawing everyone's attention. "Does anyone know?" A twinge of fear rippled through Eleanor but eased when she realized they were not asking about Bowman, but the brazen hero who died fighting a dragon.

"I don't have a clue," Nigel answered. "It seems we should know." The innkeeper stood and shook off the tremors of fear as he scanned the room. When his gaze fell upon Black Samuel, he shouted, "You! Black Bastard!"

"Samuel," the dark-haired man corrected, unable to meet Nigel's gaze.

"Your name is no matter," the innkeeper responded. "What we want is the name of that man. You must have picked it up during the game."

"I did not," Black Samuel admitted.

"Did none of you know?" One by one they shook their heads, ashamed of the simple act of decency they overlooked, had always overlooked, and would continue to overlook.

"To die unknown," Valun said. "I shall beseech Petra to welcome him to her vineyards."

"Grint," Annabelle blurted out. "His name was Grint." She touched her lips as she spoke, perhaps imagining the kiss given before departing this world.

"Well then, let us raise a mug to Grint," Nigel said waving a hand. The bouncers went behind the bar to fill mugs with ale. This aroused everyone's attention, and they gathered to accept their free drink. Eleanor watched, unable to shake the notion that something was missing. The back of the bar, battered and disheveled, looked somehow barren. A silly observation given the attack, but very few of the mugs and casks fell from the shelves. So, what was she missing?

"That means you, Black Bastard," Nigel shouted, noticing that Samuel was not taking part. Under the scrutiny of the tavern, Samuel shuffled forward and accepted a mug. With drinks in hand, Tahr and Grag rejoined the group and as one lifted in honor of their unlikely savior.

"To Grint," young Marcus shouted. They each took a drink and bowed their heads. Eleanor took a mug, but did not drink or bow, content to observe, her lips quivering with amusement.

"To Grint!" came another shout from behind the bar. Everyone raised their eyes. Several mugs shattered on the floor as their contents spilled over leather boots before flooding the cracks between floorboards.

The foam head from a hastily poured ale covered Grint's upper lip, and he smiled at the crowd of people staring awestruck, their mouths agape. "Are we not toasting anymore?" Still receiving no answer, he tilted the mug and drained the rest of its contents. As he slammed his mug onto the bar, he wiped a sleeve across his mouth, leaving a muddy streak in its wake.

Eleanor found herself both shocked and pleased. How had he survived? How had he returned and gotten behind the bar with no one noticing? Without her noticing? That he had done so only reinforced her desire to take him instead of Black Samuel.

Grint refilled his mug and hopped onto the bar to sit with his legs dangling over the edge. Grag leaned on a chair beside him, blood caked around his crooked nose. Grint reached over and rubbed the bouncer's bald head. "No hard feelings about the nose?"

"You killed a dragon," Grag replied, wide-eyed and in awe.

"That I did," Grint nodded as if it were nothing. He took another drink and let his smile falter. "Now, who here was calling me a cheat?"

That was all it took for the gathered mass to collect every bit of copper, silver - even gold - from their pockets and offer it to the dragon slayer. Grint beamed as he held open a fine leather coin purse for them to deposit their homages. Eleanor surmised the amount of coin he now held was close to thirty times larger than what he would have won playing Cheat Me. As the last coin clinked inside the bag, he tied the string and made the pouch disappear up his sleeve. *The very cheek!*

Annabelle shoved past the loggers to stand beside Grint. She held her chin high as if named the Queen of Upper Anghor. Eleanor stifled a laugh.

"I could use a room," Grint said to Nigel with a wink.

"Of course," Nigel stammered. "Anything you want!"

"I have one," Annabelle said and blushed at the roar of laughter. Embarrassment did not stop her from taking Grint's hand and coaxing him from his seat atop the bar. The man shrugged and smiled as the loggers parted to let them through, slapping his back while making lewd jokes.

"I want my knife back," Black Samuel called out. The crowd quieted and Grint pulled his hand free.

"Why don't you go on up," Grint said to the girl. "I'll be along." Annabelle hesitated and then skipped up the stairs.

"My blade," Black Samuel repeated.

"This blade?" Grint asked as he drew it and flipped it back and forth through the air. An appreciative gasp and hoots of laughter filled the room as the showman continued to make the blade dance with ease.

"I'm keeping it," he announced. "It's nice."

Black Samuel blinked first and lowered his eyes. The crowd laughed and Grint sheathed the blade in a belt loop, then tipped an imaginary cap to the crowd. Many voices cried out for him to remain and drink, but he motioned toward the stairs with an apologetic shrug. They bandied a few more jokes about, but before anyone else objected, he disappeared.

Eleanor sat back down and nursed her ale. Now that Grint had returned, she would await him here. The party did not die with his absence as the loggers and gamblers milled around, drinking, toasting, and telling stories. Even the surly innkeeper seemed happy and uncaring of the gaping hole in his tavern.

"I object to him taking my blade," Black Samuel glowered when pressed. Those around him laughed with great delight, which only darkened the man's mood.

"Should have told him that when you had the chance," Toothless shouted, spit spraying with each word.

"He preferred to stand there pissing himself," a rotund man with little left of his hair chimed in. Men who would never have dared insult someone like Black Samuel no longer feared doing so. The bestial figure had proven himself weak. But she sensed him using the ridicule to stoke angry fires deep within. He was not the man for the job at hand, but perhaps there were other ways to make use of him?

Annabelle returned, clopping down the stairs with a sour twist to her mouth. Eleanor reckoned that her footfalls, exaggerated as they were, sounded much like a mule on a cobblestone street.

"Done already?" Nigel laughed. "I guess being a dragon slayer doesn't mean you're good at everything!" There was uproarious laughter throughout.

"No," Annabelle pouted. "Nothing happened."

"What?" Nigel asked, confused.

"He came in, smiled at me and then climbed out the window." She sat at the bar and dropped her head into her arms while pretending to cry. Eleanor stood and shouldered her bag. There was no need to remain for the theatrics. Grint vanished and she would need to find him.

Exiting the tavern, Eleanor heard someone ask, "Nigel, where's that ugly statue you keep behind the bar?"

"What? It's gone!" Nigel sounded despondent. "Everyone look around, the dragon must have knocked it over. Family heirloom that is."

Eleanor laughed as she stepped into the cold Upper Anghor night. A purse full of coin wasn't the mark at all, but a statue of jade. Dawn neared, but she felt confident that her hounds could find where Grint had gone.

"Mistress," Bowman said as he fell in beside her.

"A man left the inn through a window," Eleanor said. "Find him."

"As you wish," he said and whistled for the others. Eleanor smiled as she looked up at Effulg and the shattered remnant of Nacinth. The hounds would find the thief for her. This turned out to be a fine night.

"A fine night indeed."

3

"In the art of negotiation, it's the one who thinks they're getting the deal that always gets fleeced."

- General Mackius
The Tragedy of King Mezzer

Only an hour remained until dawn's red kiss would paint itself on the eastern horizon and wake the world. Grint fought against the exhaustion burning behind his eyes, his displeasure at being kept awake manifested itself as an aching bloom in his chest. All he wanted was to lie beside a warm fire and count the coins from his haul. Instead, moldy bark crumbled against his back as he listened for the fools hunting him. In the pre-dawn gloom, the dark and light conspired to trick the eyes, but his ears told the truth. They were out there and tracking him with enthusiastic fervor.

A long howl hung in the air until answered by another, sending ripples of goose flesh along Grint's arm. This wasn't a lone man, but a group sweeping the forest; and they brought dogs with them. *The night had been going so well,* Grint thought as he shifted the sack's strap and repositioned the jade statue so the serpentine arms stopped jabbing his ribs. It hadn't been hard to steal, not with everyone's attention on the dragon. The only concern was the cold woman spotting him. There was something about her. A demeanor? A sense of superiority? Grint knew the type; with eyes that saw nothing but watched everything. Yet the dragon shook her, pulled her onto the street and while everyone thought Grint was sacrificing himself, he snuck through the tavern's back door.

The kry-damned statue was heavy. Heftier than any jade he'd encountered, and his shoulders ached every time he shifted the sack from one side to the other. The weight slowed his pace, but he couldn't leave the ugly thing for his pursuers to happen upon. That defeated the whole purpose of being here. Faighur needed it for a buyer and Grint owed him for the time his friend helped pilfer a cursed necklace down in Marinoire. So Grint agreed to the job and they ran the old dragon-slayer con. *Faighur,* Grint thought, *where is that bloody dragon when I need him?*

Another dog howled far to the right. It had a higher pitch than the first two and moved fast, making a lot of racket. Grint pushed away from the tree and jogged onward. The night offered decent cover, but was just as dangerous, limiting visibility to a few feet. Dense forest underbrush hid crags or shale deposits that slid underfoot, waiting to mark his position. The ground sloped southward, steep enough to make traveling with the burden of the statue an arduous task. More than once he tangled his foot in a root or stumbled over a rock.

Grint's haste to distance himself caused an awful racket, but his mystery guests weren't any quieter. Hunters always boasted of sneaking up on their prey, but those were just tavern-tales. People made a noise. Animals too. None of them could help it. That was how he first noticed they were following him. The subtle snap of twigs, shuffling of leaves, the flutter of an owl's wings taking flight, and the cry of bats atop the trees. The forest sang a song in the night - if you knew what to listen for.

Upper Anghor maintained a small military component closer to the capital, but left the mountain towns on their own, relying on locals to protect themselves. The Kambar militia formed at the sight of the dragon, but why would they be after him? Once they finished cleaning up the town, they would go south to search for the dragon carcass. They always did. That was the beauty of the con. Could someone have sussed out the deception and formed a mob to spill his blood? No, Grint thought. That wasn't this. Mobs were notorious for the noise they made, hefting torches and shouting challenges into the night. They wanted you to choke on your fear as they tightened the noose. The group tracking him maintained discipline, moving within the darkness, allowing their dogs only enough leash to...

"To keep me moving east." They were herding him.

Grint paused, placing a hand against a sap-coated maple. Closing his eyes, he listened to the night. Down the slope and to the south - the heavy footsteps of a man. A dog trailed behind him, almost on top of him, making it hard to differentiate the two. Another raced along the northern slope scaring wildlife. It barked, snapping twigs and scattering a herd of rabbits. Someone shouted a word from a language Grint never heard before. The loping trot of a dog departed from the source of that shout. *What in the charffing Hells of Astapoor is going on?* With growing certainty, Grint knew they were closing their trap.

There weren't many viable options to consider. Standing his ground allowed them to approach in unison. He might as well give up. All Grint had to fight with was a stolen statue and knife. If they were thief-catchers, the statue was damning enough for losing a hand in most places. They may even consider the knife an act of theft. Grint would argue that taking Black Samuel's knife while the man stood in a puddle of his own piss wasn't theft. Not that it would do him any good. Thief-catchers didn't concern themselves with things like details.

Hiding wasn't any better than standing. The image of hunkering down beneath the brush, hoping they passed by made him laugh involuntarily. A fool's wager. The dogs would catch his scent. Even if they were the dumbest dogs in the world the rising sun would reveal his position and that would be that.

Grint punched the maple and felt a flap of skin peel away from his knuckles. Shaking blood from his hand, he lamented leaving his travel bag beside the bedroll he longed to lie in. There were things in that bag he could use to confuse his trail, but it was out of reach and nothing more than a dream. The best and only real option was to change direction, charge a tracker, slow them down, hobble them, create confusion, and slip the trap. Maybe from there he could turn the tables and herd them.

It's a terrible plan, he told himself. There were too many variables and no way to know how many trackers on his tail. Three at least, but the noise from the dogs could hide their real numbers. Grint had only a passing knowledge of the forest from the two days spent camping as they planned the job. If the trackers were local, their familiarity with the surrounding woods, even in deep darkness, would eclipse his own. Surprising them would be tricksome enough, but the unpredictable nature of their dogs added a dangerous facet.

Any chance of success hinged on each tracker having only one dog. Any more than that and they would overwhelm him.

Sliding downhill through the trees, Grint raced towards the sounds of pursuit. The barest hint of morning lit the way, a strange half-light casting shapes on the edges of trees, creating illusions of phantoms lurking everywhere. It was unsettling and Grint's heart jumped at every shadow. Pausing amidst a small copse of rotted trees, Grint tossed the statue beneath a stone outcropping. He snapped a moldy branch and laid a piece of torn cloth over it before he set about making a racket, slapping his knife blade against the tree trunk and throwing rocks. When he heard a dog sprinting toward him, he dropped and rolled beneath the lip of the rock.

The sound of nails scratching against stone made Grint's hair stand on end. He took a deep breath as the dog leapt toward his decoy. For an instant, he saw a tangle of brown and white fur before the mutt disappeared behind drooping fern leaves. Relying on his ears alone he heard the rustling of leaves and a heavy-booted step. A man grunted, a guttural, angry sound followed by steel dragging the length of the trunk. The man? How did he get so close? A murder of ravens screamed as they took wing, and the man tossed a handful of bark mere inches from Grint's face. The fabric decoy tore as the man snatched it from the stick and then a deep, snorting inhale that painted a mental picture of the tracker jamming it against his nose. *Why is he smelling it? Why not give it to the dog?*

The answer didn't change the plan. Hobble the scout, get over the rock, find the next choke point and Krypsie willing the dog wouldn't follow. Keep at it, one by one and swing them back around, draw them north towards Faighur. The dragon would be angry, and would no doubt require Grint to pull another job as a recompense for the trouble. They could haggle that point over drinks, both very much alive. Hobbe laughed within his memory, his former mentor's voice filling the role of Grint's subconscious. *Plans only work so long as Lady Lorelai doesn't pull on her webs.* The chiding caution was right; the Goddess of Chance was an ever-present concern, and the only god Grint took care not to anger.

There was no time for liturgical rituals or runes to gain her favor. It was time to act. Grint rolled out and snatched a hunk of wood. The tracker threw down the torn scrap of cloth, seeing through the ruse, but it was too late. Grint was on him before he could shout a warning or prepare a defense. The heavy stick shattered the man's knee, bending it inward as he collapsed like a marionette against the base of the tree. The force of the blow snapped the branch, leaving the top half dangling from a thin piece of bark. Grint held on to it, searching for the dog. When the mutt didn't appear, Grint threw it aside and retrieved the statue. Hope sprang and blossomed as Grint slid over the rocks. *Maybe the plan isn't banjaxed after all!*

That hope died a quick and inglorious death under the sound of scattering leaves and the rhythmic pant of a dog in full stride. Grint rolled over the rocks, sliding through a crevice as he caught the barest flash of red fur between trees. A different color, which meant a different dog. Where was the first dog? Too many questions. Grint moved, counting on the man's screams to cover his steps. Except, the man made no sound, just a single, gravel-rough shout.

"Here!"

How is he not in agony? Grint thought as he backed away. He stepped on light feet but each crunch beneath his boot sounded like thunder. Another tracker found the first, their muffled whispers echoed. Grint needed to move - now - with or without the benefit of cover. If either tracker decided to peek, they would see him making an awkward attempt to tiptoe backwards. Groping for a tree to hide behind, he lunged around, clinging to the first he felt like a drowning man. The thick trunk worked fine to block their view. A few steps more and he could make a run before they came looking. Babbles from a nearby brook tickled the inner part of his ear - water echoing through rock. If the rock formations stood tall enough, he could use them as a natural choke point to hold these charffing fools off.

The cold press of steel beneath his chin made Grint's breath catch. *Now where did that come from?*

"Shh," her soft whisper warmed the edge of his ear and made Grint believe for the briefest moment that she might be there to help.

"Where is he?" their whispers grew to shouts.

"Here," the woman at Grint's back answered. Even as she uttered the word, a man hopped atop the rock, an arming sword in his left hand. The tangled mop of greasy black hair did nothing to hide a face crisscrossed with scars. As he looked at Grint, his upper lip peeled back, baring his teeth like an angry mutt.

"Behave yourself," the woman whispered to Grint and waited for his nod to remove the blade from his throat. "Bring him," she added with a wave of her hand.

The scarred tracker stepped off the rock, holding the tip of his sword at Grint's eye. His steps were graceful, and he moved with surprising ease in the dark. As he circled behind, he lifted the bag off Grint's shoulder with his blade, then patted him down with a free hand. Discovering only Black Samuel's knife, he confiscated it with a hasty tuck into his belt.

Shouldering the bag, he slapped the flat of the sword blade against Grint's back, urging him to follow the woman.

They rounded the rock, back to where the man he crippled sat with his back against a rotting tree. The woman crouched beside him as two other trackers lit torches for her to inspect the wound. Like the scarred man with the sword at his back, the men bore peculiar disfigurations. One with burn scars across his face. The other missing his nose, giving him a skeletal look. And with the torches lit, Grint noted the injured man's milky-white eyes. *Like a blind man. Who are these people?*

Upon 'seeing' their quarry caught, the blind one cried out in pain. "Now he screams," Grint grumbled, which earned him a strike from the pommel of the sword. Grint dropped to his knees, grabbing the side of his neck. The woman glared at him.

"Bowman displayed great discipline," she replied. "His strength is an example to us all."

Grint took what measure of the woman he could. Tall and slender with neck length black hair brushed behind her ears. A travel cloak hung over her shoulders, thick wool in pristine condition. It implied the garment was new, or the woman wasn't one for hard travel. There was something familiar to her accent. A smooth lilt from the Sandy Kingdoms, but also the hard vowels of Bar Church, and even that odd question-like lift at the end of a sentence - a Tarynese trait. This was a woman from everywhere and maybe nowhere. Not unlike Grint.

"I am not an example," Bowman said through the pain. "I am a failure, undeserving of the gift."

"Nonsense," the woman said. She ran her fingers through his hair and pet his face with the back of her hand. The affection she felt for him was clear in the gesture, but it wasn't love. It was the way one regarded a dear pet. Grint looked around for the dogs, of which there was no sign.

"We will return as heroes and the Count will bring you back to us," she continued.

"Death is the gift long promised," Bowman replied.

"Death is the gift long promised," the others repeated.

"Death is the gift long promised," the woman whispered as she drove a long-bladed dagger into Bowman's chest. His body shuddered and his arms fell upon the moss as he coughed up blood, gurgling his final breath.

Grint turned away, hiding his face behind his hands. *That won't be enough.* Brushing leaves aside, he uncovered a patch of dirt and began scratching a looping symbol. The scarred captor interrupted him with a swift kick. Grint rolled to the side and then crawled back toward the symbol, frantic to complete his work. The one without a nose put a boot down on Grint's hand, gentle at first, but harder as Grint tried pulling it free.

"Enough," the woman said, and the man lifted his boot. She wiped the blade against Bowman's chest, leaving a wet streak of blood that the fabric appeared to drink. For a few moments she inspected the symbol, following the lines with the tip of her knife. Then she cocked her head, looking over at Grint.

"Is that Parthian?" she asked.

"Trying to curse us," the burned man said.

"No," she continued looking at the symbol. "Carvo mallar behonas. It's an old blocking ward. Who are you hiding from?"

"You never know who's looking through the eyes of the dead." Grint rubbed his hand. The boot print would turn to an angry bruise in a few hours.

"No one is watching," she replied. "The dead are dead."

"Whatever you say." Grint knew better. Sometimes someone *was* looking.

The woman regarded Grint, a bemused smile on her face. It would be easy to look at her as just a pretty face with wide eyes and full lips, but that was the honey trap. Once you dropped your guard all the coldness hiding beneath her skin bubbled out to freeze you. For the first time, Grint truly saw her.

"You were at the inn," he said without question.

"The cold woman," she replied, not hiding the mirth in her voice.

"If you wanted the statue, we didn't need to do all of this."

"Statue?" she asked. The one Grint nicknamed Crosshatch opened the bag with the jade statue. She threw her head back laughing. It was a rich sound. Another weapon to disarm the unaware.

"It's for sale if you want it," Grint added.

"I have no need for that. Well done though. It will be a long time before they realize it was you who took it. If ever."

Grint looked around. If they weren't after the statue, then what was this? The men held themselves in a rigid manner. All scarred, but their bodies hardened like weapons. Not a single one bore any sigils or marks of allegiance but moved as a trained unit.

"Who are you people?" he asked, giving voice to the question.

"I like that. More concerned with whom we are than what we want."

"I like to know whom I'm dealing with," Grint replied.

"Who do you think we are?"

As much as he hated being in this position, he knew he would have to play her game. "You're not thief-catchers, because you don't care about the statue. For a moment I thought you might be from the Papality with the way you chased me, but there's no way any of you are Ropes."

"Run afoul of the Papality?" she asked.

"Who hasn't?" Grint responded as he stood, brushing dirt from his leather pants.

"Who we are isn't important, Grint." He winced at the sound of his name. "What you can do for us is."

"What I can do? Is this a job?" Grint clenched his jaw, exasperated.

"Let's return to your camp," she answered. "We can discuss all of this beside a fire. I would prefer to remove the chill from my bones."

"What camp?" Grint asked, giving his best clueless look.

"If we could dispense with games, this will go smoother," her tone was patronizing. "I would never believe you planned to wander the wilderness with just a stolen statue and knife." She held the knife out to Grint, hilt first. The men tensed as Grint accepted and sheathed the blade, remaining on guard even as he slung the sack containing the statue over his dominant arm.

"Follow me," Grint said, giving up on tricking his way out.

"Take Bowman," she commanded her men. The one with the burn - *Torchy* - slung the corpse over his shoulders while the others vanished into the forest. Eleanor walked beside Grint as he scanned the terrain. There wasn't any imminent danger from this group, but if the terrain offered an opportunity to turn the tables, was it worth considering?

"You have me at a disadvantage," Grint said as he picked his way along the rocky path.

"How so?" Her tone made him think of a cat playing with its kill.

"I don't know your name."

"The cold woman doesn't suffice?"

Grint couldn't help but laugh. Everything about her centered on the goal of disarming. "Not if you have a job for me."

"Eleanor," she replied. And even as the name left her lips, "How did you do it?"

"I took it off the shelf when no one was looking."

"The dragon," her tone less mirthful. "How did you tame it?"

"There was nothing tame about that beast," Grint replied. "I'm just glad I was there to save those people." Eleanor laughed again but this time there was no humor behind it.

A snapping branch caught Grint's attention. In his mind he pictured Faighur crashing through the trees, but it was just Torchy yanking his boot free from the underbrush. "Who is he?" Grint asked. He didn't care, it was just a distraction to pull her mind from the dragon. The story fell apart under scrutiny.

"That is Malus," she said. "On our flanks are Tamos and Callum." Hounds howled again, one on each side.

"And the dogs?" It was a valid question, but Eleanor laughed at it. Grint wished she would stop doing that.

They walked for a time as Grint sought landmarks to lead them towards camp. The sound of Eleanor's dogs followed, but they never showed themselves. Of Faighur there was no sign. At this point it was better if his partner remained away. Such a sudden appearance would stir up a ruckus under normal circumstances, and Faighur was not normal, even by this lot's standards.

Halting beside a fir tree, Grint bent a branch aside and reached into the tangle. "It's best if we keep moving," Eleanor tapped her foot. Was she revealing her tell for annoyance?

"We're here," Grint said in a grunt, groping for the pull chain.

"I thought we were through with the games," all traces of humor vanished.

"Not a game," Grint's voice strained as he started pulling the chain. The ancient metal flaked bits of rust as he yanked on it, but it refused to budge.

"He could have a crossbow hidden in there," the noseless one said, appearing from the dark with his sword drawn. Beside him a deep brown shepherd dog growled, its hackles raised. It sniffed Grint's feet, continuing a deep growl that sprang from deep in its throat. The dog's muzzle was a crosshatch of scars. And that's when Grint realized - the dog's names were Tamos, Callum and Malus.

The woman has skinlings with her. This just keeps getting better.

"Who hides a crossbow in a tree?" Grint shifted his weight to get a better grasp on the chain. Faighur had been the one pulling it before, and he was far stronger. "The latch pull won't give." He planted a foot against the trunk and used his weight - and it clicked. The branches to his left swung open revealing a covered path into a sheltered oasis.

"Amazing," Eleanor breathed as she inspected the gateway. Grint ducked under the branches, but Noseless yanked him back. The dog called Crosshatch trotted in first, sniffing the path. After a minute he returned and barked at Eleanor. Noseless relaxed his grip as Eleanor waved Grint on with a gesture that said, *after you.*

The path curved, hiding a covered campsite large enough for twenty. Towering pines ringed the grotto, grown together to form a natural barrier. In the center sat a fire pit full of charred stones and ashes with a single clearing above open to the sky. Just large enough to vent the smoke. At night, the darkness within was almost impenetrable, but dawn's light was finding its way through the wooded ceiling, providing just enough clarity for everyone to get situated. Grint suspected the ones who made this place used magic on the vent. It had been decades since anyone last stepped into this place and the branches never grew to cover it.

Eleanor's minions followed and Grint snapped his fingers to get their attention. "Be good lads and start a fire."

They made no move to listen until Eleanor echoed the command, "Light one."

"I see how it is," Grint laughed as he knelt beside his travel bag, transferring last night's coins to his dwindling stash.

"Do you see?" the tracker's voice was harsh with a strangled quality. Grint couldn't tell which it belonged to until the fire lit his features. Crosshatch, the cut one.

"I liked you better as a dog," Grint replied. The tracker drew his sword but backed down at Eleanor's gesture. Grumbling like a dog, he helped with the supplies, but couldn't help glancing at Grint, his dead eyes flecked with gold from the dancing flames.

"Prepare Bowman," she said. Her trained dogs nodded in unison as they undressed their dead companion. "Have you used this spot before?" Eleanor ignored the growing tension.

"Would it matter if I had?" Grint closed his bag, settling with quiet satisfaction on the well-worn travel blanket left beside the trees. The skinlings spat whispered curses, caring little for the disrespect he showed their mistress. Eleanor did not seem fazed.

"Having a familiarity with a place can lead to greater magical power." Eleanor walked the perimeter, brushing her palm across the brittle needles of low-hanging branches. "I've noticed elder wards carved in the bark."

"This place is old." Grint took off his coat and used the tree to scratch a spot between his shoulder blades.

"So, you are familiar with it."

"No," Grint replied. "I don't get to Upper Anghor often."

"Angry gamblers, dragon attacks, and being hunted in the night," she took a seat close to her men, but with an easy sightline to Grint. "I can't imagine why you wouldn't like it here."

Grint smiled, but nothing more. It was clear what she was doing, and he didn't intend on falling into her web. Eleanor would try to put him at ease with light conversation, humor, maybe a sly smile that hinted at them falling in love. Any connection they formed became an exploit to leverage negotiations in her favor. They were negotiating, even if Grint didn't know what the endgame was. He hoped it wasn't to slay a dragon. That wouldn't go well.

"I once used a fight to distract a rather loathsome man from my true target, much like you did tonight." And there it was. Her attempt at a connection.

"I never said I didn't like Upper Anghor," Grint replied. "You said I didn't, all I said was I hadn't gotten up here much." The cold look she gave was reminiscent of the tavern, shrewd and unemotional, but the unintended tapping of her foot told a different tale. *Good,* Grint thought, *she knows I'm not falling into her trap.*

The minions drew red-bladed knives as they bowed over Bowman's corpse. When they satisfied whatever ritual they were performing, they carved Bowman up. First, by severing each bone at the joint. Then fingers, wrists, elbows, and so on. Grint's stomach shrank, and he fought hard against the urge to sick up. He'd seen men butchered on the field of battle and dispatched some himself. It was the ceremonial act that bothered him. The methodical way they cut and placed the dismembered parts in a pile. Grint wanted to block it from view but doing so would mean breaking eye contact with Eleanor and that was not something he could do.

"And yet you found this place." The twinkle in her eye sparkled at Grint's discomfort. Taking a seat where she had held strategic purpose. Eleanor was playing two hands ahead in a game Grint had yet to drawn a card in.

"Dumb luck," Grint lied. She outmatched him in every regard, but he wasn't rolling over.

The oasis was easy to find for those with an unscrupulous background. Decades past, smugglers ran contraband through Lake Tarsis and created the hidden camps to rest and lie low. Anghor's unified navy once patrolled the channels between lakes forcing the smugglers to adapt and find overland routes to avoid capture. Once safely past the patrols, they could load their goods onto new boats at Lake Urthery. That was all before the Papality took control of the region and snuffed out illegal trade markets. Camps like this faded into obscurity but the markers and language remained for those who knew how to read them.

It wasn't knowledge he planned to share with his new friends. Hobbe taught him several rules for negotiating and chief among them was never playing your hand first. Grint could wait for Eleanor to move on from the idle conversation. It was a game of chicken where the first person who asked what the other wanted would be at a disadvantage. Unfortunately, Eleanor learned the same lessons and wasn't in a rush to give in. *No meat here. Just a lot of fat.* Thinking of meat and watching the minions at work made Grint's face pale. Eleanor cocked her head and smiled.

"Are they making you uncomfortable?" The triumph in her tone was that of an owl spotting a field mouse and deciding on how best to prepare the meal. "I understand that death and violence frighten you."

Grint's understanding of her approach deepened. It wasn't about putting him at ease but scaring him, making him beg for his life. In a state of panic, he would do whatever job they offered - for free - if only they would let him live. Mutilating a body, albeit gruesome and dramatic wasn't unlike the tactics of the brokers or fences Grint often dealt with. When starting a new partnership, they always made him watch their muscle beat someone bloody before sitting down to talk business. The 'cross me and this is what will happen' routine. Once he looked at it in that context her antics became less frightening.

"I try to avoid the killing part," Grint said, letting the tension melt from his shoulders. "Have nothing against death and violence."

"This is tiresome," Crosshatch whispered to Noseless. "Time is of the essence."

That was the thing with smugglers. They were all paranoid about plots behind their backs. Dens like this were enchanted to amplify even the slightest whisper. The magic came from the runes Eleanor saw carved in the branches. When Crosshatch spoke, every word echoed as if he stood and shouted. Eleanor's mouth thinned to an indiscernible line.

Grint beamed as he broke eye contact, looking past Eleanor to the huddled men prostrating themselves before her. "Well, there it is," Grint laughed.

"There what is?" Her response was a final, desperate attempt to regain even footing.

"Time is a precious commodity, and if you want to keep using mine, it will cost you." Grint put his right arm behind his head making himself comfortable. Eleanor watched for a few moments, weighing her choices behind those frozen eyes, and then tossed two silver squares. Grint snatched them from the air and with a deft flick of his wrist, made them disappear.

"Sufficient for a few words?" she asked. Grint nodded and so she continued. "I have a job that requires a man of skill."

"And what skills do you think I have?" Grint slid his hand under the latch of his bag, releasing the secret catches, and sifting through its contents.

"Don't sacrifice the ground you won being obtuse."

"Your silver is running out," Grint pulled a hunk of cheese from a wax wrapping and popped it in his mouth. A poor choice considering the dismemberment occurring across the fire.

"I need someone who can make a tavern full of people intent on killing them, give away all their money instead." She leaned forward, baring the slightest amount of cleavage. "Someone adept enough to rob them blind while their eyes are wide open."

"You want to talk to the thief?" Grint made a show of untying the top of his shirt and leaned forward, exposing his own chest. "That's fine, but this conversation just got a lot more expensive."

Eleanor leaned back, tapping her feet. She inhaled. Held it. And exhaled as she produced a hide pouch which she tossed at Grint's feet. The jingle of coin as it landed satisfied his ears. Grint snatched the pouch and ripped open the drawstring. A gorgeous assortment of silver and gold from all over Terragard twinkled in the firelight. He couldn't help but lick his lips.

"What's the job?"

"What we seek," Eleanor said, "is an urn possessed by a bitter rival. We have a man on the inside, so all you need to do is bring the urn back to us."

Grint tore his eyes from the coin, observing Eleanor from under his brows. "I've been doing this most of my life. Long enough to know there's more to it than that. Always is for a purse this bloated."

Eleanor drew a map in the dirt. "There's a city in the mountains where the nobility go..." Her words cut off as the purse full of coin landed in the middle of her drawing.

"I know what the Terrastags are." Grint stood and hung his coat on a branch. The action gave him an excuse to prepare for a fight. Saying no would turn this thing bloody. The minions were already on their feet. Knives dripping with blood gripped in their meaty paws. Grint's new blade was close at hand, and now his bag as well with more than a few tricks tucked away inside. Getting to the exit felt reasonable if the men didn't turn into dogs. In hindsight, he shouldn't have given the coin back.

"Sit," Eleanor commanded. "Everyone." The minions did, but Grint continued standing. "Please."

Grint compromised by leaning against the tree, digging at a piece of bark. "Not doing it. It's suicide. That place devours thieves."

"If you would allow me to elaborate," Eleanor's voice dripped with honey. "We have a way in and back out. Your role is more like a courier than a thief. A courier we don't want seen."

Grint stabbed the tree with his knife and stepped away, shaking and nodding his head in a silent debate. Losing the private argument, his shoulders sagged, and he chewed his lower lip before he faced Eleanor and said, "I get paid the pouch and..."

"And whatever else you steal. As long as I get the urn."

"The pouch," Grint held up a single finger. Eleanor tossed it at his feet. "Whatever else I steal," he held up a second finger. "And ten thousand gold triumverates after the job is done." A third finger went up.

Torchy laughed, then Noseless and Crosshatch. "What is a thief going to do with that much gold?"

"Buy my own Terrastag manor," Grint said still holding up his fingers. "Now shut your mouths before I hold up a fourth finger and demand that all of you get dismembered to match your friend." Torchy looked ready to snap, but Noseless put a hand on his shoulder.

"Why would I pay you ten thousand?" Eleanor responded as if the outburst had never taken place.

"Time is of the essence and I'm your only option," Grint didn't hide his satisfaction.

"You're far from my only option," Eleanor laughed.

"Head back to Kambar then," Grint shrugged. "There were two other thieves at that Cheat Me table, but my guess is they'll soil their britches when you say the words Terrastag Manor. Price just went up to eleven thousand."

"Three thousand," she countered. "While we wish to acquire the urn with haste, Tamos is not an expert on our timeline."

"Death is the gift long promised," Grint said. Eleanor gave him a dangerous look. "I've been around necromancers before."

"Is that a problem?"

"I don't care if you enjoy dead things," Grint waved his hand. "You want the urn for a ritual? I'll get it for you, but don't tell me there isn't a timeline. Not when the Stabbing is what? A moon's cycle away?"

Eleanor's shoulders dropped a hair as her foot stopped tapping. The Stabbing was a convergence of the moons Effulg and Nacinth. Once a decade, the shard of the shattered moon Nacinth crossed into the mother moon. Effulg turned blood red when it happened, as if stabbed. Spiritual fanatics and necromancers used the time to perform some of their most powerful rituals. Hobbe said it was a bunch of guff and all in people's heads, but by Eleanor's reaction, she believed - and the urn was essential to that.

"Five thousand. Final offer," she said as she stood.

"Fifteen," Grint replied. "It's still my neck. I don't care how good your way in or out are. It's the Terrastags."

"Then we have an accord," she held out her hand. Grint spat into his and they shook. There was no further commentary or argument from her minions. They knew to hold their tongues.

Grint picked up the statue, tucking it into his bag before walking toward the exit path.

"Where are you going?" Noseless asked.

"To finish my first job," Grint replied, already looking forward to handing off the burdensome statue. Noseless appeared ready to follow but Eleanor cleared her throat and that stopped him. "Sorry pup, my buyer doesn't like the unknown."

"And you'll be back." Eleanor's cold eyes expected an answer.

"I always finish my jobs," he winked.

*****

Making his way through the forest was much easier with the sun up. And no one chasing him. But he still felt the need to pause and listen for Eleanor's hounds just in case. Either they were better at sneaking than they let on, or Eleanor felt content to let him conduct his business. Half a mile north of the oasis, along the steepening slopes of the mountains was the clearing he sought. A lonely sentinel sat on the slope staring at the new sun. A thick, gray cape draped over his shoulders and his frayed woolen arming cap pulled over pointed ears. Faighur had owned the hat for as long as Grint knew him - which was most of his life.

Faighur did not stir as Grint approached or even when he sat in the grass beside him. It was not until Grint produced a bladder of fire rum that his old friend moved. He smiled, eyes wide and mouth open in anticipation of a sip. Faighur's skin was smooth, almost slick, and colored the faintest hue of grayish-green. Beneath that ratty, old cap was a bald head, a trait Grint assumed extended everywhere else on his person, though he'd never gotten drunk enough to ask.

"Drink up," Grint said.

"Torsha," Faighur replied in his monotone way before drinking.

"Remind me what Torsha means again. Is it Thank you? Or burn in Parthia?" Grint leaned back on his elbows looking at the final few stars that had yet to accept the dawn.

"There are many I would tell to burn in Parthia," Faighur replied. "You are not one. It means 'thank you'."

They sat in silence as they passed the skin back and forth, but it wasn't uncomfortable. It was the relaxed silence that good friends knew how to share. With the skin drained and a warm buzz in their chests, Faighur turned his attention to the sack containing the jade statue.

"Did you have trouble stealing it?"

"You took your time bashing your giant ugly head through the wall." Grint smirked as Faighur made a disgruntled sound. "But after my incredible heroics it was easy. No one was watching the back."

Faighur was a skinling like Eleanor's dogs. Except his change allowed him to transform from man to dragon. The suicidal risk in becoming a dragon made him the only person of any race to accomplish the feat. The rituals involved in skinling magic were odd and beyond Grint's desire to understand. Not that Faighur would talk about it even if Grint wanted him to. His friend was tight-lipped about the story. The costs were great to become a normal animal. Krypsie only knew what it cost him to become a dragon.

Much like all the thieves Hobbe collected, Faighur was an orphan. A cult looking for warrior blood butchered his family. When the God of Thieves found him, Faighur had been surviving by stealing food from vendors in Barro Dineer. Grint remembered him as a shy boy with a penchant for laughing in awkward situations. Crews always had their fair share of infighting but no one ever fought with Faighur. That was his strength. At least until he underwent the change.

"You neglected to answer my challenge question outside the tavern."

"I've told you a hundred times, I'm not replying to those. We don't need a fiddle-dragged code because we know who each other are!"

Faighur made a non-committal sound and whistled at the statue. "Still, my buyer will be quite pleased. A sylph of this magnitude is scarce."

Grint dropped the statue when he heard the word sylph and rolled away. Faighur caught and set it on the grass while

Grint hopped around shaking his hands and wiping them against his pants.

"Brau fallah geihanid," Faighur hissed, inspecting the sylph for damage. "This one houses over a thousand souls."

"You had me steal a pox-horned sylph? With a thousand ghosts inside of it?"

"Yes," Faighur said, looking up. "What did you think it was?"

"A kry-damned jade statue!" Grint shouted.

"The things you get upset about," Faighur replied, cocking his head.

"I had that thing around necromancers," Grint growled, pointing at the statue. "Do you know what they could have done to me if they knew what it was? Or what was inside?" The thought made him ill.

"Is that what they are? I could not tell." Faighur admired the statue as the first rays of sunlight struck its side.

He couldn't tell? It meant Faighur knew they were chasing him. Knew they caught him and brought him back to the oasis. All of that and he hadn't done a thing to intervene. Instead, he sat on the hill looking at the horizon - because it wouldn't have occurred to him to help. That was Faighur now. Most things didn't occur to him. The thoughts of a dragon's mind were far beyond a simple man's understanding. The affable boy Grint knew was long gone.

"I have been human too long of late," Faighur said as he stood. "I long for the winds. Would you like me to fly you somewhere away from those people?"

"No," Grint said emphatically.

"Your fear of heights is amusing," he replied in a voice bereft of amusement. "And contradictory of the feats I have seen you perform."

"They have money. And a job," Grint responded.

"Sometimes that is enough," Faighur nodded. "Yet this group smells wrong. They will try to kill you."

"I'm sure they will," Grint smiled.

"Is it worth it?"

"It's the Terrastags," Grint lifted his eyebrows and beamed a smile. Faighur's eyes widened in the first spark of emotion Grint had seen in years.

"Ma'harata," the skinling breathed.

"You want in?" Faighur nodded but looked down at the sylph. "Go meet your buyer. I'd prefer this group doesn't know about you. Let's plan to meet south of Tarsul; before the mountain passes. Oh, and let Marm know I may send word."

Faighur removed his robe and hat, placing them in the bag with the sylph. Beneath he was naked, so Grint averted his eyes, lest he get his answer on the coverage of hair. "Be careful, my friend," Faighur said. "I do not long for the day when I will have to avenge you."

"That's a long time from now," Grint replied. Dragons lived for centuries. Who knew if that held true for skinling dragons. Either way, Faighur would outlive Grint. It didn't take a seer to scry that.

"I hope so. Gerahast!" he shouted and broke into a sprint down the slope. As he neared the trees Faighur leapt into the air and rose much higher than Grint could have managed. As he cleared the treetops, great wings sprouted from his back and a serpentine tail emerged. The neck lengthened as thick scales rippled into existence. Where once there had been a man, there was now a dragon flying low across the horizon. Grint sat back on the grass and watched.

It always helps to have a dragon up your sleeve, was his last thought before sleep took him.

4

"The Papality have their pilgrimage of nine towers. Parthians their seven glories. For a thief it's just one: The Terrastags."

– Blue Fingered Hobbe

"Wake," the gruff voice commanded as a hard boot dug into Grint's side.

Grint rolled over and hopped to his feet, drawing the stolen knife. In his mind, it was a nimble and awe-inspiring move. In reality, the fire rum running through his head skewed his equilibrium, so he stumbled and dropped the knife. As he recovered, he squinted against the light and found Crosshatch shaking his head.

"Krypsie's sake, Crosshatch. You're not a sight I want to wake up to."

"Did you pass out?" the minion was incredulous.

"Maybe," Grint answered as he stretched and cracked his neck. "Has she summoned me?"

Tamos grunted, pointing their way down the hill. Traveling with a hostile at your back was never a wise way to continue living, but they weren't foolish enough to kill him with the job unfinished. That didn't dissuade an image of Crosshatch burying a dagger in his back as they walked.

Gold given is gold they'll kill you to get back. An old lesson Hobbe taught over and over because there was truth to it. The more gold someone offered for a job, the more certain it became they would kill you to take it back. In the world of thieves, the stingy brokers are the ones you could trust. Fifteen thousand gold triumverates for a job was an egregious amount. Even with the Terrastags involved. Grint knew with certainty they would dispatch him once he delivered the urn.

I have until then to figure out how to avoid that, Grint thought. They won't try anything until then.

Every plan you make, expect your opponent has made two. Another of Hobbe's lessons came to mind. Grint could even picture the smug look on Hobbe's face, nodding as he spoke.

"Shut up," Grint said, swatting at the imagined voice.

"I wasn't speaking," Tamos replied as he shoved Grint. Grint listened to the sound of the morning birds as his breath puffed out before him. Tree sap ran thick across the bark as small critters darted about under the brush, emboldened by the light. It wasn't often he found himself awake at such an hour to experience these things. The morning was a rude time of day.

Grint yanked the latch to open the oasis. Eleanor and Torchy cut their conversation short, having learned their lesson from the night before. A flat iron pan sat over the smoldering embers, frying a pile of meaty-hash that filled the oasis with its rich aroma. Grint opened his mouth in a cavernous yawn and sat beside his bag, leaned back, then closed his eyes. One more hour of sleep and he would be right as rain.

A tin plate slapped the dirt by his feet, followed by the word, "Eat."

"I'm sleeping," Grint replied as he waved his hand to shoo them away, eyes still closed.

"We're leaving," Crosshatch said as he nudged Grint with a boot.

"Have a good ride," Grint wished they would just shut up and let him sleep. The urn would still be there whether they left now or in an hour.

"I'll drag you if I must," Crosshatch nudged him again, his glee at the prospect of doing just that was plain in his voice. Not wanting to test the hound, Grint sat up and wiped the sleep from his eyes as best he could.

"I'm a thief. A nocturnal creature. Only monks get up at this abominable hour." He reached down and collected the plate. It smelled good at least. A fork stuck out from the hash, so Grint scooped a heaping pile, but paused before it reached his mouth. Should he be suspicious that their dead compatriot's body was absent? All that remained of the departed was a puddle of red-hued mud. Had they cooked him up for morning vittles? Grint looked at the hash.

"We're not eating dog?" he asked as he looked over at Eleanor. Her expression remained flat, showing neither annoyance nor amusement.

"It's kipper," Torchy answered. His face sagged, insulted by the suggestion.

"That's good then," Grint said. "Death is not a gift I want for breakfast." He shoveled a forkful into his mouth and choked. Kipper hash was a simple dish used to feed military units. The primary ingredients being potatoes, peppers and kippers; which were small rodents not unlike a squirrel. If memory served, the dish originated in the northeast. If you ever wanted to know where someone came from? Look to what they ate. Food always told the tale. This lot hailed from Taryn or Cattachat. Grint put that tidbit in his back pocket in case he needed it later.

As he swallowed the first bite, he jammed the fork back in the hash and tossed the plate to the ground. "I didn't poison it," Malus commented.

"With as much garlic as you used, Torchy, I would disagree." Grint filled his mouth with water, then swished and spat it back out. Anything to clear the taste.

Grint knelt in front of his travel bag, a constant companion on all his adventures. Upon a cursory glance it was unremarkable, a simple burlap bag with two straps to sling over the shoulders. It had once been gray, but years of travel stained it a multitude of colors, including blood - of which only some was Grint's. Frayed seams lined the edges and three sewn leather patches sealed up holes that would otherwise dump the contents onto the ground. Only the latch, a flat piece of tarnished copper looked out of place and a bit too grandiose. Grint ran his finger over the odd symbol etched into it; three daggers falling to the right. He never found out what it meant, but he cared a great deal for what it did.

The thief cocked his head at the latch sitting just a tad askew. Glancing over his shoulder, he looked first at Eleanor, then to her hounds. Torchy busied himself wrapping a hand burnt to match his face. Grint allowed himself a chuckle, then cupped his fingers under the latch and used his body to hide what he did. The bag unhooked, and he tossed the flap over the back.

"An interesting defense." Eleanor stood behind him and he flinched. He hadn't heard her approach.

"It does the trick." The first thing he pulled out was a simple necklace of black string with a bleached knob of wood hanging on the end. The hand-etched carving depicted a man and a woman embracing, but was faint. The image almost worn clean away after years of running his thumb across the surface. Grint put the necklace on and tucked it into his shirt. Next, he grabbed a small pouch of seeds and dried fruit. A half handful would be enough to satiate him until lunch.

"What else is in there?" Eleanor craned her neck, curiosity getting the best of her.

Grint closed the latch and slung the bag over his back as he stood. "Clothes, food, and more than a few things that help me along the way. So, keep your paws off it if I'm not around." Grint pointed at Malus's hand, which he tried to hide behind his back. "There're things in here that can level the mountains."

Tamos laughed, "Which mountains?"

Grint stopped at the mouth of the exit path and turned toward his new compatriots, all humor gone from his face. "All of them." And then exited.

Outside the oasis, the crispness of the morning struck him anew. A breeze picked up, and the chill cut through his coat until he tied it shut. There would be a storm in a few days. The air had that quality. Eleanor stepped out next, fastening a thick purple cloak around her neck. The wind rippled the fabric and blew strands of hair across her face. For a moment she reminded him of Jessua, so he turned away.

"Are we waiting for Noseless?" Grint peered around for the missing minion.

"Who?" Eleanor sounded confused.

Grint made a hand motion around his nose, "Noseless. The one without the nose." And then under his breath, "I thought it would be obvious."

"Callum," she said, enunciating his name, "has gone to get you a horse and will meet us at the base of the mountains. I think it wise to avoid the roads until we're well clear of Kambar."

Grint leaned against a tree and closed his eyes waiting for the minions to finish breaking camp. Fire rum and a sleepless night made poor travelers. A short nap followed by a cup of coffee would go a long way towards getting him down the mountain, but it didn't seem his benefactors were much inclined to allow that.

"Next time, clean your own dish." Grint opened his eyes to find crosshatch waving a tin plate in his direction. The moment, combined with the alcohol became too ludicrous for Grint, who threw back his head and laughed. It wasn't the reaction the minion expected, and Tamos lowered the plate while looking at his mistress in confusion. Grint shook his head and walked away.

"Where are you going?" Eleanor called out.

"To the Terrastags. You coming?" Grint answered.

For a blessed time, they walked in silence, carving a new trail through the trees. Paths on the mountain were rare and overgrown from decades of disuse, making the going slow. Crosshatch lugged the gear on his back as Torchy scouted the woods. In his dog form, Torchy was a mastiff with blood red fur. It made Grint wonder what Noseless looked like as a dog.

Around midday, Grint pulled a few sticks of dried beef from his bag and gnawed on them. Eleanor walked a few feet to his right, wiping the back of her neck with a kerchief.

Sparse tree cover on the lower slopes let the sun through, baking the land. The temperature warmed enough to cause a thin sheen of sweat to break out. Grint walked up beside her and offered her a piece of jerky, which she accepted.

"Venison?" she asked and Grint nodded. "I've been wondering," which was never a good statement to hear. It meant the conversation would go in an unpleasant direction.

"About?"

"You don't have your own horse."

"I don't have a pet dragon," Grint rolled his eyes.

"Interesting that was your first thought."

"That's where you were heading," Grint answered. "Sure, you'd twist and turn your way there, but that's what you wanted to say."

"And yet..." she began, but Grint cut her off.

"I'm not Zorn, flying around on the back of a dragon."

"Zorn flew on racs," she corrected.

"Rac, dragon, flying lyzan," he waved his hand in the air. "The point is, if I tamed a dragon, why didn't I have it eat you and your dogs last night?"

"A fair point," she said, considering the words. "It is just odd that someone who may need to escape in haste does so on foot."

"When I need a horse, I steal one," Grint said. "When I need coin, I sell the horse. It's worked my whole life, so why try anything different?" Eleanor nodded, perhaps satisfied by the answer, perhaps not. It was difficult to read her expressions, but she remained silent which suited Grint.

As the sun set, they reached the base of the mountains and found Noseless waiting with the promised horses. Eleanor conferred with her scout as the others unloaded a large tent and set it up. Grint found a patch of grass warmed by the sun and put his bag down before retrieving a shirt from within. He balled the garment up and put it under his head. Within moments he was asleep.

*****

During the night, the sound of whispers woke Grint. Sleeping light was a necessary skill every thief learned, but Grint took it a step further and trained himself not to flinch when he awoke. Two figures stood by the horses, obscured by a thin layer of fog and swirls of mist. Grint could make out one of them; Eleanor. The other had their hood up, but he reasoned that it was one of her minions. The stature. The deference they paid her. The barest hint of conversation floated on the wind.

"Don't rest until you..." their muffled words were difficult to piece together without the benefit of reading their lips and cut off as an owl hooted. Eleanor turned her gaze towards Grint, who planned only to feign sleep but fell back into the real thing.

He woke again in the morning, leaving him to wonder if the encounter was a dream. Dew slicked the grass and soaked his hands as he sat up. One hound sat close by, lying on his belly, panting with its tongue hanging out.

"Crosshatch, you need to stop watching me sleep." The hound bared its teeth, hackles rising. Grint yanked free a moldy piece of wood, half buried in the mud and tossed it over the dog's head. Crosshatch watched the stick but didn't move.

"Fetch," Grint said. The mutt barked at him. Eleanor whistled and Tamos quieted, trotting across the camp to sit at her side. Skinlings were odd, even Faighur. They often preferred their animal form to their humanity.

Grint brushed himself off, then picked up his bag and the shirt he used for a pillow, slinging each over a shoulder. Torchy was cooking breakfast again. More kipper hash by the smell. *What a treat.* Eleanor stood by the flames, warming her hands. Behind her they had raised a fair-sized, white tent. With the entrance secured, Grint couldn't see inside, but it wouldn't surprise him if she had a bed.

"Where are you going?" she asked as he walked past the fire.

"Washing up," Grint replied.

"Food is almost ready," Torchy said over the hiss from the frying pan. Grint waved his hand and kept walking. Noseless had disappeared again, and they were shy a horse. Not a dream. *Where did you send him, Eleanor? What goal demanded 'no rest' until completed? Or found?* Whatever it was, it meant trouble for Grint, that much he could surmise. But he kept turning it over in his mind as he left the camp behind.

The birds were talkative, their calls filling the air, but not so loud that he couldn't hear the babble of a creek. He adjusted his path a little to the right and kept going until he found the serene, little stream. A tree sat atop the embankment where he hung his bag and coat. The necklace was next, hung with a gentle hand on a small knot, followed by his shirt, boots and socks. Rolling his pants above the ankles, Grint stepped into the water.

It was cold, no doubt feeding from a majestic mountain reservoir, but also refreshing. Grint wiggled his toes in the silt as the water brushed past his shins. The creek deepened an eyeshot downstream, but there was no time to dive in. Instead, he reached down and splashed water on his chest and arms, scrubbing the grime away. He finished by dunking his head and loosening all the dirt and bits he could from his hair. As he stood and shook his tangled locks, he imagined looking like a dog drying itself. The irony wasn't lost on him.

Grint sat with his back to the tree, drying his feet with yesterday's shirt and contemplating the midnight conversation. A riddle with no answer. None he could fathom without more to go on. "Just keep your head up and eyes open," he warned himself. Putting on the shirt he used for a pillow, Grint grabbed his belongings and strolled back to camp.

Eleanor and her minions exposed a weakness without realizing. It was after all not a weakness one often considered. They may be travelers, but they weren't rough travelers, preferring the comfort of camps and cook fires. Each knew the song of battle and fought hard, but in the dull moments between brawls they stayed at inns and took baths. Grint would make a goblin's wager that the hounds slept at the foot of her bed. Too bad for them, the road was a tough place and Grint had every intention of making it harder.

Torchy had a plate of hash waiting for Grint while a pot of coffee simmered over the flames. Grint availed himself of both and smiled at the rich, refined taste of the coffee. Not at all like the bitter stuff he choked down when he had the coin to buy some. The hash also had far less garlic and was close to edible. Shoveling the last heap into his mouth, he washed it down with coffee and then dropped the cup and plate.

"I told you to wash your own dishes," Crosshatch said in a voice sounding like a bark. He may be in human form, performing mundane chores, but there would always be a part of him that remained a dog.

"That's not what she's paying me for," Grint said with a wink. "Now which one is mine?"

"The gray," Torchy answered.

It was clear why they chose that horse for him. At his approach, the gray bucked and stamped its feet. The horse flared its nostrils as Grint reached into his bag and pulled out a chunk of dried apple. The stallion sniffed at it and then took it from Grint's hand, nipping him. Grint didn't scold him. Instead, he reached up and stroked his nose, which seemed to calm the beast.

Opening the saddle bags, Grint pulled out a brush and brushed the gray, avoiding the bruising on his flanks where some muck-coddled rider kicked him often and hard. The gray danced as Grint neared the bruises, but some calming sounds and the promise of more apple put him at ease.

"And what's your name?" he asked.

"It's a horse, what need does it have for a name?" Crosshatch mocked.

"One could say the same for dogs," Grint said as the horse bobbed its head and whinnied. People underestimated a horse's intelligence at their peril. Crosshatch grumbled but let him be after that and Grint continued brushing down the stallion. Along with the bruises were a plethora of scars from arrows and sword. The horse had seen battles through the years. Some scars were a decade or more old. As he finished, he took another bit of apple and let the stallion eat it. This time he didn't nip the hand.

"Every horse needs a name," he whispered as the horse chewed its reward. "What do you want yours to be? Thorny? Kingston? Marble?" The horse seemed to pay little attention to the names he listed until he reached, "Storms?" At the sound of that name, he bobbed his head again.

"Storms it is then," he said with a satisfied smile. "You'll rage like a tempest when you need to. I can see that."

"Are you about done?" Eleanor sat atop her horse and looked down at Grint with impatience.

"Yes," Grint said and mocked a bow. "Right away, mistress."

Eleanor rolled her eyes as she wheeled the horse around. Grint stowed the brush and mounted Storms, who only bucked a little at his new rider. Reaching forward, Grint pet the horse's neck to ease his tension and then slapped the back of his own neck with both hands. The blood drained from his face. Eleanor and her minions trotted a few lengths ahead, talking about the best route to Tan Tan, but their voices trailed off as Grint galloped full speed towards the creek he'd bathed in.

Torchy screamed in alarm, but Grint didn't care. His heart pounded against his chest as he raced headlong towards the trees. Storms whinnied with pleasure at the pace and only shook his head when pulled to a stop. Grint leapt from the saddle, breaking into a run as his feet touched the ground. The horse pawed at the dirt as Grint darted between trees to the edge of the creek. Hanging on an old knot swung the necklace he forgot to put back on. Grint pulled it down and put the loop over his head. It was the last thing Jessua had given him. The last bit of her he had.

"I didn't take you for sentimental," Eleanor said. Grint froze mid-motion.

"I'm not," he answered as he finished tucking the necklace into his shirt. Eleanor never bothered to dismount her horse at the edge of the trees. Miraculously, Storms remained there too. Only now did he stop to think the horse might bolt.

"For a moment I thought the gray had gone rogue," Eleanor said, her face full with a sinister smile. "Tamos thought you were trying to run and wanted to shoot you with an arrow. Neither instance was true. Such a spirited run for a simple trinket. Must hold great value?"

Grint ignored her as best he could as he walked back to Storms and swung his leg over the saddle. "Or is it more witchcraft?" she continued. "Something to protect you from the all-seeing eyes?" Her tone was thick like honeyed syrup.

He gave no answer. Let her work out her own story. People were arrogant enough to believe their answers were always the correct ones. Give them the barest nugget and soon enough they would hand you your own alibi.

Foolish boy, Hobbes' voice laughed. *You've betrayed your own weakness!*

Grint wished for the second time in as many days the old voice would shut up. "How about you tell me this plan of yours?"

5

"Leverage, my boy. Leverage is all you need. With the proper leverage one can open a door, move a log, or topple a King. Leverage!"

– Master and Apprentice, Volume 1

The plan. It was a simple enough idea. Within the Terrastags was an urn her master required. It was solid gold and the size of a man's forearm with ancient runes carved along the base. The current resting spot of the urn was the subterranean vault of Lord Ballastrine, which was where the need for a thief came in.

A cover story provided by the count would allow Grint to enter the city unmolested. From there he needed to break into Ballastrine's manor, find their contact within the vault, and take possession of the urn. If he was everything he claimed, Grint should be able to get in and out before anyone was the wiser.

Once he delivered the urn, the hounds would kill him. That part she would hold back for obvious reasons. The discovery of his mauled body beside fragments of a shattered replica urn should be enough to close the circle, eradicating any trace of Count Danghier's involvement. Thinking of the thief's demise brought a smile. His inane banter spilled forth without end and wormed its way under her skin.

On their second night of travel, towering storm clouds swallowed the moons, darkening the land. Eleanor knelt beside the campfire, drawing a diagram of the Terrastags in the dirt. Fresh rabbit meat sizzled over the cookfire as Tamos set up her tent. The thief stood over her shoulder asking questions, but Eleanor couldn't focus. Each time he shoveled food into his mouth the fork scraped against the tin plate. And each time she imagined taking the fork and stabbing him with it.

"It is not to scale," she said through gritted teeth, "but it is close."

"There's plenty of dirt if you need to make it bigger," he said. The fork scraped again.

"It need not be bigger. What you need to know is that there are five boulevards running north to south and five running east to west." Eleanor jabbed a stick at each as she spoke. "At each intersection is a public square. If you lose your bearings, find the one in the middle. It's called Divinity Square and has a fountain depicting the gods."

"All one hundred of them?"

Eleanor dropped her shoulders and exhaled, then looked over her shoulder at the thief. "I doubt very much that the lords and ladies of Terragard put much faith in the bush spirits of the commoners."

Grint shrugged, "Sounds less impressive. Just show me where this Bardo lives."

"Ballastrine," she said, turning back to the map. "I have told you his name three times. Bardo is the alchemist you are meeting in the vault. The manor of Ballastrine is here."

Eleanor stuck the poker into one of the grid segments near the upper right corner.

Grint nodded as he walked over to ladle more hash onto his plate. The thief tore a piece of rabbit meat free and dropped it on top, sucking the grease from his fingers. The meat burned while the hounds worked on the tent leaving the stench of charred rabbit to linger in the air. Grint made a face as he chewed but said nothing as he took the plate over to his bag.

"You still haven't told me what the story is that will get me through the gates," his words close to unintelligible under the chewing.

Eleanor produced a fine, dark lacquered disk the size of her palm and threw it to his side. "The Dueling Spiders?" he asked as he inspected the intricate carvings on the sigil of two mirrored spiders holding swords above their heads, each pointed towards their counterpart. "House of the Geldens?"

"You know of them?"

"I've robbed them," Grint answered.

Eleanor laughed, until she realized he wasn't joking. Was she impressed? "The Crown of the Seven Kingdoms have no holdings in the Terrastags. You will enter as a representative of the Geldens to appraise a manor for purchase."

"The Geldens are rich," Grint replied. "Won't that draw attention from someone wanting to impress them? The Governor?"

"Governor Ardon is a self-important narcissist. He won't leave his manor for anyone shy of Krypholos. He will expect the Geldens to attend him once they arrive."

"You know a fair bit about the inner workings of the Terrastags." Grint looked up from the disk. "How?"

Eleanor produced a second disk, this one with the carving of Danghier's sigil; eight snake heads blossoming out from a single stalk. "Not one I recognize. I must not have robbed your master yet."

"I would not advise you try." It was a warning the thief laughed at.

"If you have a disk, I would assume you have a manor?"

"My master does," Eleanor answered.

"Why the story? Why not give me yours and skip the potential for a mess?" It was a fair point, but one that had an answer.

"Our house cannot connect to the theft," Eleanor said.

"They're rivals," the thief worked out. "The urn goes missing and Master Snakeheads will be the first one blamed."

A pot of water slammed to the ground, spilling liquid that hissed as it ran into the fire. Tamos stood over the mess, his eyes ablaze with fury. "You will not demean or disrespect the name of Count Danghier!"

"No offense," Grint said, holding his hands up. "I meant no disrespect to," and then he looked at Eleanor with a hidden smile, "Count Danghier."

Eleanor stared back, her face made of stone. It did not matter if he knew the count's name as it was not something she was trying to hide from him. It was the ease at which he whittled out information that rankled her so. There would be no need to punish the hounds as the information had no value - unless one considered that names themselves held power. Eleanor needed to know what the thief had in that kry-damned bag of his. The trip would give her opportunity to charm him and then he would spill his secrets. They always did.

"Big storms coming in tomorrow," Grint said as he tossed his plate against the overturned pot. "Will make traveling fun." And then closed his eyes.

*****

The thief's prediction was as accurate as it was frustrating. In the hour before dawn the storm started and refused to let up. For two days they traveled under a deluge of rain and sleet, each keeping their own company in miserable silence. It didn't take much to draw a person into themselves. Save for the thief. Nothing appeared to bother him.

They crossed the border into Greater Anghor on the first night and camped beneath a canopy of trees. Even within the tent the moisture seeped into everything. Eleanor woke up feeling leaden and irritable. A mood that worsened as she stepped outside. The thief remained dry, a remarkable feat for laying in the tall grass with nothing but a bedroll. Everything else in the camp was terribly waterlogged, so it was a puzzle she worked through her mind as they rode.

At dusk they set up camp, cursing the unending storm. Eleanor commanded Malus to remain outside with the thief. To see what magic he employed to remain dry. It must have been magic. The hound lay outside the tent whining without end, so she relented and allowed him in, where he curled up beside his brother. Eleanor took the time to dry his red fur before laying back. The slap of rain on the canvas made sleep a stranger for many hours and when she awoke, a chill had once more settled into her skin. As before, the thief appeared unaffected by the weather. She found him leaning against a tree, smoking a wooden pipe that he chewed as often as he puffed.

"What is that?" she asked.

Grint pointed the end of the pipe at some bushes. "Nestel," he said. "It's flavorful," and held the pipe out to her. She refused. It smelled like a dead skunk. Tonight, Malus would remain with the thief no matter how often he whined.

With the Anghor Mountains now at their back. The quartet of riders sat atop a rise that sloped across several miles to the shores of Lake Tarsis. The rain turned to a fine mist that bit at them from whichever direction the wind blew. A town sat on the shore, faint firelight twinkling in the growing darkness.

"Ten, maybe twelve buildings," Tamos said, holding a hand over his brow to shelter his eyes.

As miserable as she felt, Eleanor wanted to limit the number of interactions they exposed themselves to. A small copse of trees further inland caught her eye. "We'll make camp there."

"And mark ourselves as bandits," Grint said. "More natural to go into the town. Besides that's swampland. Gators and snakes."

"Dinner," Malus said, sounding excited. Grint laughed.

"I'm ready for a bed and a hot meal that Torchy hasn't butchered."

"You can cook your own meals," Malus said, sounding insulted.

Bickering aside, the thief's proposal spoke to her. One night in this remote fishing village would not jeopardize their mission. Even were Ballastrine to come this far in his search for retribution, all he would glean from the encounter was that he traveled the wrong direction. "Yes, let us see what the village has to offer."

It was not much. Tamos' estimations were correct. Ten buildings; all ramshackle heaps of roughhewn planks jammed together with pitch and spikes. A dirt road ran through the center of the village with five houses on either side. The anatomical origin of each house - a tiny square shack - was visible beneath years of repairs and additions. Of the ten, only one appeared suitable for occupants. It was the largest, boasting a second-floor, glass windows, and a railed porch around the front and sides of the structure.

The rains turned the dirt road into a thick mud good for snagging the horses' hooves as they stepped. Half sunken in the morass was an overturned boat, propped up at the bow. Two dogs sheltered themselves from the storm beneath it as they fought over a bone, their battle stopping when they noticed the mounted strangers. Angry barks filled the night. The thief turned to regard Tamos and Malus with a giant grin. No doubt his ceaseless flippancy would soon follow.

"Quiet down, ungrateful mutts!" The porch door swung open, and a man of medium build and middling age stormed out. In his youth he may have been attractive. Now he was balding, tired, and flabby with an inordinate number of scars along his forehead. More troubling was that he wore only a long nightshirt, buttons askew. Thank Krypholos, it hung low enough to cover his bits. But not by much. The man jumped when he saw the entourage, but recovered with a slap of his ample belly.

"We're traveling south," Eleanor answered the unasked question. "The weather has been unfriendly. We thought perhaps a night beneath a roof might reinvigorate us."

"Don't get many visitors," the man said. Other villagers opened their doors enough to peek through the crack. Their curiosity at the sound of voices tempered by a mistrust of outsiders. They were rough folk, hair in tangles, clothes torn and sullied. True fisherfolk who saw little of the outside world.

"We need a room if you have it."

"A room? Yes," the man answered, his face splitting wide in a smile. "Where are my manners? Plenty of room here. Plenty of room. No place to stable your horses, but you can tie them to the rails. Plenty of room. I'm Jacken, the mayor of this village."

"We can pay," Eleanor said, reaching for her coin purse.

"Unnecessary," Jacken said. "Plenty of room. Only the one spare room in my home. Which I insist you take. Best room in the village. Nothing less for the leader of this bold expedition. The others can find rooms with my people."

"I know which room I'm taking," Grint said, dismounting. He smiled at two women leaning against a rickety doorframe, giggling as they whispered to one another. Twin sisters, and even without all their teeth Eleanor could recognize a comeliness to their appearance.

"No. No, no, no," Jacken said, stammering and spluttering. "No. Lonnel! Lonnel, come out here!" The mayor came down the steps, his bare feet squashing in the mud.

Another door swung open spilling bright firelight onto the street. A bent, angry looking old man stepped out and spat something dark that landed beside one of Grint's boots. "What?" the codger said.

"Need you to take this one in," pointing at Grint. "Show him our heartiest hospitality. Can't have reputations besmirched."

"No," Lonnel said. When his door slammed shut the entire structure shook. The mayor gathered fistfuls of mud and began throwing them at the side of Lonnel's house, shouting for him to come back. A loud crash sounded inside the hovel and the door re-opened. "Come on in if you're coming."

Grint shrugged and wandered in. The door closed once more.

"Now that's settled, we can get out of this rain," Jacken pointed a muddy hand at his door. Eleanor dismounted and tied her horse beside Grint's. Jacken offered her his hand in ascending the two steps to the porch. Eleanor accepted the gesture as to not be rude. Tamos and Malus followed, but the mayor blocked their way. With a wide smile he directed them to an empty house with a collapsed roof across the street. "Plenty of room. Plenty."

Jacken wasn't an obstacle to the hounds, but a roll of the eyes and nod from Eleanor sent them on their way. The mayor puffed his chest as if it was his antics that dissuaded them. Ridiculous. "After you," she said, but before she entered, Eleanor paused. Was that laughter coming from Lonnel's shack? Had the thief's quick charm worked on the old man? Or was this another game? It was difficult to tell with that one.

"Yes, yes, please come in," Jacken said. Eleanor let it go, not seeing the potential harm if this was a game.

The interior of the mayor's abode did not subvert her expectations. The pungent stench of lake fish lay thick on the air. It emanated from a small room to the left where she could see fish hanging from hooks over barrels of salt. It drowned out the underlying smell of mildew and rot that settled into the wood. Mold bespeckled the floors and lower walls while many boards had disintegrated from the moisture, exposing large gaps between rooms. It looked a long time since anyone tried to repair the damage.

"How did you become mayor?" Eleanor ran her finger across a board which folded in on itself like parchment. How is this house still standing?

"I own the boats," Jacken replied. The ass of a man even sounded prideful at the admission. "It gets cold at night. Perhaps you would prefer to..."

"You mentioned a spare room," Eleanor said in a tone that demanded his pursuit of the subject go no further.

"My pleasure," Jacken said with no sign of rejection. "Through the door to the right. I can't speak to the freshness of the linens. A lady like you deserves much better."

"This will do," Eleanor said as she entered a room barely bigger than a closet. The bed was small with a lopsided mattress on an old wooden frame. Pieces of straw stuck through the threadbare cotton sheet, and around the half-sized fur they placed on top as an afterthought. A rice sack had been used for the pillow casing, and as Eleanor placed her hand against it, she realized it was not a casing at all, but a sack of rice used for a pillow. The comfort of sleeping in the tent set a low bar. This room failed to best even that. But it was dry, so she would accept the hospitality for what it was.

Sleep was difficult to come by as the hours dragged on, but she did not find herself afraid. There was little to worry her in a place like this. Even if the entire village descended on the room, the cost they would pay in blood would outweigh their baser desires. No, the insomnia came from the creaking floorboards outside the door. From the heft of the steps, she judged it to be the mayor. Though there could have been someone else in the house she hadn't seen. Eleanor spent years training her mind to alert her of noises at night. Catching her unaware was near impossible. While the mayor was the least threatening man she encountered on this journey, his cacophonous footfalls were akin to a two-ton bell clanging in a city square.

As night stretched toward morning, she reached the limit of what good manners allowed. Swinging her legs out of bed Eleanor stepped like a wraith. The first blade she pulled from her bag was a dagger with a barbed edge that hummed when unsheathed. Opening the door, she found the mayor a few steps away, wringing his hands and mumbling something unintelligible. His eyes opened wide when he saw her, and Eleanor couldn't help but wonder what imaginings raced through that simple mind.

She grabbed his filthy shirt in her left hand and shoved him against the wall while bringing the barbed blade to rest against his throat. The metal sang and whined for the blood hidden just beneath his skin. It had been long since the singing blade last fed. The smile melted away from the mayor's face as the blade scratched his throat.

"Keep away from this door." Eleanor's words were toneless, allowing the man to insert whatever malice he desired.

"Just checking on my stocks in the other room," the mayor said, his voice strained. "Didn't mean to disturb." His eyes darted back and forth as he spoke. Eleanor felt the frantic desire to escape radiating from his flesh.

"Then you best pray to whatever mud-covered water god pisses in your lake that those stocks keep until morning. If you pass by my door again, I will feed you the tool you seem so desperate to use." Eleanor used the blade to lift his chin, forcing him to look into her eyes. She was careful not to draw blood. Even the smallest drop would incite a bloodlust within the blade that would require exsanguination. The mayor nodded with a quiver, so Eleanor removed the blade and shut the door.

She was not disturbed again, but sleep remained out of reach. Incensed by the denial of bloodshed, the dagger made discordant sounds that stung her ears. In hindsight, she should have used a different blade or even her sword. The additional intimidation of the singing blade was overkill. Hubris now caused her sleeplessness. Eleanor wrestled with killing the mayor outright. It would shut the blade up. A simple thing to accomplish, but the fisher people would form a mob. Maybe even hire a constable. Remaining anonymous - discreet was still the most important part of the mission. Fantasizing about his death would have to suffice.

At the first hint of morning light, Eleanor collected her things and left. Mayor Jacken did not come to bid her farewell. That victory would have to be enough to curb the foul mood she felt. The hounds were by the horses readying them to ride. Much to her surprise, the thief was also up and ready. He knelt in the mud, rustling a young boy's hair. Grint gave the boy a coin making Eleanor wonder if the child was now the richest person in town.

"Such a waste," she said as Grint mounted his gray. "These people don't understand money. That child will end up throwing it in the lake."

"Kings and queens think they rule their little kingdoms," he replied as they trotted up the road. "You want to see true power? Find the children born in gutters and tremble if you find them watching you."

Children? The thief held such odd notions.

6

"The network of thieves throughout Terragard are so pervasive and well organized that one cannot help but wonder at a God of Thieves overseeing them all."

– Wizen Alanna, Magicai of the Third Order

It was a two-day ride to Tan Tan where Eleanor planned to hire a boat. The weather remained against them, slowing their pace. Time was not yet short but only just. Traveling by water would fulfil her desire to make up time and give a much-needed break to clear her muddled mind. Half a day's ride from the city her thoughts wandered to a warm bath with suds. A plate of hot food prepared by someone other than Torchy. *Malus!* Eleanor gritted her teeth. The thief's way of thinking had seeped into her brain like poison. Even now she heard him calling her faithful pup 'Torchy' as the two bickered over recipes.

"Malus," she called out. "Take point and watch the farmhouses." A pointless command, but it would separate the two and give her a break from their infantile arguments. Malus trotted past and slowed after a few hundred feet. Scanning the horizon as he muttered retorts to a discussion he was no longer having.

The road beyond the fishing village widened. Large, flat stones buried beneath the mud kept the horses from getting stuck. *Someone had once tried to build a road here,* Eleanor mused. An ancient attempt at creating something permanent. *Had it been Zorn when he conquered the world?* Whoever the architect, the job remained forever unfinished. *Perhaps the moneylender realized the futility of the goal?* Small farmhouses dotted the countryside, sitting on open fields that stretched for miles. It was poor, agrarian land that would never yield a return from civilizing it. *Pitiful wretches. What point is there to your existence?*

"Settle a bet," Grint said, easing up beside her. His words pulled her from the first peace she had in days.

"If you continue to annoy my hounds," she said without waiting to hear what this bet was, "they will rip out your throat."

"They won't do anything without you telling them to," Grint laughed.

"Then perhaps I will tell them to."

"Torchy would kill Crosshatch if you told him to."

"What's your point?"

"It doesn't matter if I infuriate them. They'd kill me on your say so, even if I was their best friend. Might as well have some fun." Eleanor opened her mouth to spit an insult but nothing meaningful came to mind. She remained quiet. A poor retort was a worse defeat than silence.

"So, the bet Torchy and I have is..."

"Quiet," she snapped when she saw Malus held up a hand.

A rider approached from the east. As they grew closer, she recognized it as Tamos. Was he being pursued? The horse labored with exertion, its chest heaving in full gallop. Tamos stood in the stirrups, whipping the crop for speed.

What creature in Terragard could make him travel with such haste? No. He knew better than to lead anyone to her. His urgency came from purpose, not fear. Tamos slowed as he approached his brother. There was news to impart.

"Wait here," she said. The thief heeded the command with a cheeky wink. At least he didn't comment. *Insufferable!* Eleanor kept the horse to a trot as the hounds rode to meet her. "What news?" she asked. "Ballastrine?"

"No, Mistress." Tamos glistened beneath a sheen of sweat. His voice breathy and incoherent as he tried to speak between drinks of water.

"Take your time and compose yourself," she commanded. Tamos pulled a rolled piece of parchment from his coat and handed it to her. Words were unnecessary. As she unfurled it, Eleanor closed her eyes and screamed silently at all the demons in Astapoor. Something sour woke in her belly and raged in response. She wanted to breathe dragon's fire and topple castle walls like a stoneskin giant. Pulling on the bridle, she turned the horse and walked it back to the thief.

Grint leaned back in the saddle as he stared skyward, humming a somber song Eleanor did not know. He sat up at her approach, the smile on his face faltering under the storm in her eyes. That was at least a victory. Hollow as it may be.

"Everything alright?" Grint asked, looking past her to the two scouts. Like Tamos, Eleanor did not vocalize an answer. The parchment would say what she could not. The thief took it, and for a few moments studied it. A smile returned as he did. When he turned the wanted poster towards them, he was outright laughing.

"If you look at it in the right light it almost resembles me," he said of the drawing. Eleanor thought it captured his likeness well.

"It is you," Tamos said, snarling his upper lip.

"What?" Grint looked again, his brow crinkling. "How can you tell?"

"It says your name under the picture," Eleanor rolled her eyes.

"Huh? So that's how you spell my name," Grint used a finger to trace over the letters.

"You can't read?" Malus asked, appalled.

"And you can?" the thief sniped back.

"Yes."

"Oh," Grint said, embarrassed. "Good for you." He handed the poster back to Eleanor and trotted past them.

"You never told me you have a bounty in Tan Tan," Eleanor said, following.

"I didn't know there was one," he answered as he snapped his fingers. "Wait," he continued, mumbling a litany of names. When he got to one sounding like 'Marm' he snapped again. "Could be her, but that was years ago." He shook his head.

"The wronged have long memories," Malus said.

"Perhaps you had best tell me where else you're wanted," Eleanor said, lamenting the death of her plan to hire a boat.

"It might be easier to tell you where I'm not," Grint smiled.

"Do I appear to be in a humorous mood?"

"Knob Junction for ransoming a countess. Although she hired me to kidnap her, so that one isn't fair. Then there's Dirty Gull for thirty counts of larceny. Mount Kahlick and Undertwa. Bisserby..."

*****

Eleanor and Tamos rode into Tan Tan side by side. It was a small city, boasting only a few streets on an upper plateau with a dozen more by the water's edge. There, a spider's web of docks reached out into the frigid depths of Lake Tarsis. Only a few of the buildings reached two stories and their overlapping cedar shakes rattled in the wind. Molded steel oak supports etched with the intricate symbols of an outlawed religion adorned the corner of each home. The narrow cobblestone streets made their ride uneven but were a nice change from the slow drudge through the mud. Worse, the city had a stink that stung the nose. *Rotting crab?*

Along the docks stood a lone barracks house flying the sigil of Duchess Aerienne. None of the four chimneys smoked on this chill day, giving Eleanor reason to wonder if the flag was an ornamental affectation. There didn't appear to be an actual garrison presence. The size of the barracks could house a mighty force. Five, maybe six hundred? She doubted anything more than the local militia used it now. Trade through the lakes had suffered since the Papality claimed the Anto Republic and Baltrude fractured into civil war. Everything came overland from the south now, crippling the once thriving lake towns.

Tamos led them along the main thoroughfare. A handful of people stood around reading the wanted posters. Dozens of notices lined each post they passed. Those gathered turned to watch, hopeful to match their face with a bounty. Between their heads, Grint's poster looked back, his stupid grin mocking her. Sometimes his poster was on top. Other times obscured by newer crimes. One thing was certain, they had wanted the thief for a long time.

The pair stopped at an inn called The Drowning Turtle. A line of horses whinnied, pulling against the hitches as they dismounted. With no sign of a pass-through to the stable, Eleanor believed they were to leave their horses here. Against better judgement, she left Tamos to tie the horses and started up the steps. Tan Tan reeked of a city rampant with thievery, so Eleanor paused and flicked a hand signal for Tamos to remain with the horses and their belongings until she negotiated a room for the evening.

A smattering of locals sat at the tables, eating and drinking while two lanky boys sang and step-danced. A thick man with scarred cheeks leaned against the bar tapping his foot in time with the music. The white towel slung over his shoulder and interest he showed marked him as the one to speak with.

"Are you the proprietor?"

"I am at that," he answered. "McCauley. Welcome to the Drowning Turtle."

"Tell your livery man I have two horses outside." She removed her gloves and looked around the room.

"No stable, so no livery," McCauley said. "You can leave your beasts tied outside. Or there's a stable a street down that charges a fair price."

"An inn without a stable? That's ludicrous," Eleanor's voice was as sour as her glare.

"Never needed one," the innkeeper answered, uncaring of her tone.

"With all the wanted posters, I would say you do." Eleanor felt triumphant in her response.

McCauley laughed, "No one steals in Tan Tan without paying the price." Tamos entered with a saddle bag draped over each shoulder. McCauley looked past her, appraising the scout. "You needing two rooms then?"

"If you offer them," Eleanor replied. "Or should I look elsewhere for that as well?"

"Two silver ladies," McCauley gave her a flat look.

"I don't have any ladies," Eleanor said. Ladies were the local currency. Coins etched with a curvy woman meant to resemble the Duchess Aerienne. "I can give you silver daggots."

"Don't know what those are," McCauley gave her a questioning look. "I'll take four though."

"Four?" Eleanor stepped back. "Daggots are from Cattachat and thicker than your ladies."

"We don't get a lot of foreign trade. So, I'll need someone who can take them to a bank in Edelgrah or High Grace. Lot more effort."

"Three then, and I would like a hot bath and meal brought up," Eleanor countered. McCauley took time to consider the offer and then nodded as he held out his hand. Eleanor deposited the funds.

"Up the stairs, last door on the left." The patrons clapped as the boys finished their dance. McCauley waved a hand at one who jumped off the dais and led them.

The boy lit an oil lamp on the side table illuminating the modest room. There was little in the way of comfort aside from the single bed and a chair beside the table. The mud-caked window afforded a view of more mud in the alley below. It was warm and dry. Those were the main comforts Eleanor sought.

"I paid for a bath," Eleanor said to the child.

"I'll run it now," he said with his hand out.

Eleanor dropped a copper bit there. The thief's warning of children running the world echoed in her head. It would be a joyous day when she rid the world of Grint. The boy trotted away closing the door behind him.

"Watch the horses," she said, feeling a cold chill run up her spine. "And make sure no one is watching us."

"Mistress?"

"An odd notion," she traced her hand along a splinter in the wooden door. Or a carving. "Just be sure."

*****

The bath was as lovely as she hoped. The copper tub kept the water at the perfect temperature to soothe her aches. There was danger in relying too much on comfort and the softness it created. A truth her younger self would scream at her. But the higher she rose within the ranks of Count Danghier's service, the greater the comforts afforded to her. Eleanor was not stupid. It was a purposeful manipulation meant to make her reliant on the count. One she bought into with a deep, unwavering loyalty.

The bed was the softest she laid in since beginning this journey. Sleep came quick yet ended before morning. A man's voice roused her from her slumber. She reached for the dagger she forgot to leave beside her pillow. A sloppy mistake borne of exhaustion, but she wasn't helpless. Eleanor's left hand circled the man's throat in a grip that left him gasping for air until the word, "Mistress," choked out. Without hesitation she released her faithful hound and listened as he sucked in air. Then got up and lit a candle. Tamos backhanded the candle, knocking it from the table.

"What's wrong?" she asked.

"There's been a theft," his said, his voice strained. "Instrument of importance. A mob formed. Eyes downstairs. All on me."

"Gather our things," she commanded. The mob wouldn't find a stolen instrument, but there were things in her possession just as damning. Necromancy was tantamount to heresy this close to the Papality and looked down on most everywhere else. The forceful use of spirits and communing with demons who fed upon the living was the antithesis of every religious belief. There were also irreplaceable items she would not want grubby, inconsequential mud fishers pawing over.

Tamos shouldered the bags and opened the window. "I'll bring the horses round to the next block. Follow the alley to the next street and we'll ride out of town." Eleanor nodded in agreement and the scout dropped through the opening. He waited for Eleanor to join him and then pointed her way through the back alley while he disappeared to gather their horses.

Eleanor stood in the dark mouth of a far alley, waiting for Tamos. A flurry of activity buzzed as townsfolk rushed about, forming into mobs headed towards the Drowning Turtle. A few glanced her way as they passed, and it made Eleanor sick to think her face would end up on one of these silly posters. When they found her gone from the room, they would conclude she stole this instrument and perhaps send a thief-catcher after them. Such a person did not worry her. Losing time covering their tracks did.

Escaping the city unscathed, Eleanor sat atop a hill south of Tan Tan, watching torches bob through the darkened streets. A beautiful tapestry of stars covered the night sky, but Eleanor kept her focus on the mob. A frigid wind bit at her cheeks, so she raised her hood to give some meager shielding from the cold. It was an hour since they fled, and no one yet came to look for the travelers who disappeared from the inn. What were they waiting for? They had to have discovered she left by now.

"I located Malus's camp," Tamos said as he rode up. Eleanor yanked on the reins to spin the horse round.

Tamos rode with his shoulders squared and eyes forward. Eleanor knew her hounds and when something upset them. Tamos kept his eyes on the path, neck tight with strain. "What is it?" She asked.

"It is," he paused and considered his words, "It is best you see for yourself."

Eleanor despised circumvented explanations and riddles, but her desire for an answer would not have to wait long. As they approached the dull light from a smoldering campfire, Malus stepped from the shadows to greet them and take the reins to Eleanor's horse. None of her worst nightmares manifested as she glanced around. There had been no attack, no fire, no discovery - and then she heard the twang of a stringed instrument and stared wide-eyed at the thief sitting amidst a pile of furs. He strummed a long-necked guitar with small round body as he chewed on a long stick of dried meat.

"What is that?" she asked as Grint adjusted the knobs to change the sound.

"Banjo," he answered without looking up. "They come from the old dust towns out in the Frontier. Worth a lot of money in some places."

"Where did you get it?" Her words trailed off as she pieced together the answer. She felt the blood draining from her face as he plucked at individual strings to create a tune. Malus brushed down her horse trying to remain out of sight, but she caught his eye, compelling him to look her way.

He dropped his head under her glare, letting the brush hang at his side, "Mistress, he left before I knew it."

Eleanor wanted to erupt for the second time today. To spew ash and let the molten fire in her chest bleed through her pores. She wanted to eviscerate Malus and feel his entrails slide between her fingers; to tear off his burn-scarred flesh and burn him again. Each pluck of the banjo's strings magnified her rage.

"Stop that," she snapped at Grint.

"I also stole furs," Grint said. "None of you seemed concerned that we'll be traveling in cold mountain terrain without warm clothes." And then played a somber tune that would have made the demon lords of Astapoor weep.

Eleanor breathed in, held it, and exhaled. Malus and Tamos stood in a static pose somewhere between pouncing on the thief and falling at her feet, waiting on whatever command she issued. "Ready my tent," she said, her breath clouding the air in front of her face. "And put out the fire. You and the thief sleep in the cold tonight."

*****

The journey was no easier the next day. Or the one after. The thief returned to his endless list of places the authorities sought his head. No matter how often she stated that was sufficient; he continued. Worse yet, he concocted a jaunty tune on the burgled instrument that wormed under her skin.

A ruby ring here, a silken dress from Bashere. Fifty stones and a copper bone in the Sandy Kingdoms I fear.

The storms returned at night. Whipping winds shook the canvas of her tent, sounding as if a great battle were being waged. Hail stones and freezing rains abated by morning but left her with little in the way of sleep. The thief remained unfazed and woke with a smile and fresh tune. The only bright spot she found in those days was that no thief-catcher trailed them from Tan Tan. And the city of Bryce was close at hand.

In far Mont Challice, I stole a young queen's kiss, along with her gold in a state of bliss. Now I'm wanted for that and for this. So, I no longer ride through far Mont Challice.

Hope disappeared in the thick fog surrounding Bryce. Tall-masted ships flying the Papality flag sat anchored in the harbor. Soldiers and Ropes roamed the streets hanging the priests of whatever minor gods they could find. One of the murdered priests was the object of affection of a salt witch living on an island in the bay. In her anger, she conjured a thick fog over the city. According to the guard Tamos spoke with, the Papality were mounting an offensive against the witch. No one thought that would end well for them.

The streets of Bryce were silent as they rode through. No streetlamps were lit, no hearth fires burned in the windows. The residents hid behind locked doors while ghost-like bodies swung from ropes along the boulevard. The Papality were thorough in their executions. Even the jester's school fell to their might. The splintered door swung in the wind. A broken, steel latch tapped against the stone, its sound magnified by the silence. Students laid in a heap against the wall, each run through with methodical proficiency. The Papality hadn't bothered to hang them. They would find no aid in Bryce. So, Eleanor set her mind toward Tarsul, the last of the lake cities.

In Edelgrah, In Edelgrah, I robbed old Saint Shaw. Ten golden teeth from his crusty maw. In Edelgrah, In Edelgrah.

Tarsul has promise, she allowed herself to admit. Nestled against the cobalt blue waters of Lake Tarsis; Tarsul was unlike her brothers to the north. Tan Tan and Bryce were creatures of steel oak and brick; while Tarsul's structures were soft lake stone dug up from the shallow drafts. In sunlight, the lake stone shimmered. A vision to behold, making the city appear as tranquil as the waters it sat beside. It was both a breathtaking and dizzying display.

The walls of Tarsul had no wanted posters, no Papality thugs to incite the ire of witches, and it filled Eleanor with a sense of calm. Yet, she knew taking a boat was now pointless. South of Tarsul they would follow the Duchess Highway until they needed to cut across the lowlands. There they would head east into the mountains. But a bed and night of quiet sleep would be enough to rejuvenate her. As they entered an inn called the Praying Priest of Payment, Eleanor's desired only to climb the oak staircase and fall into a deep sleep.

"The infamous Grint!" the burly, dark bearded man behind the bar shouted as he slammed the wooden tankard in his hand, splintering it into a hundred pieces.

Grint squinted and cocked his head. After a moment he smiled, "Beauregard? Well, I'll be a shameful lock pick!"

"You've got a cheek coming in here!" Beauregard stepped from behind the bar as all eyes fell upon Eleanor and her traveling retinue. Beauregard stood at least seven feet tall and walked with a grace that belied his size. Chairs scratched as patrons acted in haste to get out of the way of his lumbering strides. He walked the length of the tavern, his face darkening with each step. Grint waited with a stupid smile - as if this man meant to buy him an ale rather than bury him beneath the kegs in the basement.

"You look cross," Grint said.

"Do I? What would give you that idea?" Beauregard clenched both fists tight. Droplets of blood squeezed between the fingers of his left hand and spilled to the floor. Sprouting from splinters of the mug he smashed digging into his flesh.

"Did I steal from you?" the thief scratched his head and looked around. Eleanor gave him a flat-eyed glare. Grint shook his head and said, "No. No! Never stole from you." The smile returned.

"No, but you slept with my wife," Beauregard said in a booming voice. A hushed whisper echoed through the onlooking gallery of drunks and degenerates that comprised the patronage of the Praying Priest of Payment. Even as the innkeeper announced this, a statuesque woman of a height with Beauregard stepped from the back room looking confused. The woman was gorgeous with flawless skin and a long blonde braid that fell almost to her feet. She had the look of a wolf woman from the Frozen North. The patrons looked at her and then the two men and back again. Eleanor didn't need to be a scholar to know this was the wife.

"Come on, Boory! I didn't know she was your wife when I slept with her!" Grint replied.

"The first time," Beauregard said. "What about the other times?"

Grint shrugged, "I mean, look at her. Can you blame me?" Beauregard followed Grint's gaze to the wolf woman, and his face turned the color of a winter's fire.

"That's not Mabby, you mud-choked idiot! That's my new wife!"

"In that case," Grint said with a smile at her, "it is a great pleasure to meet you. I'm Grint."

The milk-witted woman had the audacity to smile back and even blush, which was more than enough to set Beauregard off. His right fist was a battering ram that collided with the thief's face and sent him cartwheeling across the floor. That wasn't enough for Beauregard. His greed for destruction still unquenched, he cracked his knuckles with a mind to satiate himself.

Grint, ever nimble, leapt to his feet before Beauregard got three steps and yanked a torch from the wall sconce. The innkeeper stayed out of reach as Grint waved the torch. "I don't want any trouble," Grint said. "My companions and I need rooms."

"There are no rooms for you here," Beauregard shouted, a blood vessel in his temple throbbing. "Out!"

Grint stepped towards the door, careful to keep the innkeeper far enough out of reach. Twice before he reached the door, he had to swipe the torch towards some industrious fool who thought to intercede. Ultimately, he reached his goal unmolested. Pausing within the doorway, Grint smiled at Beauregard once more and said, "I didn't catch your new wife's name."

"Selane," the wolf woman said with a smile.

"Out!" came Beauregard's bellowed response. Grint tossed the torch in the air and slammed the door shut. Beauregard caught it and a moment of silence fell over the tavern as no one knew quite how to react. As the silence stretched on, Beauregard turned until he stared straight into Eleanor's eyes.

"Was I being unclear?" he asked.

"We only have the misfortune of traveling..." she began.

"Out," he said with a snap. "I don't care if you just met him on the street. You walked in with him. By Krypsie, you're walking back out with him."

On another night, in another place, Eleanor would cut through the collected gathering without effort. Beating the innkeeper would require skill, his wife too if she was a wolf woman, but they would both fall. This was not another night or place. Such a violent outburst could cost a hound, the thief, or the most precious commodity - time. Eleanor bowed and led her hounds outside.

Grint sat on his horse, looking at the darkened buildings lining the street. Eleanor swallowed another violent outburst, squeezing her eyes shut. The night air was crisp and someone close by was baking apples. *I could still salvage something from tonight,* Eleanor thought as she opened her eyes.

"Find us a new inn," she said. "I'm tired and hungry. Find whoever is baking the apples."

"No," Grint said.

"What?" Eleanor asked. Grint wasn't looking at her but pointing her attention to the rooftops. The lights inside the tavern blinded her, so it took a moment to adjust to the dark. Small, shadowed shapes crouched along the edges of the taller buildings, whispering amongst themselves.

"Goblins?" Malus asked, which elicited a laugh from the thief.

"Children," Eleanor corrected. The eyes and ears of the city.

"There will be no inns open to us tonight," Grint said as he walked his horse towards the eastern gates. Eleanor shook her head. Her exhaustion would need to wait.

The streets stayed silent save for the clip-clop of hooves upon stone pavers. They passed other inns, all lit with warm fires and the sound of merriment. Each with a huddle of children skulking in the alley or hanging from the eaves barring them from any thought of entry. As they continued, an unbidden thought wormed its way into her head. Was it a coincidence that the first inn they rode to had a man looking to confront Grint? The theatrics of it was not dissimilar to what drew her to him in Kambar. Had he manufactured the incident? Was there a Beauregard in every inn? Waiting to begin a confrontation that would send them away?

Eleanor continued to chew it over as they rode south along the Duchess Highway. If true, what was Grint gaining? *Comfort,* she thought. *He knows my weakness and is denying me comfort.* Eleanor needed to follow this thread. There was something more here she was missing.

Grint pulled out the infernal banjo and played a song about unfaithful spouses. The shape of the puzzle manifested in her mind. When had the thief taken the upper hand? It was so subtle she failed to notice. The fishing village where he suggested they stay, and in the morning, he gave a coin to the child. The pieces fell in their appointed pattern from there. Wanted posters and a theft with no thief-catcher to pursue them. Even now, every note from the stolen instrument caused tension and anger amongst her pups. In Bryce, a foggy city with hung priests lining the street. But was also the home of a jester college. So tired by then, she never thought to check the dead or consult them for guidance. For all she knew they were scarecrows stuffed with straw and draped with vestments.

So why? Not to be a nuisance. The thief acted with a purpose, that much she knew. He wanted her tired; making mistakes. Not to escape the work, but because he knew finishing the job meant his demise. Clouding her judgement, he could maneuver events toward an outcome where he got paid and kept his head. Smart, but infuriating. If she hadn't already been planning to kill him, she would now.

"Malus," she called, and the scout fell in beside her. Eleanor leaned over and whispered a command. He moved to complete it with great fervor, galloping into the darkness.

"I guess he didn't like my song," Grint said as he watched him go.

"None of us do," Tamos answered.

Eleanor would keep quiet about her discovery. Best to let the thief think he was still pushing her. In the meantime, she would have her own fun and see how far she could swing the pendulum back.

An hour later, Malus returned and led them into the forest. They climbed a steep hill and though the horses needed rest; they managed the task.

Cresting the top, Malus dismounted and called out, "Here."

A rejuvenating smile curved Eleanor's lips as she surveyed the new campsite. There was a small clearing with an overhang of trees that would protect them from any rain or sleet, but best of all, just within the trees was a small statue upon a pedestal. At the base were three skeletons, peppered with arrows and chipped bones. Torn, stained furs hung in tatters off the bones. The statue was old. The wear of years leaving little but the vague impression of a hunched man draped in robes. A newer mark drawn in blood obscured the faint remainder of an ancient inscription carved on the base. The bloody mark of a Brotherhood Knight.

Eleanor wanted to laugh. She sent Malus to sniff out a shrine to the God of Thieves but had not expected him to find one littered with the dead. This was so much better. "Kin of yours?" she asked as she dismounted.

Grint brushed down his horse, pausing long enough to look over his shoulder at the skeletons before continuing his task. "One of them may be my cousin, Dodger."

Sarcasm was not what she expected, but she pushed on. "And is this your God? What do they call him? Tinder Hobe?" Grint threw his head back and laughed.

"A God of Thieves?" Grint stowed the brush in the saddlebag. "You've been out in the woods too long. Believing the folktales."

Grint picked up the banjo out and plucked the strings. "Blue Fingered Hobbe, the God of Thieves..." The song continued, but Eleanor heard no more amidst waves of racking pain shooting through her right arm. Pulling off her glove, she found a black mark on her palm. A spreading shadow that followed the lines and crevasses. Somewhere far away, Tamos yanked the banjo and smashed it on the ground. There was an argument, but the words drowned beneath an ocean of pain.

"Enough," she screamed, unsure if she meant the argument or the pain.

"Crosshatch owes me money for that," Grint said.

"We need the camp," Eleanor ignored him. "Find somewhere else to sleep." The thief stood his ground, perturbed by the loss of the instrument. "Go, or I'll allow them do what they've been wanting to."

Grint cracked his neck to the side and spat. Without another word he shouldered his bag and draped a fur over his shoulders. As he disappeared into the trees Malus stepped beside her, watching him go.

"Shall I follow?"

"No," she said, fighting the pain to speak. "Gather those skeletons around the fire."

"Mistress?" Malus replied, his concern for her growing as she fell to her knees.

"Do it." Looking at her hand, she found it swallowed by the inky mass beneath her skin. "The count wishes to make contact."

*****

Grint walked through the woods, making no effort at stealth. Twigs snapped, leaves crunched, and stones scattered down the slope to his left. At one point he whistled a tune he'd concocted on the banjo, but he was terrible at whistling and the sound was uneven. Most of the time it sounded more like an old man trying to cool his tea than an actual song. Had that kry-damned mutt not smashed the banjo he could have played it. Losing the banjo would be a problem with Marm. At least it was one for another day.

"You sound like an angry giant stomping around," a monotone voice said.

"And you smell like a badger that died, got eaten, and crapped back out," Grint answered.

"Rude," Faighur said as he conjured a flame from his finger to light the long pipe sticking from his mouth. Grint smiled and dropped the remnants of the banjo to clasp hands with his friend.

"Is that Marm's banjo?" Faighur asked, pointing the pipe at the wreckage on the ground.

"It was," Grint replied.

"That will be troublesome. Marm loved that banjo."

"She can take it from Beauregard's cut," Grint said as he placed his bag against a tree. "His penance for not knowing how to stage a punch."

"He's angry that you slept with his wife." Faighur puffed smoke, watching Grint rummage through his bag.

"I never slept with her," Grint said.

"He thinks you did."

"Not my type." Grint sat back on his heels clutching the necklace through his shirt.

"I liked Jessua," Faighur said. "She was sweet. And good for you."

"Yes, she was." Grint continued sifting through the contents of the bag. "Where the bloody grief is it? I can't find anything in this milk-sotted bag."

"Did it work?"

"What?" Grint asked, and then realized that Faighur was asking about the plan. "Yeah," then, "I think."

"I remain unconvinced," Faighur said in the closest thing he could to frustration. "I promised a lot of coin. The jesters seem especially greedy."

"It was working," Grint said. "Where the blaze is it?"

"It is not now?"

"I think she's on to me," Grint admitted. "There it is, got it."

"What makes you think that?" Faighur asked, trying to look over Grint's shoulder.

"She tried to get a reaction out of me with a shrine to Hobbe." Grint pulled a red jewel, the size of his palm out of the bag. An amulet wrapped with an intricate gold weaving and a single loop where a chain could attach.

Faighur sniffed at the air, "I do not sense a shrine."

"A Brotherhood Knight desecrated it," he said as he polished the jewel. Faighur made an angry sound. A dragon's sound.

Grint knelt, facing Eleanor's camp. He closed his eyes and placed the jewel against his forehead. The cold stone warmed, but wasn't unpleasant. No, it was quite the opposite. The amber glow coming off the jewel filled his mind, melting away all cares and pains. Melting him away.

When Grint opened his eyes, he was not in the forest, but back in the camp. At least his sight was. His physical form stayed with Faighur, but the magic tore a piece of his spirit free to wander. That was what the jewel did. Now he stood just a few feet from the firelight watching Eleanor and her hounds perform a strange ritual. They stood in a triangle around the fire with the thieves' skeletons interspersed between them. Crosshatch and Torchy knelt while Eleanor stood before the growing flames, clutching her wrist. From this distance, Grint couldn't tell what was wrong with her hand, but it had turned dark. He didn't dare get closer. Without knowing what magic was at work, he wouldn't know if they could sense him watching.

As the flames reached skyward, Eleanor took the darkened hand and plunged it deep within. Her head leaned back and shoulders tensed. "Ortium," she stammered through clenched teeth and then relaxed as the flames retreated, releasing a gaseous purple cloud. The first of the three skeletons rose and rotated as the cloud fed upon it.

The vapor hung over the fire, pulsating with the rhythm of a heart. Her heart? Grint did not know but continued to watch as a figure took shape. Was this tall, gaunt man, with angular features sharp enough to cut, Count Danghier? His eyes, colored purple by the vapors danced with a promise of madness and forthcoming anarchy. There was something beautiful about the count. If you considered the moment of your own death beautiful.

"Count Danghier," all three spoke at once. It was him. The puppet master stood with his arms held wide in all his imposing glory.

"My dear, Eleanor," he said in a smooth voice that ran like oil atop water. "I expected contact much sooner than this. I was beginning to - worry." As he paused, his smile broadened, betraying the sentiment as a lie. This was not a man who felt emotional connections, this was someone who exploited them. Eleanor ate up the attention like a starving child. So besotted with her benefactor she ignored the chains he shackled her with.

Eleanor dropped to her knees and tried to kiss the hem of her master's robe, but the smoke slipped through her fingers. "All is going according to plan, Master."

"Good," Danghier replied and touched her head with an intangible pat. "Have you prepared Black Samuel on how to gain my prize? Where is he? I do not see him." The count's gaze swept across the camp and paused for a pregnant moment at the spot Grint watched from. Grint wanted to flee from those eyes, terrified this madman would inhale his spirit and swallow him forever. The count's gaze moved back to Eleanor.

"The thief is ready, Master. We will have the urn and return home before the ritual time." Eleanor kept her head lowered as she spoke, awaiting a response that never came. When she looked up, it was to find Danghier wagging a single finger in her face.

"You're being obtuse, little girl," he said, and her head jerked sideways from an invisible strike. "Be plain with me."

"There was a slight deviation," she stammered.

"Go. On."

"I found Black Samuel to be an inferior specimen. Incapable of accomplishing the most basic of tasks," her words were quick as if she were trying to get them all in before punishment rained down upon her.

The count replied, but a wave of pain and nausea passed through Grint, obscuring the moment. The magic was turning on him. Soon it would require more of his spirit. He would not have much longer, but needed to hear what their plans were. How they intended to kill him. The second skeleton was now being consumed. He had to hold out against the growing pain.

"I have given you leeway in the past, Eleanor, but I thought I made myself clear. Was I unclear?" Danghier asked as he struck Eleanor again with invisible hands.

"No, Master," she said through tears. "You were not."

"There is naught to do now," The count continued. "The choice is made. Who is he?"

"His name is Grint," she said.

"Not a name I have heard," The count said as he considered it. "Is it a surname or familial name?"

"The only name he goes by."

"Odd. And you have prepared him for what we require?" Danghier asked. Eleanor nodded as the third skeleton rose.

"Yes, but he is aware we intend to kill him," she answered.

"Will he complete the job?"

"The prestige and the gold are too much for him to pass on. I also suspect he now owes money..."

This was it, yet the magic was not cooperating. A vibrating quake grew from the center of his chest as the magic hungered for more of his spirit.

"Pray your failure is not beyond the measure of pain I can inflict," Count Danghier was snarling. What had he missed?

"No, my Master," Eleanor shook her head. "I have sent Callum..." More pain, sharp as a needle un-threading the stitching of his spirit. "He will bring..." The camp sight flickered. "That will be the end..."

The vision dissolved. Faighur yanked the stone away and threw it on the ground. The world rushed back like water from a broken dam and Grint choked on reality before catching his breath and falling onto his back. A pile of half-frozen leaves cushioned his head, and they felt wonderful against the inferno of a headache raging through his skull.

"They were about to tell," Grint said.

"You were under too long," Faighur replied. And then after a few moments, "Keeping an eyesighter in your bag is a poor idea."

Grint laughed. "If you knew everything I had in that bag, you'd leave this continent and never come back."

"What did you learn?"

"She sent Noseless to get something," Grint answered, but Faighur didn't know who that was. "And her boss is a jack-ape."

"That does not seem worth the risk," Faighur admonished.

"We're about a week's ride from the Terrastags," Grint said as he sat up. The world doubled over, and he rubbed at the bridge of his nose until the sensation settled. "I need you to get there ahead of me and wait inside."

"Inside the Terrastags?" Faighur said with the first spark of emotion Grint heard in a while. "You are the jack-ape. I do not see how I'm expected to gain entry."

Grint pulled a wooden disk from his breast pocket and held it out to his friend. The sigil carved on it was of eight snake heads blossoming out from a single stalk. "I lifted it from one of the skinlings. Their master has a manor in the city."

Faighur took the disk and looked it over. It looked so small in his oversized hand. "And they will let me in? I am barely passable as human anymore."

"They're necromancers, and I've gathered that the Terrastags don't care how you make your gold as long as you pay it to them. You'll be fine."

Faighur nodded and pocketed the disk. "I will get the lay of the land and meet you when you arrive."

"You best get moving," Grint said as he picked up the eyesighter and put it into his bag. "She'll send the dogs to find me once they've recovered from their ritual."

"Be safe, my friend," Faighur said as he disappeared into the forest.

Grint smiled and set his back against a tree to wait for the dogs. Eleanor knew what he had been up to. "This job is anything but safe."

7

"And so Myralee, Goddess of Hope bore unto the world a child and named him Zorn. When he conquered the world, he broke her heart. When he died, he shattered it. Beware, youngling, the Tears of Hope."

– Tennebrue, the Rogue Wizard
inscribed by his 53rd apprentice

Grint squirmed within the silken confines of the emerald green coat and trousers Eleanor foisted upon him. There was also a matching, white silk shirt that wasn't white but had some absurd name like egg-skin. The material was too thin, allowing the cool mountain air to cut through, leaving him in a perpetual state of freezing. It made him feel uncomfortable, exposed, and in danger of sliding out of the saddle. When she presented it, they argued over the thing until Grint relented. Hate it or not, Eleanor's explanation for wearing it made sense. The guards would never believe he served a great house like the Geldens dressed as a vagabond thief.

At least the woman and her dogs allowed him to do this part on his own. That was a tradeoff he could live with. They parted company a day earlier where Eleanor, Crosshatch, and Torchy could cut through the forest and connect with the road running south towards Dook. When Grint had the urn, he was to bring it there and complete the exchange. That part was a lie, and all the players knew she would kill him, but why speak plain and invite the chance to let the 'how' slip?

Thoughts of Eleanor fled from his mind as the towering one-hundred-foot wall came into view. The massive barrier made of clay, stone, steel - and as some legends stated the shattered bones of giants - made his skin crawl. It ran for miles east, south and west of the city. The city sat against a thousand-foot cliff that comprised the northern wall. The sheer-faced stone rose into the mountains and rumors spoke of traps for anyone foolish enough to attempt scaling down its length.

Guards who looked no larger than ants, paced back and forth atop the ramparts and would do so all day. The difference in the Terrastags was that those guards were looking into the city rather than watching out. No force ever attacked the city. There was no point to do so. The area held no tactical advantages and it would be next to impossible to march an army through the thick forest and tight stone crags. This was a resort for the rich and powerful with the simple rule of 'behave yourselves.' The retribution befalling a monarch who betrayed that rule was a strong deterrent.

The guards watched the streets in a constant vigil against thievery. A fact that occupied Grint's thoughts as he rode closer. For a thief, pinching a modicum of the wealth buried in these vaults was the heist of heists, and the one way to get your name said in the same breath as Blue Fingered Hobbe. The deadly allure of this place enticed thieves for generations, spawning a multitude of tavern tales about those who failed spectacularly. While the God of Thieves may not know them, their names had become infamous. Termund the Tunneler tried to dig beneath the wall, but found the fortification continued underground. He dug so deep the tunnel collapsed on him before he ever found the bottom. Hackne of Marlowe tried to catapult himself over. The splatter of blood still painted the southern wall. Yallo, a wild woman from Tandana set a herd of pigs on fire to distract the guards, but only set herself ablaze. The list went on and on. In fact, the only story ever told that came close to a success involved a Parthian barbarian who stole the heart of a queen.

A friend from the old days - *Poor, dead Tebbs* - once dared Grint to rob the Terrastags. Being young and stupid he accepted. He made it no further than a few miles from the Red Goat Inn before Hobbe caught up and cuffed him for intense stupidity. Had he made it to the city, chances are he'd be just another name on the list. Instead, Hobbe brought the whole crew to the Barrows where everything would change. That was where Grint would meet Jessua. He touched the necklace beneath the dreadful, silk shirt.

Many people camped beside the road in a make-shift tent city all its own. Just a few at first, but the number grew the closer he got to the gates. Trade workers, potion makers, stitchers, and hunters. People of all trades. A man fixing the wheel of his cart looked up at Grint and took his hat off in a gesture of deference.

"What are you doing here?" Grint asked.

"Waiting to get into the city." From the look of his wagon, the old man had been waiting a while.

"How long do you have to wait?"

"Longer than you will," a young man said sitting up in the driver's seat. He glared at Grint, stifling a laugh at the silken suit's expense. The old man struck the side of the wagon with a long pole and startled the kid who went back to adjusting something under the seat.

"Forgive the brashness of youth, m'lord." Grint almost laughed at being called a lord but held it back. Instead, he waved a hand in what he imagined was a gesture of forgiveness and rode on.

A line of people formed, waiting on the guards at the gate. Everyone on foot. Grint wondered if he should dismount and walk Storms from here. A man with shaggy hair and a coat of stitched pelts swatted an arm as Storms bit the back of his collar. He brandished a wood axe as he turned around with fire in his eyes. Whatever words he wanted to sling died in his mouth as he measured the station of the man atop the horse. Grint smiled and gave him a nod.

Two guards appeared, dragging a man through the gates. Whatever his crime, he struggled hard to free himself. The man kicked and screamed until the guards heard enough and threw him to the ground. They stomped on him with their heavy steel boots, silencing his cries. A squire ran through the gate and finished dragging the man's limp body toward the stocks. It would be a miracle if he lived the night. A chill ran through Grint. If he died, there were a lot of eyes to see through. He tried subtly to hide his face.

The guards spotted Grint and eyed the line ahead of him. "Look lively," one shouted as they turned their boots onto the men and women standing ahead of him. They kicked a handful aside before others got the hint and moved without the gentle prompting of steel boots. With the way clear they waved Grint forward. He did his best to ignore the hate thrown his way as he stepped Storms past.

"State your business," a fat, sweaty man said without looking up. Grint knew the type. Only on rare occasions did he deal with anyone of higher social status, so he carried a bored tone and a predisposition towards making people wait.

"I represent Prince Oryn, of the Geldens," Grint said as he removed the token from his coat pocket. Hearing the word 'Prince' the guard looked up and straightened his uniform.

"Pardon," he said as he took a kerchief from his coat to wipe his face. Grint passed the token to him for inspection.

"What is this?" a man of higher rank stepped from the gatehouse. He wore the same dark coat as the others but also crossing sashes of golden scales. Grint doubted it was real gold or even gilded. The closer the man came, the clearer the brush strokes on the scales became. Some fool painted it. Did he know? Atop his head was an ill-fitting helmet with a ridiculous purple plume that waved in the wind as he walked.

"A representative of the Geldens, Captain. Sir." The captain snatched the token from his underling and took his time inspecting it before squinting at Grint.

"And are you a Gelden?" The captain's tone held a hint of disbelief. Grint pegged him as a self-important man who wanted to catch one thief before his sad, bland life ended. The irony was that his opportunity had come and would soon slip right past.

"Me? Krypholos, no," Grint laughed. "I am but a valet for Prince Oryn. His Majesty sent me ahead to prepare their arrival."

The captain nodded along as Grint spoke. "Wait here," he said and took the token back to the gatehouse where an old man slept sitting up and appeared displeased at being woken. Unlike the others, he wore a plain gray robe with a simple rope tied around the waist. He was bald save for a few wisps of white hair scattered amongst the liver spots. Those eyes though; they were sharp and peeling away the layers of

Grint's story. The token sat in his palm where the old man spat and waved his right hand above it. A blue light shone from the token as he whispered an incantation.

"What's that?" Grint asked.

"Authenticating," one of the rough guards answered. They were flanking his horse, ready to pull him down if the coin proved false.

"Dillard," the captain said with a snap. The guard grumbled something before taking his frustrations out on the next merchant in line.

Once the old wizard completed his examination, he handed the token back to the captain and nodded. "You check out," he said as he brought it back. "If you're looking for lodging, try the High and Might Inn. No better rooms in the whole city." Given the captain's state of dress, Grint doubted the claim.

The gates creaked open after the captain pounded his steel gauntlet against the wood. The old wizard locked eyes with Grint as he passed by. A dark twinkle lingered there saying, *the token may have passed the test, but not you.* The silk shirt stuck against beads of sweat running down his back. As much as he hoped it wasn't the case, he knew the old bastard would cause a fair bit of trouble for him if he let his guard down. Grint rode on with all the noble swagger he could muster and lost his breath at the first sight of the splendor waiting within.

The streets were a flurry of activity. Merchants hawking their wares filled every space imaginable. *No wonder there's a line to get in.* The upper echelon of society browsed and took in the street performers. Jugglers, puppeteers, magicians all working for tips and careful to step clear of guards who looked to brook no nonsense. Manor houses, some three to four stories tall, hid behind alabaster white walls ornately crowned with gilded steel bars weaved in circular patterns. *Now that is real gilding,* Grint grinned at the thought.

"Five apples for a golden mayor, my lord." Grint wasn't used to being looked at as anything more than a drifter and almost passed the man by without remark.

"I'll give you a silver pip for one." The hawker thought it over and tossed the apple to Grint.

Grint took a bite and swore the juices tasted sweeter. Was it the grandeur of the place coloring his mind or was it something more? The air felt warm. Temperate enough to take his coat off. And the sun was shining. Was it his imagination? He could swear the morning sky outside the gate was slate gray, but it was a beautiful summer's day within. Magic.

At the first square beyond the gate, Grint dismounted. The crowds thickened, and trying to navigate from horseback was tricky. The merchants were more than happy to move aside, but the nobles wouldn't budge. Their looks of self-important entitlement despite their rank were worth more trouble than Grint wanted to deal with. The fountain in the middle of the square glistened in the sunlight, white marble streaked with grays and blacks that almost appeared to move when water spilled over the edge. Two tiers of carved statues adorned the monument. They looked to be wrestling in the old Zornish style. Storms pulled gently toward the fountain, eager to taste the clear water trickling like rain.

Before they reached the edge, a man in a plain brown jerkin, and knitted hat knelt by the edge trying to hide a bottle he dipped in the water. Without hesitation, two guards emerged from the crowd, yanking him to his feet. They slapped the bottle from his hand with a cudgel and dragged him off amidst protests. "It's for my pregnant wife!" Nobles, dressed in their finery followed the trio, waving coin purses and calling for wagers. Two drunks in silk shirts to rival Grint's shoved at one another which escalated into fisticuffs. More guards appeared as a fresh call for wagers rang out.

Grint went south from the square unsure if the rules allowed nobles to drink from the fountain. Storms pulled at the lead line, reluctant to leave the water behind. "Best not to test it, boy." The horse dropped its head, pouting. The new street they walked had fewer manor houses but no shortage of guards dressed in house colors. Intermixed between the gates were small shops named such things as 'Terastaggered: Wines & Fine Spirits' and 'Twitch's Coinery'. Each place hung a small sign out that read: Token Holders Only.

Ahead on the right was the place the captain recommended, The High and Might Inn. Grint's nose wrinkled at the punnery. Aside from its attempt at comedy, the inn appeared to be a well-appointed building of red brick and aged oaken beams stained a brilliant golden-red. Gas lamps lined the walkway between flower boxes full of white roses. Two imposing red doors dominated the front of the inn, but Grint walked past and turned down the stone, horse path just beside the building. Behind the inn he found the stables where a young boy, bucktoothed and squinting against the sunlight, came out to greet him.

"Welcome to the High and Might Inn, I'm Jabe. I'm happy to stable and feed your horse." The boy had a rote way of speaking.

"Double rations for him," Grint said. "I'll make it worth it."

"This is the High and Might Inn. All horses get double rations." The boy was fighting between instructions and his desire to see what Grint's definition of 'worth it' meant.

Grint handed the boy the reins and removed his bag from the saddle. When Storms was in hand, he flipped a small bit of unmarked copper to him. Jabe looked at it with flat, expressionless eyes disappointed by the meager amount. When he realized there would be nothing more, he took the horse into the stable and left Grint staring at the back of the inn. While not as ornate as the front, the rear was still well-to-do with intricate stone patterns and well-tended topiaries. Beyond the hedges, he glimpsed a white gate leading to a larger garden area that offered privacy for the guests.

Grint entered to find a bored looking man in silver velvets staffing the front desk. He had a pinched face, stuck in an expression of dissatisfaction as he judged the world through half-lidded eyes. That judgement came down on Grint, who he no doubt categorized as an undesirable because of his entry through the back door.

"Yes?" The question dripped with incredulity. *How dare you enter this fine establishment* was what the man wanted to say but decent decorum forbade such rudeness. Even the man's smile mirrored the subtext of the greeting.

"I'd like two rooms." Grint took off his coat off and shook a plume of dust free. The act offended the steward.

"Stop that at once," he demanded. "And leave! We do not allow those who do not have a tok..." The steward's jaw stopped spewing out words but continued to open and close as he looked at the token Grint presented. He quickly realized who the sigil upon it belonged to. "Is that?'

"Prince Oryn. Of the Geldens."

"The Geldens?" And then, "You?"

"No," Grint shook his head and gave a winning smile. "I'm just their man. The prince doesn't care for waiting. I'm here to procure accommodations. The gate captain seemed to think this was a place I could do so. Unless he was mistaken?"

"It would be my ultimate pleasure to serve you." The steward gave a stiff-backed bow and smiled. "My name is Montrouse."

"Of course, it is," Grint replied, leaving the steward at a loss for words. Montrouse bowed again and led them up two flights to a resplendent hallway. The decor would not be out of place in a palace. Golden frames encrusted with jewels displayed priceless pieces of art, a small table at the top of the stairs with solid gold candle holders, and an ornate glass bowl filled with pearls. It was difficult to remember that this was just an inn. There was a king's ransom in wealth, and this was just the hallway.

"Our rooms draw the finest nobles waiting to meet with the governor." Montrouse's voice came out in a slow drawl that connected each word to the one before. "I don't have full suites, but there is half-suite with a small servant's room. I trust that will suffice?"

Montrouse paused by a door on the left side of the hallway, a golden key in hand, The left side faced out the back with a view of the western wall. What Grint wanted was a view out the front. He jerked his head toward the door on the right, "What about that room?"

"The Grand Adjutant is occupying those rooms. A royal judge of the Trinian Provinces," he added in response to Grint's frown.

"And a prince, my prince, should stay in the smaller room while an adjutant..."

"Grand adjutant."

"...grand adjutant stays in the larger?" Grint let the words hang in the air while a battle raged within the steward's mind.

"I see your point," he said after a time. "But the grand adjutant has been waiting weeks to meet with the governor."

"And Prince Oryn is meeting with him the night he arrives. It would be a pity for his first comments to be about lackluster service at the High and Might Inn."

That was enough to change the steward's disposition. He unlocked the door and entered without invitation. Grint waited in the hall as the shouts grew in volume and intensity. Words such as 'impropriety' and 'lack of decorum' flittered about before the door opened depositing the grand adjutant into the hall. "Now see here!" the portly old gentleman cried, his golden robes shaking as Montrouse shoved him through the opposite doorway. Two young servants, a man and a woman poked their heads out. They were both dressed in white robes wrapped tight around their bodies. The grand adjutant was from the Trinian Provinces where a major fortress of the Brotherhood Knights stood. Grint hoped one of those steel bastards didn't appear next. He'd run afoul of their kind one-too-many times.

The grand adjutant rang a bell from his new room. The two servants hurried his belongings to him. Grint brushed past them as they exited and walked straight to the window, thankful that there were no knights in their service. Three blocks east and one to the north he found Ballastrine's manor. The view wasn't clear, but he could see a tower and widow's watch rising above the walls and other manors. It would be enough to learn the landmarks around the manor while he searched out Faighur and figured out how to get inside.

"As you can see, there are two full rooms and a private dining area in this suite." Montrouse was giving the full tour, but Grint's attention remained outside. The old wizard from the gate wandered along the street outside, two guards in tow. Grint's heart pounded in his chest, seeking escape. This was not the place to get caught up in. Directing the guards to spots that gave a good vantage of the front door and stable path, the wizard nodded and waddled away. The tension eased, but his throat remained bone dry. *That wizard has concerns and nothing more, otherwise they'd kick in the doors.*

"We decorate all the walls with it," Montrouse said, pride in his voice. Grint realized the steward was pointing his attention to the obscene amount of velvet covering the room.

"I once knew a duke who covered his walls in velvets," Grint said looking around. "Not just one layer, but two." As he looked up at the ceiling, he whistled. "He never put it on the ceiling though."

"Our guests enjoy it." Montrouse's shoulders stiffened. What didn't offend him? A small gold box filled with coins sat against the window. Grint took a coin, closed the lid, and tucked the box in his bag in one smooth motion. *Thank you, grand adjutant.*

"No offense meant." Grint flipped the pilfered coin to the steward who let it fall to the floor as his expression turned from offended to horrified.

"This is not some brothel where we fling money about!"

Grint paused before leaving the room. "Keep it or don't." And then kept walking. It was a sloppy move. Civilized persons of noble blood didn't go about throwing things at one another. At least not in public. The wizard and guards occupied his mind, not notions of propriety. Another of Hobbe's lessons intruded on his thoughts, *Best not to spend too much time looking at the right hand and missing what the left is doing.* The old man was right. Making a mistake with Montrouse could prove as deadly as one with the old wizard.

The inn's builder shaped the doorknob on the front door into a golden lion's head. It was awkward to hold and even worse to turn. The guard across the street tensed and pretended to browse a vendor's stall filled with scarves as Grint stepped out. It was a better cover than his partner, who stood by the stable path studying the sky. Grint considered exiting on the roof and slipping them, but if the wizard posted a spotter, there would be no way to talk his way out of it. He also couldn't hide in his room. Slip the noose and snap the trap. Leaving through the front confirmed what he suspected. Their orders were to watch him. For now.

It was not yet midday, but the streets of the Terrastags overflowed with shopping nobles, street hawkers, and traveling performers. Grint paused at a cart selling wine flutes, pretending to fix his hair in a looking glass. A two-man patrol passed from the opposite direction without looking at or acknowledging the two following him. Grint tilted the glass to get a look at the roofline, continuing to preen until satisfied no sentries watched from on high.

Grint continued along under the pretense of shopping. Another two-man patrol passed by but this time one glanced at him. How many were watching him? Was this the same patrol that passed by him before? *No, their gaits are different.* Were they? Of that he was not sure. Three young maidens laughed as they browsed the fabrics of a blind merchant. Grint tucked himself in beside them, running his fingers through a translucent sash, watching. The patrol walked by his escorts with no words or hand movements. Escort, only one guard now, not two. Where had the other one gone? *He's gone back to fetch the wizard.* Grint rubbed his neck as he felt the noose tightening around it. How blind had he been? *Blind enough I couldn't see I'm already standing on the gallows.*

Grint took a corner of fabric with his left hand and looped it through a maiden's belt while he perused fabric with his right. As she walked away, she pulled the bolt loose.

The fabric maker shouted, and the silk strip blocked the road. It would be a momentary distraction, but maybe enough for him to lose the guard. Slithering through the crowd was difficult, the throngs only accommodated a path for the patrols. A street awning collapsed onto a stall of bird cages, releasing a flock of exotic Parthian birds. The chaos it unleashed was more effective than Grint's silk trick. People ran around in blind panic as if the colorful birds had any interest in feasting on their eyes.

Grint turned left at a fountain depicting a mammoth bear on its hind legs and kept a brisk pace without breaking into a run. Guards appeared from every direction, sorting out the mess and restoring a modicum of calm. His tail would catch up soon, so he needed to keep changing direction and let the sea of people swallow him up. Could he make it to the next fountain? Grint eyed the alleys on the right and left. Slim, dark passages running between or behind the manors. The problem was slipping into one without a multitude of eyes seeing him. There were at least three patrols on the street, two guards in front of a manor gate, and a half-dozen more on the steps of a magnificent-looking bank. Grint blended in beside a street magician waiting for the opportunity to vanish. The magician wasn't bad, his sleight of hand was almost fast enough to fool Grint. A fireball jumped into the air and the crowd applauded. Grint stepped into a shadow as their heads turned but moving further could draw the guards on the bank steps.

A rickety cart full of kegs lost its wheel and the whole load crashed onto the street. Another timely distraction drawing everyone's attention. Grint moved further into the alley. The smell of baking bread was all that followed. *Lady Lorelai is smiling on me.* It was a happy thought which turned sour. If the Goddess of Luck was here and bending events in Grint's favor, it would amount to no good. A god's involvement was always more trouble than it was worth.

Grint came out one street to the south and fell in beside a trio of lords well into their cups for the earliness of the day. "Good day, sir!" The lord beside Grint noticed him and smiled with the half-lidded stupor that accompanied drunkenness. Still, he appeared a man of pleasant demeanor.

"Good day." Grint gave him a tip of the imaginary cap.

"I am Abner, Lord of Linglewood." Abner slurred his words, but Grint remained confident he said Linglewood. "These are my cousins, Crayven and Billis."

"Crayven, like the Wolf King of old," Crayven added, sloshing his cup as he spoke. "Not craven, like a coward."

"I'll make a note of that." Grint smiled and accepted the skin of wine passed to him. "That's an interesting coat. I met an acquaintance earlier who loves velvet," he said after he took a drink. Abner wore a coat of blue velvet and looked to be Grint's size. Getting out of the green might throw off the guard. So, he took it off and held it out to Abner. "A gift from the Prince of Geldens."

"Oh ho! A Prince!" Abner stumbled as he took the coat and examined it. Then he removed his own and handed it to Grint. "Let it not be said Linglewood gives what it gets."

"That makes no sense," Billis said.

"Quiet now, or we'll send you back to the manor."

Over the bickering, Grint heard a female crier calling out for patrons. Something she said caught his ear. "All are welcome, even the Tebbs' of the world!"

"This is where we part," Grint said as he slapped Abner on the shoulder.

"It was a pleasure. If you are ever in Linglewood, come feast with us!" The trio bumbled on as Grint donned the new coat. The arms were spacious, meaning poor Abner was in for a tight fit. Guards and patrols walked past, but none paid him any mind. Their eyes watched the common folk, not token carrying nobles.

"All are welcome here. All welcome," the woman continued to shout. The crier was a buxom woman standing in front of a tavern called the Southern Dawn. It was a shabby establishment, in stark contrast to the surrounding opulence. "You sir," she said, addressing Grint. "You look like one of our sort."

"Looks can be deceiving." Grint held up the wooden token, and the woman laughed.

"So they can. Our regulars don't carry those, but all are welcome."

"Even Tebbs," Grint said, pocketing the token. To that remark, she squinted.

"You steal that token?" Her voice was a whisper.

"I only steal hearts," Grint said. As the woman barked a throaty laugh, Grint went through a series of hand signals. Four fingers, two, then three. Pinky, then thumb tapping against the thigh. She responded in kind as she finished her lengthy guffaw.

"That is not good. Not good at all. Has that ever worked?"

"I promise they get better when I've had some ale."

"I doubt that, but go on in," she said and returned to her calling. "The only thing you can steal in the Terrastags are hearts! Steal mine and win an ale. All are welcome!"

Grint walked up the steps to the tavern but didn't enter. Instead, he stepped through a small curtain to the left of the door. The path beyond led into a thin alley, heavy in shadow, thick with mud, and full of a stink beyond description. A tavern band rumbled on within, accompanied by the rhythmic thump of the patrons stomping in time. A hooded man sat on an overturned crate taking bites from an unpeeled onion.

"That's disgusting, Faighur."

"This is one of the few things I can still taste," the skinling replied. "I take what I can get. You're welcome, by the way."

"For what?"

"The awning and the cart." Faighur slapped a hand on his thigh, shaking the empty sling draped there.

Grint threw back his head and laughed, "Krypsie be praised! That was you?"

"Who did you think it was?"

"Lorelai." Grint pulled a small bit of beef from his bag and gnawed on it.

"You think too highly of yourself."

"What's with the tavern? Out of place for the Terrastags." Grint kicked at the brick wall, watching chunks of mortar shower the alley floor.

"There is no fountain to Hobbe. There is a tavern."

"Lucky him," Grint replied. "You learn anything interesting?"

"If I knew how wretched a place this was beforehand, I never would have let you talk me into coming here."

"That's helpful. This place is madness, I'll grant you that. I've been here two hours and they're already following me." Grint scratched his head and looked both ways down the alley. The itch between his shoulders telling him he hadn't lost that guard.

"They are," Faighur replied, his voice flat. "Someone delivered a letter to the gate after you went through. They've been following you since."

"Who even knows I'm here? A seer?"

"I don't think it's that deep a mystery," Faighur said, looking disappointed. "You're an Apple Filling." It was an old assassin's term for disguising poison in a drink or food. In thief lingo, it meant a decoy who distracted from the real plan.

"Maybe," Grint admitted. "It makes little sense. Eleanor spent a lot of effort to bring me here just to use me as a distraction."

"I hope you're right." Faighur popped the last of the onion into his mouth and swallowed, then stood. "There is a gate two blocks south. Say the word and we go. We'll do to those necromancers what we should have in Upper Anghor."

"We finish the job," Grint said.

"For as much as you hate Hobbe, you sound just like him."

"What have you learned about the manor?" Grint's tone was harsher than it should have been, but it bothered him when anyone compared him to the old bastard. Or did it bother him that Faighur was right? They should cut and run. He had for less misfortune than this. The job hadn't gone sideways yet. It was sinking like a dying boat, but they could still make it to land.

"Come," Faighur said, and they continued through the back of the alley. "I have not gotten too close to the manor. There are wards everywhere and they become more pervasive the closer you get to the governor's mansion. They've even warded the sky so I couldn't fly out if I wanted to."

The alley came out in a small tent filled with wood carvings. An old, blind woman sat on a stool whittling at a block and gave no mind to Faighur. Yet, when Grint passed she reached out and snagged his wrist. No words passed between them as she pulled a small figure off the shelf and tried closing it in his hand. Before she could, Faighur pulled him from the tent. "Don't dawdle, there's a small window for what I want to show you."

"How does everyone living here get past the wards?" They passed through a square whose fountain depicted stone boats fighting in what looked like the Provincial Wars between the Orrish and Sandy Kingdoms.

"Keep your voice down. They train the guards as thief-catchers. Thank Krypsie you haven't been here long enough to steal anything." Grint hissed and slapped his bag where the bulk of the small golden box sat. Faighur grabbed him by the coat and pulled him to the side of the street. "Grint?"

"There was a golden box full of coins just sitting there," Grint said.

Faighur shook his head and grumbled something unintelligible before saying, "Ditch it now and it may buy us some time."

"It's a golden box. Full of coins," Grint reiterated.

"Inno janoi," Faighur spat and stalked off. "Anything that's not nailed down."

"That's the point," Grint said as he followed. "Now, the wards?"

The pair paused by another alley and waited for the patrol to walk by before stepping in. The alley systems were a different world from the rest of the city, dark and seedy. Dirty in a way that seemed impossible when compared to the streets. "Do they glamour the streets?"

"In a way. Keeps the common folk from looking into the alleys or entering them."

"So how are we doing it?"

"The tokens," Faighur replied. "It's the same with the wards as I can tell. The tokens let you pass, but for the manors you need the specific one to the house."

Getting in to Ballastrine's manor would require getting one of his tokens, which could take time. Why hadn't Eleanor prepared him for that? "What about the waterways? You can't ward water."

"From what I learned in the tavern, the water in the streets isn't what goes in the manors." Faighur slowed his pace as they neared the end of the alley.

"Why?"

"Their water comes from a special system running through the governor's mansion. Something magic about it or there is when the governor gives them a taste. There are claims the water flows from the Tears of Hope. No one can say if that is true."

Faighur pressed Grint against the wall and pointed into the square. The large fountain depicting a dozen prominent gods rose taller than any of the other fountains Grint saw. The square was larger still with a score of stalls and performers entertaining. Tables covered by massive umbrellas let the self-important nobility sit in the shade while enjoying a repast. The skinling drew Grint's attention to a young man sitting backwards on a chair as he surveyed the square. "Ballastrine's son. He comes here each day to gawk at a young lady from another house."

"And he has a token," Grint smiled and chewed on his lower lip. "I'll go snatch it. You run interference." Faighur shook his head and pointed to the three house guards a few paces behind the lordling. Grint shrugged. "I've done more under worse conditions. You remember the Chalice of the Moons?"

"I'd feel better if there weren't a hundred thief-catchers within a knife's throw."

"So, what then? A Donnel Berrybright? I win him the girl's heart and get invited to dinner?"

"That could take weeks."

"True." Grint tapped a fingernail on his teeth as he thought. "Do the guards carry tokens?"

"I don't believe so," Faighur said, the hint of a smile on his lips. If the guards could get in without a token, it meant the cancellation was an area effect. Was that why Eleanor hadn't told him?

"The Goblin Tailor of Garr." Grint snapped his fingers.

"While we could approximate their attire, would they not recognize you as an imposter?" Faighur sounded doubtful.

"Not if they don't get a look at my face. Once through the gate, I'll duck to the side, move slow. I think it could work Right? Faighur?" His companion had fallen silent, and worse yet, was no longer beside him.

"Who you talking to runt?" Black Samuel asked as he shoved Grint against the alley wall and pressed a dagger against his throat.

"Black Bastard? What in Krypsie's name are you doing here?"

"Watch what you call me while I have a knife to your throat." When he smiled, he showed off his decaying, black teeth. "Speaking of knives. Where is mine?"

Grint smiled back as he tapped Blackblade against the man's precious jewels. "You mean my knife?" Black Samuel hissed and tried to pull away, but Grint held him in place. There was someone else in the alley, hiding themselves behind Samuel's massive frame. Grint knew Eleanor and her sniveling hounds well enough now to know when one was lurking close at hand.

"Noseless? So that's where you went."

It took Black Samuel a moment to piece it together, but when he did, his face turned sour – more sour than usual. "You know him?"

Grint squinted as the moment dragged on. "Which one of us were you asking?"

"You?" Black Samuel did not sound at all sure.

"His leash holder hired me to steal an urn which I now see was not an exclusive contract. Breaking a lot of rules."

"It's my job now," Black Samuel said and then after a mental struggle added, "How much is she paying you?"

"Twice what they offered you," Grint said.

"Twice!" With Black Samuel distracted, Grint dropped a knife from his left sleeve and pressed it against his rival's jugular.

"Two knives to one." Grint pushed Samuel back, clearing himself of the wall.

"Idiots," Noseless whispered. "The guards will see."

"You're paying him twice what you're paying me?"

Noseless sighed. Grint imagined many instances of this stupidity as the hound traveled with this dullard. "He doesn't know what you're being paid, so how can it be double? Think."

Being called an idiot was enough to raise Black Samuel's anger to its full splendor. Knives or not, he shoved Grint once, twice, and then with his ample size a third, which sent Grint stumbling out of the alley. The first thing he hit was a large pole over a baker's tent, which collapsed. Next was a chair that sent him flailing into a table where he scattered glass bottles and a carafe of wine. The wine found a new home on the dress of a pretty young woman out for a stroll. Grint hit the ground hard as he made the knives disappear up his sleeves before anyone saw them. The girl shrieked, mostly out of surprise but was composing herself even as Grint sat up.

"I am very sorry," Grint offered her a silken kerchief. The girl smiled, handling the moment much better than Grint could have hoped.

"Clumsy dog of low birth," a young man shouted. "Offender of beauty and destroyer of purity!" As the voice grew closer, the girl's eyes widened. Grint looked over his shoulder to find little lordling Ballastrine descending on him with his sword drawn.

Of course, he thought. *This is the girl he watches. Maybe I can convince them to fall in love? Donnel Berrybright anyone?*

"I challenge thee to a duel," young Ballastrine shouted to raucous applause. The girl, meek of voice tried to object but no one heard her.

"A what?" Grint asked. Black Samuel skulked in the alley's mouth, a giant grin painting his ugly face while he made a rude gesture of three fingers pointed down. Go die was the rough translation. *This sinking ship of a job just sunk.*

8

"Grint, for the last time. Don't steal for the right reasons."

- Blue Fingered Hobbe

Grint hadn't woken up this morning intending to duel the Lord's son he'd been hired to rob, but you played the hand dealt. Eleanor played her own hand. Black Samuel. What an unexpected displeasure that was, but proved Faighur's theory of Grint being an Apple Filling. *Where in the sour crack is Faighur? I'm not an Apple Filling. More of a Full Hand with a Shot of Clear.* Eleanor doubled down on her original wager by bringing in Black Samuel, using the rival thief to keep Grint off balance the way he had with her.

"Do you even own a sword? Rat-tailed wretch!" The little lordling played up to the crowd who now encircled the duelists while providing them a healthy berth. More onlookers joined, crowding the square as word of a duel spread. Those who could not see climbed like spiders onto the edge of the fountain, shouting bets in time with catcalls.

"Let's do this with fists," Grint said, cracking his knuckles.

"Swords." The little lordling had a temper. The girl he sought to impress stood at the edge of the crowd holding a thin shawl over the damp stain on her dress. The look on her face wasn't hard to read. She wanted to be anywhere but here.

"Your daddy never taught you when to back down, did he?" Grint let two knives drop from his sleeves, Blackblade in his right and a blunt-bladed, swatter in the left. "Allow me to rectify that."

The lordling's eyes widened at their sudden appearance, but composed himself by making a joke to the crowd. "He wishes to fight with dinner knives!"

"It's not too late, kid. You're not winning yourself ground with the girl." Young Ballastrine glanced her way, but she averted her eyes as the surrounding crowd clapped her shoulders. His face flushed a deep red Grint never saw before. There was no way out of the duel now, besides, the crowd wouldn't let him leave with money on the line. Instead, Grint would use the opportunity to goad the boy close and find the kry-damn token to his house. The lordling rushed forward, shrieking an unintelligible battle cry as he bandied his rapier. *He looks like a mud-drowned maniac.* Grint slapped the attack away with his swatter and slashed the young man's ribs with Blackblade on the follow through. It wasn't deep, just enough to remind the boy that combat wasn't a game.

Grint's one advantage over Black Samuel was that neither possessed the proper token to get past Ballastrine's gate. The little lordling did and Grint would have it before this duel ended. Ballastrine jumped back and then forward, thrusting his rapier. The tip of the blade wavered an inch from Grint's chest as he side-stepped it, pinned the blade under his arm. Ballastrine struggled to break away, but not before Grint slipped a hand in the right pocket of the kid's coat. *Nothing.*

Are you sure Black Samuel doesn't have the proper token? It was Hobbe's voice, speaking with that know-it-all inflection. As if he knew secrets he couldn't share until you figured them out. *Odd that Eleanor never told you what the tokens were for. Funny to find him traveling with Noseless when Eleanor said they needed to avoid suspicion. Funny.*

"Real bloody funny." Grint didn't mean to vocalize his reply to Hobbe. Even during a fight some might judge him mad for talking to himself, but the words never rose above the clamor. The lordling pushed Grint away and straightened his coat. *Can't have a wrinkle during a death duel.* With a flourish of his left hand, the kid danced, stabbing the rapier toward Grint's left eye. *No one will hire a blind thief,* Hobbe laughed. Grint jumped back as a second thrust came close to his right eye.

"Enough," he grunted and charged. Impatience threatened to overcome his desire for caution, something he chided himself for as he checked young Ballastrine's left pocket. This mummery grew tiresome, but he couldn't let the lordling know what he was really after. *Breathe you fool and do the job,* he thought as he patted down the pants with the flat parts of his blades. Still no token. There had to be one on him. Did the guards have it? Did he have a bag Grint missed at the table?

Grint ducked below a clumsy blade swipe. As the lordling's jacket fluttered open, he saw the subtle circular outline of the token within an inner pocket. Making the blades disappear into his sleeves, Grint clenched his fists and slugged the kid in the gut. The blow took his feet out from under him, and the lordling fell forward. Grint punched him again and snatched the token while the boy crumpled. The slap of flesh against stone sounded when the kid hit the street, losing whatever air remained in his lungs.

"Stay down, kid. Yield. Quit." Even as Grint spoke, the lordling searched for his sword, struggling to his knees. "This is over." The crowd swallowed the words or maybe the kid had too much pride to give up. Either way, he had to end this. Grint kicked the sword out of reach and shattered Ballastrine's knee with the thick heel of his boot. The joint bent the wrong way with a sickening crack. The crowd gasped, then roared with animalistic pleasure.

House guards in Ballastrine colors paced at the edge of the crowd. They bounced on their feet, torn between rushing to the side of their charge and risking interference. When a fight involved betting, stepping in could earn them a trip to the gallows. Grint counted three. Were there more before the duel? It didn't matter. They knew Grint now - at least by sight, and Black Samuel had earned himself a healthy head start while keeping his anonymity. The house guards would follow if Grint ran; making the token in his pocket all but useless without some way clear.

"Dragon," someone screamed. The crowd quieted, no one quite believing the claim. A few people laughed. A heckler made a lewd remark. The deafening roar and rising spout of fire changed everyone's minds. *Faighur, you idiot. You'll get yourself killed.* True or not, the result was widespread panic as the crowd ran in every direction. Ballastrine's guards started toward Grint, who wasted no time in running the opposite way. He danced past a gaggle of young girls and jumped on the lip of the fountain to stay above the frenzied crowd. Leaping off blindly, he fell onto a man in a chef's hat and had to roll back onto his feet. A cloud of flour puffed into the air.

Grint let the flow of the crowd pull him from the square, moving within the herd until the chaos died down. A fresh cry from the dragon renewed the panic, pushing him further along. Grint hoped his friend's plan factored in an escape. A cadre of wizards trotted toward the beast, the crowd parting to let them past. Flakes of ice snowed around them as powerful magic danced between their fingers. For a moment, he considered rounding back to help, but knew that would infuriate the skinling. Faighur had done this to get Grint out of that square, not pull him back. He hated leaving him, but the dragon was on his own.

Looking back, Grint saw that a single house guard remained on his tail. *The others must have stayed with the lordling. I hope.* The crowd's flow carried him toward his goal, which in some respect was a good thing. *One street left, then another to the right at the statue of the frog.* Grint ducked around a large group of women in green dresses and shed the blue jacket, hanging it across the shoulders of a frightened young boy.

Another left and then straight on. Was the crusty wizard still out there looking for him? The guards he assigned? Too many unknowns. How far ahead had Black Samuel gotten? Was he ahead? Was he biding his time hoping Grint would get himself killed or caught?

Grint stopped behind a cart of leather boots, ducking down as he pretended to check his own. A few dozen people ran through the street, but most had now taken shelter indoors. Their faces pressed against windows as they looked for signs of the dragon. Five vendors gathered in a cluster, pointing at columns of smoke while wishing ill on their competitors. A large retinue of soldiers made a racket as they marched double time. A noble on horseback charged out of his manor, flanked by two dozen guards, forcing people to leap out of the way or get crushed. Grint was sure the man would have run anyone down who got in the way. The banners carried by his men bore the sigil of Ballastrine. Grint watched the lord ride past, a gaunt man with a pointed black beard and ashen face. The column of guards continued pouring from the manor, fifty to sixty strong. How many did that leave in the manor? *Not enough to stop me.*

With Lorelai's luck, the trailing house guard would fold in with the rest of the men. Grint waited for the last of the guards to trot past. A short dash along the walkway led him to a spot where he could slip into an alley beside the manor's southern wall. Many of the manors had trees on their grounds and Grint hoped to find one hanging over the ten-foot walls that he could use to climb over. The alleyway was narrow, and though it had been a while, he was confident he could leap off one wall and up the other if he had to.

That plan ended up being unnecessary as he came across a servant's door built into the alley wall. A smooth wooden door he estimated to be of considerable girth as he tapped a finger against it. There was no exterior latch, something that would have proven problematic had someone not already kicked it in. Hanging off a hinge, the wood had splintered where the inner bar tried to hold it closed. Black Samuel beat him here after all. What need did he have for a token if he could kick a door in while the wards let a column of guards out the front gate? Smart. Too smart for Black Samuel at least. An entire night of gambling with the man and he never once showed this level of ingenuity. Eleanor did. Was she with him now? Had they been together the whole time?

Run, stupid boy! Hobbe's voice banged like a bell. *Get out!*

No, this was still a Terrastag manor. Stolen gold sat fat in his pocket and the promise of more lay inside. After that was the urn and Eleanor's payment - which he would see doubled when he figured out a way to finish the deal while keeping his head. *You'll be too dead to enjoy it.* Grint shut the voice from his mind. Faighur risked himself to get Grint into position. The thief would not do any less to see the job done. *There isn't a shiny coin in the Hells of Astapoor that I'm letting Black Samuel become the first thief to rob the Terrastags.*

Beyond the gate sat a small guard house of white stone large enough for a single guard to sit on a stool. On the other side of the structure, Grint found the man in a pool of his own blood. Black Samuel had snapped his neck and gutted him. Dead eyes stared up at Grint. The thief couldn't worry whether the God of Murder watched through them. It wasn't his kill. Another hope. Another maybe.

A small garden path led to the manor. Pebbles crunched underfoot as he jogged toward a row of hedges encircling the house. Two guards stood at the front gate, their attention focused outward for now. *Probably mad they didn't get to go.* The path hooked right as it neared the manor and led to a door - also kicked in. The sounds of a struggle echoed from within. Black Samuel had no subtlety. He was what they called a basher. A thief who broke anything in their way. A blunt object with no sense of stealth.

Grint found a secluded window behind a hideous hedge cut in the vague shape of a four-legged animal. A large, multi-paned window with hinges that opened outward. Only a single silver latch held it closed. Easy enough to unlock with a blade, but first he pulled a flat copper disk from his bag and tapped it against the wooden frame. A sparkle of red light wound around the latch. Grint nodded, *warded.* A trip ward like this one was easy enough to disarm. Grint pulled a bulbous, black rock from his bag and scraped it with Blackblade. Agot stone shavings deadened most magic. The scraping sound raised a few goosebumps on the back of his neck and left a greasy streak along the already blackened steel. The latch sparked when he touched the blade to it, a brilliant blue color that meant the ward had fallen.

Grint climbed inside, the sounds of a struggle still audible from here. Black Samuel could bash his way in and draw all the attention. All the better. Grint would be the shadow who slipped away before anyone knew he was there.

"Speaking of robbing," Grint whispered as he looked around the room. He found himself in a study with shelves full of old tomes. Certain dealers would pay a year's wage for just one book, but unless you knew what you were looking for, it was best to pass. In the center of the room sat an oak desk that glistened from the oils used to wipe it down. On it sat a quill, ink pot, wax stamp, and stacks of paper, all arranged in meticulous order. A large, golden bust of Ballastrine dominated the edge of the desk. It would be too large to take, but the string of pearls wrapped around its neck fit neatly in Grint's bag.

Four colored gems the size of a fist sat on a glass shelf by the window. Each placed in such a way that the sun would glitter through them as the day moved on. Grint tapped the copper disc on the shelf and smiled when nothing happened. The four jewels went into the bag along with the golden prongs used to display them.

The fighting in the hallway had fallen silent, so Grint opened the study door and peaked out. A thick red runner embroidered with ornate golden thread ran the length of the wide hallway. Ruby encrusted candle sticks sat in sconces between framed paintings and a crystal vase. Far to the right, a pair of feet disappeared as someone dragged their body away. While Black Samuel wasted time covering his tracks, Grint went the other way, stepping on soft toes toward the main staircase. Eleanor said the urn and her contact were in a sub-basement. The door for it would be somewhere in the basement larder.

Grint squeezed himself into a thin alcove housing a statue as he heard a woman's voice nearing. A door to his right opened, and a maid dressed in a baby blue dress stepped halfway through. She was turned in such a way that her back was to Grint as she yelled into the kitchens. "I've got to get the charffing eggs."

"What for, Marna?" Another woman replied. Far back in the kitchens from the faint sound.

"You know Lord Ballastrine will want an afternoon egg when he gets back." There was irreverence and disdain in her voice that Grint admired.

The unseen woman laughed. "With all the strutting he'll be doing at his brat's duel, you'd think he could lay his own egg. Krypsie knows the cold bitch he married can't."

"Quiet now, you'll get us both switched." Grint found the exchange amusing, but hoped Marna didn't turn and see him. What he would have to do to her would be less funny, and that was nothing compared to what Black Samuel might do if he came around the corner. Thankfully, neither of those scenarios occurred and the jocular maid continued out the door without spotting Grint. Marna pressed a flat panel beneath the master staircase. It must have housed a hidden switch as the panel slid open to reveal a much rougher door. The basement door whined in protest when she opened it.

A flame flickered to life, spreading its light across Grint's face. Wood scraped against metal as she pulled the torch from its sconce and started down the steps. Grint waited in the alcove, one eye on the hall and the other on the doorway. When the light faded, he stepped on tiptoes toward the stairs. It was a darkened recess, lit only by the torch Marna carried.

From the top, he could see the faint outline of two doors below and hear the vague sound of running water. Faighur had mentioned the governor doled out water to the manors. *That must be where it comes in.*

Something hot blazed to life in Grint's chest. The thieves' gut come home to roost. It was a poor time to feel antsy, but the urn being so close gave it life. No. There was no time for fear, and he wouldn't give it a chance to grow. With a deep breath and a moment of silence, he calmed himself enough to hear the heavy steps of Black Samuel as he stomped around the corner. Grint had but a moment to turn his body to meet the charging bull.

The basher slammed into him, his meaty hands clambering for purchase around Grint's neck. Unable to pry the larger man off, Grint began blindly punching fist after fist into the bull's side, trying to shatter a rib or break him off. The pair kicked and punched one another as their bodies shifted on the upper landing, and Grint could feel his heels slipping over the edge of the stairs.

As they thumped down the first step, they heard Marna singing. Her voice was distant, coming from somewhere deep in the cellar but the tune carried. The melody was light and as she reached the chorus; he realized the song was Harfordshire Maidens. It was the sort of drivel they sang at spring festivals to get the young girls excited for love. Jessua hated it.

Grint kicked a foot out from under Black Samuel and they slid down half the staircase clutching at one another's throats. "***All the maidens know when it's time to come home.***" They stopped falling when Samuel's large frame wedged into the tight space below the railing, allowing Grint to pull free and land a punch against the basher's right eye. "***All the maidens know when it's time for love, love, love.***" Black Samuel cursed in a hushed whisper and put the flat of his foot into Grint's belly, launching him down the staircase. "***Find that boy, spin him round. Make Mama proud. Sing out loud.***" Grint fell the rest of the way down without touching a step, landing on his back in such a way that he knew he'd bear the bruises for a month."***The first boy to fall will be the one who is yours.***" His head slapped the cold dirt floor and stars appeared where none could be. Grint hated the song too.

Wasting no time, he pushed himself up while fighting the spins that threatened to pull him back down. Black Samuel righted himself and stomped down, ignorant or uncaring of the truth they were not alone in the cellar. Grint stepped backwards through the larder doorway, fists raised and ready for a fight. The maid had stopped singing and held up her torch, straining to see what caused the noise.

Through the door were two rows of shelves reaching the ceiling, each stuffed full of food. A center aisle divided the larder running from front to back. Grint stepped to the right and as Black Samuel spotted the woman, he stepped left. The rivals glared at one another while the maid scanned the cellar. "Duhast? Is that you? Duhast? You know you're not allowed down her. Come here, boy."

Grint could see his breath coming out in frantic puffs. The unnatural, frigid air bit at his skin, courtesy of a chilling spell, cast to keep the food cold. The arctic temperatures made Grint recognize the odd, hot sensation pressing against his side. He looked at his trusted travel bag with the horrified realization that something inside had gone amiss. As he flipped open the cover, Black Samuel looked on with morbid curiosity. Something inside glowed white hot beneath one of his balled-up shirts.

Dear Krypsie, Grint thought, *it's the kry-damned Tricorn of Emblazoning.*

Such a ridiculous name, Hobbe added.

The Tricorn was composed of three crystals, all worthless on their own, but each imbued with powerful magic. As the story went, the Tricorn, if assembled correctly, could start an unstoppable fire. Grint stole it from a wizard and expected a sizable return for the trouble. Except no one knew how to make it work beyond a few simple sparks, and no one wanted to buy something useful only as a curiosity. For the past three years, Grint used the crystals to light campfires and as fishing lures, and had eaten well. Something during their struggle had set them off. *Of course,* Grint thought. *Now is the time they're arranged correctly.*

"Come here, Duhast, and I'll give you a treat." The maid kept calling for what Grint assumed was the family dog and had moved on to bribing it. Then in a more forceful tone, "Come! Now!" The Tricorn glowed brighter and Grint knew he had to take it out or risk setting off much worse items stashed away in the bag. An unquenchable fire was not something he wanted blazing beside the eyesighter.

The maid sighed and lowered the torch as she walked toward them. "If you've gotten into the water again, I'll tan your hide as dark as Lord Ballastrine will mine." She passed by the pair without seeing either crouched in the dark, and stepped into a chamber across the hall.

With her back to them, Grint pulled out the Tricorn and tossed it to Black Samuel. It glowed dimly, but the heat coming off it was enough to sting Grint's hands when he touched it. The big, dumb animal that Black Samuel was, stared at the glowing crystal with awe and greedy anticipation. As he caught it, he offered a smile that said, *I don't accept your bribe.*

I'll keep this beauty and kill you too. Then the burning heat sank in. Grint climbed through the shelves as Black Samuel dunked the Tricorn and his hands into an open barrel of chilled mead. His groans of pain and mewling whines faded as Grint put distance between them, crawling and leaping from shelf to shelf.

As he reached the back of the cellar, Marna reappeared waving her torch against the darkness. Grint quietly shifted a heavy crate to watch as she turned toward the mead barrel. He expected cries or sounds of alarm, but the maid said nothing. Black Samuel had moved and so should he.

Eleanor's meager directions were to find a rack of shelves against the back wall that served as a secret door. Behind he would find a spiral staircase leading to her contact. Grint counted three racks against the back wall, but only one had sweeping scratches in the dirt beneath it. While the maid was still distracted, he pulled on the shelves, but the kry-damned thing wouldn't budge. There wasn't time to pull everything off, so he slid his hands over the wood, feeling between bottles as he searched for a pull lever or release. Instead, he found a keyhole. A bloody, ram-baked, sour-cracked keyhole.

The maid heard the noise and came closer, waving her torch down each aisle she passed. "Duhast?" she whispered each time.

Grint pulled a skeleton key and pick from his bag and jammed it in the keyhole. He picked locks like this in his sleep. *Not like this,* Hobbe warned. *Test it,* he thought and pulled out the copper disc. It tapped blue. No traps. The girl was now only two rows away. The light from her torch casting the barest flicker on Grint's arm. And where was Black Samuel? Grint put the skeleton key back in and worked the pick. He went to a place in his imagination like Hobbe taught him. A place he could see the inner workings; the cogs and pins as he manipulated them. Marna was only one row away, but Grint almost had the lock, he could feel it giving in.

It clicked, and the shelf opened a crack. "Duhast? Who?" The torchlight shone bright on his back, painting his shadow on the shelves. The maid stood behind him. Grint cursed and turned. To her credit she didn't appear panicked; just confused.

"Sorry, Marna," Grint said, and she cocked her head. Throwing a right hook, he struck her. He'd pulled the punch, but still she went down and rolled until she came to rest against a shelf, where she lay unconscious. Somewhere in the dark, Black Samuel's laugh echoed off the stone walls.

Grint slipped through the hidden door and closed it behind him. There was nothing to bar on the inside, so he hoped it locked on its own. It wouldn't buy him more than a few moments, even a basher like Samuel knew how to pick an unwarded lock. Grint ran down the steps, staying close to the inner wall, leaping two to three at a time. Once he reached the bottom, he could lay a trap for Black Samuel. *I can...*

Grint ran into the guard before he knew what he was seeing. Wearing heavy leathers and a burnished skull cap the guard craned his head towards the noise on the stairs. When he saw Grint, he reached out a hand and smiled. Grint planted a foot against the outer wall and launched himself into the man. Knuckles against teeth, the guard grunted. They stumbled through a small hallway as Grint punched him again, his knuckles wet with blood. When they slammed into the door, it swung open, depositing them on the other side. Grint hopped to his feet, fist cocked back, but the guard lay still.

"What did you do to Mullens?" There stood a man with shoulder length white hair, black goatee streaked with gray, and a burgundy robe tied neatly with a silken cord. The studious look on his wizened face belonged to someone who knew they were smarter than you.

"Barlow?" Grint asked as he turned to look for something long and sturdy to block the door with.

"Bardo," the man corrected. "But, Mullens?"

"I don't know who Mullens is," Grint answered. A metal pipe the length of five arms balanced atop two pieces of wood with a dozen glass ampules dangling from it. Grint yanked the rod from its perch, uncaring as the glass shattered on the stone floor.

"Now see here," Bardo's voice squeaked as he pointed at the tendrils of smoke rising from the mixing liquids. Grint ran to the door and stood left of the opening. Black Samuel, ever the basher, pounded down the staircase with reckless abandon. When he breached the door, Grint swung the pipe and caught him in the throat. His head snapped back while his feet continued forward, and he slapped the ground with the flat of his back. Grint straddled his chest and punched him a few more times for good measure.

"Go to sleep," he said as he struck Black Samuel into unconsciousness. Satisfied, Grint tossed the pipe aside.

"Who is that?"

"There're a lot of names here. Grint. Bardo. Mullens," Grint said as he pointed to himself, the contact, and then at the unconscious guard. Bardo nodded with each name.

"And him?"

"An assassin sent to kill you. Now if you don't mind, I'll take the urn." Grint looked around the room. There were four tables situated around the space, all covered with books, glass jars, small fires busy boiling liquids. Tubes thick enough for a mouse to run through snaked around all of it. A tall curtain obscured the back of the room, burgundy like Bardo's robe. Did he plan that? Grint spotted the urn on the table furthest right.

"Yes, that's it, but it's not ready yet," Bardo said as Grint walked over to the prize.

"What is all of this?" Grint ran a finger along the tubes filled as they dripped a viscous crimson liquid into the urn. He tried following the tubes back to their source but lost the trail in the maze of tables and bottles.

"That's what I mean. I began filling it after my morning meal. It's not ready yet."

"No. No, no, no. No." Grint shook his head as he turned toward Bardo, who he assumed was an alchemist. "I'm here for the urn. I don't care about the rest of this."

"The urn is useless without the blood," Bardo said as he shuffled through some papers.

"That's blood?" Grint almost asked if it was an animal's or human but decided he didn't want to know.

"Yes, and when it's done, I need to seal it with rituals to prepare it for activation. I explained all of this to Eleanor. I can do most of the sealing and activations while we're on the road, but the blooding must occur now." The alchemist found a sheet of parchment and held it out to Grint as if that would explain everything.

"We?" Grint's eyes went wide.

"Yes, of course," Bardo said, quite surprised by the question. "I am the one who knows the rituals."

"I had a bad enough time getting in here and you expect me to take you back out?"

"That's what Mullens was for. Our escort." Bardo looked around the table at the still form of the guard. "Did you kill him?"

"No," Grint answered as he looked at the tubes. If they dripped any slower than this, Grint would lose his mind. "Can you hurry this up?"

"How do you know he isn't dead?"

"Because the God of Murder isn't here. How long will this take to finish?"

"What an odd thing to say. The God of Murder."

"How long?" Grint asked again.

"You're early," Bardo said, and then jumped as Grint slammed his fist against the table, shaking the urn. "Half a day."

"Half a day?" Grint stepped around the table as he drew Blackblade from his belt. "We don't have half a day. Ballastrine and all his men will be back soon, and when they get here, they'll kill us."

"You see, you're early. I wasn't expecting you." Beads of sweat ran down Bardo's temples and into his eyes, making him blink.

"They'll kill us. You. Me. Mullens."

"Mullens?"

"Mullens too," Grint said poking the tip of the knife against the underside of Bardo's nose. "All of us."

"I'll collect my notes and see if I can complete this any sooner." Bardo gave a weak smile and shuffled over to a pile of books. Grint sheathed the knife and saw one of Black Samuel's legs twitch. Retrieving the pipe, he hit the basher again and tossed the weapon aside. Bardo jumped as it clattered against the floor.

Hobbe laughed at Grint, *Should have run, boy. Should. Have. Run.* He couldn't argue. The teachings of Blue Fingered Hobbe were immutable truths. He should have run. Would have if it hadn't been for Faighur. *Don't blame the dragon. He was the only one who hasn't made a mess of this. This is all on me.*

Grint stared at the urn hoping that it looked fuller than before. It wasn't. The sinewy tubes did what they needed, but the pace was all wrong. In fact, one worked against the rest as drops of blood seeped through a crack, falling onto the table. "Is this supposed to be like this?"

"I'm working as fast as I can," Bardo called out.

Grint snorted. Working as fast as he could. They were all working their way - in a hasty manner - towards old Jim Gallows. Mister Longtimbers and the Motherly Hug if you please. What had he expected? This was the Terrastags. Did he think he would just walk in, rob them blind, and walk back out while double crossing the necromancers? *Sure. I'm Grint. I can do anything.* The kry-damned hubris.

Grint held a finger under the dripping blood and rubbed it against his thumb, smearing it into the skin. It felt warm to the touch. He felt warm. ***Help her.*** It was a whisper of the mind, a forgotten fragment of memory, a voice so familiar and doubly missed. Grint reached down and touched the snippet hanging around his neck. He pictured a moonlit dell in a blanket of fog. A girl in white, and felt compelled to follow the sinewy tubes if only to find Jessua waiting at the end.

Bardo was deep in his books and oblivious to the thief's movements. Grint followed the tubes one way and the other until finally he found where they disappeared under the burgundy curtain. It was a thick, soft material. *Velvet,* he thought. *Montrouse would approve.* He pushed at the curtain until he found a seam to step through. Beyond was darkness with only a single candle to provide light, but it was strong enough to illumine the towering marble pillar with crossing chains wrapped in tight circles. Slumped at the base was a little girl on her knees with manacles around her wrists that kept her arms raised high. Blood stained her arms through skin rubbed raw by the metal. Where they attached to the girl, the tubes looked more like living things, latching onto her with leech-like teeth as they sucked at her blood.

Sweat dripped from the tangles of her dark hair, landing within the pooled fabric of soiled white robes. Grint reached out and brushed her hair aside. She was little more than a child, ten, maybe twelve years old. Her heavy-lidded eyes blinked listlessly, but she managed to glance up with. ***Save her,*** Jessua said as if whispering in his ear. Had the girl's lips moved when Jessua spoke? Grint stood outside himself, watching as he used Blackblade to cut the tubes. The leech tubes writhed in pain before the toothy mouths opened and dropped to the floor, leaving purple bruises on the girl's arms. ***Free her.***

"Thief? Thief?" Bardo called out for him, unaware of Grint's discovery. Knife in hand, Grint stepped through the curtain and strode toward the alchemist. He felt both in and out of control as he argued with Jessua. *This isn't what I do!* Bardo stared, a stupid look on his face for such a smart man. Grint struck him across the side of the face with the butt of the knife, then grabbed his long white hair at the top, slamming his face into the table. Warm blood sprayed from his shattered nose and Grint let him slump to the floor. Bardo looked up and mouthed something through shattered teeth. "Why?"

Grint pushed open a door to his right and smiled as Bardo tried to crawl away, but the attempt was futile. Grabbing him by the boots, Grint dragged him, taking pleasure in Bardo's pain as the alchemist's head bumped against each mismatched stone. The room Grint had discovered was a privy large enough for one, with a marble bench and a deep hole. It was here that Grint deposited the alchemist. The smell wafting out of the hole was rank. A ten-foot fall into two feet of putrid waste. He wouldn't die. Not unless his wounds got infected from the sludge, but that wouldn't happen right away. And it had nothing to do with Grint.

Stalking across the room, Grint upended tables and smashed glass bottles. Some of the candles flickered as the spilling liquids doused them. Others started a blaze. The urn sat on the last table. Grint dumped out the girl's blood and threw the metal thing into the spreading fire where it spit and sparked. The curtains ignited and Grint decided it was time for them to go. The girl remained where he left her, and she slumped into his arms as he picked the manacle locks open. She was a tiny thing weighing less than the bag across his shoulder.

The curtains fell from their hooks into a pile of ash as smoldering threads floated through the air. Grint edged around the flames, careful to keep the girl's thin gown clear. Bardo's moans floated up from the privy. Mullens lay still, yet Black Samuel was missing, along with the urn. Did that matter? Grint didn't think so. From Bardo's explanation, the urn was only a small part of a bigger need. *I need it! To finish this bloody, cursed job!*

The job is over, Hobbe said. With his mentor's voice back, Grint felt himself again.

A single vial of blood with a cork stopper rolled along the floor. Grint lifted his foot to smash it, but picked it up instead. Every instinct said to dump it, get rid of it, leave it behind, but he put it in his pocket instead. Better to keep it with him than leave it for someone to use as part of a tracking spell.

The ascent to the cellar felt never ending as the full weight of what happened tried to crush him. The seeds of doubt crept in. Was this right? Panic once fed became a voracious beast, so Grint beat it back down to let it starve. There would be ample time to think about it later. Grint reached the hidden door and with a twist of the handle the door swung out. A roaring fire reached for Grint and the girl, forcing him back down the steps.

The larder was aflame as thick smoke rose from burning shelves of food, spreading into the rafters. Grint looked back; the winding staircase remained dark and still save for the smoke clinging to the ceiling. There was no way the fire could have beat them up or even spread this far. Was there? *No.* It was the Tricorn and its unquenchable hunger. After it evaporated the mead - it lit the barrel. Caught between two fires, staying still meant certain death.

Grint wet two shirts from his bag and wrapped one carefully around the girl's face and the other his own. They almost tripped over Marna, who had yet to wake up. Wherever Black Samuel went, he didn't feel the need to save Marna. Grint did. Readjusting the girl in his arms, he slung Marna over the other shoulder and walked in a crouch, trying to keep them all beneath the acrid smoke. The Tricorn's fire raged on in the larder but hadn't yet spread into the hall or stairs.

"Inno janoi," he grumbled as he contemplated a climb up another staircase, this time carrying two people.

The sounds of a fight stopped Grint's progress halfway to the door. Metal on metal and the signature growl of one Black Samuel. The heavy footfalls of steel boots clanged over someone shouting orders. The basher had run straight into the hornet's nest. Grint was careful with Marna as he laid her in the doorway and retreated down. There had to be a place to hide and wait this out. The larder wasn't an option and the alchemist's dungeon was now out of reach.

More smoke poured from the larder and billowed up the stairs to the main house. Fight or no fight, they wouldn't be able to stay here much longer. Grint reached into his bag for the waterskin to wet the shirts with the dregs of what remained. It wasn't much. If he had more water, he could douse their clothes and find a corner to hide in.

The last place left to them was the room opposite the larder. A doorless arch of ancient stone led the way into a dank, cool chamber untouched by the Tricorn's fire. The only meaningful feature was the convex wooden surface running horizontal against the far wall. It was a tiny room. You could take two steps in any direction to touch a wall. With no places to hide - unless Grint made them invisible behind a few discarded buckets - they would get caught the moment someone came downstairs.

There was nothing in his bag that could make them invisible, but he felt a hum beneath the wood piping, a vibration both soothing and consistent. The surface chilled and wet his palm as he laid his hand against it. Rivulets of water trickled onto the dirt floor. This wasn't something decorative installed by a madman with too much gold, but an aqueduct. Grint laughed as he slid the hatch open, revealing a small river of water flowing past. The governor doled out water as he saw fit, and the maid was afraid the dog had gotten in to it. It was dark and wet and as good a place to hide as any. If he hid with the girl inside, they could wait for night and sneak out after everything calmed down.

Grint slipped the bag off his shoulder to lower the girl inside, then turned back to grab it. In that one instant with his back turned, she disappeared. A wisp of white fabric vanished beneath the surface. The water flowed, but the current didn't look strong enough to take her like that, so Grint jumped in. When his feet touched the bottom, a hidden force yanked at his boots pulling him under. The firelight receded as the current dragged him deeper. Grint raked his hands along wood slick with algae and could find no purchase to halt his momentum.

An absolute darkness blinded his vision, so when he struck a metal grate, it was a shock that forced all the air left in his lungs out in precious, wasted bubbles. The girl's white dress tangled around the bars, her bare feet slapping his legs as the current ebbed and flowed. A choking sensation wrapped around Grint's throat as he fought for the breath he was so desperate to take. There was a way out, he just needed to think. Feeling the bars, one shook in his grip. They weren't wide enough for them to squeeze through, but perhaps he could force one loose. It was an exercise in mind over situation as he gripped the grate and kicked. It took all of his energy while trying not to black out. His face, shoulders, chest, belt; each a battle against oblivion. The moment the bar came free, the current yanked them again.

As he struggled to extricate himself, he hooked a leg on the bar and pulled the girl through. He had no notion if she was alive or dead. They flowed through the tunnel until Grint couldn't hold out any longer. Water flooded into his lungs as his brain forced a breath. Convulsions racked his body, violent tremors carrying the certainty of death. And then all the water shot out in a savage cough. Grint's throat burned as he sucked in air coated with dank mildew and old rot. Somehow, he was above water, but still couldn't see.

Pulling the girl under his arm, he groped for a wall, a ceiling, but neither were within reach. Nor could he touch the bottom any longer. The small passage opened in a larger aqueduct it seemed. The current remained strong, so Grint floated on his back and pointed his feet into the flow as he pulled the girl onto his chest. In the dark, he heard her cough out a spray of liquid that slapped against the water. Other than that, she remained lethargic.

They drifted in a blind man's dark, unable to see their own hand in front of their face. Water splashed all around, drainage from other ducts feeding into this larger body, causing ripples that rocked Grint. The roar of water grew louder, echoing and reverberating from every direction until it disoriented every sense. *Sounds like a waterfall*, Grint thought. He felt both proud and stupid as they fell over the edge.

There was no telling how far they fell. Maybe fifty feet. Maybe more. Somewhere on the way down, he lost hold of the girl. He scratched at the air but came up empty. When he hit the water, his shoulder wrenched backward threatening to pop. The waterfall shoved him deep below the frigid depths twisting and flipping him around. As his momentum slowed, he found himself unsure of which direction up was. He held his hands out and kept them still. A down current pressed against the back of his right hand. He was upside down.

Grint flipped himself over and swam to the surface, his lungs hungry for air as he broke through and breathed in. "Kid?" he croaked but couldn't hear his own voice over the thunder of a dozen waterfalls. Grint swam, feeling for any trace of the child but coming up empty. In his mind he painted a picture of this place as a giant mausoleum. Here, his waterlogged corpse would float in this place of interment for all eternity. Panic was all too happy to feast on the thought.

Think, Hobbe screamed, but it was too late. Grint was tired, half-drowned, and desperate. Panic took over as he flailed around - swimming in circles for all he knew - in some vain attempt to find the edge of a vast underground reservoir. When a strong current pulled him down, he thought, *Good, at least I don't have to panic anymore.*

The water sucked through a tighter tunnel where he could feel rough stone walls on either side. It was a small comfort, but not the only one. Before his breath gave out, he realized he could see the faintest silhouette on the stones growing more pronounced every moment. The flow of water leveled out, giving him a breath of air above the surface just as it slammed him into another set of metal bars.

The girl struck him in the back a moment later and he reached around to pull her above the waterline. Her face was pale, eyes closed, and water trickled from her nose. Beyond the bars the water fell into a flowing river running through a giant cave. Not a cave exactly, the far wall dipped low, but the shine of daylight peeked below the lip. Grint wedged himself between the ceiling and floor and kicked at the grate. The mortar was old and gave way after a few solid tries. The grate crashed in a shallow pool. They quickly followed it.

This time Grint kept hold of the girl even as they went into the river. The current wasn't strong here and the water only hip deep. Grint swam with the girl to a rocky shore where his fingers dug into sharp stones that littered the bank. They cut open his palm, but he ignored the pain as he struggled upright and checked the girl's heart. For a moment he thought her dead, but then heard the faint beat. She was alive and began coughing up water. Her eyes fluttered and she blinked at him before passing out.

Grint walked toward the light beyond the cave leaving the girl to rest. The overhanging rocks dipped low, but Grint could crouch beneath them with little trouble. A cold wind cut through his wet clothes, specks of ice already forming on his sleeves. A gray sky hung overhead while a light flurry of snow fell, coating the surrounding trees. Had he forgotten it was autumn in the mountains? Being in that place, even for a short time had mangled his perceptions. The Terrastags were not far. He could see the imposing wall a half a mile to the west, where it rose above the trees, dominating the horizon.

Grint laughed as he ducked back into the cave, causing him to cough up another lungful of water. He had done it. He was the first thief to rob the Terrastags and get out alive. The jewels and gold in his bag were proof. And the girl, the girl was too. The girl. What in the seven depths of Junkar's Palace was he thinking? Grint wasn't an altruist. All he had to do was take an urn full of blood to the necromancers and he would have been swimming in rivers of gold from here to the Sandy Kingdoms. Instead, the voice of his childhood love told him to save an imprisoned girl, and he had done it. A voice. Or was it something else?

Grint retunred to where he left her and stood over her. The cave blocked most of the wind, but the chill remained heavy in the air. When night fell, it would get worse. Worse, the child was barefoot and wearing only a thin, torn white dress that would provide no warmth. The dress wasn't suitable for traveling, and they would need to move fast. How was he going to do that with a kid who would die from exposure on the second day? What if he left her? They would find her. Ballastrine. Eleanor. And if they didn't? The world would eat her alive. A kid on their own never stood a chance. You could ask Grint's dead sister if you didn't believe it. Could he even trust the girl? The feeling that she bewitched him still plagued his mind. Something had happened in that cellar, because nothing went according to plan.

Grint drew Blackblade and knelt over her listless form. He put both hands on the hilt and held it high. *This is the right thing to do. Quick and clean. Hobbe said it - the job went to the dogs. I'm faster on my own.* And yet he couldn't do it. It wasn't Jessua's voice telling him not to, and it sure wasn't Hobbe. It was just...

Grint rolled off and fell on his back. The blade clattered against the stones and scattered a few pebbles into the water with a tiny plip – plip – plip. In his bag were a handful of caras sticks; small twigs really, brown with white striations down the length. Grint took one and broke it in half, holding one end while closing the girl's hand around the other. The ends smoldered red and burned like a candle's wick. The heat started in their chests and warmed outward until even their clothes were dry.

With a sigh, Grint pulled out the few travel clothes he carried and covered the child. His gut rumbled, and he felt the bile in his throat. A lot of people would want him dead for this and he had no next move. "What have I gotten myself into?"

9

"No one fails me. Let alone twice."
- Count Danghier

Eleanor stood with her back against a curved marble wall watching the final test of a makeshift gallows. The structure straddled the Great Grizzly Fountain so that the bean-bag man they tested it with would drop; stopping just short of the crystal waters each time. The hooded man operating the lever gave the city officials a salute. This was the first public hanging in twenty years and the crowd frothed with excitement for its commencement.

Noseless whimpered at her side until she yanked on his chain. Calling him that was not an accident this time. The name would remain in her thoughts and on her lips until she felt he served his penance for failure. Just as he would remain in his hound form. It always interested her how the skinling magic worked on her pets. Tamos with a scarred muzzle, burned Malus with fire red fur, and Callum, her noseless boy took the form of a black mastiff with a flat snout.

Guards bedecked in red and black sashes appeared, shoving the crowd out of the way as they cleared a path for the doomed prisoner. Soiled, burgundy robes hung in tatters off his shoulders which shook with each step. Was he crying? The guards stabbed at his back with their spears as he protested, but Eleanor missed his words over the pleasured cries of the gathered crowd. Although his face showed like a map of giant bruises and the scabbed cuts oozed puss from infection; she knew this to be Bardo. And Bardo walked alone. One noose, one hanging. Both thieves had so far escaped capture.

A Papality priest waited atop the gallows, chanting an inane liturgical ritual as he sprinkled Bardo with blessed water from an aspergillum. Eleanor was not the only one to roll her eyes. The cadre of wizards watching did not appreciate the priest's inclusion. For Eleanor, it was that she did not believe in Krypholos and marveled at how others could. There were no Gods. No Krypholos, no Lorelai, no Death. Just the insatiable realms of the demon lords or the spiritual oblivion awaiting you upon dying. Given those choices, how could you not follow the demons?

The crowd roared their approval as the executioner pulled the lever, releasing the trap door beneath Bardo's feet. The rope snapped tight, and his body jiggled in a one-man death dance no one else would join. Stones, debris, and other assorted junk continued to strike his body until he stopped moving. The crowd cheered again.

Two guards in Ballastrine colors took an interest in Eleanor. She was careful not to look back, but watched them from the corner of her eye. They disappeared when Bardo's life did, leaving her to wonder if they were reporting her appearance to their lord. It was a paranoid line of thinking, but likely true. She should never have come into the city. There should never have been a need. Eleanor yanked on Noseless's chain eliciting a whimper.

Bardo was dead and the two thieves remained in the wind. That was why Noseless was being punished and why her own punishment would be worse. When she instructed the hound to fetch Black Samuel, it wasn't with a plan in mind. Plans were fluid things shifting with the terrain as whims and decisions unfolded, often outside one's control. When the thief played his games, she formed a countermove. Put Black Samuel in his path. The idea was to spur Grint on, force him to make rash decisions. Change the terrain, take the urn, and kill them both to leave a tidy end to the tale.

Callum's failure was three-fold: allowing the thieves to meet too soon, losing Black Samuel before the duel, and then Grint after it. Eleanor walked away from the gallows, clicking her tongue in a command to Noseless. *Find a scent.* Bardo being the only one hanged meant the thieves escaped Ballastrine's manor. Or he had them, and they were being interrogated. There had been a fight in the manor, a nasty affair. The informants could tell her that but not what happened to the fighters.

Noseless pulled at his chain, leading them along the causeway. Scorch marks and rubble littered the alleys. Cleaning and repair work was well under way, supervised by a cadre of wizards cloaked in red and black leathers. The hawkers and performers gave the men a wide berth, looking down or away when they ventured close. It was a sentiment Eleanor did not share. Stories of a dragon appearing interested her more than a need to defer to the governor's wizards. Long had she suspected the thief's valiant confrontation in Kambar had been a sham. This confirmed it while asking new, disturbing questions.

Dragons could not appear and vanish at will. Yet that was the story everyone told. One moment the red-scaled monster had raged through the city, the next it was gone. Dragons were mindless, greedy animals incapable of deception. They sought gold to sleep upon, easy food, and avoided human contact. Eleanor kicked a piece of charred half-melted marble with her foot. The street cleaner who witnessed it choked in horror and fell to his knees, begging her forgiveness as he chipped away at the debris. Noseless growled, but the man continued unperturbed in his duty.

Never once, in the history of Terragard, had there been an account of someone taming a dragon. Such a feat, while nigh impossible, may not have been outside the realm of possibility. Eleanor beheld enough oddness in the world to keep her mind open to possibilities, but the simple answer here was Grint had not tamed a dragon. The thief used illusion magic. It was a kind she had never seen, but it was the only logical truth. The dragon came and went at his will. How an illusion affected its surroundings was a curious question and one she intended to ask when she found him.

Noseless whimpered as he sat and pawed the air. Did he have one of their scents? Eleanor knelt at his side and scratched his neck. His gaze focused on a commotion in the street. Thirty city guards and three hooded men. Wizards of a different sort to those at the gallows; these were Truth Scryers. The High and Might Inn must have housed one of her missing thieves. Grint, she believed. Callum would have told her if Black Samuel came here. In confirmation, two guards led a gray horse from the stables. The mount was the one Grint called Storms. Moments later a Scryer shoved a thin man through the front door, spilling him spread eagle onto the street. Issuing a cacophony of wails and babbling incoherent protestations, the man refused to shut up until a guard mashed his face under their boot. The lead Scryer gave a command for the guards to shackle him. They passed Eleanor in a procession towards the governor's palace and the deep dungeons waiting below. Many begged for the gallows after a single day in the governor's care.

From the street, Eleanor could see the front door had been cracked in half and now swung loose on its hinges. A single guard remained stationed beside the door ignoring anyone curious enough to peek. "Inn is closed," he said as Eleanor walked up the steps. A flash of her house token and a piece of silver in the palm changed his mind. Now he ignored her too. Eleanor let go of the chain allowing the hound to dart inside. A boy screamed as Noseless cornered him behind a podium.

"Inn no be open." The boy had a stunted, simple way of talking that grated Eleanor's ears.

"I trust you are not in charge?" Dressed in burlap clothes, both torn and dirty, the child was not an ideal candidate for greeting new guests. Neither was a broken door or city guard.

"No-no, they took him away." Noseless drooled as he bared his teeth, nipping close to the boy any chance he could. "The dog?"

"Was he the owner?"

"The dog." The boy's tone was more forceful, bordering on an order. That was not something she would brook. A tap of her foot and Callum stepped forward, barking just inches from his face. The boy wet himself.

"Was he the owner?"

"No, ma'am. Montrouse think he being the uh-uh man. He no-no be."

Satisfied with the respect, she whistled, and Callum heeled at her side. "What can you tell me about the business with the city guards?"

"I get beat for talk about the inn." The boy shook his head as he spoke.

Eleanor took out a small golden coin and rolled it across the back of her hand. "Boy..."

"Jabe," he said with wide eyes. This would be more money than he had ever dared to see. If it were real. It was not. A simple piece of iron painted gold.

"Jabe. Tell me."

"The guards take him because the guest upstairs. Said he should have know-know he was a thief." The boy spoke in a strangled series of sounds, his throat fighting between greed and a forthcoming beating.

"Is the man upstairs now?" Eleanor's face flushed with wrathful excitement.

"That man? He no-no here. Don't come back last night. That's why the wizards say Montrouse should have told them."

"How did the wizards know to look here?" Eleanor knew the answer, even as the boy confirmed it.

"The mean wizard got a letter at the gates." A pang of regret fell like a weight from her chest into her gut and lit it ablaze. The letter seemed such a good idea. Another way to put coal under the thief's feet and make him rush his preparations. Take away his time to get leverage over their trade and avoid certain death. Now it proved to be the folly Tamos warned it might be.

"What did he look like? Red hair? Unkempt?"

Jabe nodded. "Green silks."

"Are any of his belongings still upstairs?" Jabe frowned at her. A stranger coming in off the street and asking questions aroused suspicions. "I am a thief-catcher," she replied. "Hired by an outside individual."

Jabe, oblivious to the working of the world, accepted the explanation without thought. "Coin for the key," he said, holding out a wrought iron key. Eleanor nodded, and the boy snatched the coin from her as he dropped the key in her gloved palm. "Third floor, left then right." Jabe bolted out the back door.

"Stay," she said to Noseless, who laid down beside the stairs to gnaw on the leg of an ornamental chair.

Third floor, left then right. The key turned out to be useless. The wizards who came before her melted the lock. A useless show of strength. The steward would have given them a key. They wanted to show what they could do and instill a little fear while doing it. Wasted potential. True fear arose from engineering a situation to show your target that control of the outcome was never in their hands. Once you did that, they could never look at you as anything less than an immovable wall. Melting locks was a parlor trick inviting challenge.

Rooms at the High and Might Inn were beautiful, well appointed, and regal. How Grint secured them with just a token and a tale reminded her of why she chose him over Black Samuel to begin with. That had been the first mistake. The second was in believing the sacrifice of Bowman would paint her as an immovable object in his mind. It did not. Grint was a different breed of man. Underestimation had been her third mistake.

"Too many mistakes," she said as she ran a finger over a lacquered wood table. The room was bereft of any effects personal to the thief. Grint left nothing behind or perhaps the Scryers took it. The bed looked unused, so the former seemed true. This was a dead end.

Eleanor walked down the stairs, holding in her rage and a desire to smash the High and Might Inn's very tasteful décor. The only part of the day to give her any cause for smiling was knowing the useless stable boy would be dead by sunrise tomorrow. The coin, which she handled with gloves was laced with a tactile poison already working in the boy's system. In an hour he would have a fever and in two his throat would swell shut, rendering him speechless. As the night wore on, the fever would burn every organ in his body. And he thought he was being so clever trading the coin for the key. Eleanor whistled and Noseless fell in beside her carrying the leg of the chair in his mouth. It wasn't an act of pure malice. She needed to cover her tracks in case the boy took someone else's coin to talk about her.

The guard was no longer stood at his post outside the inn. A street recently full of gawkers was now clear for a block in each direction. It disconcerted her that someone could arrange this in the short time she investigated the inn. Something or someone powerful was at work and Eleanor despised being the object of scrutiny.

As she stepped into the street, a dozen armed guards trotted from the alleys and stable paths. Gold and red tabards emblazoned with black skulls and white lightning bolts decorated their chest pieces. These were Ballastrine's men, and they formed a circle around her, swords drawn. A covered rikshaw carriage appeared from down the street. The runner pulled it forward, the clicking of steel soled boots echoing off the cobblestones. The carriage came to a halt outside the circle where the runner turned it sideways and stepped around to open the door.

"Hello Eleanor." Lord Onor Ballastrine stepped out, stretching his arms as if he had fallen asleep on an afternoon stroll and wasn't the author of this situation.

Eleanor crouched down and scratched Callum's ears, unconcerned at the number of guards the Lord of Grauss brought with him. "Onor."

The informal use of his name rankled Ballastrine's guards as they muttered in disapproval. Ballastrine dropped the pretense of stumbling onto her, the smile fading. "The happenstance of finding you here a day after a grievous theft is bitter fruit in my mouth."

"Did you lose something? Was that why your alchemist got hung? Perhaps additional hangings would instill proper motivation in your guards."

"I'll hang you," he said in a low, angry voice. "I'll do it from the roof of this inn if you don't return her!"

"Her?" The question and the confusion were real. As was the concern over who Ballastrine was referring to.

"I could accept the theft of the urn Danghier and I quarreled over." Ballastrine paced as he exhorted. "All part of the larger game he and I play. But to take the urn and the girl is tantamount to a declaration of war! Worse to find that his dogs appear to be in league with the coward who crippled my son. The games have ceased, and my rebuttal is at hand!"

Ballastrine was a prize fool. Without the slightest prompt he vomited out most of the answers she sought. The urn and mysterious girl were not in his possession. One, if not both thieves made it out with them. Why had they taken a girl? She was not part of the contract. It was another question she intended to ask when she found them.

"Would you like me to find the thief for you? My hounds are most capable. I must warn you, Count Danghier gouges on prices."

"Find them?" Ballastrine was apoplectic as drops of saliva shot from his mouth. "You will go nowhere. Find no one! My men will beat you, hold you down, and make you watch as they cut your mutt's head off. Then they'll shove the beast's head over yours and watch you die the death of the thousand drowning cheetahs!"

That took things too far. "Which of these men is your favorite?"

"What?" The change of topic and her uncaring, bored demeanor took Ballastrine by surprise.

"Onor, which of these men is your favorite?" Eleanor pointed at the men in the circle.

"You will address him as Lord Ballastrine!" Eleanor turned her head and smiled at the young man shaking in rage at the lack of propriety she'd shown. He had the same ashen skin as Onor and a pinch on the bridge of his nose.

"Your nephew, yes?"

"Yes, what are you getting at?" Even as Ballastrine asked, Eleanor went to work. As Onor spoke the word *getting*, Eleanor's sword sank into the throat of the man to the nephew's left. On *at?* she spun and drove the singing dagger through the exposed armhole of the guard opposite, puncturing his heart and pleasing the enchanted blade. Past that came the screams.

Eleanor was an assassin and danced around the circle with graceful pivots and timely dips. Each strike of her blade was precise without a single superfluous movement. Ballastrine's guards were nothing more than paid bullies. Bottom of the barrel men whose only job was protecting a house in an un-robbable city. The talented killers in Ballastrine's service were off fighting a war for their lord. Eleanor outmatched the men and cut down each; except for his nephew. By the time Onor's back pressed against the rikshaw door, his guards twitched the last drop of life.

The nephew stared at her in wide-eyed disbelief, shaking with cowardice, yet he still lifted his sword. "Stefane!" Ballastrine shouted and urged him to the rikshaw. Callum snarled at the young man as he ran to his uncle's side. The runner opened the door to usher Stafane in and held it for Onor, who did not seem ready to depart.

"If we're done, I have things to accomplish today." The singing blade squawked as Eleanor re-sheathed it.

"This is not over." The blood drained from Ballastrine's face. "You and Danghier have maneuvered poorly." The Lord of Grauss stepped into his carriage. Eleanor watched the runner pull them back the way they came.

"What is all this?" Eleanor turned to see three wizards and dozen city guards from the corner of her eye.

"Civil dispute,"she replied and held up Danghier's token.

"What interest do you have with the inn?"

"None." Eleanor stepped over the corpses as she walked away. There was nothing the city guards could do, a conflict between token holders was none of their business. In fact, she could walk down the street, cutting the throat of every merchant she found and they wouldn't lift a finger against her.

What tormented her was the depth of misfortune she found herself wading through. Lord Ballastrine would make his displeasure known and inevitably draw the ire of her own master. Of all the commands he issued, keeping the master's rival in the dark - while maintaining a certain level of deniability - had been paramount. And she still did not even have the prize to offset his forthcoming anger.

Wandering the city streets was not a plan. For now, she would return to Danghier's manor and set all three hounds loose to find a scent. The thieves must still be in the Terrastags. The moment the dragon appeared the wizards locked and warded the gates. She just needed time to squirrel them out before the thief-catchers did. In a day, they would cut Bardo's body down from the gallows. A few silvers exchanging hands and she could jam his spirit back into that meat prison and get answers. Her deepest fear was that Grint and Black Samuel had been working together since the tavern. Would she have been so blind as to not see it? Could she have been?

The gates to the manor opened as she approached and shut of their own accord when she passed through. It was a small manor compared to many others but being ostentatious was not a quality the count possessed. The manor was a family holding passed down through generations. The only reason Danghier maintained it was for the cover it provided. Anything to draw attention away from his rise in the necromantic arts. In complete contrast to that discretion, a wight in boiled leathers stepped from behind a bush, long spear held in its left hand. Bits of hair and flesh covered the skeleton, mummified to the bone. The creature chattered as she walked past. Somewhere in that noise was a language the things used to communicate. Noseless paid the creature no mind.

"Garas! Garas!" The doors to the manor opened as Eleanor shouted for the necromancer who kept up full-time residence. "Garas! I've told you to keep those kry-damned wights out of view. Garas?"

Eleanor entered the study where Garas liked to read by firelight, hoping to find the man. Far to the right, her hounds sat beside Garas, who wore a look of consternation. Eleanor opened her mouth to ask what was going on when the necromancer pointed to the couch. There sat a mammoth figure with bushy, black hair, stitching up an open wound, and bleeding over the vintage, white velvet cushions. Black Samuel.

"You." Eleanor's lips curled back, and she wished she had fangs to tear his throat out. The man grunted as he jammed a needle and thread through his skin. "What happened?"

"What happened?" Black Samuel looked up from his efforts and let the needle dangle against his arm as he pointed a meaty finger in Eleanor's face. "You hired another thief to do my job."

"What I hired you for..."

"I got your vase," Black Samuel interrupted her as he tapped a burlap sack that had been laying behind his feet. When he went back to stitching the wound, he kicked it towards her. It clanged with a metallic thump as it rolled end over end. Eleanor snatched up the sack and pulled out what might have once been the urn.

"What is this?" What she held in her hands was a scorched bent thing with a single recognizable glyph on the side. Melted slag obscured the rest.

"The urn thing," Black Samuel grunted again as he finished closing the wound. "And I want double for it. That's what you were paying the other guy." Callum walked around the couch with a low growl that angered the thief. "No, he never said what you were paying, but he said double. I want double."

"For this?" Garas came over and took the urn from Eleanor. His study of the artifact elicited several displeased sounds. Eleanor tried to tune it out as she stared down Samuel. "The urn alone is useless. I needed it filled with blood. Is there any blood in that urn?"

"Never said anything about blood."

"What I said was to take it from the other thief when he came out of the manor." Eleanor was fuming.

"I don't recall that." Black Samuel did not seem to care or feel threatened. "If you need blood, just kill one of your dogs."

"It requires the blood of a certain sacrifice." Eleanor couldn't believe anyone was this thick. How had the count's seers named him?

"A certain sacrifice? You mean the girl the runt found?"

Eleanor's interest in what Black Samuel had to say was renewed. "The sacrifice was a girl? Did Grint take her? Where is he?"

Black Samuel stood and brushed past her. The count's bar was stocked with expensive wines and rums that the thief had the gall to help himself to. "That man is a cheat and a coward. Hit me as I walked in the door. When I woke up the room was on fire. I took the urn and left. I saw him for a moment carrying a girl. Also saw a lot of guards. They're dead now, like Grint will be."

At least she didn't need to worry about the two of them being in league. Grint had the girl Ballastrine wanted and was somewhere in the city. Where though? Could he still be in Ballastrine's manor? An interesting thought. "If you drink that, it's worth more than I owe you." Black Samuel paused with the glass to his lips and stared at the translucent brown liquid.

"Mistress," Garas whispered. She left the thief to contemplate the drink. "The urn itself is useless, but there is a small amount of material within."

"And what can you do with it?" The hounds barked, Eleanor looked back to see that Black Samuel had consumed the rum and was pouring another glass. The poor, stupid fool didn't know when he was being fattened for the slaughter.

"A base direction. The strength of which will give us an idea of distance." Even as he spoke, Garas began preparing herbs in a mortar and grinding them up. "Will only last a moment, but it will be a starting point."

"The girl alone, can she be useful?"

"To the count's ritual? Oh, yes. The magic will be more potent with the girl, but we thought getting her out was impossible. Whoever this Grint is, he has done what the scryers could not foresee." A pinch of oil. Snake poison. With the scale of a salt fish, Garas scraped out the material and dropped it in the mixture. A smoky haze rose, the stench of ancient life and seaweed, and like a finger the smoke pointed east. Eleanor walked over to a map of the city stitched into a mural on the wall. Three manors to the east, some alleys, and two stores. A place to start.

"Mistress, if I may," Garas whispered. "The smoke was faint."

"Meaning?"

"The girl is outside the city walls. Miles outside." The thief took the girl - an impossible task - and then got her out of the city. Another impossible task. She chose her thief too well. But east? There was nothing between here and Cattachat. Not even a hedge kingdom. Not with the Dire Lands so close.

"Black Samuel," she said as she walked over to him. His eyes already bleary from the drink. "Where would a thief go to ground if they traveled east of the Terrastags?"

"Want me to find him for you? Going to cost you triple." He stumbled as he stepped away from the bar. "No. Four times. Pay me four times what you paid him, and I'll take you."

"So, you know?"

"There are places," Samuel slurred.

Eleanor stepped behind him and drew the singing blade across his throat. The blood soaked into its blade, and it cheered at another feeding so soon after the first. Black Samuel gurgled as he swung a giant arm around. Eleanor ducked and cut again. And again. The blade sung so sweet. When his head came loose from his body, she sheathed the knife and seared the neck closed on the fire.

The body twitched on the floor until the hounds descended and feasted on the succulent meat. Eleanor slapped Black Samuel on the cheek. "Garas, be a good chap and wake him up. Black Samuel here may be of some service to us yet." A chance existed for her to come out clean. Eleanor poured herself a glass of rum and allowed a smile to form on her lips.

10

"In the past, the line between a thief and catcher blurred. The empathic requirements of the thief catcher often led to the hunter turning to the life of the hunted. With a simple inhale of Calystro, the path you seek will open before you and your prey will have nowhere to hide."

- Dorre Tantanno, Chief Orrish Alchemist

It was near midnight when a thief-catcher interrupted Grint. Another few moments and he would have finished carving the last warding glyph at the base of the knotty pine. The snow turned to rain during the day and then back to an icy mist that swirled around in looping sweeps. The forest offered little respite from the elements. In the mountains, the weather did as it pleased and offered only a perpetual chill that sank beneath your skin. Grint's breath blew out in a great gust, clouding the face of a thief-catcher as he choked him out.

It was their second day on the run and the first of many thief-catchers to come already caught up to them. Thank Krypsie the catcher concerned himself with speed rather than stealth. Grint heard his boots crunching in the perma-frost from a half mile away and ambushed him by a ravine outside the glyph circle. They struggled until Grint took the advantage and pinned the man's arms under his knees. As he weakened, Grint grabbed him by the hair and punched him several times. When something in his cheek gave way, Grint stopped. The thief-catcher fell unconscious but was still breathing. Grint dragged him further from the camp, and the girl, looking for an ideal spot to leave him.

The thief-catcher had carried a club and wore a brown backpack that Grint tore from his back. Rummaging through it he found a rope intended to truss up the girl and decided, *what works well enough for the girl will do just as nice for you.* The man moaned when Grint tightened the knot.

"Shut up," Grint said, returning to the backpack. He found it full of useful items; furs, a bedroll, dried beef, and water skins. The man tried to hide a small pouch in the bag's lining. Grint cut it free and smiled at the silver coin. Not enough to settle his debts with Marm, Beauregard, or Dirty Lonnel; but it was a start. At the bottom of the backpack, he found a tightly wrapped rag containing two milky-white crystals, each the size of a knuckle. *Calystro.* The kry-damn thief-catcher used Orrish drug magic to hunt them. That explained how he found them so fast. There was a time when Grint could find a market to resell the stuff. Until thieves realized what it did. Then an unspoken rule fell into place. Anyone caught trading in Calystro ended up dead or marked. Grint hefted a giant stone and smashed the pouch, satisfied by the glass-like crunch.

The thief-catcher wept. One half lidded eye watched him destroy what must have been a sizeable investment. Grint tossed the bag to the side its contents spilling out and rolling down the hill. "Your keepsakes are yours. If you have any skill, you'll be free in a day or two. Don't follow me." Before

Rent, Grint would have killed the man to cover his tracks. Too big a risk now.

"Next time I kill you." The man didn't need to know it was a lie. For good measure he took the man's boots.

Grint listened to the night as he walked back to camp. Ice falling from trees, critters in the underbrush, nighthawks in the sky, but no hounds. More thief-catchers would come. The list of people who wanted a piece of Grint grew longer every day. What worried him most were the necromancers. In a fight he could take the hounds one on one, but not Eleanor. There would be no stopping her. Understanding that truth, Grint wasn't afraid to light a fire for their camp. Those who came looking would find them with or without it, so he might as well die warm if that was what Krypsie wanted. Except, according to Hobbe, Krypsie wanted nothing except the taste of wine, but that wasn't as colorful a saying.

Ducking under a low-hanging branch, Grint entered the escarpment that served as their camp and dumped the new supplies and firewood by his bedroll. The girl sat cross-legged in front of a pile she arranged around herself. Grint noticed with growing horror they were the items from his own bag, now upended like the thief-catcher's backpack.

"What in all three salty serpents are you doing?" Grint snatched up his bag and crouched just outside the circle. The girl skittered back pulling her knees to her chest while wrapping her arms tight around them. Grint hadn't meant to frighten her. Or had he?

"It's just. You shouldn't play with these things. Some of them are very dangerous, kid." Why was he apologizing? What was she to him? A victim? A job? A bauble to sell to the highest bidder? "How did you even open the bag?"

"Lark." Her voice was little more than a whisper. "My name is Lark."

"Right. Lark." Grint picked up the red glass cylinder with spiraling gold snakes and began carefully wrapping it in the glyph covered cloth that contained its magic. "Want to tell me why they had you in that dungeon, Lark?"

"What is that?"

"Turns people to stone," Grint hefted the wrapped cylinder and shoved it in the bag. The girl flinched and put a hand over her mouth. "I stole it from a drunk wizard."

"And this?" Lark pointed at a red jewel hanging from a gold chain.

"An eyesight. It lets you see things far away." Grint wrapped it alongside a cluster of multi-colored crystals and small black orb filled with lightning.

"Like a looking glass?"

"No, it shows places you shouldn't be able to see. As if you were right in the room."

"Does it hurt to do that?" The girl looked around at the items, eyes wide with wonder. Curiosity was a killer.

"Yeah, it tears at your spirit and makes you want to use it more. The last owner got so he couldn't take it off. Mober was dead when I found him." With the more volatile items packed away, Grint gathered up Ballastrine's jewel collection. "How long did they have you chained up?"

The girl shrugged. "Does all magic hurt?" Lark looked at her arms, tracing the bruises from the worm tubes.

"Not all." Grint held up his copper disk. "This detects magic wards. These stones help deaden magic. This key can pick most locks. All harmless." Grint packed up his clothes and stolen goods, leaving just a deck of Cheat Me cards for the girl to play with and a box of herbs.

"Is that food?"

"You hungry?"The girl nodded. Grint threw her an apple and wished they had Storms with them. Lark kept looking at the box as she ate.

"You don't want to eat anything from this box. They're poisons. There was a girl; a friend who taught me about herbs. She was a natural." Grint sighed as he looked at the box. Lark wore a sympathetic smile that unnerved him.

The Cheat Me deck she could keep. The cards were easy to come by. Grint sat with his back to a tree and started dissecting the confiscated boots with Blackblade.

"Hold up your foot." The girl looked up from the cards; confused. After some consideration she leaned back and lifted a bare foot in the air. Grint shut one eye and estimated the size. She dropped her foot and resumed flipping through the cards, giggling at the pictures.

The fire crackled. A pleasant sound and he hummed himself a tune while he worked. Keeping busy, the tension fled from his distracted mind; and he forgot for the briefest moment that the world was out to get him. Grint finished stitching the first boot and tossed it to her. "Try that on and let me know if it fits."

Lark put the cards down and yanked the boot on with the exaggerated effort of a child. Wiggling it around, she gave him a smiling thumbs-up. Grint went to work on the second.

"Who was the man you beat up?" Grint looked up, shocked that she'd heard their fight. The girl's focus stayed on the cards, flipping them one by one. What else did she know? *She knows enough to open my bag.*

"Someone bad," he replied.

"Will there be others?" Grint stabbed his thumb with the needle as his attention drifted.

"Yes." The questions were natural he just didn't want to answer them. Or rather, he wanted her to answer his questions. It hadn't gone unnoticed that she avoided them.

"Will you let them take me back to the bad people?" This time she looked up.

Honestly? I should. He tossed the second boot to her and stood up. "Walk around in those and let me know if they need adjusted." The fur he took from the thief catcher would be too long for her, but he draped it over her shoulders to get a feel for how much he'd need to take off.

"I'm not cold," she pouted under its weight.

"You will be when there's no fire. And you need to get used to moving in it. For when we're traveling. How are the boots?"

"Loose," she answered. Grint waved his hand for her to give it all back to him.

"Eat the mash in the cook pot," he instructed. A fair bit of the fur would need taken in, but he could use the rest to make them hats or scarves. "You lost a lot of blood. That will help."

"It's not poison?" The girl looked at the box of herbs.

"No," Grint laughed.

Between bites of mash she asked, "Where are we going?" Food spraying with each word.

"I don't know. East." Blackblade cut through the furs with ease. *How in the greasy grip of Grummand did Black Samuel come by it?* The boots needed just a few stitches to tighten their grip on her feet. Their travel options were pathetic. West was the Terrastags. *Death.* To the North sat impassable or inhospitable mountain ranges that could take weeks to climb. If they survived. *Death.* South would take them through Dook and right into Eleanor's lap. *Death and more death.* The necromancers might even bring him back to life just to kill him repeatedly.

"You don't know? Or east?" Grint appreciated her sarcastic tone. Had she picked that up from him?

"Somewhere the bad people won't follow." Such a place didn't exist, but the kid didn't need to know it. They would head east until someone ran them down. It would happen. The pace they needed to maintain would tire them out even though he felt strong now. And the hunters would keep coming. One after the other. More once the contract circulated.

"Will you sell me to someone bad?"

I should. "Rest up, we'll head out at first light. Maybe before."

"There are dark shadows around you, but not in you," Lark said as she laid down on the bedroll. The fire lit her face as she watched him through the flickering flames, using her left arm as a pillow. "That's why I'm not afraid of you."

Grint shoved a few scraps of fur under his head and closed his eyes. It had been absurd madness to take the girl from the dungeon. Not that he didn't care; it just wasn't the contract. *Contract? The entire job was a lie.* Objects to venerate demon lords were one thing, but human sacrifices another. Freeing Lark was the right thing even without Jessua's voice telling him, but what had he pulled out of the dungeon? Was she even a human? They wanted her blood. But why? With necromancers, the reasons were too many to count. Still, there was something unsettling about her. She opened his bag without setting off the trap. Maybe she got lucky? The glyphs on the bowl and herbs he put in the mash didn't affect her. *Maybe she's something I don't know about?* Grint fell asleep hoping to hear Jessua's voice again. Hoping for an answer that never came.

*****

They made good time the next day as they descended the mountain slopes toward a deep eastern valley. The storms that hung over them as they fled the Terrastags dissipated, leaving the sun to shine in a deep-blue sky. Yet, the winds remained unpleasant, forcing them to bundle up against its bitterness. Lark, at least, kept up with the pace Grint set. She even appeared deft of foot as she darted around trees and hopped over exposed roots. Along the way she hummed a snippet of song that Grint recognized as 'The Enchanted Fountain'. A jovial tune about a boy who freed a woman trapped in the fountain by an ancient lord. The woman later reveals herself to be a monster who tries to devour the boy. With his doubts about Lark, the song conjured visions of himself as the boy and her the monster. *How does the boy defeat the monster?* Grint hummed along, trying to remember the words.

Thunder boomed far to the southeast. The forest obscured the sky, except what was overhead. *Odd*, Grint thought as he looked up. There hasn't been a cloud all morning. The wind blew south so any storms forming should stay clear of them. As the rocky path turned into a grassy slope, Lark gasped and smiled with the wonder of a child seeing something for the first time. Along the northern mountains, a faint, orange smudge painted the horizon from east to west.

"Is that a second sun rising?"

"No, that's the Dire Lands," Grint said. Getting close enough to see the perpetual fires was too close for his taste.

"What are the Dire Lands?"

"Long time ago they called it Zorn. Then their King, also named Zorn, made himself an Emperor and conquered the world." As they got towards the bottom of the slope, Grint climbed onto a fallen tree and lifted Lark over.

"Did they name him after the kingdom or the kingdom after him?" Grint laughed. Not because it was a stupid question, but because he never asked and didn't know the answer.

"I don't know. Are your boots loose?" he asked, seeing them wiggle as she walked.

"A little," she said. "So, why is it the Dire Lands now?"

"When Zorn died the wizards in his kingdom fought to see who would rule next. A lot of bad magic got unleashed. Fires that never go out, monsters that grow from the ground, magic storms. No one lives there anymore."

"When did that happen?"

Another crack of thunder to the south. This time it sounded close. Jutting mountain peaks cut into the sky in every direction, but no clouds. The thunder gave him an uneasy feeling. "Long before us," he finished, and they continued.

Climbing the next slope took longer. The girl's boots slipped loose every few feet as Grint kept pausing to listen for the thunder. At the summit, a small spring trickled beneath what could have been the ruins of a giant statue. Grint filled their water skins while they sat to eat. Erosion claimed the statue's features, but Grint thought it could have been a soldier holding their sword on high. An old partner once claimed the mountains near the Dire Lands hid Zornish fortresses full of gold. Was Seve right? The gold-itch fell on Grint as he ran a hand over the rocks looking for a passage.

"Grint," the girl said.

"What?"Was that a draft? There, just by the trickle of water?

"Grint?" The fear in her voice chased away the gold-itch. Grint turned to see a muscled man in wolf furs stepping around a tree. His shaggy hair slick with sweat and streaked with gray. The pock-marked edges of his sword gave the blade a misshapen form. Then he bared his teeth, a mouthful of glittering sharp things cut into daggers; all chiseled to a fine point. The sunlight caught a gold medallion resting among the thick carpet of chest hair between his furs. *Kry-damn Tall Company!* The next thief-catcher had found them.

*****

Night had fallen by the time they found a suitable place to rest. Grint carved more glyphs into the trees and slumped beside the fire with a pained grunt. The battle against the thief-catcher had been brutal. The salty bastard bit his forearm and even tried for his neck a few times. Grint matched his brutality and came out on top, leaving the man tied to the faceless stone statue. There wasn't much on his person, just the sword and medallion. Both would fetch a meager price, but one coin was as good as fifty. They didn't find a travel bag but Grint didn't take the time to search either.

Grint poured water on the wound, then a healthy splash of fire rum. He squeezed his eyes shut and gnashed his teeth. The next bit of rum went into his gut. Lark watched as he heated a needle over the fire and stitched the wound closed. He smiled at her with a flat piece of leather clamped between his teeth. A piece with well-worn teeth marks. When he finished, he wrapped it with a thin piece of white cloth and stitched the bandage shut.

They needed to eat, needed to set traps for critters or they'd risk running out of food. There were many needs but what he wanted was to shut his eyes for a few moments...

*****

The hill crested like a lazy wave in the deep ocean. Sky-blue flowers covered the landscape and fluttered in the warm summer's breeze. The sun beat down on his shoulders. It felt nice after having been cold for so long. On top of the hill was a young woman, her short, brown hair a thorn bush's tangle that did not quite reach the simple, white dress she wore. Her back was to him, but he would know her anywhere. The freckles dotting the back of her neck were a well-studied map. The softness of her hands, the scent of lavender flowers, her warmth. As he ran up the hill, reaching a hand towards her, Jessua turned and screamed, "Wake up!"

*****

Grint opened his eyes, unsure how long he'd slept. The question would go unanswered as he heard the girl scream and leapt to his feet. She stood a few feet away, Blackblade held in her tiny hands as she struggled to keep the heavy dagger pointed toward the shadows. Grint used a hand up to block the firelight and saw a dark shape moving between the trees. Not the hounds, he thought with a relaxed sigh.

Grint got up and rested a hand on her shoulder. The girl jerked. Gently, he removed Blackblade from her grasp and ushered her behind him in case the creature charged the wards. It poked its head around a tree, giving Grint a better look. A golem, midnight black with sinewy skin stretched over its distorted frame. This one tried to walk upright, but kept falling onto all fours, its hairless skin glistening. It wore a human face with an elongated jaw that jutted out. Serrated teeth snapped the air around the glyphs and flinched back as the air crackled with energy. A noise in the woods drew its attention, so the golem darted off for easier prey.

Grint went back to his bedroll and sat down, letting Lark nuzzle against his side. "Was that a harquin?"

"What? No, just a golem." Grint didn't like her bringing up harquins. Not with the phantom thunder booming to the south. "What do you know of harquins?"

The girl shrugged. "Just something I heard. Was the golem from the Dire Lands?" She dangled the gold medallion and let it sway back and forth. The thief-catcher carried the markings of the Tall Company. They weren't too bad. Drunks and misfits. Easy to bribe - except for this one who seemed more beast than man. When one of the collectives came looking there would be hard choices to make.

"Maybe. It wasn't like most." Golems were usually hairy and stood on two legs. This one could have grown in the sour soil of the Dire Lands. Traveled a long way if it did. Sleep would be light in case it came back to test the wards.

"You're a thief." It wasn't a question.

"Yes," Grint wondered where she was going with this.

"Do you decide what you steal?"

"Sometimes. Sometimes someone hires me." Grint averted his eyes from the medallion in case the girl was trying to mesmerize him. *A lonely life, not trusting anyone.* It was something Jessua said to him the second time they met.

"I want to hire you," Lark said as she dropped the medallion in the dirt and pulled away to face him.

"And what do you want me to steal?"

"Me," she said as if it were the dumbest question in the world.

"I already stole you," Grint laughed.

"And now I want you to return me."

Grint frowned, "How could you want to go back there?"

"Not there. Home."

Grint picked up a stick and scratched a rough outline of Terragard in the dirt. Where he estimated their camp was, he jammed a dot in the dirt then handed her the stick. "Show me where that is."

"I...I don't know," she stammered. Grint shook his head. "It's called Teal...Thiel. It's called Thiel."

"Never heard of Thiel," Grint said. Was it made up? It could be real, and someone could pay a tidy finder's fee for their long-lost child.

"I was in the dungeon for years," tears fell from her eyes. Grint squirmed, ever uncomfortable around feelings. "I don't remember where it is, but my parents are the king and queen." Now, if that was true - *if* - a monarch would pay a heavy ransom for the return of an heir.

"We can play for it!" Lark pulled the Cheat Me cards from her pocket and held them up. "If I win, you take me home."

"You need dice for Cheat Me," Grint laughed.

"Then we can draw cards to see the highest. The guards in the dungeon used to do that."

Grint motioned for her to hand the deck to him and shuffled. He did some elaborate tricks that made her giggle and then placed the deck face down. "You go first."

Lark picked up a card and chewed on her lip as her shoulders sagged. Grint picked his card and dropped the twelve in front of her. Lark tried to throw hers in the fire, but it fluttered well short of the flames. Two points. Grint swept up the cards and handed them back. She shuffled through them for a short time in silence and then looked up eyes red from tears.

"You...you cheated, didn't you?"

"Of course," Grint admitted. The girl cried again. "Listen, kid. I steal things to buy more things I don't need. Or I get drunk. I don't do quests."

"Then I'm dead," she choked out. "You should have let me drown or stabbed me with that knife in the cave." Grint flinched, he hadn't realized she was awake for that. Reticence turned to shame, and he took a big breath.

"Okay."

"Okay?" she sniffled. "What?"

"When we get somewhere civilized, I'll see if we can find where Thiel is." The girl jumped on him, wrapping her arms around his chest. "I said we'd try. I'm not promising anything." Grint wasn't even sure they'd live long enough to find civilization. "And I'm not doing this for free."

"My family will pay you a mountain of gold," she said, her voice muffled by his coat. "It has my face on it, so you can remember me."

A flash of lightning lit the campsite. Closer than ever. "That's the harquin," Lark said as if she was pointing out a cat sitting on a fencepost. Something deep and cold ran through Grint, who spent the rest of the night staring into the darkness.

*****

A harquin was a person once. Usually, a wizard or witch who drank too deep of their magic. Sometimes they weren't magical to begin with but unlucky enough to touch a cursed object that overwhelmed their frail, human vessel. Whatever the cause, they became mindless wretches no longer identifying with whom they had been. In populated areas, they hunted harquins. In the wilds, they could wander for decades unchecked as their bodies twisted and their magic corrupted the land.

Before the sun rose, the harquin stumbled through the mist, hurling lightning bolts at their camp. Grint had dozed for a moment but shot up, Blackblade at the ready. This was a fight he couldn't win, but he could run. He tried to shoulder his bag, but it slipped off when grabbed the girl and shoved onto the path ahead of them. Leaving it behind broke his heart, but there was just no time. Lark pulled away, becoming an indistinct shape in the fog ahead of him.

They ran with reckless abandon, uncaring of the dangers hidden in the morning gloom. Lightning snapped like a whip at the ground throwing Grint against a tree. His injured arm bled, the stitches snapping as his arm scraped against the bark. A cry, both a mixture of anger and pain filled the morning. Blood oozed into the bandage as he pushed himself up. Loose stones scattered as he stood but he kept his balance.

"Grint!" he heard Lark call. A purring gurgle cried back. The harquin moved, swirling the fog.

There was no path underfoot. No deer trails to follow. All Grint had to guide him was the faint bit of Lark's fur cloak swimming in the mist. Had he not focused on that he would have bashed into her when she skidded to a stop.

Grint dove to the side and landed against a steep incline of shale stones that rained atop his shoulders. They'd run themselves into a ravine buffeted on all sides by steep slopes. How high did they go? Grint couldn't say, the fog hid anything beyond a few feet. Grint tried to lift Lark, help her climb, but there was no purchase and she fell on top of him amidst another shower of stones.

The snap of lightning ceased, and the morning grew deathly quiet. An electrified buzz raised the hair on the back of Grint's neck. Lark tugged on his coat as they heard shuffling steps and a labored wheeze growing closer.

"When I hit it," Grint said, twirling Blackblade in his hand, "run past and get back to the camp. Get that red cylinder from my bag."

"No," she whispered.

"Don't argue," he said as the harquin came into view. Each step a shambling agony that twisted its face. It looked to have been a young boy, maybe a few years older than Lark. Now its skin turned was gray and sunken. Its hair thinned to a few wisps, hanging over eyes crackling with the promise of mayhem. What remained of its clothes had melded to its skin. Puss oozed from wounds around the petrified fabric and tore open with each movement.

Grint hoped that killing this thing wasn't murder, that Rent wouldn't see. *Kill it? I'll be lucky to survive this!* The harquin's mouth cracked as it bit the air. Grint darted forward cocking back the knife as he ran. He was of such little consequence to the thing. The harquin snapped lightning from its fingers. The surge threw him into the stones. Static tingled through his limbs, biting with a thousand tiny stab wounds that sapped the air from his lungs.

Through sheer force of will, he fought off the embrace of darkness. Blackblade lay in the dirt beside him. He picked the knife up by its tip and tried to decide which of the four harquins his blurred vision presented was the real one. All he needed was one clean throw. The harquin ignored him and focused on Lark. Its shambling steps took it closer to the girl, who froze in terror. Then it opened its mouth, intending to feed. Grint threw the blade, but his strength fled and the knife skittered across the ground. He wanted to scream but had no air. There was nothing he could do but watch the harquin wrap its arms around Lark. The world flashed white, and a warmth filled him like the flowered field from his dream. And then darkness.

*****

When he woke, it was midday. Dark-bellied clouds raced through the sky leaving behind sweeping shadows and a light drizzle that carried an understated, cold ferocity. He sat up and wiped the moisture from his face, then winced as thundering drumbeats of pain bashed against his temples. For a moment, he struggled to recall who he was or why he was waking up in the dirt, but the sight of Blackblade brought it all back. There was no sign of Lark. Or the harquin.

"Lark," he tried to call out, but the sound was little more than a scratch in his throat. Pushing himself to his feet, he took a step and fell sideways onto the shale. It took some time to dig himself out of the stones, and he took a more cautious approach to standing. When he could take a step, he did; and then another. Jolts of lightning passed through his muscles leaving a tingling sensation in his fingers. He fumbled with the knife as he picked it up and shoved it in his belt.

Where he last saw Lark, he found a dark scorch mark on the ground that had turned to glass. The falling rain beaded on the surface and rolled clear. "Lark," he yelled again and this time it came out as a hoarse whisper. *Better.* Grint retraced his steps through the forest trying not to think about the kid becoming a molten puddle in the dirt. *That wasn't her.* When he got back to camp, he would regroup and track her. The harquin was dead, it had to be, otherwise it would have eaten him too, to put it indelicately.

Grint started a mental list of magical creatures that could destroy a harquin. There was more to this child than innocence. The necromancers wanted her blood for a reason. Dragonfire could destroy one; burn it to cinders. Lark wasn't a dragon, even a skinling one. Grint thought of his friend. Faighur's appearance would be welcome, even if he was angry about him mucking the Terrastag job. The skinling invested a fair amount of gold into it, only for Grint to run off with the bank. Given their longstanding friendship, Grint hoped it would earn him a moment of explanation, but among thieves there was little forgiveness.

"Grint," Lark shouted as she ran towards him, her fur cloak whipping behind. She barreled into his chest, causing him to stumble back a step. Lost in his thoughts, he had wandered into camp without realizing it. Lark beamed at him; arms wrapped tight around his waist. Purple stains ringed her mouth and the spaces between her teeth. Back by the dying embers of the fire sat a pile of berries and some dried meats the girl sat on a kerchief. The red cylinder sat beside the food, the glyph-stitched cloth wrapped around the base.

"I thought you were dead. Which was very scary, but then I saw you were breathing, and I wanted to come back and get you something to eat and so I gathered..." The girl's words came out in a rambling slurry until Grint put a finger over her mouth.

"What happened to the harquin?"

"I...I don't know," she answered as she stepped away from him and shrugged. "It tried to hit me with lightning, and I think it destroyed itself."

Grint nodded as he walked across the camp. "Pack the cylinder and the meats. Leave the berries. Some of them might be poisonous."

"You should rest," she said and sounded concerned. So was Grint, just about different things. A harquin couldn't destroy itself. That was half the problem with the things. They were immune to their own magic and most other magic besides. Was the girl lying? Or did she not know what happened?

"We've lost half a day. It's too dangerous to stay put." Grint gathered everything he could and stuffed it in his bag. The numbness in his extremities faded slowly, but it was fading. If a thief-catcher caught up to them now, it would be an easy slaughter. *What a grand thought.*

As they walked, Lark took his hand and hummed a new song. Something about it sounded familiar but he couldn't find the lyrics in his muddled mind. *Did she use emberstalk venom?* The emberstalk was a parasitic snake that burrowed into the skin and wrapped itself around a person's spine. They were common in Lyzan swamps. The venom was lethal to wizards, but it wouldn't turn a harquin into a glass puddle. Besides, the girl didn't show signs of host sickness.

The question plagued him as they navigated through the low hills at the base of the mountains. That night they camped beneath a rocky outcropping beside a babbling brook. Grint walked around the trees and drew the normal glyphs along with a few new ones that eliminated more monsters from his mental list. The girl wasn't demon possessed. She wasn't a banshee, a veyhex, a stregau, or even a goblin in human skin. The last was a mental joke for Grint, who needed the laugh. He pictured the alchemist fumbling about, trying to get the goblin out of the girl's skin. Goblin blood was no more magical than any human, but it was an amusing image.

"You drew more sigils than before," Lark said as he started the fire.

"We've found more things to worry about." A better lie than, *I have no clue what you are and that worries me.*

Lark smiled as she chewed on a piece of dried bread that somehow survived at the bottom of Grint's bag without molding. That night she slept beside him. In fact, she hadn't left his side since the harquin. Contradicting emotions ran through him as she twitched in her sleep. A deep desire to run. That was how he preferred things. Alone save for short stretches where he worked with a partner. But somewhere below that was the disturbing need to keep the girl safe, and it spread through his mind like a disease. Was she influencing that feeling?

Some nights you got to sleep. Others, it wasn't in the deal of the cards. Grint spent the night listening for hounds, thief-catchers, harquins, and golems. For monsters known and unknown. Every time he came close to nodding off, he started awake, expecting the monster in his lap to wake up and devour him. It was the second longest night of his life.

Dawn broke, and he woke Lark with instructions to smother the fire while he packed up. As he finished, he found she'd wandered off and felt a stone drop in his stomach. "Lark?" he called out in a loud whisper. Images of a thief-catcher behind a tree with a knife to her throat filled his mind. The sound of her laughter was not at all what he expected. Lark sat beside a brook dangling her feet in the water as she traced a carved image on the tree beside her.

"Did you carve this last night?" she asked as he approached.

"No," Grint replied, looking at the carving of a rudimentary goblin head with three waving lines beneath it. "That's old." Old and faded, easy to miss in the dark.

"What does it mean?" She continued tracing it and then pulled her hand away as if she was touching fire. "Should I not touch it? Is it dangerous?"

Grint smiled. "It's fine. A symbol for a rambler town. See these three marks," Grint traced the wavy lines with his fingers. "It's a direction. Southeast."

"Is a ramble town like where they kept me prisoner?"

"If there's an opposite of what the Terrastags is, it would be a rambler town." The girl still had a questioning look as they walked back to camp, so Grint went on. "They're towns built by people who don't want to live in a place with rules or under a lord's thumb. Sounds happy, but it's not. It's full of criminals, convicts, killers..."

"Thieves?" she asked with a wry smile.

"Thieves too," he gave her a playful shove. "Pick up the furs. It's for anyone who wants to disappear."

"Should we avoid it?" Lark asked, looking up to him for answer. Grint thought about it. It wasn't part of the plan. *There's a plan?* They would have missed it if Lark hadn't found the symbol. The sky darkened under the weight of thick clouds. Yesterday's storm was just the first touch of something worse.

"I don't think we'll have a choice. The coming storm will be bad and we could use the chance to outfit ourselves." Grint ushered her from the camp. There was no guarantee the rambler town was still there. Sometimes they disappeared as quickly as they popped up, but if it was, they could wait out the storm and get their bearings. *Maybe someone there has heard of Thiel. Maybe there's a fence for the jewels and gold box. Maybe we won't get killed.*

The rain fell in thick sheets as Lark ran through a verdant field, spinning around. The hill sloped up towards a pine forest. At the top, Grint paused beneath the shelter of a fir as he scanned the landscape behind them. There had been no sign of Eleanor or her hounds. Did she even know he was alive? That he had the girl? The thief-catchers knew, but Ballastrine could have sent them. He never asked. Not that they would have given him the truth. It was possible Eleanor didn't know or guessed his escape route wrong. None of that sat right. Eventually she would be there.

"How far away is the town?" Lark held her tongue out trying to catch raindrops. The words took a moment for Grint to decipher.

"Shouldn't be far. They never mark the towns more than a day's hike out. Why?" Lark lifted her left boot, which came apart at the seams. Grint whistled between his teeth and thought, *Just like my life.*

11

"Papa Deego is the wolf
When he eats the chickens and hens.
Papa Deego is the storm
When he drowns them in fives and tens.
Papa Deego is the man
Who approaches with grit and grim
Papa Deego is Death
And you can't run away from him."

- Rhyme from a children's game

A slat of wood leaned to the right, and the wind shook it as it creaked against the rusted iron nails holding it together. Grint wiped a thick layer of mud off the face. The inscription read: **Here be Finder's Lot.** The rambler's town sat upon a butte surrounded by a bottomless crater. A hundred crooked buildings rose above the crumbling stone foundations of an ancient fort while narrow rope bridges spanned the gap between. Strong gusts swayed the bridges. Grint felt sick just looking at them.

Crumpled stone buttresses littered the hills, all marked in the old architectural style of Zorn with looping curves. Etched reliefs depicting the heroic exploits of Zornish generals lay forgotten in the mud. Before the imperial expansion they would have used this as a border fortress. After the death of Zorn and unfortunate creation of the Dire Lands, no one remained to man it. When the ramblers had moved in was anyone's guess. Places like this had short memories and cartographers knew better than to put them on a map. Hobbe said the first rambler was a goblin which was why they used the goblin glyph to mark the path. Grint had been a child when he first heard that story and always assumed the thief master told it as a bedtime story.

The tattered remnant of an old tent, entangled in the bare branches of a tree, ruffled and snapped. Grint shielded his eyes against the dust from the long dormant soil and looked at the skies. The coming storm would soon drown the land, but Finder's Lot didn't care. The city came alive with dancing fires as the skies darkened. The sun dipped below the mountains and the remaining light faded fast. If they didn't move soon, they would have to navigate the bridge in the dark.

"Can we cross?" Lark asked. Laid out on her stomach, the girl poked her head over the edge of the chasm.

"Soon," Grint said, watching a bulky man struggle to cross the bridge. Passing someone on the small bridge was an easy way to get yourself robbed or killed.

"How deep does it go?" Lark plucked a stone from the mud and tossed it down.

"I don't know. Deep enough to kill you. Come away." Grint drew Blackblade from his belt and shifted his body to hide it behind his right thigh. Lark ignored him and threw more rocks, laughing with nervous excitement each time.

The temperature dropped fast as the sun set and fat raindrops slapped against his hair, chilling him with water that ran down the nape of his neck. The wind kicked up again, carrying with it the aroma of char, old wine, rot, and the unwashed. All the smells you'd expect from a place like this. The bulky man stepped off the bridge, stumbling drunkenly. Stretched across his frame and tearing at the seams, the patchwork vest he wore didn't look like it belonged to him. *Probably stole it off someone's corpse.* His cheeks, flushed red with exertion, highlighted a nasty scar where someone had tried to chew off his face. Glassy eyes blinked at Grint as if he didn't understand why a person would be standing in the mud. Then he offered a wicked smile that never touched his eyes.

"Spare some coin?" He slurred the words as he licked his lips with a swollen tongue. "Going to Little Lot."

"No coin here," Grint said. The drunk stepped toward him but halted when he heard Lark's voice.

"Do you think there's a big lake down there? With mermaids? I hear water."

"Hello little one," the drunk changed his direction with almost fluid grace and took a few shambling steps toward her.

Grint grabbed the back of the vest and pressed Blackblade against his throat. "Keep moving or you'll find out what's down there."

The drunk nodded when Grint let him go. He stumbled a step or two and turned, madness alight in his eyes. As he smacked his lips, Grint could see the internal battle raging between leaving and killing them both. The thief was always ready for a fight but fighting drunks was unpredictable. It would be a nasty bit of squabble even without the worry of Lark lighting the world on fire or turning them all into little black puddles of glass. *Praise Krypsie,* Grint thought as the drunk stumbled off with a half wave. Grint watched to be sure it wasn't a ruse, but the drunk never looked back. He disappeared into the gloom. *Off to Little Lot. Wherever that is.*

"Who was that?" Lark asked, standing by his side. Her hand slid into his smearing mud across his palm.

"A fool who will get himself killed. Let's cross." That was all he needed to say. Lark yelped with joy and ran onto the bridge. Grint took a more cautious approach planting his feet after each measured step. Holding the rope on either side in a white-knuckled grip, he could feel the rough fibers digging into his palms. *A thief with a fear of heights? How droll,* Hobbe mocked. Grint scaled towers, rode the back of a dragon, and even swung across an impossible canyon on a fraying rope. All in the pursuit of gold. But that didn't mean he liked it. He couldn't abide heights. Something about falling to one's death just struck him as a daft way to die.

"Do you remember Grint?"

"The thief who stole the Hungering Blade from the Demon Lord Anastassus?"

"That's him. Do you know how he died? He fell off a bridge." The laughter filling the tavern would be grand and Grint's place in history would forever be the punch line of a drunkard's joke.

Lark's bare feet slapped against the planks as she ran back and forth in blissful ignorance of the danger. Grint wanted to shout at her but his throat felt tighter than his grip. Storm winds rocked the bridge and one of Grint's feet slipped, dangling over the abyss before he righted himself. *Some kry-damned god is having fun with me,* he thought as he furrowed his brow. Sheets of rain began pouring down, drenching his face as distant thunder boomed.

Which god controls the wind? Grint couldn't recall their name, but also thought there were four. One for each direction. *Leave it to the gods to contrive a system where four gods do what one should.* Mocking the gods helped occupy his mind long enough to get across the bridge and onto solid ground once more.

"Can we go over again?" Lark stared back from where they came, a mad elation in her eyes that reminded Grint of the drunk. A disquieting comparison, and one that made him believe this entire misadventure was taking place on a rope bridge, *and I'm one strong gust from toppling into the abyss.*

"Later," Grint said, fighting down an urge to be sick.

The rope bridge fed onto a small street barely large enough for a cart. Discarded shards of pottery and heaps of bloody clothing lay along the length of a crumbling wall leading up to the main avenue. An overturned horse cart propped against the building on the corner housed a family of tabby cats. Paving stones from the old fortress lay buried beneath inches of thick mud that covered the top of Grint's boot when he stepped. Lark sank into her ankle and laughed as it squished between her bare toes.

"Better hope that's not horse dung you're stepping in," Grint said and the girl froze.

"No," she replied, disbelief creeping into her voice. "You're joking, right?"

"Stay close," was all he said as they turned onto the main avenue.

Finder's Lot didn't make improvements on the original layout of the fortress. They built whatever they wanted wherever they could find the space. The main thoroughfare curved in both directions, following the outer edge of the butte in a giant ring. Each building along the road was unique, built with whatever materials they had on hand. Woods of different size, type, and thickness; stone or brick and sometimes both; hemp sheets for doors; and some fool even used a massive sail for their roof. Finder's Lot was a patchwork puzzle that didn't fit together with thick smears of tar filling the gaps between boards and crooked windows illuminated by the red glow of candles. Rain poured off the roofs in gushing waterfalls, falling into barrels that overflowed onto the sodden streets.

"What's that?" Lark tugged on his sleeve as she looked over her shoulder. A raven-headed man, bare chested with tattoos, a necklace, and scars crouched atop a barrel. Iron manacles clasped his wrists while chains bolted to the barrel shook. The creature opened its beak and screamed as he made quick hand gestures at them. "Is he a harquin or golem?"

"No," Grint said, imaging a scene of white fire scorching the rambler city from existence. "He's a malicant. An animal bonder who took his gift a little far."

"What's he doing?"

"I don't know," Grint said, trying to tug Lark away, but she resisted. "Whatever it is, it's not good." The gestures went too fast for Grint to decipher. They could have been wards, castings, even curses. It wouldn't surprise Grint for a rambler town to curse someone as they entered, just to make them pay for the cure.

"Can we free him from the chains?"

"No," he tugged her again.

"You freed me from chains, why not him?" The girl stomped her feet, refusing to move.

"He's not a prisoner." Grint directed her eyes to the key on the malicant's necklace. "He chained himself up." Lark didn't understand the why of it any more than Grint. "Maybe he's afraid someone will steal his barrel?"

The girl giggled and then clapped a hand over her mouth when she noticed the attention it drew. A scream ripped through the storm as a man stumbled from a tavern, clutching his belly. Mud splashed as he dropped to his knees and his intestines slipped out between his thumb and forefinger. Another man appeared, the rain matting his wild, black hair. Dark shadows hid his face until the lightning flashed, illuminating the elongated scar across his mouth. It made him look as if he wore a permanent sneer. Mr. Gutless tried to crawl away, but Sneer yanked back his hair and drove a small blade into the base of his neck. The rumble of thunder drowned out the death rattle as Sneer wiped the blade on his victim's shirt and walked away. Lark buried her face in Grint's coat, shaking. All Grint cared about was that Gutless didn't look their direction when he expired. *We should be safe.*

Gales of laughter filled the night punctuated by the rhythmic pounding of feet. Muddy urchins appeared from dark alleys to squabble over the dead man's pockets. A child no older than Lark ripped off the boots and ran, chased by two others who meant to claim the prize. Grint kept Lark close as they passed.

What Grint sought was a tavern close to the main bridge. A dozen horse carts parked along the street led him to believe there must be a crossing large enough to accommodate wagons. Taverns by the main gate were always the tamest. The people passing through frequented them, and someone with miles of road still ahead was less inclined to kill you. What passed as tame in Finder's Lot remained to be seen.

Few buildings they passed had covered porches, but those that did looked unsafe. Slanted things sinking in the mud, but that didn't deter dozens of shadowed figures from using them. Whispers and laughter followed them as they walked. The alleys were dark webs spun throughout the city and filled with hungry eyes that hated and watched. The creak of rope and sway of a body caught their eyes as fire-light glinted off silver armor.

"Shiny," Lark whispered as she reached out to touch a boot. Grint pulled her hand away. A Brotherhood Knight, foolish enough to have entered this place. *Such unbelievable hubris to think he could deliver justice in this place.*

"This is what we want," Grint said, looking past the knight, into the tavern his corpse decorated. A wide-mouthed arch stood across the street and a sturdy bridge beyond. They stepped on to the porch where Grint tapped his boots against the wall to knock loose the mud. The rotting wood splintered. No one seemed to notice or care. The heat slapped them across the face as they walked in, but at least it was dry.

Lark covered her ears as the shouts reached uncomfortable levels. Tables crowded the tavern, filled with men and women drinking, gambling, threatening, and swearing. The way they jammed the tables together left little room to walk. Servers as rough as any patron pointed meat stickers at anyone who got too friendly.

"I'll give you ten culls for an hour with the girl," a man shouted.

"Something that sweet, I'll give you thirty!"

The low taverns, places of ill repute, were all the same. Tables, servers, a bar, and then somewhere in a corner the man who ran it all. This establishment was no different. Under a torch suspended from the rafters sat a thin gentleman in baggy, gray clothes, his hair slicked back. The napkin tucked into his collar was a map of blood splatters that Grint hoped came from the slab of beef he cut into. Thick muscled goons with cudgels looped in their belts circled the table, shoving aside anyone who ventured too close.

"Little girl, I'll give you thirty for your friend!"

Grint didn't need to pull Lark as they walked toward the back. She attached herself to his arm the way he held on to the rope bridge. Sneer watched them, sitting against the wall, hair still wet, knees stained with mud and blood. His stare was reserved for Grint as they passed, never sparing a glance for Lark. Was Rent looking through those eyes? Why did that scar make him think of Eleanor? Her hounds were all scarred, but that didn't mean everyone with a scar was one of her hounds.

"What do you want?" a goon asked, freeing the cudgel from his belt.

"A word with the gentleman of the tavern," Grint replied. He knew the proprieties of speaking to a fence.

"Why would he speak with you?"

"Because even at a glance, I recognize a man of opportunity."

"Are you a believer?" asked a wiry young woman with red and black-streaked hair and eyes as sharp as a falcon. A small cutting blade danced between her fingers, highlighting the scars earned from learning the trick.

"Krypsie is a tired old drunk who doesn't care about us," Grint answered. "So, no."

"Do you believe in Blue Fingered Hobbe, who gives us the gift and makes all things possible?"

"I believe in what I can steal and the profit it brings, which is all the belief Hobbe wants," Grint answered. The woman stopped smirking and held the blade between her middle and ring fingers as she closed her fist.

"Let him through, Abbitha." The gentleman fence sat back from his meal, watching the exchange. Abbitha relaxed and waved Grint through but closed off her arm as Lark tried to pass. Grint looked from the guard to the fence who smiled and said, "The girl too." Lark stood behind Grint's chair as he sat down.

"I am Tzivo, of House Artus," he extended a hand in greeting as a servant removed the dishes.

"Grint. Nothing else."

"I doubt that," Tzivo said with a smile. "You spoke of opportunity?"

Grint opened his bag and took out a few of his low yield items. A crystal pendant on a rope necklace, a thimble of silver, and a ring of bleached bone. Tzivo smiled as he put a magnifying monocle on his eye to examine each.

"I pay in culls."

"Is that the local currency?"

"You are new here," Tzivo replied.

"Passing through," Grint said. Lark stepped away from the chair, feeling braver in the confines of the fence's company. She jumped at any loud noise but remained curious about everything happening around her. Grint wondered if she had ever seen a crowd this large.

"Culls are what you'll want to use in outfitting yourself. If you use anything else, you're like to get your throat cut. Will you need a horse or shoes for the girl as you head towards...?"

"Thiel," Grint turned back toward Tzivo. "Ever heard of it?"

"As in Senethiel? Bad luck to name your town after the world breakers."

"It's a kingdom. Don't know where it is though."

"Neither do I," Tzivo answered as he put the monocle down. "I will take the crystal for the information."

"What information?"

"About Thiel." Tzivo scooped up the necklace and handed it to a servant who put it in an iron lockbox.

"You knew nothing about Thiel." Fences were notorious for their frugality, but this was bordering on the egregious.

"That it had no value to you does not mean it did not cost for me to give." Tzivo spread his arms wide and smiled. "I can give you one hundred culls for the other two pieces. Enough to outfit yourself."

"They were offering me thirty for a turn with the girl, I'm sure your lockbox opens wider than one hundred."

"An offer you did not consider," Tzivo smiled and tapped a finger under his right eye. "Tzivo sees all. One hundred is more than generous for the remaining pieces. I'm happy to give you less."

Grint hated dealing with new fences. It was always the same. Endless bargaining for a tenth of what the items were worth. Worse yet, Grint had no frame of reference for a cull's worth. The offer could be a copper's weight for gold. If he needed more, he could come back. There was still the gold box and the jewels from Ballastrine's manor. It would be an affront to sell them so cheap but continuing to live would be worth the price.

"I'll take it," he said with a deep sigh. Tzivo scooped up the items as before and handed them back. The servant retrieved ten iron coins from the box and set them in the center of the table. Culls were octagonal coins with ten raised pips on one side and smooth on the other.

The gentleman fence snapped his finger, summoning his servant back with the whole chest. With nimble fingers he dug out ten new coins and put them down beside his wine glass. These culls had a raised copper edge and a single copper pip. Grint took the hundred culls while looking at the new pile.

"One thousand culls," Tzivo answered.

"For?"

"The girl." Grint shook his head and dropped the culls in his pocket. "Not for any purpose as base as what you imagine. I would feed and clothe her. Educate and train her as Abbitha was." Abbitha sat on the edge of the table to his right, her blade dancing once more. "Or, you can continue your journey towards the fictional kingdom of Thiel."

Grint considered the offer. Tzivo was right that Thiel didn't exist, but Grint always knew that. There was no King's bounty waiting for the little princess to return. And this... this would be a better offer than anything Grint could arrange. Wasn't it always going to come to this? Lark wasn't his apprentice, she wasn't his ward, and she wasn't his daughter. She was the side effect of a job gone wrong.

"Why her? There're a hundred urchins in the streets."

"Monsters," Tzivo spat. "Couldn't trust them and couldn't train them."

Tzivo added another five hundred culls to the pile. Finder's Lot wasn't paradise, but she would be safer here than with him. No thief catcher would step across those bridges. If he could leave her here, maybe he could lead Eleanor away until the Stabbing came and went.

"Two thousand," Grint countered. Tzivo considered the offer and then scooped up all the culls and put them back in the chest.

"No girl, no deal," the gentleman fence smiled.

Grint jumped out of his chair and looked around. He had forgotten Lark was there. How much had she heard? There was no sign of her. "Where?" he asked Abbitha who smirked and pointed at the front door. Grint looked past the guards and saw a man leaving as he pushed his way through the crowd.

"Get her, Mikael. I'll catch up," a drunken man shouted as he fumbled with his coat. Grint planted a boot in the man's back and sent him face first into the wall beside the door. The oil lamp over his head shattered and a flower of fire blossomed across the tavern. Grint heard screams as he burst through the door but didn't care.

Ankle-deep puddles dotted the street, rippling in the light drizzle that now fell. Grint slid in the mud as he jumped off the porch and fell onto his side. Picking himself up, he watched the man named Mikael run into an alley. Grint gave chase his shoulders rubbing both sides of the claustrophobic alley. Deeper in the walls narrowed further, so he ran sideways while jumping over debris and rats. Street urchins hooted as they watched from nets strung between buildings.

Grint ran blind until the alley opened onto a street only an arm's length wider. Mikael stood still a few feet ahead, his focus drawn elsewhere. Unable to stop, Grint rammed into his back, the force shoved him down. The scoundrel flopped like a dying fish as he coughed up chunks of mud that poured into his open mouth. Grint fell as much as he jumped on Mikael, mashing his face deeper in the mud. An incoherent scream bubbled up from the muck before Mikael was able to throw Grint off, wavering as he tried to stand.

The thug needed to clear his eyes, wiping vigorously at the grime. Grint took the advantage and struck with a right hook that sent him tumbling into a ruined stone wall. *A gift from the old fortress,* Grint thought as he smashed Mikael's face into the image of a knight on horseback. Bits of shattered teeth fell from the thug's mouth while others remained embedded in the stone. Bloody bubbles formed on his lips as Mikael dropped, twitching and mewling. Grint pulled Blackblade, no longer caring what gods watched.

Lark yelped, a squeaky, surprising sound. Grint hadn't seen her at first, but she stood in the street, hair matted against her pale forehead, and legs a muddy mess.

"Lark," he said as he stepped past the man. With each step he took, she retreated until her back pressed against an iron door surrounded by gargoyle heads. Grint held up his hand and sheathed the knife. "Kid," he whispered urgently, waving for her to come away, but she shook her head.

"Lark," he repeated, "Listen. You need to get away from..."

The stone gargoyles opened their eyes as the imposing iron door opened. Deep shadows coalesced around Lark and yanked her inside. Grint cursed as he sprinted toward it, knowing he had to get in before it closed. *Iron door means salt witch,* Hobbe warned. *I know,* Grint answered as he led with his shoulder. Pain shook his body as the door fought back, but he rolled through the threshold before it clicked shut. Tumbling face first onto a cold, dirt floor he heard the lock slam shut. Then nothing else.

Two candles flickered on a table in a small room forgotten by the world. Cobwebs swung against a draft whistling as dust swirled and skittered with the mice. Ancient scrolls sat on crooked shelves. The paper so delicate they would no doubt crumble at the touch. The room smelled like rotted meat on a summer's day and Grint gagged.

"I did not invite you, the man of many threads," a scratched, disembodied voice whispered.

"Give me back the girl," Grint said. He reviled these creatures; and creatures they were. Nothing else in Terragard was as nasty as a salt witch.

The shadows in the far corner moved as something dragged itself across the floor. It leapt onto the table, joints snapping with every movement. The salt witch was old, maybe as old as the fortress itself with stringy white hair so thin it did little to hide the jaundiced skin beneath. Her body bent in odd ways, popping audibly as she settled into a crouch upon the table.

"The gods are upon you," she moaned.

"There are no gods here," Grint answered with a shudder. Had he killed anyone in his haste to reach Lark? He almost killed Mikael. Wanted to kill him. How sure was he that no gods were present?

"Silence," she screeched. "Webs upon webs and strings with no end. Even a marionette does not dance to so many tunes." The excitement in her voice palpable and stressed by the stream of urine loosed on the table.

"Filthy," Grint spat on the dirt floor. "Just give me the girl."

"Girl is mine now. Mine, mine, mine," her tongue, a dry, black thing licked the air. "Come to my door she did. They all come, one by one and two by two. The urchins feed Hattie, take care of Hattie."

"I can pay."

"Metal coins hold no interest. Make your offer sweet." The witch was open to bargaining, that was a good sign. It also meant, if he made a poor offering, she would unleash whatever hells she had squirreled away in this dark abattoir.

Grint went through a mental inventory of what he carried. And went through it again. There was one thing she would want, and he didn't want to offer it. Hattie wasn't interested in the jewels or even the magic baubles. A salt witch fed on things of spirit and life. Reluctantly, he grasped his necklace by the trinket and yanked it off. Hattie sniffed at the air and quivered in divine pleasure.

"Now you interest us," she cackled. "Such pure emotion. Love! Loss! A feast for a century."

"This. For the girl."

The scream started as something small and erupted with such a vibrating force that the very sound assaulted. "The girl is mine! We bargain for your life."

"Kry-damned witch," Grint gritted his teeth against the pain.

"Keep your bauble," she said as she hopped off the table, disappearing beneath. When her face reappeared from the shadows, the candlelight danced across her many wrinkles, making them sway like the ocean tide. "What I want is a name. One little name. Of all the strings tied to you, I want the one so thick and dyed with misery, tied right to your heart. Give me the name."

"I'm walking out of here. Whether you're alive when I do will depend on you giving me Lark."

"Give me his name. Speak the name."

"Give me the girl!"

"No! The dennel is mine! Give name to the God of Murder!" The witch flicked her hands and a thousand spiders, each as big as a rat descended from the ceiling. Their silken webs floated on the air wrapping around Grint's arms and legs.

Fighting against the restraints he swatted at them with his knife, but there were too many. Eruptions of puss splattered the walls with each strike, smaller spiders birthing from the goo. The room overflowed with spiders, dropping, crawling and biting. A numbness spread through him, slowing his movements. Hattie cackled from her hideaway, her bones snapping and resetting with every movement. *Hobbe, for once if you can hear me...*

A flash of white light shattered a wardrobe from the inside. A second filled the room. Two short pulses but they were enough to chase the spiders. Grint expected to be covered in webs, but when he looked down, he saw it had been an illusion. The white light flashed again, and Hattie skittered from under the table, hissing at the wrecked wardrobe it came from.

Grint grabbed the rotted edge of a bookshelf and pulled it down. Hattie screamed as it collapsed on her and struggled against its weight. From the splintered wardrobe Lark emerged and jumped into his arms. Together they ran towards the iron door. With the witch distracted, it opened easily enough, but slammed like a tolling bell as they tumbled into the street.

Grint breathed a deep sigh. Mud oozed into the folds of his coat, but felt cool against his neck. The sun shone down, beginning to dry out the mud and he blinked against the light. Was it morning already? How long had they been in the witch's home? Lark knelt an arm's length away looking down at him. As he propped himself up, she reached out and punched his arms with her little fists. It didn't hurt but the pain on her face hurt him in other ways.

"Lark," he said, which just prompted her to hit him again, tears streaming down her cheeks.

"Shut up." Her punches grew listless as she tired and she wiped at her face with the sleeve of her dress, spreading mud across her cheeks. Grint wanted to say more but stayed quiet. *At least she isn't hitting me with light,* he thought.

Lark looked down at the mud and punched it sending drops in every direction. Something moved in the street, just past her shoulder, Grint could swear it. Leaning to look, he saw two glowing yellow eyes in the dark. Whatever it was, it cocked its head. Squinting, the nightmare he long dreaded materialized. Not one, but two hounds stepped from the alley and split to flank them. A canvas of scars covered the one on the left as the other shook drool from its jowls; the sunlight setting fire to its blood-red fur. *Crosshatch and Torchy.*

Scooping up Lark, Grint ran. They stumbled through the twisting maze of alleys as she squirmed in his arms, hitting him in the chest, and trying to wrench herself free. She didn't understand. She'd never met Eleanor or her hounds. Grint held her tight and kept running, hearing the panting breaths of the hounds in close pursuit.

Any chance to turn, he took. First right, then left, and then right again. They needed to lose the hounds, steal a horse on the main street, and make a run for it. After making another left, he could see the open boulevard just beyond a few loitering locals. One of them stepped into Grint's path, and the mud sloshed around his boots as he skidded to a halt.

"You owe me a cull, Mabry. I told you he hadn't left town." Abbitha lounged against the alley wall with two thugs and a man named Mabry; the one Grint had nicknamed Sneer. In the bright morning light, his scar shone a deep purple, making it look somehow more sinister.

Lark squirmed free, all spit and fire until she saw Tzivo's crew. She took a step back. Grint turned his attention from Abbitha to look for the hounds and when he did, she put a boot into his back. He went face first into the mud, banging his chin, and biting a chunk from his tongue. Grint coughed, tasting the blood filling his mouth.

"Bloody iron pigs." He spat a wad of red. "I don't have time for this."

"We have all the time in the world," Abbitha's laugh sounded sweet. Nothing like the woman. Sneer drew his blade and threw it. From his knees, Grint tossed himself to the side, and struck the wall at an awkward angle feeling something snap in his shoulder. A vibrating tingle passed through his right arm before it went numb. Another blade struck the mud a few inches from Grint's face.

"The girl is ours now. Recompense for the damage to Tzivo's tavern. Took an hour to put all the fires out and by then the cutter had to put poor Abrim out of his misery. Burns all over his body." Abbitha produced a sword and waved it around in a flourish. "All Tzivo wants of you is your head. I think he plans to stitch it on that Brotherhood Knight."

"Don't have time for this," Grint repeated as he grabbed the blade from the mud and flung it underhanded. Even thrown lefthanded it caught a thug in the chest. At this distance it was hard to miss. Derelict crates shattered under the man's weight, and he smashed his head against the wall.

Grint had just gotten to his feet as the other thug drove a knee into his groin, and thankfully, he missed the important parts. Slamming his head into the man's nose, Grint maneuvered him like a shield as Sneer threw another knife. The blade struck bone with a thick snapping sound, and the thug tensed. Abbitha crouched out of view and popped back up, striking Grint from over her man's shoulder. Pain blossomed as his nose bent sideways under the blow, filling the back of his throat with blood and snot. Grint spat a mouthful of the crap into the muscle's face and shoved him. Bloodyface fell back taking Abbitha with him. As they hit the ground, her sword ran him through, sprouting from his stomach like a magic tree.

"No more!" Lark shouted. The color drained from her eyes as her hands glowed. It was happening again.

"No!" Grint jumped in front of her, hoping her fear of hitting him with the light would calm her. Sneer drove a fist into Grint's kidney, then his ribs. Still, he refused to move. Maybe it was fear of her wiping the whole place clean. Maybe she was just too young to have real blood on her hands. Whatever the reason, he stood his ground even as Sneer drove punch after punch into his torso.

Lark dropped her hands, color returning to her wide eyes as she pled in silence for Grint to act. He nodded toward the knife in his belt which might have been a million miles away with the way his right arm hung dead at his side. She jumped toward him and pulled Blackblade loose, shoving it in his left hand. Grint smiled and spun, the knife slicing open Sneer's face. The good half. The thug's eyes rolled back as blood fountained from his mouth.

Grint was vaguely aware that Lark held his right hand as she led him out of the alley. Abbitha freed herself from Bloodyface's dead weight as Eleanor's hounds stalked past. They'd watched the battle, content to let it play out. Now they advanced ready to take on an injured Grint. They growled at Abbitha and sniffed the surrounding air. Holding up her sword, she pressed her back to the wall, looking to

Grint with pleading eyes. When they transformed to human form, she dropped the blade and fainted.

"Give her to us, and I'll kill you quick," Tamos said as he and Malus walked naked onto the street. Grint limped on, his knee a throbbing mass of fire. Dozens of onlookers parted to let them pass. There was no need for the hounds to rush, so they followed at an even pace, believing that escape from them was an impossibility. His right arm hung limp, moving only because the girl pulled on it. Blood flowed from his broken nose, giving him the red beard he always wanted. Somewhere along the way he dropped Blackblade, his grip too slick to carry its weight.

Eleanor waited ahead with Noseless at her side, his tail wagging. The hound licked its lips, anticipating an easy victory. Grint blinked, not quite believing what he was seeing. The woman held a large head aloft like a night man's lantern. The severed head's mouth moved, whispering as its milky, dead eyes darted back and forth. It was Black Samuel's head, Grint realized. Eleanor killed him and used her necromancer magic to bring it back. What secrets had she pried from him? Of course, Black Samuel knew this place. Eleanor never needed to chase him through the woods. Not when she could wait for him to bring the girl to her.

"End of the story," Grint coughed as he stumbled to the side of the street. They could get him, but not her. He ushered Lark toward an alley and blocked the mouth. Half dead - almost fully dead - he would face this on his feet. Balling his left hand into a fist, he held it up. Eleanor and her hounds gathered before him and had the audacity to laugh at the gesture.

"Run, little bird. Run far and run fast," Grint said as Lark fought against his last stand.

"Papa Deego," she said, tugging on his sleeve. "We have to go before Papa Deego reaches us."

Grint didn't understand. "Papa Deego?" Dizzy and struggling to stand it was all he could do to keep his fist up. "Papa Deego is a children's rhyme. There is no Death. No god of death."

The town of Finder's Lot went still. No boisterous shouts, no bets on how long Grint would last. No laughter or tears. Just the steady sound of boots crunching in the mud as they hastened closer. Eleanor and her hounds looked left. Everyone looked left. Grint's mouth went dry and filled with ash. He didn't need to look to know who walked the streets of Finder's Lot, but he did anyway.

Striding up the avenue, four deadly shades at his side, bedecked in a long black coat and wide-brimmed hat was Calabassus Rent. The God of Murder. The divine bastard held out a hand to Grint as he approached, victorious smile from ear to ear.

Grint looked down at Lark and whispered, "Do it."

The world turned white.

12

"A Bhanyu and a Willen walk into a tavern..."
-Joffer the Mummer

Grint hadn't known what to expect when the white light enveloped him. Would it burn or be cold? If the energy tore him apart, would he have time to scream? Death was not a journey Grint prepared himself to take. Not that anyone did, but Grint had seen the loom behind the stitch and gotten the story straight from the bull's arse. As the saying went. There was nothing after, no Palace of Light or battle lodges for the brave. No flight of dragons or rebirth. When you died, whatever intangible piece of spirit that made you who you were just stayed where you fell. Shoulder to shoulder in an infinite crowd of spirits as far as the eye could ever see. It must have been nice to be one of the first spirits with room to wander.

Spending eternity crammed in the melting pot of Finder's Lot and old Zorn was not what Grint desired. It was a stupid, romantic notion, but he wanted to die on a small stretch of beach just off the eastern coast. Within a stone's throw of where Jessua died.

The sensation he felt when the white light enveloped him was far different from anything he imagined. It felt as if someone tied one end of a rope around his waist and the other around a tornado and then let it loose. A tornado filled with wild horses pulled him sideways. Grint wanted to vomit but had no stomach or throat to do it with. He was part of the light but also moving through it. How far? How fast? There were no points of reference, just light. The pressure of the movement grew stronger and squeezed him through a miniscule space no larger than a blade of grass. And then darkness.

*****

Air rushed into his lungs, and he coughed up chunks of phlegm that splattered onto his chin and ran down his cheek. Grint's head pounded like he'd lost a drinking contest with a goblin, and the sunlight burned his eyes when he opened them. A blue sky filled with fluffy, white clouds crawled lazily along. *That one looks like a rabbit*, he thought as he lay in the grass watching the clouds like a child. The rougher blades poked against his neck and hands. Thinking back on the last sensation before he blacked out, Grint was relieved to feel anything.

Small hands hit his stomach. "Ow," he said flatly. The hitting stopped.

"Grint?"

"Hi kid," he replied. "Are we dead?"

"I hope not." Her voice was full of worry.

That doesn't sound promising. Grint pushed himself up, forgetting that his right arm was next to useless and fell back. The ground spun beneath him bringing back the nausea. After taking the time to make sure everything remained in his stomach, Grint tried again and took a physical inventory. *I dislocated my right arm at the shoulder. Left leg feels numb but not broken. And the knee burns when I flex it.* Dark purple bruises painted a map across his ribs, tender to the touch. He could feel his nose swelling and used a light touch on the scabs clotting around his nostrils. He had to keep spitting out mouthfuls of sludge draining down his throat. There were times he had been this bad off, but always in different company.

"Never a dragon around when you need one."

"What does that mean?" she asked.

"Nothing." Grint looked around. They were on top of a squat hill surrounded by dozens more all similar of size. They looked like the swells of an ocean of grass during a storm. "Where are we?"

The girl shrugged, but he hadn't expected her to know. It was a question for himself. Craning his head as far as he could, Grint spotted the squat butte and Finder's Lot miles in the distance. The rambler town was little more than a smudge with tendrils of smoke snaking above. *The God of Murder will burn that town to the ground.*

They were miles from Finder's Lot now. The light moved them in seconds. The kid moved them. Pulled them out of certain doom and given them a head start. How much of a head start was questionable. Grint knew he wasn't moving anywhere fast.

"Hand me my bag." There were herbs in there that when combined could dull his pain for a short time.

"Lark?" The girl sat in the grass staring at him with tears welling up in her eyes. Grint didn't need to ask what was wrong. That much he remembered.

"You wanted to sell me." She was angry. She would always be angry when this part came.

"No, I wasn't going to. Hand me my bag." Lark didn't move. "Please?"

The girl dragged the bag over and hit Grint again. She punched his left shoulder, which was the one spot on his body that didn't hurt. So, he let her. "I heard you. Two thousand gulls."

Culls, but no one likes to be corrected. So, he kept quiet and dug out the alchemy box. Annamourn for the pain and Gissel for taste. Grint shoved a pinch of each in his mouth and dry swallowed, then used the blood filling his mouth to swish the grunchles down his throat. As Lark continued punching, her hands flickered with light. Grint grabbed her waist and tossed her onto the grass before she obliterated him with magic. She sprang to her knees, a hateful twist to her face.

"Stop," he said. "Listen, kid. Look at me. I'm busted up. If we make it to that forest south of us it will be because Krypsie flew down from the sun and gave us a ride on his golden steed."

"You weren't busted up when you tried to sell me."

The kid has a point, Hobbe added.

"I thought you'd be safe there. Safer than you are with me."

A weak argument. You wanted rid of her and two thousand culls buys a lot of booze to drown the guilt.

"I am safe with you. Look how far we've gotten."

"On luck. And luck runs dry." Grint grabbed more Annamourn. "I'm a thief. I survive because I don't stand in anyone's eyes and when I leave, they never know I was there. This bag," he grunted as he lifted and shook it. "It's a bunch of tricks and I'm about out of them."

"You promised to take me to Thiel!"

"Leave off with Thiel. We both know it's not real." Grint saw that her hand was bleeding and waved her over, but she didn't budge. "Come here."

"Why?"

"You're bleeding," he said. Lark relented and walked over on her knees. "How did this happen?"

"That lady threw a knife at me," she said holding her palm out. It was a minor cut. The blade must have glanced her. Eleanor wouldn't kill the girl. Not yet. Grint cleaned the blood and wrapped her hand tight. It might need stitched whenever they got somewhere. *And where is that?* Grint washed the girl's blood off his fingers and got to his feet, laboring with the effort, but feeling somewhat better.

"Can you do that thing again? With the light to, uh, move us?" Did she have enough control of the magic to know what to do? Or would she vaporize them if she tried again? Lark held her hands out from her sides and closed her eyes. Nothing happened.

"I can see it, but I can't touch it," she said, flicking her hands. Tiny strobes of white light danced between her fingers, but nothing else. Giving up, she shook her head.

"It's fine. Let's go. We need to get out of sight of that town." If Rent left anyone alive, they would come looking for the pair. Eleanor would be at the front of the posse. Tzivio right behind. *Krypsie help us if those two start to work together.* Slinging the bag's strap over his neck, Grint fashioned a loose sling for his arm. It jostled as he walked but would keep most of the pain at bay until he found time to pop the shoulder back in. Lark wouldn't be strong enough to manage that.

The hill sloped on all sides leaving no easy way down, so it was slow going. One wrong step and he risked injuring himself further. In contrast, Lark bounded down the hill with great ease. His ribs stung with each breath, and he found himself winded by the time he stepped off the hill. An old path covered by dead grass wound through the hills and connected with others. They looked like giant infinity symbols all lined up. These weren't just goat paths. Something about them felt unnatural.

"Thiel exists. You'll see." The kid hadn't even given him a chance to put both feet on flat ground before she started in again.

"Fine," Grint replied, trying to catch his breath.

"Not fine. It's true."

"I'll make you a new deal. If it is real, I'll only take half a king's ransom in payment for your return. If it's not, I'll find the lowest, nastiest piece of human filth to sell you to. Deal?" Grint stretched, hiding a wince of pain as he held out his left hand. Lark glared at him and stomped off.

"Stay to the path and keep heading south," he yelled after her. The pace he set was slow, weighted down by his dragging leg. Fighting against the symphony of pains battering his body was constant. The annamourn cut it back, but not enough. Taking more would make him dizzy and want to sleep. Maybe when they got somewhere safe, he'd be able to rest for a day or two. *Does such a place exist?* Lark stayed in sight but carried a mean grudge, refusing to look back.

"What are you going to do with her?" Jessua asked as she fell in step beside him.

"I don't know," Grint replied as if talking to your dead love was not strange at all. "Keep us alive until the Stabbing. The necromancers will lose interest after that."

"And then what? Leave her in a basket outside an orphanage? Retire from the life and raise her as your own until you succumb to the need for another fix from the one joy you can't deny? Train her as your apprentice?"

"Not bloody likely," Grint laughed and regretted it as the pain bit at his side.

Jessua walked in a white dress with a pale-yellow coat over her shoulders and matching yellow silk ribbon in her hair. Grint smiled as he watched her, forgetting how much he missed this part. "What?" she asked with a blush.

"Yellow suits you."

Jessua adjusted the coat, wrapping herself tight. "I'm cold and you're dodging the question." Grint flinched when she mentioned being cold.

"There is no answer," Grint said as he swatted at a foy fly buzzing around his head. "I didn't put any thought into this. I'm just trying to survive. But she's dennel, so even if I escape what's behind me, what's ahead will do me in."

Dennel. Child of a god. There were dozens of myths and fables about such beings. All of them cautionary tales about the corruption or overreach of power. Even Zorn, the most well-known dennel in history fell in that category. Grint knew little beyond the stories. Hobbe had always been reticent to expound on the subject, but offered a crude explanation one drunken night. Dennel didn't come into the world in traditional fashion. The god formed them inside themselves and laid them like an egg. Hobbe's explanation made more sense than that, but the image of a god crapping out an egg never left Grint's mind. Once born, the dennel became its own being and led a normal human life. When they died, the god reabsorbed them. Hobbe never created one, so he said, but he was also unclear on their powers. It varied wildly by his estimation. Even though Lark used light, it didn't mean her father was Krypholos, God of Light. It could just as easily have been Maguire the Bargainer. Regardless, the sheer strength of a dennel's power could make the most adept witch look mundane.

If the salt witch told the truth, Lark was a dennel. It added context to the value of her blood and answered why the harquin focused solely on her. Her power would be a beacon for anything with sensitivity enough to see it. Knowing what she was gave Grint no comfort. It made it worse.

Their path took them back and forth around the hills. Grint monitored the sun to make sure they weren't going in circles, but without being able to see the horizon, there was no telling how far the forest was. His energy to keep going had run out, so Grint paused and sat against the hill in an unceremonious heap. When Lark realized he wasn't following her, she came back, kicking stones around the trail.

"Still not speaking to me?" Grint asked as she kicked another stone, but at least this time she looked at him. "Can you go up that hill and tell me how far we are from the forest?"

Lark nodded and stepped through the vision of Jessua as she climbed. The hills weren't tall, maybe twenty feet, but even that would have been too much for Grint to manage. The annamourn fogged his mind, but there was also an itch telling him that he'd missed something. Grint felt the chills spreading through his body and watched his hand tremble when he held it up. A bad sign.

"Too early to be bone sickness," Jessua said. He couldn't see her any longer, but her voice remained. It wasn't bone sickness; it was something else. A crutch inside him that was fading.

"Do you want me to count back and forth or by rows?" Lark was already at the top and shouting back down. Grint stared at a floppy leafed purple flower with black veins running through the petals, trying to recall where he had seen it before. "Which one?"

"What do you mean back and forth?" Grint called back. Lark made a pointing gesture at the hills left, then right. Left then right. "Is it like that all around?" Lark spun around, shading her eyes from the sun when she needed and then nodded.

Grint looked back at the flower. "Raven's Tears," Jessua answered for him. "Decorates cairns of the dead."

These weren't foothills, it was a burial ground, and each mound was a tomb. Grint waved for Lark as he forced himself back to his feet. When she reached him, she opened her mouth, but he put his hand over it and made a gesture for her to remain silent. She nodded that she understood. Grint felt a surge of adrenaline giving him new reserves of strength, and they continued along the path. A necromancer could do a lot of damage within a graveyard, and the dead didn't care for visitors even without a necromancer's help to wake them up. With the age of this place, he'd win a goblin's wager that the tombs were filled with Zornish soldiers.

Grint quickened his pace and was wheezing by the time they reached an old, dead tree just outside the cemetery. "Can I climb it," Lark whispered, and he nodded. She jumped onto the lowest branch, kicking her feet as she tried pulling herself up. Grint sat in the shade and shut his eyes. It was midday, and the heat felt unbearable. If he could rest, the afternoon would cool enough for him to travel again. Just a little while.

Except it's not hot out. It was Hobbe's voice. Jessua had gone. Grint thought on that statement as he fell asleep.

*****

"There's a cart," Lark said as she dropped out of the tree. The thud of her feet woke Grint, and it took a moment to remember where they were.

"What?"

"A cart," she repeated as she pointed down the old stone path beside the tree. "Do you think it's bad people?"

"Out here they're all bad people." It was a nihilistic view, but the girl needed to learn the world would tear you down if you weren't careful. Take what you could when you had the chance. "Help me up."

Lark grabbed his left hand and tugged. There was no chance she could budge him, but he didn't need her to lift him, just to give him enough leverage to fight through the pain. The treeline across the dirt road was sparse, with fifteen to twenty paces between each trunk. The forest thickened deeper in but getting there before the cart would be impossible. Even now, he could hear the horse's hooves on the packed dirt and the distant creak of a wheel in desperate need of oil.

Grint limped across the cart path, needles of pain stabbing every inch of his body. They made it to the second tree before the cart appeared. Keeping themselves hidden behind a pine as it approached. Grint looked for the driver but couldn't see them through the brush. If it kept its pace the cart should pass them by in a few moments. Instead, the creaking axle slowed until it stopped altogether. The horse stamped a foot with impatience and snorted. A low-hanging branch obscured the driver's chair, and no one had gotten down. *What are they waiting for? Are they taking a break?*

"Do you think they saw us?" Lark whispered. Grint reached down to his belt for Blackblade and felt sick to find it wasn't there. A vague recollection of dropping it in Finder's Lot came back. Grint almost asked Lark if she had it, but the knife tip poking against his ribs dissuaded him. The person standing behind him whispered a shushing noise into his ear. Grint nodded. *People need to stop sneaking up behind me.*

"Hello there, young lady." The voice of the stranger was nasally, almost childlike. Lark jumped at the suddenness of the greeting and the stranger who offered it. "No need to be afraid."

"We're alright, sir," Grint said. "No need for you to stop." The poke in the ribs became more pronounced.

"The way the two of you limped through that graveyard, I would beg to differ." Grint had yet to see the stranger, but the way Lark frowned made him think there was something here that didn't jibe.

"Made me say, Spiru, those folks look like they could use a hand." Spiru kept the knife against Grint's ribs hidden from her view.

"How very considerate, Spiru," Grint said and earned a deeper jab of the knife and a subtle push forward.

"The Papality offers blessings to those who help travelers in need." Spiru gestured at Lark as they walked, but she refused to move until Grint gave her a nod. "There, now we can all ride in the cart. Spiru will be happy to take you where you need to go."

The stranger changed his position to keep the blade hidden, giving Grint his first look. His skin was the color of old, faded copper and etched by the weathering of age. Slate-gray eyes, hidden beneath the permanent squint of a man who spent years in the sun, watched Grint carefully. Long, silken gray hair fell behind his shoulders and as he smiled, Grint expected those stone etched features to crack. Spiru looked like an old bhanyu, an ancient one from the etchings Hobbe kept in his vault.

"My daughter and I are from a hamlet called Praetore. We got lost during a hunting expedition and set upon by thugs from that town there." Grint made it up as he went, hoping this encounter was random. Maybe the old man would let them go.

"Dangerous place, Finder's Lot," Spiru said in that child-like voice, sounding out of place from someone so old. "I know Praetore well and can put your feet on the right path."

Grint's stomach turned as the pieces of a puzzle fell in place. This wasn't random, and there was no talking their way out. Kind old Spiru with the child's voice was an assassin of the highest order. A krau assassin. On his best day the fight would be a longshot. This was not that day. When they reached the cart, the stranger smiled and offered a seat up front for the girl. Lark stood her ground, but at a knife's urging Grint nodded, and she hopped up.

Smart girl, he thought. She learned enough to follow his lead. With her magic too weak to use, they needed to stay alive for a day or two. Then they could unleash it and keep moving.

Hobbe laughed in the back of his mind. *Already using her to your advantage. That's my bo...*

The assassin slammed Grint's face into the side of the cart once Lark was out of view. It caught him off guard; the blow dazing him. The strength Spiru exhibited was as alien to his body as the voice. Grint blinked, trying to stay conscious. Spiru slammed his face again. From a dark recess of his mind, Grint felt himself being lifted into the cart.

"Is he okay?" That was Lark. The cart lurched forward.

"Your father fell. He needs rest."

Kry-damned krau assassin!

*****

Krau assassins were dangerous beings, having honed their craft over thousands of years. They weren't immortal in the traditional sense. You could kill them, but when you did their spirit went into another body. The krau could then continue their mission, safe in the anonymity of a new form. The bodies they inhabited came from nests forged from their dark magic. Anyone who stumbled into a nest suffered agonizing pain while the magic tore their spirit apart. When the process completed, the body became an empty vessel perfectly preserved until the krau needed it.

The krau were by-products of old De'Krau magic even the gods didn't understand. There was no hierarchy or honor among them, selling their skills to the highest bidder. And some madman had put marks on Grint and Lark.

*****

Grint struggled back from the darkness. A laborious process, but one that gave him time to listen. The crackle of a fire, the call of a night bird, the distant rush of a river, and the mumble of voices close by. Children's voices? Lark and Spiru. A thick crust formed around his eyes and cracked as he forced them open. He was in the back of the cart. Thick with must and old rot. The burlap flaps opened with the breeze. Grint saw nothing but darkness on the other side except for the occasional spark from a fire. Was it the same day? Without knowing how long he slept, there was no way to gauge that. If enough time passed, perhaps Lark's magic was ready.

Grint wanted to time his movements with the call of that kry-damn bird, but even the slightest movement made his body angry. Wretched pain became a constant thing, reaching every point in his body. As yet, his injuries hadn't healed.

The dislocated shoulder, cracked ribs; and why were his feet cold? Shifting to look, he wiggled his toes. Spiru had taken his boots. *Charffing deranged fish-swiller.* Whoever hired the krau didn't want them dead or they would be already, but Spiru didn't want them running either. Grint had one good arm to feel around with. His bag wasn't here. The many knives he carried on his person were all meticulously searched for and removed. Without weapons, what hope did he have against the assassin? Spiru even took the small pig-sticker he kept in his boot. Being covert in this current physical condition was pointless, so he focused on climbing out of the cart without falling on his face.

Nausea gripped his gut as he stood, but he found comfort in leaning against the wagon. Charred leaves and roasting acorns led him to the fire. Grint limped, dragging his leg and stretching to get the blood flowing. Spiru sat on a log with Lark beside him. As Grint appeared, he took the crossbow resting by his feet and placed it on his lap, pointing the bolt at Lark. The girl ate a bowl of soup, looking at Grint for directions he wasn't able to give.

"I hoped you would sleep through the night," Spiru said. "I feared the smell of food would wake you, but poor Lark was so hungry. We had to risk it."

It was the same day then. Maybe a few hours past dusk. *How long does the kid need to recharge the magic?* Grint didn't think they could hold out the two or three days he hoped to. Not against a krau.

"She told you her name?" Grint asked as Lark looked down into her soup, avoiding his glare.

"We've talked about many things," Spiru said in his high-pitched way. Grint settled himself onto a log opposite the fire as Spiru spoke. "I regaled her with my recollections of Praetore. A town she seems woefully ignorant of. Have you been keeping her chained in a basement?"

It was the Terrastag job then. Not a surprise. Marm wouldn't send a krau after him over a broken banjo or a handful of promised gold. This was about Lark. Which one had done it though? Ballastrine or Eleanor? Spiru smiled at him, a cat playing with the mouse before dinner.

"What sort of monster would do a thing like that?" Grint saw his bag by the fire. Thankfully, it remained closed.

"When you've been around the world as much as I have, the things people do stops surprising you." It was the first true thing Spiru said.

"Do you mind?" Grint asked, pointing at his bag. If the assassin had tried opening it and failed, he showed no signs. Spiru drummed his fingers on the crossbow and nodded. With exaggerated groans, Grint dragged the bag over to a log opposite the fire and sat. Spiru cleared his throat, showing Grint the finger held firmly on the trigger. Although neither had ever met one before, Faighur had believed that a krau would be overconfident and sloppy due to their immortality. Grint counted on that as he obscured what he was doing with the flap of his bag.

"Here we go," Grint said after rummaging through the bag. Wagging a water skin in the air, the assassin watched on with a smug look of amusement. The skin often held fire rum, but Faighur drank what remained back in the Anghors. The krau didn't know that, and what he didn't know would be useful. Spiru lifted the crossbow, making Lark aware of the danger for the first time. Grint mimed a look of surprise at the weapon and offered the skin. "It's just fire rum. Would you like some?"

"No, and neither should you." The assassin liked games,

but his tone said this one was over. "Not while you're healing. Have tea instead. Young Lark can pour it for you."

Good, keep biting little fishy. Soon enough you'll find my hook.

Lark put down her soup and brought over the teapot and a clay cup while Spiru kept the weapon pointed at her. Her hands shook as she poured, so Grint put his good one over hers to help steady it and gave her a wink. Steam rose from the brown liquid and even with a broken nose, the pungent, sour smell presented itself. Grint took a sip and swished it around his mouth before swallowing.

"Juniper leaf."

"An acquired taste to be sure," Spiru held his own cup out for the girl to refill. When it was, he took a deep sip and smacked his lips in appreciation.

"You mentioned being chained in a basement," Grint said. Spiru looked at him over the rim of the cup. "How is Ballastrine? Is it Lord Ballastrine? I can't recall. There's so many counts and dukes and lords wrapped up in this. I can never keep them straight. A queen or a king, those I understand. What on Terragard is a viscount? Do they make these titles up?"

"We're dropping the pretenses then?" Spiru finished his tea and aimed the crossbow toward Lark again.

"I don't see the point in them. We all know who each other are." Grint finished his tea and held the cup out. Lark gave him a look and stood to refill it. "It seems I've acquired a taste after all. And you don't need the crossbow. It's a nice affectation, but a threat is only useful if you can back it up. You won't kill the girl."

"But I could still kill you," Spiru replied as he swiveled the crossbow in Grint's direction. Before Lark sat back down, he nodded for her to refill his cup too.

"You won't kill me, or you would have by now." The tea was terrible, but he needed Spiru to keep drinking his, so he kept talking. "Ballastrine wants me alive with the girl. Or you want me for your nest."

Spiru threw his head back, filling the air with laughter. "You know what I am? Wonderful! What gave it away? Was it the voice?" He rested the crossbow on his lap as he drank his tea. "No matter how many bodies I jump to, my voice always stays the same."

"How much does it cost to hire one of you," Grint asked. "I've always been curious."

"More than a thief like you could afford," Spiru mused. "Ballastrine has coin to spare and then some. Wasteful fool called his forces in the south to join the hunt for you. Hired a mercenary group called the Tall Company and even has his house guards sweeping the countryside. I told him, 'Onor, all you need is me.' And here we are."

"I met one of the Tall Company. He bit me." Grint rolled up his sleeve and exposed the bandage. Spiru clucked.

"Such savagery. Ballastrine wants the girl back, that's without doubt. You? All he wants are the how and the why of it all. I don't think you'll survive the process." Spiru finished his tea and lifted the crossbow again. "I'll make you a deal. If you tell me, I can make it easy for you. My nest will make it feel like going to sleep."

"How magnanimous," Grint rolled his eyes. Spiru smiled and gave a shrug.

"The choice is yours."

"Give me a day or two to think on it?" When Grint asked, Spiru bobbed his head back and forth and then shrugged again.

"Just be sure to make the choice before the choice makes you." That appeared to conclude the matter as the three sat in silence, enjoying the sounds of the night. The crackling fire chatted with the river. And the kry-damn night bird must have gone to sleep or found somewhere less populated to sound its hideous cries.

Breaking the silence, Spiru said, "You know, I seem to recall an old brother named Corrado. Haven't seen him in fourteen hundred years, but he tried changing his voice. It always sounded forced. Still, unless someone knows what to look for, they would never qurdfgtun..."

Spiru's voice trailed off as he lost the ability to form words. Next, his jaw flopped open, and the crossbow slipped out of his grip, firing into the dirt. The bolt shattered, its pieces scattering across the ground. A moment later he fell off the log, causing Lark to yelp as he hit the ground.

Grint stood, feeling less injured than he had let on. The shoulder was still out of whack but everything else felt better than he had in days. As he approached the paralyzed body of Spiru, the only thing he saw moving were the eyes, which darted back and forth, vascillating between bewilderment and outright fury. Grint loomed over him, listening to the assassin's long, wordless whine.

"I wasn't sure it would work," Grint said, tapping Spiru's cheek with his toes. "I use agot stones to kill magic traps. Shave a little off onto a knife or my lock pick and I get right through. You have to keep them dry, otherwise they crack and dissolve. I dropped a small piece into your teapot."

Grint limped over to his bag, splinting his arm in the strap. "Lark, do me a favor and load anything useful into the cart." The girl nodded and grabbed an armful of furs too large for her to carry, tripping over the dragging ends as she walked. Grint picked up the teapot and swished it. By the sound of it, there were a few cups worth left inside.

"It doesn't affect me because I'm not magic," Grint poured the rest of the pot down Spiru's throat. "But you? Everything about you is magic." Grint closed the assassin's mouth for him, but it fell back open. "I had been hoping it would kill you. Kill the krau part of you, but paralyzing you is just as fine. I'm happy it did. If it hadn't, I was giving your offer with the nest serious consideration. Lark?"

The girl poked her head through a hole in the burlap at the front of the cart. "Yes?"

"Bring me some rope if he has it." Spiru did. Lark dragged a long coil, the ends trailing in the dirt behind her. With her help, they tied the assassin to a tree.

"I mean, can you imagine me in a krau nest? Or with that squeaky voice?" Spiru whined in response, the inflection changing as it went on.

"What's he trying to say?" Lark asked.

"Who cares?" Grint tore a piece of fabric from the assassin's shirt and tied his mouth shut. "So the spiders don't crawl in. You can thank me later"

Lark loaded the last useful thing in the cart and hopped onto the front seat. Spire hadn't hobbled the horse, just tied it to a nearby tree. Grint untangled the line and climbed up beside Lark. They took a moment to look at Spiru, tied to a tree in the dying firelight. "Will he come after us?"

"I'm hoping we're far enough away it won't matter," Grint said. The assassin wouldn't forget this. A krau's memory was long.

Grint yanked on the reins, but the horse resisted them. A slight whip of the lead lines and the cart lurched forward. They would need to turn around to get back on the stone road. Something snapped behind them, a deep, angry noise that upset the horse. The beast became restless, rearing its head and ignoring the reins. The snap came again and turned to a burning sound as an amber glow lit the night. Grint and Lark looked back at the cart to see a swirling red light tracing glyphs along the wooden panels. From the light, thousands of fireflies erupted into the sky.

"What kind of salt swilling pig puts a trap on his cart?" Grint shouted. The horse screamed in terror as it bolted, dragging them through the forest. The cart rocked and jumped as it ran over roots and bashed against trees, but the horse had the bit and wanted nothing more than an escape from the swarming fireflies. Grint realized with great horror what they were. Fire wasps. The wasps darted back and forth, slashing at them with razor sharp wings. Great burning welts rose where they stung.

Lark buried her head in Grint's lap, and he did what he could to shield her. The sound of the river grew louder. *Good,* he thought. If they could get to the water, they could get away from the bugs and maybe find the cart again when the magic passed. Grint did his best to hold on while covering Lark in a blanket. The trees thinned and disappeared. Grint looked past the horse but saw nothing ahead of them. *Nothing?* The ground fell away beneath them and they floated awkwardly in the air before gravity reasserted itself, plummeting into the icy currents of the river below. The horse had run them off a cliff.

The horse and cart crashed into the water first, followed by Lark and Grint. A shock from the cold water gave him renewed clarity and new depths to the pains across his body. The bag that saved his life many times had him wrapped in its embrace while dragging him down. Grint struggled out of the strap while fighting a current that bashed him into hidden rocks.

Lark struggled to stay above the water a few lengths away. A spray of white foam swallowed her as she hit a rock and when he saw her again, the girl floated motionless. Grint kicked toward her, but the bag held him back. He couldn't swim with one arm and hold it. That bag was his life, his tricks, his tools and the summation of his wealth. He screamed in rage as he dropped it. The tears running from his eyes conveniently masked by the river; he swam to the girl. Somewhere in the night he could hear Hobbe laughing at him.

The girl spat up water as he pulled her onto his stomach and together, they floated on their backs with the current. *At least I can see where we're going this time.* Not that the sight was helpful, not when each step of the journey robbed him of something else.

"Canoes," the girl whispered. Grint saw them too and kicked hard to get them close to the shore. When the riverbed was shallow enough to touch, they crawled through the muck and fell on their knees beside a few anchored canoes. Grint traced a hand over the hardened burlap hull and recognized the symbols painted there.

"Let's not go swimming again," Lark said with a smile. Grint felt no joy. Not with what he'd lost and what they'd just found.

Leaves rustled as the first small man appeared. They moved quick, darting back and forth as they ran. A warrior Grint never saw coming struck him across the face with a painted leg bone. Three others emerged from the forest and shoved Lark onto her back. Tying their ankles with rope, the little people dragged them along a path.

Grint protested, "We weren't going to steal them!" But the orange-skinned man ignored him. As he repeated it, a trailing warrior pointed the sharpened end of their bone spear against his throat. He thought better of arguing and did as they wanted.

More little people emerged from yurts in the village as they dragged the prisoners in. The orange-skinned people were the willen, a diminutive and tribal culture that migrated like gypsies. Bone magicians, spirit callers, and fierce warriors. They were reasonable unless you somehow offended their sensibilities. Trying to steal their canoes might do it.

The tribesmen and women who dragged the pair fetched the elders. One, in particular, stepped out of a yurt wearing a disgustingly large wooden mask. He looked at Lark and then did a double take at Grint. The masked man and the elders exchanged words, and he laughed before coming over to kneel beside Grint.

"Bsshlngtmme."

"What?" Grint asked. The mask muffled what the Willen said.

The Willen shook his head and removed it. "I knew you were ugly, Grint, but what happened to you?"

"Hello, Tin Boots," the thief replied, dropping his head into the dirt.

13

"The Willen have no home, no recognizable gods and no interest in the sharing of culture. Is it not clear they are the children of the Great Deceptor?"

- Pope Gaius Demarcus
Living Embodiment of the Papality

"Take good care of that one," Tin Boots shouted over the music. "He's very important." The one-time thief raised a mug in Grint's direction then quaffed it in a single swallow, a gesture Grint would have reciprocated had the bone priestesses tending his wounds allowed it. Instead, they made disapproving sounds and resorted to slapping his hands when he tried to drink.

"You should stay clear of the Crowing Priest," the eldest of them said as she dabbed the fire wasp welts with a soothing balm. From their chatter, he believed her name was Dry Twig. The willen practiced spirit and bone magics, but rudimentary herbal reliefs had their uses. Dry Twig and her assistants tapped runic bones against Grint's flesh as they chanted. Blue sparks jumped with every tap. Grint liked to avoid magical remedies, but each time they made the sparks fly he could feel his wounds knitting back together. Given what he'd been through, he'd take the help.

"I've known him most of my life," Grint replied.

"Not something you want to admit to these women," Wet Snake poked him harder than necessary, eliciting laughter from the other priestesses. Their work continued. All the while chattering away in their language, pointing at scars long healed. Each had its own story, but they'd have to let him drink if they wanted to hear them.

Dry Twig scolded them in their native tongue. Grint knew a few willen words, most of them profanities, but also enjoyed how they named themselves. In willen custom, their names came from bones rolled by the elders. Often, they adhered to no known standard of sense. Tin Boots, Dry Twig, Wet Snake, Angry Leaf, etc.

The village came alive with activity as willen men and women ran about with torches, lighting great bonfires. A tired-looking man barked orders at two younger boys who hurried to fill cauldrons with water from the river. Three broad-shouldered willen spitted a salted boar over the central fire. The rich aroma filled the air, creating a long rumble in Grint's belly. Shaggy dogs with stumpy legs drooled as they gnawed on discarded bones but scattered as the Willen rolled out massive clay pots filled with fermented milks and wines. The band plucked the strings of small banjos, blew on flutes, and slapped leather wrapped drums. An hour earlier, they had all been asleep.

"It is our custom when we have guests," Dry Twig whispered to Grint, who watched the preparations with great appreciation.

"Even in the middle of the night it seems."

"Even then." She examined his nose and not gently. Then grimaced each time he flinched. "Do you want it fixed or not?"

Grint nodded. He would take healing, the feast, and a moment of time with an old friend. The road hadn't been kind.

"Try some of this mare's milk," Tin Boots said as he held a cup out to Grint.

"Away with you, charlatan." That was Oily Shell, working on his leg.

"Come now, Shelly," Tin Boots said in a sweet coo. The women laughed.

"You'll not trick her into your yurt again," Dry Twig grunted. "Be away." Tin Boots grumbled, waved a hand, and jumped into a line of dancing willen.

"He thinks he is fooling everyone with his piety," Wet Snake said, and the others agreed.

As the priestesses finished, Dry Twig walked around and inspected their work. She was not shy about pinching and prodding his flesh as she went, but Grint took it in stride. Satisfied, she made an affirming noise and her assistants put their bones and tools back into bags hanging off their hips. Dry Twig reached a calloused hand up and checked his eyes before putting her own tools away.

"You should be well as long as you rest." After a considered pause, she continued, "You should have told us there was other magic working in you. It did not conflict with ours, but if it chose to, it could have been troublesome."

"I didn't use..." Grint stopped and looked across the camp at where Lark played with the willen children.

Dry Twig looked too and jammed a finger into his chest. "You have a good heart," followed by a poke to the temple, "and some intelligence. Choose better friends and divest yourself of all those gods weighing you down. They'll get you killed."

"I know. If you have any ideas how I can get rid of those two, I'm listening." Grint tested his shoulder. It felt better than it had in years.

"Two?" Dry Twig cocked her head and laughed. "He said two." Shaking her head, she walked away. Grint stood, but the magic they used made him dizzy.

Unable to follow the priestess, he shouted after her. "Why is that funny? How many kry-damned gods are tied to me?" He knew of Hobbe and Rent, but who else? Krypholos? Lorelai? Whoever Lark's parent was? He was still turning it over in his mind as Tin Boots came over and put the aforementioned cup of mare's milk in his hand.

"Quite the scrap you got yourself in," and then, "Hey!" as Grint put the cup to his lips.

"What?" Grint looked over the top of the cup with confusion. Tin Boots lifted his cup high. "Oh," Grint caught on. The two clanked their cups and recited the toast the old crew concocted:

Thief in the street
Thief in the gutter
One coin, two coin, poor as butter
Thief on the roof
Thief in the night
Three gold, four gold, all is right
Thieves getting drunk
Thieves like to skim
All gold everywhere, the drinks are on him!

They finished with another clink of cups and drank deeply. Grint hadn't tasted the willen mare's milk yet, and it was not at all what he expected. The dominating flavor was a sour, creamy texture, but also tasted hints of wild berry, forest moss, and mushrooms. No one ever accused him of having an adventurous palate, but while he was here, he would accept a refill. The milk spread through him like a warm blanket and eased any lingering pains.

"I thought maybe you had forgotten that." Of all the old crew, Tin Boots was not the one Grint thought of as sentimental.

"As often as we all recited that, I believe our spirits will babble it in the Afterwards."

"To the good old days," Tin Boots smiled. "How is Hobbe?"

"Not dead."

Tin Boots choked on his milk and coughed it out. After he wiped his mouth against a sleeve, he looked at Grint. "Still with the two of you?"

It was a friend's question, borne of concern. It shouldn't have made Grint angry, but it did. Any mention of Hobbe had that effect. *Then why do you talk to me in your head?* Tin Boots still saw Blue Fingered Hobbe as a benefactor, guiding wayward children towards their true callings as master thieves. Grint did not share the interpretation.

"Do you have a shrine to Hobbe in that yurt of yours? Or some token around your neck? I'll take my advice from those who haven't turned away from the life." The words came out harsher than intended. Tin Boots turned away, so Grint softened his tone when he continued. "What is it you do here, with all of this? What do they call you?"

"A Crowing Priest," he replied, the red in his cheeks fading. "It's an easy job. Now and then they want me to incant over something. I do and then we celebrate."

"The priestesses called you a charlatan."

"I am," Tin Boots laughed. "They know it, I know it. Everyone in the tribe knows it, but no one cares. They've had good fortune since I arrived, so they're content to let me keep doing it. I think some of them hope the Spirit Lords are working to make me a believer." Tin Boots waved a hand, dismissing the idea. "There's nothing in the Afterwards except for a mountain of the dead ten thousand generations deep."

"What do you get out of it?" Grint watched some willen girls braiding Lark's hair as she laughed. Since their travels began, all she'd seen were monsters and death. And almost drowned twice. *Have a laugh, kid.*

"I don't have to look over my shoulder for thief catchers, Ropes, or Brotherhood Knights. No getting double-crossed by thieves looking for a larger share. I don't get mugged by fences who don't want to pay or hunted by brokers who can't accept it when a job goes sideways. I don't wake up from a drunken stupor wondering where all my coin went. Best yet, I don't have to plan a hasty job just so I can eat." It had been a long time since Grint had seen Tin Boots, but what he described was the day-to-day life of being a thief.

"Sounds nice," Grint lied. Some thieves just got tired. That wasn't Grint. "We all die penniless and alone."

"Not me," Tin Boots said, raising his voice over the music. The silence stretched between them until Tin Boots asked, "What's the story with the girl?"

"Don't you know? Since there's a festival, I assumed you incanted over her."

"That sounds obscene!" Tin Boots laughed, the melancholy moment passing away.

"It's a long story, but I got hired to steal an urn. When I got there, it was being filled with her blood. So, I took her out and we've been on the run." It left out a lot, but he didn't have the mental energy to relive the whole saga.

Grint stood and put weight on his left leg for the first time since Finder's Lot. It still felt stiff and needed more rest, but the smell of food made him want to eat. Besides, another cup of mare's milk on an empty stomach and he would pass out for a week. The willen priestesses were miracle workers, but even they wouldn't be able to wake him from that.

"Grint the rescuer," Tin Boots said in a sing-song voice. "I guess I can understand. The kid does kind of remind me of Jessua."

At the sound of her name, Grint's chest burned and face flushed. He reached for the necklace and almost fell to his knees when he didn't find it there. A vague recollection of pulling it off in the salt witch's home came back, but he hadn't given it to her. Tin Boots continued talking, but Grint retreated into his mind, retracing where it might have fallen. Had it fallen in the river? Did the krau take it? Had he dropped it on the witch's floor without realizing? Did Eleanor have it?

Tin Boots was tugging on Grint's sleeve. Time must have passed. Tin Boots had been right beside him, and now the willen handed him a plate of food. The appetite which had been there moments before fled, but he accepted the food. They walked to a long stump where Grint sat, holding the plate in his lap and a vacant look on his face.

"Were you in the Dire Lands?"

"What?" Grint shook off his thoughts of the necklace. Grease ran down the Willen's chin as he shoved handfuls of pork in his mouth.

"The girl, was she being held in the Dire Lands?"

"No," Grint replied, nibbling on a carrot. The food looked good, even if he'd lost all sense of taste. "The Terrastags."

Tin Boots dropped the plate, splattering the contents in the dirt. Two willen ran over and cleaned it up with promises to bring a new plate. Tin Boots ignored them, staring at Grint, working his mouth open and shut. "You. Took her. From the Terrastags? You got in? And back out?"

"There were jewels too." Grint held his hand out like he still had one of the giant things in his clutches. "A ruby, a sapphire, and an opal. All as big as a hand. Worth twenty thousand barsuls in the Orrish Bank easy. Each."

Tin Boots slapped his own face, salivating at the thought of that much coin. "Where are they now?"

"In the river," Grint said. The words hurt his mouth and his head. Tin Boots moaned. Grint felt no better about it than him. "We went off the cliff and into the river. The jewels went in the drink. Poof."

Tin Boots recovered from the news as a new plate landed in his lap. After scarfing half of its contents, he asked, "Why did they want her blood?"

"She's dennel," Grint said. This time Tin Boots threw his plate into the dirt and waved off the willen who came to clean it up.

"She's what?"

"The necromancers want it for some ritual at the Stabbing. I've been trying to keep her alive. Making it up as I go." Grint folded a piece of ham and put it in his mouth. Once the juices ran down his throat, his appetite returned, and he shoved it in hand after hand.

"Is she Hobbe's?"

"No," Grint said between bites. "I don't think so. Maybe? She doesn't know or hasn't told me if she does." He wouldn't put it past Hobbe to create a dennel and orchestrate some convoluted way to cross their paths.

The willen brought a new plate to Tin Boots despite his earlier protestations, and he set it down between them. "Abbas samaha," he whispered. It was one of those bits of willenese Grint knew. It translated into awestruck disbelief with profanity attached. Three willen women scoffed at the foul language, but then urged Tin Boots to join them in a dance. He looked at Grint with a sly grin.

"Go," he said. Tin Boots hopped up before the words left his mouth. Grint's burdens weren't his friend's. Best to let him enjoy the party.

"Watch my plate," Tin Boots said and trotted over to dance with the women. Along the way he stopped a server and must have told them to bring Grint some wine as a mug appeared in his hand moments later. Grint watched the revelry as he ate and when he finished his plate, he started on the one Tin Boots left behind. He allowed himself a smile as he imagined the mock outrage the willen would spew at finding it empty. *As if he hadn't left it for me to eat.* That was how it was with old friends. The interactions became rote. He thought about Faighur and wished he was here. Not for the dragon part of him, but the man he had been. Grint, Faighur, and Tin Boots were once a part of Hobbe's crew. Chances to see them - and the others - were ports in a long storm.

After a few more songs, the music died out, replaced by the rhythmic rattling of willen maracas. The crowd quieted as the chieftain, a woman named Empty Candle climbed onto a stump. She waved a blue flamed torch back and forth and the willen swayed in time. The priestesses joined the chieftain, arranging themselves around the stump.

"This young child has come to us with a grand tale and request for aid." Empty Candle didn't speak standard, so Dry Twig translated her words for Lark. A young willen boy in white robes stood behind Grint, doing the same. The chieftain's voice was as soft as a feather drifting upon the wind, but her words stung. He lost his entire life in the river saving Lark and the first thing she did was ask the willen for help.

"We have agreed to supply that aid," Dry Twig announced. The willen cheered.

Calls rang out to "Roll the Bones!"

"Give her a true name!"

"Little Lark," Empty Candle said as Lark stepped out of a yurt to stand beside the chieftain. Even with the willen woman standing on a stump, Lark stood taller than her. Grint noticed that they'd braided Lark's hair to match the chieftain. "The tribe has called for you to become one of us. Will you accept?"

"Yes," she whispered, her nervousness clear. The village went silent, so even her small voice boomed throughout. The willen erupted in shouts when the drums and rattles began anew. Two muscled willen bonethrowers carried a lacquered box and set it down before her. Tin Boots followed them, once more wearing the ridiculous wooden mask. *He must be in constant danger of tipping forward.* The Crowing Priest splashed water on the chest with a wooden spoon, dousing Dry Twig in the process to great gales of laughter. *No wonder they love him.*

"Who is this that seeks to join the tribe?"

"Lark," she answered.

"Lark no longer. We shall now entreat the Spirit Lords to choose your true name." Empty Candle reached into the box and pulled out a handful of rune-etched bones, each no larger than a knuckle and cast them into the dirt. Dry Twig gathered them up and conferred with the others before presenting their findings to the chieftain.

"The Spirit Lords have spoken! Your true name is Thundering Toad!"

"A grand name," someone shouted in standard. Grint didn't know what made it a grand name, but most of what the Willen did was foreign to him.

"We shall now beg the Spirit Lords for one final gift. The destiny of our Thundering Toad."

Grint heard telling of this ritual, but never witnessed it. Few outside of the willen tribes were permitted. The bone priestesses would channel their magic, opening a glimpse into someone's destiny. With a positive vision, the willen believed a life lived in service to the Spirit Lords would ensure the events unfolded. If poor, it warned of how not to live. The willen relied on their belief of the Spirit Lords, which Grint knew weren't there. Or maybe they were and Hobbe never admitted it. What kind of vision would they see from a dennel? Lark looked expectant, even excited. Grint wanted to fill a skin of wine, maybe go drink in peace; but leaving the ceremony would be an affront. Friend of the Crowing Priest or not.

The ritual began as willen in white robes fanned the massive bonfire. Chanting bone priestesses danced around the flames which spewed a multitude of colors swirling around in the smoke. The colors fanned out like paint on a canvas and coalesced into an image of an island surrounded by crashing waves. Overhead, the skies darkened. Nacinth stabbed into Effulg. The image shifted to Lark surrounded by red rivers of blood. Her body floating above a portal. Demons poured out of the maw in endless columns. From within the writhing mass, a gigantic demon lord rose. The destruction it wrought was absolute.

"Inno Jamoi," Grint breathed. The willen screamed in terror. The tribe looked to the fading images, crying and shaking their fists. Their Spirit Lords commanded that all demonic forces were a pestilence that fed on spiritual energies. The necromancers desire for Lark and her dennel blood made sense. What was locked away in that little girl's veins held power unimaginable. *Enough to open a doorway for a mud-soaked demon lord.* How stupid had he been to assume they wanted to bind a minor demon or seek a double-edged boon? Demons were untrustworthy sacks of filth in the best conditions. This was so much worse.

The priestesses walked around, directing the more steadfast members to help calm the tribe. When everyone settled, the women gathered in a circle around the chieftain, discussing what comes next. Lark stood alone, the firelight dancing across the wet streaks running down her cheeks. Grint thought of going to her, but the ultimate truth of the vision stopped him. Everything he'd done to this point, sacrificed, and tried to keep her from. It had all been worthless. Her destiny was the same as it always was. He had nothing left to give her but cold anger. Grint eased himself into the shadows. With the ritual done, no one would expect him to stay or care where he went.

"Be silent," Empty Candle called out. "Be silent. There is a solution."

The tribe stifled their tears and listened. "The Spirit Lords have guided us. We will honor Thundering Toad's request for aid and embark upon a quest..."

That was all Grint needed to hear. Grabbing a skin of wine from the tables, he pulled the cork free with his teeth and drank. If the kid wanted the willen to help, they could help her. There was no kry-damned way he was embarking on any more quests. No money in quests. Just a lot of misery. Grint stopped along the sandy shore where they'd landed hours before. The night sky sparkled with a million stars. Grant sat and continued drinking what might have been wine. Dawn was in the first steps of breaking, turning the eastern sky a soft shade of pink.

It was time to come up with his own plan. He had nothing left outside the clothes on his back, which had seen better days. If the map in his mind was correct, he was well north of the Sentent Sea. *Not much here.* Perhaps he could get Tin Boots to arrange for someone to take him downriver. Or give him a canoe. Wouldn't need to be far, just to the closest farm or trading post. From there, he could work and steal his way through the hedge kingdoms until he got to Marietta. One of the few fences he trusted, a man named Penser had been haranguing him for years to do a job. This situation qualified as being desperate enough to take him up on it. Eleanor would come for him once the Stabbing passed. Grint knew it would be personal for her. Spiru would come too; and Ballastrine. They would all have to get behind Rent. *Going to need a lot of eyes in the back of my head. Maybe Tin Boots has the right idea. Get out and stay out.*

"Stay close should the camp," a willen bone thrower said in a terrible approximation of broken standard.

"Charffing goat vomit," Grint jumped at the suddenness of the voice. He needed to get better at watching his back. The willen warrior emerged from the trees, gray ash smeared across his orange face. Without a second glance at Grint he stepped to the water's edge and scanned the high cliffs.

"You haven't found a bag, have you?" Grint used his hands to give the dimensions, but the bone thrower never looked. "Might have washed up? I dropped it in..."

"The dark stirs."

"Right," Grint replied, unsure if that was what the willen meant to say.

"Human to camp and safe," even in broken standard the disdain was clear. "Will not ask again."

"So much for being an honored guest." Grint wandered off, stifling the desire to use a willen profanity. A foolish desire that would earn him the blunt end of the warrior's spear. No reason to be angry with the willen, they'd done him a great service and saved his hide. It was just easier than being angry with...

"Lark," he said. She stood in the path, big brown saucer eyes staring at him. "Shouldn't you be getting ready for your quest?"

"Our quest, right?"

"This wine disappeared quick," he shook the empty skin. "What's the quest?"

"Glagarat? To live with the Mopey Kind," she said, unsure of the words.

"Gorgolath," Grint corrected. "The Magicai." They were a quixotic bunch, but the greatest practitioners of magic in Terragard. If anyone could help a dennel it would be them. Grint's own relationship with them was tumultuous. He had both stolen for and from them. "You'll love it, they have a floating castle."

"Oh," she said.

"Not exactly Thiel though, is it?"

"No," she replied, kicking at a stone half buried in the dirt. "Will you come?"

"Not for all the boats in Abersinth." Grint tossed the wine skin aside and walked past her. Lark latched onto his waist, holding on as hard as she could. "Get off, kid."

"No! Stay with me!"

"Get off," Grint shouted as he pried her loose. Lark landed on her rear and skidded twice. The look of hurt in those eyes almost cracked his defenses. "I told you before, I don't do quests. I'm not a hero who saves people."

"Yes, you do," she challenged.

"What? You?" Grint gave her a hard stare. "I didn't save you. What did you think would happen when the bad people stopped coming? Did you think we'd buy a farm and grow turnips or milk pigs? That I would just forget about the magical land of Thiel?"

"I'm sorry I..." the girl stammered through tears.

"Stop it! I'm a thief. I steal things and get money for them. So far on this little journey you've cost me a lot." Grint counted it off on his fingers. "Fourteen thousand gold for the urn, sixty thousand Orrish barsuls for the jewels. Make it one hundred thousand for all the things in my bag, and then there's the king's ransom for returning you to Thiel. I've killed people for a fraction of that."

"You don't kill," she said as she wiped her nose on her sleeve.

"That man in Finder's Lot? The one you called Papa Deego? That's Calabassus Rent. He's the God of Murder and he showed up because he wants me as his shadow servant." Lark shook her head back and forth as he yelled. "He wants me because I've killed lots of people."

"That's not true!"

Grint got on his knees and right in her face. Defiant, she didn't back down, didn't wilt. Grint respected that. "Wake up, kid. The world is a cruel place. If you leave here with me, you're done. The moment those necromancers catch us, I'll sell you off to save my skin and make back my money."

Lark punched him with the bottom of her fist, hitting his cheek once, twice, three times. Grint took a step back, and she followed suit. They stood looking at one another until Lark screamed, thrusting her hands toward him. The white light flickered but did nothing more.

"Now you're getting it, kid. Save yourself." Lark ran away, sobbing as the night swallowed her. When her cries faded, he looked up at the morning sky and said, "Better she learns it now, right? Right?"

To that there was no answer. No Hobbe. No Jessua. "Just talking to my banjaxed, kry-damned self."

The birds sang their morning song hopping from branch to branch. With no sleep since the assassin knocked him out, he knew he needed a few hours or a few days. Whatever the willen would give him. From there he could make his way on foot. No need for the river. Somewhere along the way, he could steal a horse and ride to Marietta.

"Is there a yurt I can sleep in?" Grint asked a passing willen who didn't understand, so he mimed sleeping and pointed at the yurts and then back to himself. She pointed to the yurt on her left and went back to her morning work.

The village had begun their morning, cleaning the refuse from their revelries. Whenever they planned to leave for Gorgolath, it wasn't immediate. No travel preparations were yet being made. There was also no sign of Tin Boots, so Grint decided he would find him after he slept. Tell him his plan over a drink and get moving. No need to drag it out any longer than that.

Grint couldn't stand in the cramped yurt, but his primary goal was sleep, so he crawled. The furs sprawled across the floor were soft against his cheek. What it lacked in height the yurt made up for in length, allowing Grint to stretch out. Sleep was a comfortable shoe slipping on, so when the first willen screamed, he imagined it in a dream. Not until horns blasted did he wake, dragging his head across the hide dome as he sat up.

Nightmares from the demon realm crawled to life as he looked outside. Skeleton warriors ran amok, slashing the yurts and fighting the willen who came out. The bone throwers coordinated their attacks, but each time they struck off an arm or leg the bone rolled back and reattached itself. Grint scrambled out on all fours as the yurt collapsed. The air whistled as a pitted cudgel swung towards him. Rolling onto his back, he dodged again. The weapon bashed against the ground, bouncing loose pebbles and acorns. A massive skeleton, adorned in rings of silver armor and a tarnished, copper cudgel straddled Grint. Its bones creaked each time it moved. Grint felt around for a weapon and came up with a tiny, stone hammer dropped by a dead willen artisan.

The skeleton laughed until Grint jammed the hammer into its groin. When it stumbled, he jumped to his feet and onto it. With his thumbs in the empty sockets of its skull, Grint planted his feet against the ribs and pulled. The head came free, flying through the morning air as it escaped his grasp. The rest of the bones fell inert.

"I hate skeletons," he said. Their appearance was no coincidence. The armor was Zornish era. He'd looted enough over his lifetime to know it on sight. This was Eleanor's work. She must have awakened the burial grounds outside Finder's Lot. The horrific vision of the demon lord could still come to pass.

Grint grabbed the copper cudgel, but it was a dense thing and difficult to wield. The weight of it pulled him forward as he swung it high. In an uncontrollable run, he crashed into two skeletons disemboweling a bone thrower. One of their skulls shattered under the accidental fall of the cudgel. The other skeleton broke in half at the waist. Even as Grint lost his footing and tumbled past, he could see it beginning to repair itself. An older willen helped him up as a row of warriors pushed the advancing monsters back. Armed with a thick roller used for flattening grains, the willen cook knocked a charging skeleton aside as it flanked. Grint grabbed the roller and pointed to the shattered skull behind them. The baker smiled his understanding and ran off to tell others.

"Go get them you bloody maniac," he said, grabbing a spear and shattering the reforming skeleton's skull with the blunt end.

The village was in chaos. Fighting was widespread while skeletons set fire to anything they could. The bone priestesses threw magic, great sparks of red and blue that disintegrated the assaulting force, but there were hundreds of skeletons. Overwhelming odds against a small tribe like this. Grint saw no sign of Eleanor, but there wouldn't be, would there? She would appear when the screaming ended.

"Lark," Grint shouted as he ran. A skeleton leapt at him from a burning yurt, knocking his spear away. Grint backed up a step and charged, putting his shoulder into it. Locked in its embrace, he tore the bones apart with his bare hands. It began reassembling as he stepped past, clawing after him as it dragged itself along.

"Lark!"

A human scream differed from a Willen's. When Lark shrieked, the sound cut through the bedlam. Grint banked right, grabbing a spear stuck in the ground. Several skeletons chased him now, so he tipped over a tanning rack hoping to slow them. Through the trees, willen warriors fought against two skeletons dragging Lark by her hair. The willen swatted the arm gripping the girl, breaking it free, but it kept reattaching. Both willen fell in a spray of blood as the other skeleton slashed sharpened fingertips across their throats.

Grint swung his spear sideways and knocked the skulls off both bodies. Neither one smashed, so the headless bodies continued dragging the girl. Grint struck at the arms until one backhanded him across the face. Blood trickled down his cheek and rage overtook him. Grint picked up the thick bone staffs lying beside the dead Willen and gripped all three together. He struck at headless monsters, bone shards flying in every direction.

"I. Just. Got. Healed," he shouted as he hacked away. The skulls rolled toward him, mouths snapping at his ankles until he stomped them back into dust. The reforming bones fell lifeless around Lark, who cried and crawled into Grint's arms.

"Smash the skulls," Grint yelled at a passing willen man, not knowing if he understood. There was no time to do more. The willen would need to fend for themselves. Grint had to get the girl out of here. Lark smiled at him and opened her mouth to speak, but he covered it and shook his head.

"You're going to call me a bloody hero or say I rescued you again. Just don't." Lark smiled and nodded but the happiness faltered. More skeletons closed in on them, and they brought reinforcements. A large, skeletal bear smashed through a yurt with its gargantuan head and roared in silent triumph. The surrounding skeletons banged swords against leather bracers as they urged the beast on.

"Fuzz-lipped, blasted, horn-pocked, silken-suited sons of monkeys and..." the litany of profanity continued as he ran with Lark in his arms. She climbed onto his back, so he could swing the bone staff. They darted back and forth between trees, Lark calling out where the skeletons were. Their only advantage was that the bear was a slow, ponderous thing that had trouble navigating the confines of the forest. The human skeletons did not share its limitations. They ran with great speed and climbed the trees, leaping from limb to limb.

"Lark, your magic?" Her weight shifted, and the spark of white flashed, but nothing more.

"It's still not working," she yelled back. More profanity.

Grint knocked skeletons aside when he could, but his angle was poor. There was no strength in the swings, so the skulls never broke. He only slowed them down. They would keep coming until he found a place to stand and fight. Searching, they ran down a gentle slope, Grint's feet slipping on wet leaves. It was a losing battle. Only a matter of time. The skeletons would never tire, never stop, but Grint would.

A skeleton dropped from the trees and landed on Lark. Grint lost his footing, and the three of them tumbled another fifteen feet before bashing into a tree. The skull came to rest beside Grint, so he smashed it with a stone and stood to face the rest. One at a time or all at once, he would take down as many as he could.

A stream bed trickled behind them, leading to a small waterfall. Beyond that, he heard water flowing through rocks. Sparing a glance, he saw a large lake, its shore maybe five-hundred feet away. "Lark, run down to the water."

"What about you?"

"I'll be behind you," he said. The skeletons stopped advancing and massed in front of him, banging their swords again. Grint looked for the bear. It stood further back, still as a statue. The swords continued.

Thump thump thump. Thump thump thump. Swords they never used. We're being herded again.

"Lark, keep running!" he shouted a moment before the hound blindsided him.

14

"Of all the men I've killed, you were my favorite."

- Wolf General Appa to the Rope of Naringham

Eleanor strode through the forest, watching as Callum tackled the thief. The magnificence of the hound's form was on display as he leapt. Such beauty and grace wrapped in a deadly skin of muscle and teeth. Both hound and human tumbled, kicking up scraps of dead leaves until they splashed in the shallow remnants of a dying stream. Callum barked, his jaws snapping mere inches from the thief's exposed neck. Grint's arms strained under the weight, and he rocked them back and forth into a roll. Together, they disappeared over the edge of the waterfall. The little thing they hunted had the audacity to scream at Eleanor before chasing after her guardian. It would please her to watch the girl die, but did it still please her to watch Count Danghier rise in power?

The skeletons gathered behind her, hesitant to move without her command, but the dead fidgeted. They inched toward the edge of the falls, restless to move, to act, to live again. Eleanor waved her hand to dismiss them. Their appearance, the necessity for them, rankled her to the core. Skeletal teeth chattered as they ran up the slope, herding the undead bear with them. She thought the situation to be well in hand when she arrived at the rambler town. It was not her fault a god intervened. *It was not my fault!*

"The most pathetic excuse of the failed is that it was not their fault," she said with a promise to punish herself further. Perhaps the count would view her pro-active punishment as an act of contrition.

As soon as she left the Terrastags, cowardly Garas contacted the count and informed him of all developments. *The sniveling, mewling traitor!* Had she found success in Finder's Lot, forgiveness may have been hers. Escaping that bloodbath with her life and those of her hounds felt like victory. *The God of Murder is real!* Eleanor fought her way to the bridge, staying well clear of the deity, his shadows, and the death they dealt.

The count waited outside the town, smiling at the sounds of carnage as if he were an old dog basking in the morning sun. Crossing the bridge drenched in viscera, she approached her master. The count tilted his head, a look she knew too well. Walking out of the town empty-handed left her no room for reasonable discourse. Victory turned to ash. At the count's command, Garas and a fist of necromancers raised the Zornish warriors from their slumber. To Eleanor's great shock, the count did what he had never done before. He gave her a third chance.

A blood red hound and brindle brown with scarred muzzle padded up beside her to sit at attention. Sinew hung from their jaws. They'd eaten well of the little folk Eleanor clapped her hands, and both hounds transformed into armored soldiers, ready for battle. Malus and Tamos knelt on her flanks as she ran fingers through their hair. Even as men, she preferred treating them as dogs.

"Callum has our prey," she said. "Let us finish this business."

They drew their swords, pleasure radiating off them. Killing the thief had become a personal goal for each of them. They put that aside and remained by her side as she stepped to the edge of the falls. Calling it a waterfall was a fallacy, the forest stream did little more than trickle over the edge where it splashed into a muddy pool. A dried-out river bed of stone and puddles of brackish water extended toward the shores of a lake. Eleanor lifted her face to the rising sun. The warmth kissed her cheek as cool air, thick with the smells of pine and wet stone blew past. On this day, the sweetest sense for Eleanor was the taste of victory.

Callum was a few hundred feet away, running and fighting with the thief who struggled to keep the hound apart from the child. A wordless yell echoed as Callum tore a chunk out of the thief. The little thing threw rocks and darted into a cave when the hound turned its attention on her. Faithful and ever dutiful, Callum loped after her, sniffing the air as he vanished inside. The thief stood, mouthing a curse as he picked up a giant rock and followed. Eleanor watched as he paused, chest heaving and slick with sweat. Was he considering leaving? *Escape shall not be yours, thief. Our business goes beyond the child.* As if he heard her thoughts, he looked their direction and smiled. Then entered the cave.

"Always insufferable. Come," Eleanor commanded. "Callum will either finish this or flush them out."

Descending the rocks in a series of lithe steps, Eleanor avoided the muddy pool. After all the trials, humiliations, and failures she'd endured and continued to endure, it would be a great vindication to hold the child out for her master. As they neared the cave mouth, she issued hand signals for the hounds to flank the entrance. Eleanor basked in the sunlight, sword drawn to await the outcome.

*****

The weight of the rock strained the bite wound on his left arm, tearing the skin, but it was the only thing he had left to fight with. A deep darkness filled the cave, making the footing precarious at best, as narrow walls brushed against his shoulders. He hoped he wouldn't have to drop the rock and crawl. Twice his foot slipped on rocks slick with algae and once in a crack that twisted his ankle. Yanking it free, he rotated the foot, thankful he didn't snap the bone. Echoes danced off the rock, playing tricks in the darkness. The hound growled, and the girl screamed. Sounds intertwined and surrounded him, making him dizzy. The light dimmed the deeper he went until it resembled a cloudless night when Effulg waned. Vague shapes moved through the dark. Grint hoped it was Lark, or even Noseless. Krypsie only knew what else could live in a place like this. *Cave trolls. Red tips. Basilisks.* The kid grunted by the back wall, trying to wriggle through a crack too small even for her.

Noseless had a midnight black coat, making him difficult to see as anything more than a shadow within a shadow. The girl screamed when the hound bit into her leg. Grint rushed forward, kicking a scatter of stones as he entered a larger chamber. The hound turned, the movement nearly imperceptible, but enough light had seeped in to cast a highlight on the edge of his fur. Grint swung the rock and connected against the hound's head. The mutt tumbled left, followed by the thump of stone as he struck the wall. Without his full vision, Grint relied on sound and brought rock down where he heard the beast's snorting breath. Its fur grew wet with blood after each strike. Noseless whimpered, making half-hearted attempts to fight back. A sharp crack of bone ended the struggle. Grint tossed the rock away, a dull sucking sound came from the hound as it labored for air. Warm blood dripped from his hand as Grint shuffled backwards, breath heavy.

A small hand reached around his and squeezed. His gut reaction was to strike at it, but he blinked and saw the silhouette of the girl. The sounds of pain changed from canine to man as Grint led her away. A wavering shaft of sunlight came through the crack, teasing them with a point of egress in an otherwise dead-end cave. The crack was long but narrow. Too small for him, but if he could widen it, maybe he could squeeze Lark through. Grint found another stone and struck the wall. Sparks flew, after brief flashes of light. He pounded until the stone broke apart in his hands, leaving his knuckles swollen and bleeding.

A flash of white light shocked him and then another. Grint felt a momentary surge of hope that she could spirit them away. It faded as her light did. Lark's power hadn't returned. The darkness settled over them like a death shroud.

"I'm sorry," she whispered. The apology echoed back.

"We'll go out the front," Grint said, knowing it was suicide to exit the way they came. Callum laughed and coughed something in the dark. knowing the truth, the same as Grint. Escape meant getting past Eleanor, hounds, and the undead. They couldn't remain here either. How long before Eleanor sent the other hounds? Before the skeletons? Before Eleanor came in herself?

"Grint," Lark whispered as they neared the cave mouth. The fear in her voice shook him because it was also his.

Eleanor stood at the ready, ten feet from the cave, holding a long sword to the side at an angle. Her expression flat, unreadable, but that made it more menacing. The woman didn't need to scowl. Didn't need to gloat. Her actions were her emotions.

"Everything we've been through, this will be easy." Grint ruffled the girl's hair as he spoke, but she had met Eleanor in the streets of Finder's Lot. Witnessed her brutality. The other reality he hid from her was how tired he felt. Dry Twig ordered him to rest, and he hadn't abided the rules. All magic had rules. A cold fire spread through his chest, radiating out from his heart. This wasn't the thief's gut, it was a raging inferno burning down a forest. A small voice scared to accept this fate cried out in his mind. It wasn't Jessua or even Hobbe. This was Grint; The five-year-old dirty urchin boy stealing his way across Dirty Gull in service to Hanging Ben's wallet.

Are you going to die for this girl? Do I grow up to be so pointless? Grint tried to shut it out, but its nagging was incessant. Lark tugged on his sleeve, her eyes begging for reassurance they would survive this. *You let Tebbs die. You let Jessua die. Just let this one die! Lunacy! Madness!*

"Grint?"

"Stay here, kid." Grint let her hand drop from his as he stepped out of the cave.

*****

Eleanor kept a keen eye on the cave, waiting for some sign of Callum. Nothing stirred since the flashes of light. If the thief and girl evaded capture again, it would mean her life. The rope given by the count was long enough to hang, resurrect, and hang her again. Waiting was no longer a luxury afforded her. The others would need to go in. Eleanor prepared the order, but then the thief stepped out, arms wide, and weaponless.

"If you imagine being unarmed will save you, then you have miscalculated."

"I hoped it might help in that regard," the thief smiled. "Not sure what you want with me. You have Black Samuel's head, so you must have the urn. The better thief finished the job. I concede."

"I am in no mood for your foolishness," Eleanor said. "Bring me the girl."

"When you had the head, did it talk to you? I saw its mouth moving, so it must have. He was a terrible conversationalist. I feel bad for you."

"The girl. I will not ask again." Their eyes locked, so she could see the slight shift in his posture, rocking back and forth. *He is watching Tamos and Malus.* The men stalked closer every moment. Eleanor flicked her hands, issuing a silent order to stop. Was Grint drawing them in to unleash more trickery? If so, she would deny him that strategy.

"You don't want the girl. She's more trouble than she's worth. And we estimated her worth at fourteen thousand galleons, yes?" Her men waited with tense anticipation. She could feel their desire to jump at him, but he appeared unfazed. What trickery did he have in store for her?

"How about we make it twenty-eight thousand," Eleanor smiled a wolf's grin.

The thief laughed. "That's good. I know that scam. Do you want me to sing you a song from the last time someone tried it? I recall Tamos loves my singing."

"What about the scam where I kill you a thousand different ways? Now, do what I ask."

"I don't know that one," he said, sparing quick glances and frowning at their inaction. Why did he want them close? What was he planning? "How about I counter with this? Give us a head start and I won't kill Noseless."

Tamos screamed a despairing sound through gritted teeth. Eleanor stepped forward, pointing her sword at the thief's throat. Grint threw his hands up as he stepped back. "Whoa! Hold on. Hold on!" When Eleanor lowered her sword, he said calmly, "Let's go back to the twenty-eight thousand..."

Something struck him in the back of the head, pitching Grint forward. A small rock tumbled across the ravine. The child ran out of the cave turning left towards the lake. It surprised Tamos to see her, but he recovered and reached to ensnare her. The little thing put both hands in his face blinding him with a flash of white light, and he fell to the ground, writhing with his eyes covered. Without breaking stride, the little monster scampered over him and continued toward the lake.

That was enough. Eleanor would end this herself once and for all. "Mistress!" Malus's terrified voice cracked, so she turned...

*****

She hit me with a stone! In the back of the head! Grint conceded that during the conversation he'd offered to sell her. *I need to explain what it means to wait for my signal.* Blood slicked the back of his head as he struggled to his feet. The stone barely broke the skin but head wounds gushed no matter how small. I told her the plan, didn't I? Grint's recollection on that point was vague. All he remembered was telling her to stay put as his own thoughts screamed. *She must have thought I was trying to sell her. Again.* He as much as told her he would in the willen camp.

Explanations would have to wait for their survival, an outcome far from guaranteed. Lark ran for the water while Crosshatch writhed on the ground. The girl did her part; the rest was up to Grint. Eleanor's focus strayed as she watched Lark. The distraction gave him an opening to exploit. Torchy screamed his warning as Grint put a shoulder into her midsection. They rolled across the rocks in a heap. Eleanor jammed her thumbs into Grint's eyes, so he dropped an elbow into her throat and her grip fell away. Her sword glistened in the morning light, Grint picked it up, ready to end the woman.

Skinling transformations disquieted Grint. Watching human flesh turn to beast - *and where in Krypsie's name do their clothes go?* Torchy turned to his hound form, dark leather jerkin and pants morphing into red fur. His claws scratched against the rocks as he bound toward them. Grint spun and bent his knees, ready to roll when the hound leapt. In midair, Torchy turned back to a man. Their swords clashed, and the vibration shook his injured shoulder, breaking apart the willen healing. Grint cried out, clutching the joint. Torchy went back into hound form, growling at Grint as he circled around to where Eleanor lay. Then back again to man so that he could scoop his injured mistress into his arms. Grint fought through the pain. Holding the sword with both hands, he put everything he had into it and slashed Torchy down the length of his spine. The leather jerkin tore open, driving the hound to his knees.

I can do this, he thought. I am doing this. The hounds are down, Eleanor is down. I have her sword. Run kid, I'll be along and...

*****

Rage consumed Eleanor. She had been so singularly focused on the child that she left herself open to attack. Malus screamed into the stones beside her, his back an open wound. There was a depth of violence to Grint's fighting style she had not expected. It wasn't elegant, but it was effective. As she stood to face him, a crossbow bolt whistled through the air and buried itself in his left shoulder. The impact spun him in circles before he dropped to his knees. Another high-pitched whistle. This bolt glanced off his right temple. It struck the ground and shattered into a thousand shards. The final bolt struck his stomach. Grint shuddered and coughed up blood.

With his head down, the blood in his mouth streamed onto the rocks. He gazed at her from beneath his brows, a look somewhere between his indignation at her cheating and admiration for the same. A look that reminded her of... Eleanor shuddered. The God of Murder looked at her in such a way, a baleful stare that scorched her to the core. She had never held a belief in the gods. Assumed them to be the mewling myths of the pathetic and desperate, but that man, that being who stood before her was of such undeniable divinity that the very air became a weapon assaulting her in waves. The enormity of his power in opposition to her own master was to compare the Mother Moon to a mote of dust existing at the moment the sunlight caught it. She cried in private, for her shattered idolatry of Count Danghier and the knowledge that no demon in any of the Seven Realms could stand against such a being.

So, what was it then, to kill this human the god so coveted? What retribution would they face?

"Mistress," the crossbowman called as he approached. Two soldiers trotted from the lake shore, adorned in thick, wine-colored, leather armor. A raised image on the breast piece depicted a horned demon riding a four-legged beast with a serpentine tail. Atherton's Drach Riders. That smarmy bastard would want the credit for this.

"Why are you here? This was my honor," she said as they walked past, crossbows on shoulders, to examine their shots.

"You see," the elder of the two said, "you missed the shot because you gripped the stock too hard. Pulled it on recoil." The man ran a finger along the cut above Grint's ear. The thief swatted weakly at them.

"I asked what you're doing here," Eleanor repeated.

"I heard, but I don't answer to you," the elder said. The three slashes on his shoulder piece marked him as a Sergeant, but Atherton taught his corpsmen that even the lowliest among them was above everyone else. A foolish notion. It fueled Eleanor's anger, and she was far from unarmed. The Singing Blade hummed in her belt, a hungry sound excited by its desire to feed. Eleanor drew it, filling the morning with the song of death. The younger soldier reacted first.

He lifted his head and saluted, "Death is the gift long promised." They knew she could kill them and didn't care. To them it was an honor, the next step in their misguided devotion to the count. How far had she fallen from her own devotion that she now thought it misguided?

The thundering gallop of horses approaching brought an end to their standoff, such as it was. Six riders silhouetted against the shimmering surface of the lake rode in formation. On the far left, the rider struggled with a writhing child slung over the saddle. *They have the child,* Eleanor realized. She knew well the lead rider's countenance, and she sheathed the knife to its great disappointment. Eleanor pulled Malus to his feet so the count would not see him as weak. Tamos nursed his own wounds as he limped over to bare his brother's weight.

"Your eyes?" she asked.

"The child blinded me, but the effect is fading. Do I smell the count?"

"Yes, my pup," she whispered as the riders slowed to a stop.

"Eleanor," Danghier greeted her with a delighted cackle. "I believe you lost this. Again." Garas had the girl draped over his horse and turned to pat her on the back in coordination with the count's words. All six men laughed.

"I was dealing with the thief." Her tone cool and unapologetic. "The child would not have gotten far."

"It appears my bowmen dealt with the thief, Houndmistress," General Atherton said to more laughter, but only five of the six joined in. The count frowned at her, squinting his eyes the way he did when he looked inside her mind.

Danghier kicked a leg over the saddle and dismounted with the fluid grace of a water dancer. The tight, black riding pants stretched with his movements, the intricate, silver piping along the seams added flair to his fine physique. His black, leather boots, laced to his knees, clacked on the stones as he landed. A soft breeze rustled the loose, gray shirt, half buttoned to bare his chest. The count pulled his black coat from the pommel of his destrier and slipped it on. Thick, wooden buttons jangled as he put his hands through the white, lace cuffs. His black hair always oiled and slicked back from his flawless, pale face. The small spikes woven into the long point of his goatee jingled as he walked towards her. They were no mere affectations; Eleanor once witnessed the deadly barbs exsanguinate a man in a heartbeat. They converted blood into raw magical power the count could use at his leisure.

"What is this I sense?" he asked as those slate-gray eyes bore into her. "Has your commitment faltered? Have seeds of contempt found root in the mind I created." Danghier punctuated it all by putting a single finger against her forehead and pushing. "How is that possible? Were the failures you experienced of my making?"

"No," she said as little more than a mumble.

"No, they were not. I lay the errors at your feet." Danghier circled her as he talked, the barbs in his beard coming dangerously close to her neck. "Had you hired Black Samuel, as I ordered, we would have been able to avoid this chicanery."

"I found Black Samuel to be incompetent..." Eleanor stopped speaking as Danghier grabbed a handful of her hair and pulled it with just enough pressure to keep her off balance.

"You question my omniscience and doubt my perfection. And all because you cannot accept your own shortcomings. Black Samuel would have completed the job and been easy to dispose of. Black Samuel..."

"Was a basher and an imbecile," Grint coughed more blood after he spoke. "I watched him work; he wasn't even good for a basher. Eleanor made the right choice."

"Who is this that deems himself worthy to speak?" Danghier let go of her hair and walked over to Grint. The thief swayed back and forth, fighting against unconsciousness. The count steadied him by grabbing his face under the chin and forcing him to look up. "Such a base creature. Ruled by emotion rather than money. How did you corrupt the incorruptible? Cause failure in the infallible?"

"I believe there's been a mistake." With his face in the Count's hand, his words came out as nearly unintelligible mush. "I have a deep affection for money."

"Do you now?" The count let go, sneering at the blood left on his gloves.

"We were in the middle of negotiations when those milk sauced gangers showed up. I believe we settled on twenty-eight thousand galleons." Grint spread his lips wide in a painful smile filled with blood. "For services rendered."

"The very cheek!" Danghier backhanded Grint across the face. The thief crumpled onto the rocks but laughed like a mummer as he lay there.

"When I kill you, I'll tear your skull out through your throat," Grint laughed until the bloody cough shut him up. The count shook his head, holding the glove out for an attendant to clean.

A bird of prey screamed as it rose into the sky, a fresh kill in its talons. Eleanor allowed herself the whisper of a smile. There was murder being done in this place. Was the god watching even now? Or could he see only the moment of death? Would he appear and lay waste to them all?

"What are you doing?" The count looked at her, a deep scowl on his face. Eleanor bowed.

"Apologies, Master. I was just being cautious."

"By watching the sky?" The count's voice became mirthful, a signal to the others it was time for them to laugh. "Should we worry about flying willen? Or are you still scared of dragons?"

Their laughter masked the guttural growl until it reached a terrifying crescendo. The thief moved with such speed and ferocity she'd not thought possible, yanking the crossbow bolt from his gut as he moved. The count's eyes widened in disbelief. He stood frozen, helpless as Grint slashed at him with the bloody bolt. Eleanor was a hair faster and grabbed the back of Grint's collar, pulling him away from her master. It was a close thing; The tip tore through the count's gray shirt but nothing more. Perhaps she should have let him do it, but the old training was too ingrained for her to allow harm to come to the man she called master.

The younger Drach Rider jumped when Grint first moved. The knee-jerk, frightened boy fired his weapon wildly. Having not learned from his earlier lesson, he pulled the shot. As Eleanor pulled Grint away from her master, the bolt whizzed past, burying itself in General Atherton's eye instead. The old bastard gasped and moved his mouth but nothing came out. The life gone from him; He fell from the saddle. *Death is the gift long promised.* Eleanor smiled to herself.

When Eleanor pulled Grint back, she stabbed the Singing Blade into the open wound in his belly. The blade sighed in exultation as it drank his blood. Eleanor held him close, putting her mouth against his ear and whispering, "Tell your master I would serve him. I would murder the world for him. Can he see us now? Can he hear me?" Grint flailed his arms, trying to hit her. It was a pathetic attempt with no strength behind it. When she pulled the blade free, he slid from her grasp, slumping on his knees.

Count Danghier stood over the young Drach Rider, the deadly barbs in his beard devouring the last of his blood. The desiccated husk turned to dust within the armor, piling at the count's feet. "What did you say to him?"

"Only that I was fulfilling my promise to kill him," Eleanor lied, and the count couldn't tell. The omnipotence he claimed to possess was nothing more than another story.

Danghier ran a finger through his slashed shirt as he approached. "You have failed me more than I've allowed anyone else. Yet you remain useful." He put his hand over hers and relieved her of the Singing Blade.

"I remember when I gave you this. Has it served you well?" Eleanor nodded. The count grasped her left forearm with intense strength and in one swift motion severed her hand at the wrist. There was no pain, not yet. Her mind had yet to comprehend the loss and register what it was she should feel. The blade sang so sweet and even more so as the count had it flat against the wound. With a whispered word, the barbs in his beard glowed amber and sent streaks of fire into the blade. The Singing Blade glowed with white fire, searing her wound. The pain came crashing in, but she knew enough to remain quiet. A single scream and he would kill her. When finished, he placed the knife in her right hand and tapped her cheek.

"Punishment is how we grow, is it not?"

"Yes, master," the urge to scream grew as she spoke.

"Good. Now gather your hounds, or are you unable to manage even them?"

It was an odd question, but she understood once she saw Tamos and Malus walking towards the cave. "Their brother has not come out."

"Leave him then," Count Danghier said with a lazy wave of his hand. "The next part of your penance. Someone put Atherton's body on the back of a horse. Why must I issue every command? Anticipate."

The Singing Blade was dead, the metal grew dull and rusty before her eyes. The count's magic burned out whatever lay inside when he sealed her stump. Eleanor could no longer look at it, so she dropped it beside the thief and whistled for the hounds to join her. We must leave you for now, sweet Callum, but I will remember this place and return.

"Good news, Eleanor! We have an extra horse for you. Hurry now before I change my mind."

Eleanor mounted the offered beast. Something she found challenging with just one hand, but she managed it, even under the scrutinizing gaze of Danghier and his retinue. Her faithful hounds, just two remaining now, flanked the horse as they rode east along the lake. Why had the God of Murder not arrived? Grint was dead. Atherton, the soldier, and countless willen, all dead. Yet the god remained aloof. Had she misjudged what he was? The strength of his power? *No, I know what I felt.*

The thief's journey ended in blood. Danghier had his prize, and the Stabbing drew near. Looking back, she watched the thief until tall pines obscured him from view. Her eulogy for him consisted of a single thought, *Such a waste.*

15

"His ghost in the glade, drawing her near.
Be not afraid, come and die my dear."

- *The Sadness Song*

The sound of galloping horses receded, leaving just the trickle of water, sighing of boughs in the wind, and an occasional animal's call. Grint took a breath, sucking in air that tasted like a blacksmith's forge. A burning furnace ignited in his chest, and when he sat up, blood filled his mouth. A cool wind brushed the back of his neck. The sensation felt glorious, until he vomited. With his eyes closed he didn't know if it was on himself or the ground. Dying was bad business, but still he smiled.

"I tricked you. I'm not dead yet." Maybe not, but he would be soon.

Someone left a blade laying on the rocks. A rusty thing and dull enough to have trouble with butter, but anything was better than nothing. The knife looked familiar, but it must have been here for a long time. *Perhaps a skeleton dropped it?* Whatever its origin, the pock-marked edge had the right amount of bite to tear open the seam of his coat. Something beneath it poked into his ribs as he played dead. And before he died for real, he wanted to know what it was. *No point going to the Afterwards with a mystery to solve. That's what makes vengeful spirits. I think.*

The rusty butter knife wasn't Blackblade and Grint struggled to cut more than a few threads along the inner seam. The unknown item provided a grand mystery to solve and as he thought on it more, hope bloomed. Could it be something from his old bag? Maybe something magic, one last trick for the thief. One last escape from death. Drenched with blood, he had to peel his clothes away to see beneath. His fingers fumbled with the act, tearing open scabs or removing skin each time. More blood leaked out every moment, pooling in the recesses of the fabric.

Grint's mind wandered, the mystery losing its luster. Pulling the knife out of his shirt, the troublesome seam tore with it, depositing a small vial into his lap. At first glance he thought it empty, but when he plucked it from a pool of his own blood, it too contained blood. *Lark's blood.* Somehow the vial survived the arduous journey from the Terrastags.

He fell onto his back, laughing, or what he approximated as a laugh. A pile of leather armor lay beside him, ash and dust swirling in the wind. Pieces of bone, still decaying stuck out at weird angles. A small piece of skull, the eye socket intact, sat in a mound of dust. It made it look like the skull was watching him. Judging him on his death. Grint didn't know who he was, perhaps the archer who shot him.

"We all die penniless and alone, that's what I told Dry Boots...Tin Twig. My friend. Well, Skully, that's not the case. Not anymore." Using his thumb, he popped the cork stopper and poured the blood into his mouth. The empty vial fell from his limp hand and shattered. Near as he could figure, touching her blood let him hear Jessua and sometimes see her. Drinking it had to have the same effect. He would die with her in his eyes. Penniless, but not alone.

"What?" Grint asked as he turned towards Skully. "Oh, that looks nice." Staying awake was too hard, so he laid down beside his new friend. The sunbaked warmth of the rock provided a nice counter to the cold wind.

Droplets of blood fell from his fingers as he lifted his arm. Grint petted the top of the skull and rested his hand there. It crumbled under his touch.

"Rest in peace, Skully," he murmured with his eyes closed. They murdered Grint, so it stood to reason that Rent would see this. Not having to run from the god gave him a reason to smile. "But tell Rent he's too late. Take it up with Hobbe. They can squabble over a new fool."

Grint drifted off...

*****

She lived in an old covered wagon cramped with books and clothes. What passed for furniture were planks of wood balancing over cauldrons or crates. Everything kept simple enough for her to transform it into a workbench when the need arose. Scorch marks ran up the walls like paintings, mixing with the stink of things cooked, boiled, or burned. She'd patched the hole in the roof a dozen times, but it always fell apart. The magical fire that made it left behind a residue that disintegrated wood, so even the patches fell apart after a few days. The wagon sat on the edge of a farm, nestled between two trees and a puddle-sized pond with three fish. To a seventeen-year-old thief like Grint, it was a palace. Hobbe's prized apprentice never had his own home, so Jessua's old wagon was as close to perfection as he could imagine.

Grint leaned back in a wooden chair. The one piece of real furniture she owned. Its back scraped against the little red door with rusty hinges that squawked when you opened it.

"If the edges of the hole are the problem, why don't you cut the planks out and replace them?"

"If you want to get a wood saw and some wood, you're welcome to do it," Jessua said, head buried in her work. Today she busied herself by cutting pungent swamp leaves into tiny pieces. When she had an ample pile, they went into a large bottle over heat. Grint hadn't a clue what it was for, but the alchemist asked her to do it, so she did. *The duty of the apprentice isn't to ask why*, Hobbe's voice chimed in.

"I can't. I have important circus business to attend to."

"Are we back to the circus farce?" She didn't look up as she spoke, her attention remained on the task and her hands were as steady as any thief when she cut. "I thought we agreed it wasn't necessary."

"I never agreed," Grint said. "I value your neck too much."

Hobbe brought his young crew to the Barrows intending to rob Lord Carr of his sizeable vault. With Hobbe, it was never about walking in and taking something. Any basher could do that. Hobbe's first lesson for his 'children' was to rob someone so they thanked you for it. For this job, they posed as a circus troupe. Hobbe worked every facet of the plan, re-worked it, and had them rehearse it until no variable existed - except for Grint falling in love with the alchemist's apprentice. How could he not? No matter the efforts he took, he remained unable to keep his eyes off her. And thank Krypsie she felt the same.

"Just my neck?"

"All of you, my love," Grint replied. If Hobbe found out about her...that she knew who they were and what they were doing...

Jessua got up from her bench, straightening the light green dress full of holes and patches. *It's my work dress*, she would say when he teased her about it. Taking a rare break, she sat on Grint's lap. Even the apron showed stains in a hundred different colors, but it was her eyes Grint couldn't get enough of. She linked her arms around his neck and kissed him. It was a soft kiss, filled with endless possibility. Comfortable. When she stopped, she pressed her forehead against his and smiled.

"You reek of swamp leaf," Grint laughed. Jessua stood up and pulled the legs of the chair out so he toppled to the floor.

"Nobody's perfect." She sat back at her workbench. Grint brushed himself off and stood behind her, burying his face in her soft, brown hair. She melted into him and sighed.

"I have to finish this."

"I know," Grint's voice was a mumble in her hair.

"And you have important circus business."

"Meet me.Tonight, in the orchard."

"Past curfew?" Her question was tentative, nervous. Breaking Lord Carr's curfew was dangerous. "Why?"

"I plan to pick a lot of pockets at the afternoon performance, and I'll have a bag of coins for your roof."

"You are a thief!" Jessua was as good at mock outrage as anyone. They kissed again.

*****

...and then opened them again. The sun had swung past midday. *So, I've slept for a few hours at least.* Being alive came as a pleasant surprise. That he hadn't bled out or drowned in his own lungs was a treat. A tingle beneath his skin, almost like an itch, spread through his muscles when he moved.

Grint sat up, unsure at first if he would be able to. The blood on his shirt dried in the sun and cracked as the material folded, crumbling in tiny flakes across his lap. There was no pain as he flexed his hands into fists, nor from the arrow sticking out of shoulder - or the wound in his stomach. Grint ran his fingers over the rough scab where Eleanor stabbed him. If he picked at it, he imagined a stream of blood might flood out, not unlike breaking open a keg.

Getting to his feet, he cracked his neck and took a deep breat He felt fit. Ready to run. Ready to fight. The air was full of scents Grint had never experienced before. The path of a raindrop falling from a storm cloud. How long ago was the storm? A day for some, years for others. A spot of dirt on a stone left behind by a willen girl as she ran towards the lake. The last breath of a squirrel run down by a fox at dusk. All of it was there. And the colors... this was from Lark's blood. It hadn't delivered Jessua but healed him in ways he never expected.

"It won't last," a young boy said. Grint never heard him approach and scanned the horizon, wanting to piece together how he - *they* - had done it. There were three children behind him, not one. Two boys and a girl, all wearing dirty rags tied around the waist with rope. The girl held a sharp stick, the end whittled into a point. It reminded Grint of what they used to carry back on Peach Street in Dirty Gull. They would steal the spoke of a chair from the auction house and shave it into a sticker. That had been their initiation. Do that and you could work for a crew.

"Who are you?"

"The blood won't last," the three children said in unison. More children stepped out from behind them and more behind them. It continued as they multiplied across the ravine.

"Wait a tick. What?" Disbelief was the best way to describe Grint's reaction. How could all these children hide behind the first three?

"You'll still die." It was a cacophonous sound when they said it together, forcing Grint to cover his ears. The children closed their mouths, opened their eyes wide, and ran into the forest. Something had terrified them, and its shadow loomed over Grint.

Snakelike hands slithered around his throat. Grint could feel every callus, scar, and ridge of skin on those cold fingers as they squeezed his neck like iron. The hand belonged to a man, six feet tall and slender as a stick. The stove pot hat on top of his head was missing its top, so his crusty, unwashed hair stuck out at odd angles. In his nightmares, this man always had spiral circles for eyes. It was no different now. The Proprietor of Peach Street. Hanging Ben.

"Where have you been, little one?" Hanging Ben's voice came close to the sound a dying cat makes. "I looked and looked for you. Found your sister, I did." Grint was now five years old, dangling helplessly in the gang master's grip.

"Do you know what I did with dear sister? I cooked her up in a pie." Hanging Ben danced with unencumbered glee. "Every year I've had a single piece and kept the rest on ice. Every year I've promised myself that I would find you before I finished. But your sister is all gone, boy. Tucked away in my tummy because you left her behind."

Maniacal laughter, gleeful in its malevolence ripped through the air as the boy struggled against Hanging Ben's grip. It was pointless. A child had no power against such a monster. "I'll have myself a pie made just of you. Once a year, a sweet smack of Grint." Ben pulled him towards a mouth opening impossibly wide. To go into that gullet would be a place he'd never return from.

Someone struck Hanging Ben on the shoulder, and he fell to the side, releasing the boy. Grint landed on his feet, looking up at a young woman in a white dress. The wooden oar she gripped had cracked and would shatter with another strong blow. The sun set behind her, but when she smiled, it was brighter than the celestial fire highlighting wisps of her wild hair.

"Come with me, little one." Grint followed as she danced from stone to stone, the furious scream of Hanging Ben chasing behind. Urchins, drawn forth by the Proprietor's call, crawled to the surface. Their little bodies squeezed between rocks as they fought their way up, filthy faces twisted in angry scowls. They swiped at the escaping duo with hand-carved stickers. When any got too close, the girl hit them with the oar, and they shattered into dust.

There was no escape from the army of urchins, so the girl pushed him against a tree and stood in front, jabbing the oar to keep any urchins at bay. A cave mouth called to Grint, *Come in and find salvation,* but she pulled him back when he started walking. The urchins surrounded them, chanting dirty rhymes as they laughed, staying out of reach of her oar. Hanging Ben rose from the sea of destitute children, holding his arms wide, cackling as he approached.

"You can fight them," she said to the boy, who stared in transfixed terror at his approaching doom. Little Grint shook his head.

"This is no good. I need my Grint." She knelt and pressed a fingertip against his forehead as the urchin hands tore her apart. The skies cracked, a deep sound that shook him to the bone. The urchins, Hanging Ben, and even the girl broke apart in a swirling whirlwind of ash and dust. A cloud of detritus so thick it choked him, filling his nose, his throat, and his eyes.

When it cleared, he found himself in a high-roofed tent, supported by a large beam forty feet tall. Grint was still a young man, seventeen if he took Hobbe at his word. And this was a circus tent, he came to realize, leaning against the thick support rope behind the performance stage. Rows of seats built into the hillside filled with watchers. Patrons come to see the marvels of the show. During which, the younger boys of the crew - hidden in a network of tunnels under those seats - would reach up through holes to snatch a purse of coins, a piece of jewelry, or in times of great luck, an ornate weapon. It was all bonus loot. The real target of these trips was always someone important.

Grint was the escape artist, the one they trusted to slip out of dastardly, death-defying situations, but it wasn't his turn yet. A young boy held center stage, juggling with youthful exuberance. Watching him, Grint felt sad and awash with doom. A single phrase kept repeating in his mind, *Poor dead Tebbs.* The sands of life were running out for him, but it was not yet time. For now, he juggled twelve balls in a giant circle, faster and faster.

The crowd fell silent. There were no appreciative hoots. No applause. Corpses occupied the seats, gaunt faced and rotting. They stared ahead, jaws opening and closing as strings of saliva dripped down their chins. Grint's eyes slid past them to land on an empty seat in the back row. Her seat. Why did it cause him such alarm to not find her there? Because she always came to see him. Where was she?

"She dies tonight," Poor Dead Tebbs said. His attention drifted from the juggling as he addressed Grint. Each time a ball dropped, a slash appeared on his body, blood soaking his white shirt. "She's dying right now. I'll die tonight too, but you won't care about that. You'll shed no tears for Poor Dead Tebbs."

That wasn't true. Tebbs's death hit him hard, but compared to Jessua... The crowd stood as one and shambled toward him. Tebbs, a mess of cuts and blood, reached out with broken hands, swinging his fists at Grint. The ground beneath the stage erupted as corpses clawed their way to the surface. The dead came for him, and they were hungry.

Grint shoved his way through, dead hands reaching out, tearing at his clothes and flesh. Each step was a battle as he fought through a sea of the dead. Tebbs cried out, his words the wail of a banshee, "Save me, Grint. She's already gone, but you could save me. Don't let me die like you do everyone else."

They tore the last of Grint's clothes from his body as he struggled through the mouth of the tent. He stood naked in the moonlight, the tent - having served its purpose - disappeared. Blood stained his skin from a hundred dead-handed scratches, each infested with maggots. He could feel them crawling under his skin as he looked towards the horizon. The ocean's surface sat in placid serenity, lit by Effulg's soft light. A three-masted ship waited in the harbor, disguising the singular nature of its evil in a tapestry of beauty.

Grint ran. The maggots devoured him from the inside, but he did not care. This time he would save her. It wouldn't be too late. This time he would catch the cart before it reached the boat and save her. Tree limbs spread wide across the path, clawing as they sought to ensnare him. A root snaked from the dirt to wrap his ankle. Grint went end over end, an unfriendly tumble that left him feeling broken as he came to rest at the bottom.

The shoreline was a scatter of rocks in small coves dominated by overhanging trees. The waves, small and weak, lapped against the shore as they came in. A mound of white fabric, soaked through with seawater, lay piled in the surf. An arm stuck out of the fabric, burned by ice and cold as the grave.

"No," Grint sobbed as he crawled on hands and knees toward the tangle. "It didn't happen like this."

Grint pulled the heap onto his lap and cried over the girl who lay lifeless in his arms. With great care, he cradled her head in the crook of an arm as he kissed her forehead. Jessua's skin was pale blue and covered in tiny crystals of ice. There was no breath in her, but her eyes fluttered open; Milky, gray, dead eyes that moved like a blind person, searching through the darkness.

"You're alive?" Her eyes tracked to him as he spoke. She grimaced, and her tears became icicles as she brushed his face with the back of her hand. The gesture left streaks of frost against his cheek, but he didn't care.

"No, my love," she replied. "I'm dead, but you need not be."

The ocean rose, pooling around her dress, his knees, and then his waist. Jessua floated in his arms. "I'm not leaving you."

"I'm not here. It wants you to think with your heart, so it can devour you."

"What does?" The water reached his chest, so he stood and held her tight against his chest. Perhaps it was an answer to the question, but as the water rose, Lord Carr stepped off the ship and walked across the water, his hands held out as Hanging Ben's had been.

"One last kiss," she said as she slipped a hand around the back of his head and pulled him close. Sea water gushed from her mouth into his and the ocean swallowed them whole. Grint flailed beneath the icy waves, choking on the brine. As the calm acceptance of this fate came over him, the water receded.

Grint, now a man, stood on an island. The waves beat mercilessly against the shore as a strong breeze floated past, choking the air with smoke and brimstone. A behemoth dominated the island, hundreds of feet tall with red skin and molten eyes. The demon lord from Lark's vision.

"Here he is! Grint, the master thief. The marauder without conscience. The man who measures the worth of a person's life by the weight of a coin. Show him then. Show him the weight of that coin in the lives he has destroyed." It was Eleanor, standing at the feet of the demon, wearing ceremonial armor, lacquered, and detailed with burning bodies falling from the sky.

The image conjured reality. Bodies began falling through the thick black canopy of smoke. Corpses splashed into the ocean, the noise digging into his brain. Each one disappeared beneath the waves and resurfaced on shore where they threw golden coins at Grint. The gold felt no more harmful than an acorn, but as the bodies grew in number, so did the coins. They assaulted the thief on all sides. The coins piled up, burying him in their golden embrace.

The demon walked with great lumbering strides, crushing Eleanor. A volcano, hidden somewhere beneath the water, erupted, coughing its magma skyward in a glowing pillar. The demon transformed, first into Count Danghier and then into Lark. The dennel girl stood before him, skin red and blistered, eyes a deep pit of fire.

"How many dead bodies have you left in your wake?" Lark asked in a hollow voice. "Just in the time I've known you? The alchemist, Bardo. The basher, Black Samuel." Each time she said a name, the waves rose and formed a liquid image of the person and their death. "The skinling, Faighur. The thief-catchers. The harquin. The willen and your dear friend Tin Boots. The krau. Me. No wonder the God of Murder covets you so."

The sea churned with images. The dead stood on the sandy shore as the gold piled around him. "I'm sorry," he said to her.

"I am immune to your cries. If what you love is gold, we will see you drown in it." The dead were not just faces, they were faces he knew. Lives lost, some sacrificed, some he ended. "There shall be no escaping your fate. No tricks up your sleeve."

Think not with your heart, Jessua had said. But how could he do otherwise when confronted with all of this misery? Blackblade was in his hand, but he did not remember recovering it. *It wants to devour you,* Jessua whispered. Lark shrank, running toward him with blinding light forming in her hands. It became clear. Grint drove the blade into her heart...

...and the illusion shattered, falling away like broken glass. It had been the dennel blood coursing through his mind, consuming him with its hungering magic. Before he'd only exposed himself to a drop or two, but this time he'd consumed a vial.

Grint found himself in the lakeside cave, stabbing the rusty knife into stone. All the pain remained with him, the stab wounds and the blood oozing from his belly. None of it healed with her blood, and his body shook with the freezing grip of death that came with bleeding out. Breathing took effort, and he sucked in air with starving hunger.

A dying laugh filled the cave. "You've gone insane, thief. I shall enjoy watching you die."

"Noseless? How are you still alive?" The words sounded flippant in his mind, but the delivery was soft and broken.

"I'll live longer than you, I wager. If the master wills, I'll live long enough to watch you rot."

Grint laughed, a phlegm-wracked sound that spilled blood down his chin. The dennel blood wanted to consume him but had given him the key to his survival. The escape artist had one last trick up his sleeve after all. One last card to play. His feet fought against his commands, but he shuffled across the cave and fell beside Noseless.

"What are you doing?" Grint pressed the dull blade against Noseless's chest. The scout tried to push it away but had less strength left than Grint. "It doesn't matter if you kill me. Death is the gif..."

"I don't care," Grint said as he put all his weight behind the blade and drove it into the skinling's chest. Noseless choked, shutting his eyes tight as the pain fed on him.

Grint put a bloody hand on the man's forehead and used his thumb and forefinger to pry the eyelids open. Noseless tried to look away, but Grint turned his face each time so their eyes met. There was little fight left to the hound, and he faded fast. Death's vacancy entered his eyes. Grint let go, hearing the body slump over.

There was nothing to do now but stand and wait. The cave held a chill, but even so, the temperature dropped further. Moisture, dripping in an endless cadence from the ceiling suddenly ceased. The shadows deepened, creating new definitions to the word darkness. A man materialized from the dirt, his great, wide-brimmed hat turned down. A red scarf blew in a breeze that didn't exist. Beneath the brim, his wide smile sparkled in the faintest of light. The God of Murder had come to collect.

"Grint," he said in a soft, oily voice.

"Rent," and then Grint collapsed.

16

"Don't gamble with gods. We cheat, and we don't lose well."

- Blue Fingered Hobbe

Grint gasped as he woke from a dream about falling. Unless the Afterwards was far different from what Hobbe told him, he was genuinely surprised to be alive. And equally dumbfounded to not be a shadow puppet tied to the God of Murder. A tattered curtain covered the only window in the room and did a poor job of it. Beams of sunlight found gaps and tears in the thick fabric. Someone had tucked him into bed, swaddling the blankets beneath him. It made him wonder if the whole ordeal had been a bad dream. The necromancers, Lark, the heist, and fleeing through the woods. Moving even the slightest reminded him of the pains, wounds, and tears inflicted on the journey. *Not a dream at all.*

That same someone had also wrapped a bandage around his shoulder. The tight weave of cloth kept him from pulling it apart, but he could feel the mash of healing herbs packed against his skin. When he put pressure on it, the wound burned. It was the same for his stomach, though they dipped those bandages in wet flour to make them rigid. As he lay in the dark, the familiarity of the room settled on him. Rickety shutters with broken slats. The mattress with a soft lump between his shoulder blades, and Grint didn't need to turn his head to know there would be a door to his left with a knob that wobbled. Along the baseboard, there were crude carvings made by two young boys trying to map out their master's vault. Even the cinnamon smell remained, baked into every fiber of the place, but it was old now, like the dust in this unused room. Grint's room. *Why in the fuzzing gullet of a dragon did Rent bring me to the Red Goat Inn?*

Grint sat up, the bandage around his midsection made a crunching sound as the layers separated. He pulled a piece away to get a look at the wounds, spilling the packed herbs onto the mattress. "Why did you let him do that?" A woman stood in the doorway, backlit by candles in the hall. She carried a large bowl of water under her arm that sloshed when she put it on the chipped, blue nightstand. Sitting on the edge of the bed, she shoved Grint's hands away as she fussed over the bandage.

"Leave off," Grint said as she pushed him onto his pillow.

"Quiet," she said. The command in her voice hadn't lessened over the years, and he listened. "This will get infected if you don't let it heal."

"Hello Alanna," Grint said as she tightened the dressing.

Alanna was keeper of the inn. The one who made things run and had been doing it since Grint was a small boy. Long before then too. She may have been getting on in years, but that made her no less vivacious. Grint smiled at her once vibrant red hair now framed by streaks of white. Age settled on her face, but it was a compliment to her beauty.

"Welcome home, Grint," she said as she put her hand on his cheek and then examined his wild mop of hair. "I can trim this for you while you're here. Shame to hide that pretty face."

"This isn't home."

"If you're tending to him, you need to bloody well tend to him," Alanna spoke toward a dark corner of the room. Grint knew what that meant and scowled. When she picked up on his change of mood, she poked him in the chest.

"He hasn't left your side since you arrived, so have a little heart. It's not as if the almighty Grint is infallible." Alanna collected the unused bandages and walked toward the door. "Rest, or I'll send Gus up to make you rest."

The door closed as Grint swung his legs out of the bed. "You saucy, ox-bottomed scump!"

The shadows in the room ran together like water and formed into a frail, elderly man. It'd been years since Grint last saw him, and somehow, the immortal god looked old. Hobbe hunched forward and kept his arms wrapped around his sides. His hair had always been light, more the color of sunbaked pepper than the stark, white mop swept over a bald spot he wore now. Was it possible for a god to age so many years in such a short amount of time? To age at all?

"You should rest," Hobbe said as Grint pulled on the knob. It wobbled the way he remembered but wouldn't budge. Hobbe had a hand up, using a form of his power to hold it shut, but that didn't stop Grint. It was pure stubbornness, and he kept trying until a sharp pain in his stomach made him step back.

"You've pulled a stitch." Hobbe flinched when Grint slammed a fist against the door. "You should put your clothes on, unless you intend to regale the common room with your nature. They're on the chair by the window."

"I can see them without your help," Grint mumbled under his breath. They were new clothes, but in the style Grint liked. Alanna was too good to him.

"So, you can respond."

Grint held the new leather pants in his fist, shaking them at Hobbe as his voice got louder. "You want me to respond? Is that what you want?"

"I want us to talk," Hobbe said. His voice remained even.

"You're out of luck. We have nothing to talk about." Grint finished putting on the new clothes. Everything fit, except where the bandages bulged out.

"There are things..."

"You can make me do to listen. I know," Grint waved his hand, wishing the god would just shut up.

"No," Hobbe said, his voice rising for the first time. "Things you don't yet underst..."

"I understand that you're a god, but you're not *my* god. Not after you sold me to Rent." Hobbe's face sagged. "What? Did you think I didn't know? Or I wouldn't find out? That salt-addled banger has been chasing me from one end of Terragard to the next. And you can dispense with the theatrics. I know you too well to think you're despondent. The only things you care about are what you can steal."

Grint walked to the door. It opened on its own before his hand reached the knob. Hobbe had given up on talking. *Good,* he thought, not feeling good about it at all. They'd had a tumultuous relationship, but Hobbe was still the closest thing he had known to a father. He hated hating him, but hate was often all he could feel when he looked at the God of Thieves.

Like Hobbe, the Red Goat Inn looked as if it had gotten old in a hurry. The hallway runner had lost the vibrant colors he remembered, becoming frayed around the edges. Plumes of dust rose with each booted step. Someone had started to paint the walls but managed only half the job before giving it up. The attempt hadn't been recent. The newer paint chipped as Grint ran his hand over it, revealing the old color beneath. A fat, orange tomcat slept by the stairs. It picked it's head up as Grint approached and then watched a mouse scurry by. The tomcat tested the distance with its paw and when it saw that catching the rodent would require movement, it laid back down. *Hard to get good help.*

Downstairs sat the common room, a great two-story space with arched ceilings supported by thick beams. And it always looked cluttered. Maybe it was the two dozen tables scattered across the cobblestone floors. Or the piles of straw clumped on top of old rugs. *The good rugs are down in the vault.* A performance stage sat between two giant hearths, both lit for the autumn chill. Torches embedded in the walls would never burn out unless Hobbe willed it.

Grint took it easy getting down the stairs but could see Alanna's face twist into something angry even before he got halfway. A polished mahogany bar ran along the back of the room and Grint took a seat on a stool, readying himself for a verbal lashing.

"What part of the word '*rest*' was unclear?"

"I'm not resting in that room," Grit replied. "I'll take an ale. The amber kind if you have any."

"Not while you're healing," she said as they engaged in a staring contest.

"I'm parched."

"Have water." Neither was backing down.

A mug slid the length of the bar, the molded copper scratching against polished wood. Grint snatched it before Alanna could and took a deep swig. The amber liquid both cooled and burned his throat.

"Thank you, Gus," Grint said, never taking his eyes off Alanna. Gus had married Alanna long ago, breaking the heart of every thief who walked into the bar and got lost in her sparkling jade eyes. The couple ran the inn on Hobbe's behalf. His given name was Gustav, which he expected you to call him if you were new to the inn or on his unfriendly list. He was an imposing figure, six-foot-tall, muscles as big as boulders, and skin so dark it made the Sandy Kingdomers look pale. The bald-headed barkeep had once been a thief in one of Hobbe's previous crews and claimed to hail from a land east of the Frontier, but no one believed it. The Frontier was deadlier than the Dire Lands and twice as big as Terragard itself.

"One ale is fine," Gus said in his booming voice, standing firm before his wife's glare.

"Just the one," she relented and rested a hand over Grint's. "It's good to see you."

"You too." Grint kept a tight grip on the mug. It would be just like Alanna to try to take it from him. "Why did Rent bring me here?"

Alanna's face grew hard. "Ask him yourself," she answered through pursed lips.

There are moments in a life so important they harden within amber. Within that frozen tableau, a person can study those memories, revisit, and dissect them. Then there are moments of supreme absurdity where time races, afraid the sanctity and seriousness of life might be questioned. This moment was one of the latter.

Calabassus Rent, the God of Murder, sat at a dirty table covered in cheese crumbs as he sipped tea from a chipped cup. His signature hat, scarf and gloves sat on the next table. A patina of yellow dust covered everything in the inn, and always had, giving it a dingy appearance. The bedraggled nature of the inn was a nuisance to the god, who flicked his hand to sweep it away. Grint had never seen him without his hat, but the short, slicked black hair framed a pleasant if not pale face. Legend said the color of his skin changed depending on the person looking at him, but that could be a myth.

Grint grabbed his stomach as he stood. The walk to the far end of the inn took no time at all, but he couldn't recall a single step past the first. As he sat, Rent took a sip from his cup and put it down, flicking away the dust once more. The look he gave Grint would put any gambler he'd ever met to shame. Not a flicker of emotion.

"I have been - admiring the artwork," Rent said. Commissioned works of art adorned the walls of the common room, all portraying Hobbe's various crews over the past centuries; the oldest carved from wood, the newer painted on canvas, or stitched into a tapestry.

"That rendering contains you?" Grint didn't turn to look. He knew it well. Oil on canvas. The old crew. The Sons of Hobbe.

"Yes."

"And the others in the painting?"

"Most are alive. I think. You would know better than me."

"Poor doomed Tebbs," Rent said, relishing the name.

"Poor dead Tebbs," Grint corrected. "You remember him?"

"I remember every murder," Rent smiled from ear to ear.

Grint wanted to ask about Jessua. He knew most of the story, but not how it happened. Could he trust Rent to tell him? To give him the truth of it? Grint let it pass, afraid the god might tell him. The two sat in silence while Rent took another sip of tea.

"Why did you bring me here?"

"That was part of the arrangement," he replied in his soft-spoken tone. "When I won you."

"Yes, in a game of cards." Grint had no desire to listen to a recounting of the tale. "What arrangement?"

"Twenty-four hours, that is what I promised Hobbe. And that time has begun." Having delivered the news, Rent wrapped his scarf around his neck.

"Why do you want me? Why am I so special to you?"

"You?" Rent paused in putting on his hat and threw his head back in laughter. It was a sickening sound. "There is nothing special about you. Well, that is not entirely true, I must admit. You are a gifted thief, perhaps second only to the God of Thieves in that regard. I have delighted in the myriad ways you have slipped away as I pursued you, but as a killer you are sloppy. Brutish even. In a confrontation, you win more from luck than skill. The only value you hold is the pain it will cause him to see you become one of my shadows. You look terrible, by the way."

Grint thought the god of murder was insulting him, but it was Hobbe he addressed with the last. Hobbe stood at the bottom of the stairs, listening.

"So, I'm just a stone in a game of Fatch?"

"Stones have value in that game. You're more of a disk." It was a low insult. The disk was the game piece the others stepped on. Satisfied with answering questions, Rent put on his gloves and stepped away from the table.

"Wait," Grint said, using the chair to help him stand.

"Excuse me?" the god's voice turned to steel. Calabassus Rent was not someone you commanded.

"The girl I was with in Finder's Lot. The necromancers have her. Do you know where?"

"Necromancers kill often. No doubt I could find them, but I will not."

"Why?" Rent's hand was on the front door. "They're summoning a demon lord. I've seen the vision. If they succeed, it will be a new dark age."

"Dark ages are good for murder," Rent replied.

"I need to save that girl," Grint all but fell to his knees to beg. "I need..."

The front door swung open, slamming against the inner wall. Bright, morning light silhouetted Rent in the doorway as the wind whipped his long-tailed coat. Yellow dust from the road spun in cyclonic circles, sweeping into the inn. One of Rent's shadows lurked outside, stalking back and forth.

"I do not care what you need. Perhaps I was lax in my collection of you, but do not mistake that for any manner of fondness. I am not here to bargain or grant you boons like a common genie. Your banal desire to save a child is of no consequence." Rent stepped through the doorway and down the front steps before turning back one last time. "I will return in one day. Do not leave these grounds. There are fates much worse than death. For you and for those you care for."

The door to the inn closed, leaving Grint to stare at the stained wood. The sun grew a little brighter as his oppressive weight lifted. Grint hadn't realized it was there until now.

"Grint? Are you alright?" At the sound of Faighur's voice Grint spun around. He was both shocked and delighted to see his friend. They embraced with good cheer.

"You're alive, thank Krypsie! I didn't know if you got out of the Terrastags."

"I had to hide for two days. By the time I left - I failed in finding you. I'm sorry." True sorrow filled his voice. *Does he blame himself for me turning to Rent?*

"How did you know I'd be here?" An evasive look passed over Faighur's face. "You didn't know. This is the broker you've been working for? Him?" Grint pointed at Hobbe. The thief master placed the jade statue of the woman with snaking arms on the table in front of him. "Wait. Is that? That's the kry-damned statue we stole from Upper Anghor? All this time it worried me you might be mad about the Terrastag job going south..."

"Grint!" Hobbe bellowed, and the room quieted. "For once in your sow-sotted life, shut up." Grint did, but the scowl remained. "Do you want to save that girl?"

Without another word, Hobbe picked up the jade statue and walked out of the inn. A windstorm kicked up, obscuring the air with thick clouds of dust. The god disappeared into it after a few steps.

"You should follow him," Alanna said. "You'll want to follow him."

"Unbloody believable," he groaned as he followed into the storm.

The Red Goat Inn was a solitary building on a long, lonely road. That was how Hobbe wanted it. The inn was for thieves who - by Hobbe's estimation - earned a place at one of the tables. Across from the inn sat the only other building in sight: a large horse barn. Hobbe slid the barn door open as Grint shielded his eyes against the dust. Once Grint stepped inside, the door shut and torches lit. Hobbe stood in a dark shadow cast by bales of hay, jade sylph in his hand as he stared down at Callum's corpse.

"Noseless? Why did Rent bring him here?"

"He didn't," Hobbe said. "Rent's biggest flaw is his desire to gloat. He couldn't help himself. He reveled in telling me how you summoned him and where it happened. So, I retrieved our friend here."

"Tin Boots was..."

"...is fine," Hobbe finished. "I checked on him. I didn't want to upset the other willen, so he didn't see me, but I saw him."

"And what good is the corpse going to do us?" The stench coming off the hound was putrid.

"I'm a god, daft child. I'm going to pull his spirit out and if he doesn't talk... Into the sylph he goes. Not why I had you boys steal this piece, but it will do."

"Why do it at all?"

"I know you don't believe it, but I never wanted that girl to come to any harm." There was sincerity on his face, but Grint didn't care.

"That girl? She had a name."

"You're right. It was Jessua. I never wanted Jessua..."

"Then you should have waited!" Grint's voice startled the roosting birds who flew around in quick circles. "Why couldn't you? You're the God of Thieves! You could have stolen from Carr whatever you wanted. I could have kept her safe!"

"There's no changing the past. Not even I have that power," Hobbe said. "Maybe this will make up for it."

Grint believed nothing could ever make up for it but if it helped him save Lark, he would let the God of Thieves try. Callum's body convulsed as a sparkling red cloud pushed its way through the open wounds. A fine mist rose, twisting around until it formed into a rough approximation of the man's body.

"Even in oblivion, I cannot escape you," Noseless whined. "Put me back."

"Where did they take Lark?"

"Death has not changed my loyalties," the spirit replied. "Wait, what pain is this?" Callum's feet frayed like an unraveling thread being sucked into the sylph.

"I am selling this to a salt witch. Do you want your spirit torn apart in a witch's spell? Tell him," Hobbe said, sounding like the Hobbe of old.

"Stop the pain!" Noseless was just a torso and head now, the magic worked fast.

"Tell me then!"

"Cattachat! On the shoreline north of Dayermere. The Roosting Cliffs they're called. Stop it, put me back where I belong!"

Hobbe looked at Grint. "Finish it," Grint said and walked out of the barn, Callum's wailing cry followed him.

As he walked back into the inn, Alanna and Faighur exited a hidden door under the stairs carrying crates in their arms. Gus stood behind the bar, rolling out maps and weighting the corners down with mugs. They looked up as Grint entered, waiting for some word.

"Do you have any maps of the Cattachat coast?" he asked.

"I have many maps!" Gus's smile broadened as he rolled out the requested area. They crowded around the bar, tracing their fingers along it. "What are we looking for?"

"Here," Grint said as he jammed his finger on the port city of Dayermere. "Then the Roosting Cliffs? I don't see those."

"The bird drawings," Gus pointed at some squiggled lines meant to represent birds.

"Gulls? Ravens?"

"Racs," Hobbe answered, and they all whistled. The old god sat down on a stool and a mug of amber beer appeared in his hand. Racs were giant birds, carnivorous beasts growing as large as a dragon.

"I worried it would be too far to fly to," Faighur nodded as he measured the distance. "This should be fine."

"Faighur..."

"I insist," the skinling said. "I got you into this with the sylph job. Best we finish it together. No arguments."

"I noticed you didn't have your bag," Alanna said as she and Gus put the crates on top of the table. "It's not magic, but here's a new one and any supplies you might need. Some of my mare's milk for poisons. Sigil scarfs, they won't stop spells but will dull them. Enchanted whistle, makes animals docile. I heard there were hounds."

"Skinlings," Grint added. "Still might be useful."

"There are firejacks in the bottom, so be careful with those." Alanna stepped close and whispered. "There's some Nacinti in there too. Don't use it."

"Unless I have to," Grint nodded. The Orrish drug magic would be a last resort.

"No need to be coy," Hobbe said as he took another sip of ale. "I heard it all."

Alanna wiped the heel of her hand across her cheekbones, trying to hide the tears. "I remember the day Hobbe brought you here. Thought it destiny that he found such a sweet boy with hair as red as mine."

"I wasn't sweet," Grint blushed.

"You were to me. I doted on you more than anyone else, I know that."

"Alanna," Grint started, but found he couldn't say more. He put his head onto her shoulder and cried. Her arms held him tight and rocked him as she used to. The way she had after Jessua died. If Hobbe was a father to him, she was his mother, and he loved her as fiercely as if she was.

"Okay now," Gus said in his gentle giant's voice. "Save some for me." Gus hugged him so hard Grint feared he might re-injure the shoulder. When he let go, he had tears in his eyes.

"Come back to us," Alanna said.

"Always," Grint replied. They went through the door behind the bar where their rooms were. Faighur disappeared during the goodbye, leaving Grint alone with Hobbe. *That wasn't an accident,* he thought. Grint walked around the bar and poured himself an ale. Hobbe held out his mug and Grint refilled it for him.

"Least you can do," the god smiled. "I don't hear the clink of coins in your pants."

"I don't have a tab?" They drank in silence for a time. "Rent said he would come for anyone..."

"They will be safe," Hobbe answered. "Rent won't touch anyone. You worry about staying alive and getting that girl. Pour me another."

Grint did for them both. "How does the God of Thieves lose at Cheat Me?"

"A story for another night," Hobbe answered, which meant he lost on purpose. Grint didn't know if that made him angrier or not. Games within games. That was Hobbe. "When you get that girl, you run and hide. Stay out of his sight. I'll sort things with Rent. That's what the sylph is for."

Grint finished his ale and walked toward the staircase. Faighur could come get him when they needed to go. "Grint?" He turned toward Hobbe, who stood at the base of the stairs. "I wish things had been different."

What do you say to the man you love most in the world and hate in equal measure? "Goodbye, Hobbe," was what he came up with.

17

"How beautiful the convergence of Effulg and Nacinth must have been when both were whole. Two perfect spheres, joining as one. With Nacinth shattered, the convergence has become The Stabbing and is nothing more than a time for the wicked and the damned. Such a pity."

- Pope Gaius Demarcus
Living Embodiment of the Papality

Eleanor dipped her hand in the tepid water of a barrel, breaking the layer of grime settling on the surface. She splashed it across her face, uncaring of the quality or lack thereof. The steady rise in temperature made wearing the ceremonial armor a burden. The orders issued made no allowances for removing any piece until the ritual completed. A dozen steps to her left, a soldier dropped from heatstroke. They were not the first. *Death is the gift long promised.* The water refreshed even if it only lasted a moment or two. With the sun setting, the promise of a cool night was almost too much to hope for. A life in the fire of the nether realms was what she agreed to, so why balk at it now? *Perhaps because I no longer believe?*

The Cliffs of Cattachat towered hundreds of feet over the Krypholos Ocean and stretched for hundreds of miles in both directions. Settlements such as Dayermere dotted the coastline, tucked into small breaks in the cliff. The count's holdings were a long ride north of the city, far enough to avoid detection. Discovery wasn't a concern, not with Lord Dayermere under the count's control, but there was never a shortage of fools looking to meddle in the affairs of a necromancer.

The necromancer seers cautioned the importance of completing the ritual once it began. Disruptions could be cataclysmic, and the count, ever a slave to their notions of the future, moved the ritual from his fortress atop the cliffs to a suitable site on the small island offshore. There they would chain the child to an archway until The Stabbing occurred. Eleanor's place should have been on that island - *in a place of great honor* - but the failures of her adventurism came with a cost. Reduced to a mere spectator from afar, she would stand with the common soldiery as the count attained his lifelong reward.

A place on the island was not all she lost. After the count severed her left hand, he gave it back. In a way. Upon their return to the camp, the count made her watch as his necromancers peeled away the flesh on the severed appendage, the muscles and tendons, leaving only bone. Count Danghier forced Eleanor to her knees in front of the entire army. Performing incantations, the skeletal hand twitched to life, seeking to kill its former owner. Danghier laughed as the necromancers reattached it to her stump.

The new hand proved superior in every way. Stronger, impervious to pain, and unbreakable; But it served the count and would obey only when her goals aligned with his.

Moments of doubt incited its anger. Even now, as her mind strayed, the skeletal hand clicked together, reading her thoughts as it clawed toward her throat. Thank the netherworlds it had minimal control of her arm. As long as she kept it away from her body it would cause no harm. This was now, what about when she needed to sleep? The count's admonition to, "Get your mind right," became a constant thought running through her mind.

"That thing unnerves me," Malus said as he approached. The scout cupped a hand in the water and drank.

"It is a reminder of my failures. The choices I should have made against those I did." The ownership of failure calmed the hand.

Malus lowered his voice, "How can it be a failure when the ritual goes as planned? The thief annoyed me with his troublesome antics, but he did what no other could. I believe the count is being too harsh."

The hand lunged for Malus. Eleanor groaned as she pulled it back to her side. Malus's loyalty to her was unquestioned, and saw any pain inflicted on her as too much. Would he still stand by her if he knew her treasonous thoughts towards the count?

"It is best not to voice such things," she said, struggling against the pull of the hand. Malus was not wrong. One need only look at Black Samuel to see he would never succeed. Was there a traitor in their ranks designing a mission destined to fail? Or to succeed while bringing her low? The necromancers could be petty when they weren't getting enough of the count's attention. Had one maneuvered to remove her from the count's graces? The hand shifted from seeking Malus back to her.

"Apologies, Mistress," Malus bowed. "The hand tells me you feel different."

"Find Tamos and clear us a spot on the ridge to view the ritual." The conversation was best ended. Malus accepted the command and shifted into dog form to better track the whereabouts of his brother.

Eleanor dunked her head in the water barrel and let it trickle down her body as she stood. Cupping another handful of water, she watched it run through her fingers. It was a perfect metaphor to describe the eroding loyalty she had for the count. The hand lunged again, and she contemplated cutting it off. That action would signal the severing of her relationship with Count Danghier. Was she prepared to do that? The count's reputation for excessive cruelty was legendary. Had he stopped at excluding her from the island, she might have come back around. She could even brook the mummery of this hand business for a time. But for him to leave Callum behind? And upon their return, to dash Bowman's dust into the wind? Two of her beautiful boys gone and for what reason? *A tantrum.*

As Eleanor walked through the camp, the count's army gave her a wide berth. Soldiers sat in circles, drinking and laughing. Such a lack of discipline was abnormal, but their commanders were elsewhere, and no one felt the need to correct the behavior. Some stood when they saw her, but she passed by, paying them no mind, lost as she was in her own thoughts.

When had she become so contemplative? Where had the decisive Eleanor gone? The relentless and unquestioning version of herself? She likened herself to an arrow that once flew true, but now had a nick in the shaft so it wobbled when fired. An arrow of that sort was what they gave the infantry to use as fodder. The answer to her question was so clear, even the hand knew. When? It had been the moment she beheld a god.

A deep shadow passed overhead and for a moment she felt elation. Had her thoughts drawn the God of Murder? It was not the god, just a rac. The bird beat its great brown feathered wings as it circled the camp. Two archers drew back on their bows but did not fire. The racs were easy enough to kill, but the carnage would incite the rest of the flock, and they were restless today – an odd behavior for them. Could they sense the impending ritual?

A soldier stepped from a tent and the circling rac dove, snatching the unsuspecting woman into the air. It climbed a hundred feet as archers loosed their arrows. *Idiots*, Eleanor thought. Such panic was contagious. The rac tossed the soldier into the waiting talons of her young where they tore her apart in a cloud of red mist. A single boot fell in a torrent of gore.

Eleanor crouched as she examined the sky, unwilling to become a rac's next meal. The hand gave up its desire to strangle her, agreeing with a plan for self-preservation. More racs flocked, drawn by the blood and angered cries of the mother. Soldiers unprepared for combat would make easy targets for the flock. The camp was about to turn into a bloodbath. And then it wasn't. The racs screeched and fled over the ocean. As their screams receded a new one filled the air to the west. A roar she was all too familiar with.

"Dragon!" she shouted. A fist of soldiers running past skid to a halt, looking around in bewilderment. The captain scowled at her, whispering to his men she was just a mad woman. Eleanor ignored their glances as she scanned the horizon. In the deep recesses of her fears - she knew it was the thief's dragon come to avenge him. That was pure lunacy, wasn't it?

"Mistress?" a young private stepped close. "It's just racs." *The patronizing scump!* Eleanor brooked the abuse long enough and would not allow more. She struck the soldier across the face with the skeletal hand. An impact so severe it spun the man's head around with an audible snap. The private collapsed into a heap as the others watched. The strength of the hand would take getting used to.

"Turn the catapults west and find any necromancers still upon the cliffs. There's a dragon coming." Whether or not they believed her, they ran off. Eleanor's search continued, doubt creeping in. Had she been wrong? Then she saw it, flying low with its back to the setting sun. A smart creature. "Dragon!" she yelled again, pointing towards it, but the second warning came too late.

The dragon landed on the command tent with a bellowing roar that shook the camp, collapsing the tent under its weight. Eleanor heard strangled screams from within as the dragon quieted. General Tamood and his honor guard would have been inside. The blood red dragon stomped the tent with its claws, killing anything that moved.

Ten soldiers ran at it, the long lances they'd gathered to fight the racs now raised towards the creature. The dragon belched liquid fire and incinerated them. Only dust remained. The surrounding tents went up along with them, burning anyone foolish enough to hide there. Eleanor froze, consumed by fear and the realization that the coloring of this dragon matched the one in Kambar. Its yellow eyes focused on her, and it beat its mighty wings as it leapt forward.

The dragon landed fifty feet away, shaking the ground beneath her feet. It lowered its head in a defiant roar that struck her with a gale-force wind. She dug her boot heels in the dirt to keep from toppling over. A shadow jumped off the beast's back. A wraith, born of nightmares, come to consume her. The man rolled as he landed and came up sprinting. Mud coated the shag of his hair and clothes on his back, but there was no doubt it was the thief named Grint.

"Impossible," she breathed as he charged her, sword in hand, a crossbow slung over his back and bag slapping his side.

Had Tamos not chosen this moment to intervene, Eleanor would have remained frozen in a stupor as the thief brought his sword crashing down on her skull. Ten feet away, Tamos tackled the thief. The hound locked his jaw on the thief's forearm while Grint punched him, trying to pry the teeth loose. Their wrestling continued as they rolled around on top of one another. The thief got his feet under Tamos's belly and launched the hound in the air. Eleanor looked away from the battle as the two circled one another.

The dragon had moved on, breathing fire across the camp while using its giant head to batter scores of soldiers. Necromancers, alerted by the screams, gathered in formation. They threw green swirls of fire that rebounded off the dragon's scales. *Adapt! Find a new tactic,* she thought. They did. Scores of the dead littered the ground, and the necromancers used them to their advantage, forming the corpses into a giant writhing creature. The abomination towered over the camp and replaced incinerated bodies with fresh ones as fast as the dragon could destroy them.

The abomination reached out with what approximated as arms, and the dragon backed away. An angry screech stung Eleanor's ears as the abomination swatted the beast's leathery wings. A shower of bodies rained down, but they stood as soon as they landed and shambled back toward the abomination to re-assimilate. On the surface, the corpses crawled like ants, writhing in agony. Two thick hands grasped the dragon around the throat and the beast screamed. Then disappeared.

The suddenness of it startled her. The abomination stumbled about as the necromancers tried to discern what had happened. She recalled her theory that the dragon was nothing but a creature of illusion magic, but how could that be? The fires and the death were real. No illusion could do that. How did the thief manage it? Eleanor intended to ask.

The thief and hound battled, blood flying from a dozen fresh wounds. Tamos charged as Grint dropped to his knees, but before her hound could sink his teeth in, the thief did an acrobatic flip and jammed his sword back, catching Tamos in the ribs. He whimpered and snarled, baring his teeth.

"Come on, Crosshatch. Fight me." Grint baited the man, and he took it. Shifting to human form, Tamos stretched and moved, testing the wounds he'd received as a hound. Drawing the knife Grint dropped in the rambler town, Tamos tossed it back and forth between hands. The thief cocked his head and glowered.

"That's my knife."

"Come and take it then," Tamos challenged back. It echoed the challenge from an age past in Kambar. Eleanor doubted Grint would back down as Black Samuel had.

A man in light brown robes ran past Eleanor, someone unknown to her. The thin-bladed sword she held clattered to the ground as she watched him transform into the red dragon and devour Tamos. Her faithful hound disappeared into the creature's mouth. The beast never broke stride as it continued through the camp.

"Charffing, pox-ridden, malodorous, ogre-mouthed goat! That was my kill!" Grint shouted at the dragon as he picked up Blackblade. The ground rumbled as the abomination spotted the dragon and gave chase to its prey. The thief dove out of the way of the lumbering atrocity.

"It appears killing no longer bothers you," Eleanor said as he brushed himself off.

"It was never the killing as much as what came after," Grint answered, twirling both sword and dagger as he waited for her attack.

"And a skinling dragon. You have never failed to both vex and impress."

"Where is Lark?" Night was imminent and the moons, bright in the sky, approached the allotted time.

"Put her out of your mind. It is too late for a rescue." Eleanor swiped her sword through the air as she readied for battle. "For now, it is time for the fight we promised one another."

"You don't want to fight me," Grint shook his head.

"Why is that?"

"I cheat." In one smooth motion, Grint dropped the sword and swung the crossbow off his shoulder. As the bolt flew towards her, she imagined it sinking into her eye. Was their battle over before it began? The new hand had other ideas. It snatched the arrow out of the air. Splinters rained as it crushed the bolt in its fist. It was the thief's turn to gawk in wonder.

"That's new," he said.

"A gift from the count." She looked at the hand with a new appreciation.

"You need a new master." Grint kept his eye on her while picking up the sword he dropped.

"Perhaps you could introduce me to yours?" Eleanor charged forward, her form with a sword described as meticulous. Grint dug a boot into the mud and kicked a giant clump. The hand swatted it aside. To his credit, Grint did what he could to dodge, roll, and block with the black-bladed knife, but the battle between them was never even. His chest heaved, and he labored from fresh wounds that soaked through his coat.

"How does it feel? To know I won't relent. That you will bleed out. Knowing every cut is a marker on the path to your death."

"I've died once," Grint said. "I didn't care for the taste." He lunged, a valiant but doomed effort. The hand blocked his strike while she slashed his shoulder. As he reeled, she kicked him to the ground. It was time to end this.

The dragon roared as it charged her. Eleanor almost broke into a run but recognized how futile that would be. Its mouth opened and glowed red with the promise of all-consuming flames. The abomination fell on it, burying it beneath a deluge of bodies. Eleanor wore a wicked grin as she turned back to Grint.

"No more," she shouted. He'd crawled away but stopped when she shouted. "You will learn your place in this world. Under my boot."

Grint wore his own smile as he threw a small gem. It glittered in the moonlight, tumbling end over end. Another futile gesture. The hand snatched it from the air - and it exploded. The blast threw her back. A shoulder popped as she struck the dirt and one of her legs bent the wrong way. The pain became indescribable. Eleanor fought to her feet. Cinders danced around her face, making her vaguely aware that her hair may be on fire. Most of her clothes burned away, revealing charred flesh.

"I told you I cheat," Grint repeated, but this time it sounded sad.

Eleanor shambled toward him, each step agonizing. Even in this state, she would prove herself his match.

"Not yet, not charffing yet!" Grint yelled at someone behind her. *Who?* It hurt to turn. Someone put a hand on her shoulder and she stopped.

"I warned you what would happen if you left the inn," the man said, his voice the sound of quiet death.

Grint looked at her, "Count Danghier? Lark? Where are they?"

Eleanor opened her mouth, but the sound she made didn't match any words. Grint looked over the cliff as lightning struck upwards. *There,* she thought. *It's not hard to figure out where they are.* Eleanor watched the thief sprint toward the edge and leap off, arms and legs splayed out. What had he done? That fall was hundreds of feet.

Eleanor collapsed into the arms of the god, who cradled her. She looked into that magnificent face and tried to say, *thank you.*

"Don't thank me," he replied. "You will not survive this." The skeletal hand clawed its way toward her throat. And Rent let it.

18

"Thimmy Thommy saved the girl,
saved the girl, saved the girl
From beneath the fountain,
beneath the waves,
beneath the swirl
A hundred years he longed for a friend,
a friend, a friend
When a monster she became,
he cried to no end, no end, no end."

- The Enchanted Fountain

What in the bloody name of Krypsie was he thinking? A man terrified of heights leaping blindly off a cliff. It wasn't the dumbest thing he'd ever done, but was kry-damned close. Lightning continued to strike the sky from somewhere on the island. The moons were close to converging. The Stabbing was at hand and time grew short. There weren't other options. At least that's what he told himself.

Frenzied racs filled the sky, driven mad by the lightning and the dark energies it promised. Grint influenced his free fall to the left and windmilled his arms as a massive rac flew beneath him. He slid along its back, feathers slipping between his fingers. The bird cried and banked. Grint grabbed onto the scapular of its left wing and held so tight his knuckles ached.

The rac rolled, dangling Grint over the great nothingness below. A white-feathered flash brushed past his legs, and he heard the snap of a beak over the rushing wind. Grint lifted his legs as it returned, looking to avoid a fate at the bottom of the bird's belly. The big beast righted itself. He screamed into its feathers, praying to any god who'd listen that he was a small enough target to ignore. A shadow obscured Effulg, bright and beautiful in the night sky. The shadow grew and with it, a high-pitched scream. Talons, gleaming in the moonlight dove for Grint. *So much for bloody prayers.* He watched it drop; Blackblade held tight in his hand. Grint slipped between its talons to bury his knife in the heart. A fountain of gore showered over him.

"Charffing, dung-trolling gods," Grint coughed as the rac crashed, splattering its guts onto the larger bird. The bloody mess covered everything. Grint wiped a handful of viscera from his face, realizing his position on the food chain. Chum in the air. The rest of the flock smelled it, screaming in glorious delight as they flocked toward him. Grint fumbled with the crossbow, his hands slick and slipping on the string. It clicked and fired a wild shot. The sky swarmed with birds, making it impossible to miss. The first kill offered a momentary distraction. The flock tore into the injured bird, forgetting him. Then the rac he rode abruptly rose. Grint yelped, cursing the thing for its need to eat.

Feathers slick with blood slid through his fingers. The rac's tail rushed to greet him. No amount of arm flailing would slow his inevitable plummet into an icy death. A dragon's cry boomed behind a plume of fire. The racs scattered, their cries changing from ecstasy to alarm. *About time knowing a bloody dragon paid off.* Grint slid off the rac, shouting, "Faighur!"

Faighur dove, tucking his wings to match speed. Rushing winds battered Grint as he fell. This was his nightmare. The punchline to the joke of his life Faighur winked as he dropped below him. Grint reached, hooking an arm around a boney protrusion on the dragon's neck. No longer falling, he pulled himself tight against the dragon's back. Satisfied, Faighur banked sharply to avoid more racs, all displeased at the loss of their meal. Grint's stomach lurched as they pitched left then right. And his face ached with the effort of keeping his eyes closed.

"You jumped off a cliff," Faighur yelled. Even with the wind rushing in his ears, the dragon's voice carried.

"It seemed the fastest way down."

"You could have died!"

"The God of Murder showed up, I didn't have time for careful planning," Grint said, hoping that ended it. Talking while trying to keep his stomach where it belonged was not where he wanted his focus.

A smaller rac landed on Faighur's back, its beak poised to skewer Grint. Faighur rolled and swatted it with a leathery wing. Grint had to hook his knee around another spike to keep from tumbling off. *There's no way I won't be sick,* he thought, gritting his teeth. As Faighur leveled out, Grint threw up.

"Trying to kill me?" he shouted, wiping bile from his mouth. "This is why I need a saddle."

"If you put a saddle on me, I will eat you," Faighur roared. *Fair enough.*

Metallic sounds, like steel raindrops, began hitting the dragon's scales. An arrow shattered a few inches from where Grint's hand had just been. The dirt-blinded idiots were shooting arrows from the cliffs, hitting whatever they could. Burning feathers floated on the wind, flitting around like fireflies. Faighur did what he could to get them to the island, but the racs gathered in legion, blocking any attempt to dive.

Golden eyes blinked in the darkness. Something small moved by the dragon's tail. Grint's shifted his weight, trying to see past the protrusions until a familiar face stared back at him. "Torchy?"

Malus stalked up the dragon's back, but now that Grint spotted him he cast off the need for stealth. "I knew the dragon would lead me to you."

"Is this because I insulted your cooking?" Grint ducked under the thick club Malus swung. "It got better. You just need to use fewer spices."

"I don't know how you're alive, but I plan to close that mouth forever!" Malus brought the club down. It rebounded off the scales and almost struck him. Faighur roared and looked back. Whatever he expected to see, it was not Grint fighting another man. Distracted, Faighur missed the gray-feathered rac on his left. The matriarch of the flock matched the dragon in size and she dug her talons into his neck. Massive scales cracked under the pressure. Loose shards flew, spraying the combatants. Faighur bit the air trying to shake her loose, but she kept a firm grip and pecked at his face.

Grint and Malus held on for dear life as Faighur turned in violent circles. The dragon sank his teeth into one of the bird's wings and tore. Blood showered the sky, raining onto the dragon's back. Grint put Blackblade in his mouth and crept toward Malus. With careful steps, he reached for each spike, securing himself before his feet slipped or the dragon shook him loose.

"Here little, Torchy," Grint said through a mouthful of knife. Before the hound could react, Grint slid through the blood and slashed the backs of his legs. Malus screamed, but it was little more than a flesh wound. His thick leather pants blunted the worst of the strike. Malus used the dragon's battle to his advantage. When Faighur turned, he dropped along the body and swung himself around as they righted. The momentum carried him back and he speared Grint in the stomach with his cudgel.

They darted between the spikes, slashing and bashing one another. A small black feathered rac tried to land between them. It hovered, flapping its wings and snapping its beak. Malus shifted into hound form and barked to draw its attention. Grint jammed Blackblade into its throat.

As the bird fell away, Malus shifted back and smiled. "Too bad I have to kill you."

"Are you starting to like me?"

"No." Man became hound and lunged at Grint. In the moment before they collided, he shifted back again, driving his shoulder into Grint's chest. Falling flat, Grint slid until he slammed against a spike.

Malus pounded the cudgel against his own chest, "For my mistress!"

Faighur rose, and Malus jumped, letting gravity do the work, but this time Grint was waiting. The dragon leveled out and Grint threw a handful of the shattered scales. Enough to distract the hound. One, two, three kicks to Torchy's groin. The look on his face asked, *How could you?*

"Sorry," Grint said as he pushed the hound onto a spike. Malus screamed, staring at the bone impaling his shoulder.

Leaving the hound behind, he worked his way toward Faighur's head. They needed to land. Time was not their ally. Nacinth's tip touched the edge of Effulg. The Stabbing had begun. Before Grint could voice those concerns, the matriarch returned and slammed into Faighur's side. Grint slid to the edge. Grabbing wildly and covered in death, his fingers slipped off anything that might break his fall. The rac broke off, circled, and came in for another strike. Faighur lit it with dragon fire, but the bird's momentum carried the flaming carcass into them.

Grint jumped over the edge, plummeting toward the water. Had he not, he would have burned to death, as Faighur's back smoldered. Slowly, the dragon went limp. His eyes closed as he went into a spin. Grint had just enough time to hope his friend survived before they hit the icy-cold waters of the Krypholos Ocean. The riptide pulled him under, dragging him along the rough corral. Falling wasn't a skill he excelled at, but swimming - that was something he could handle. Grint fought through the choppy surf and found Faighur floating face down a few yards offshore. Unconscious, he'd shifting back to human. Grint pulled him onto the beach and put his ear against Faighur's chest.

"Come on!" he screamed, pounding on his friend's chest. He hit and listened. Hit and listened. Then came the faint beat of his heart. He lived.

A man coughed in the shallow water. Malus crawled out of the sea, his shoulder a bloody ruin. The hound collapsed with his face in the sand, sending plumes into the air as he struggled. He swatted the air as Grint approached, holding out a hand to keep the thief at bay. Grint slapped it aside and punched him in the face. Then again. Malus's hand fell limp. Grint picked up a stone and brought it down, over and over.

"Death. Is. The. Gift. Long. Promised."

That was the last of the hounds. Grint left the stone beside the body and sat beside Faighur, chest heaving from the exertion. Ocean salt sat heavy on the air as the cacophony of rac cries continued. The birds stayed clear of the island, only circling the edges. *The magic of the ritual must be holding them back.*

The cliffs loomed above. "I jumped off those bloody things," Grint said as he dragged Faighur to the tall grass above the tide line. A small stone outcropping looked like a good place to leave him. "Remind me not to do that again."

"You got carried away with the hound," Grint said imitating Faighur's voice.

"I know." He patted his friend's chest with a bloody hand. "I can't stay. Whenever you wake up..." Lightning stabbed skyward. "...you'll know where I am." The crack of thunder shook Grint's teeth.

It was a barren island, composed of loose stones and dirt sloping toward a high ridge. The ritual would be somewhere beyond that. Grint found it odd, there were no picket lines, no patrols, no wandering monsters. The only thing of note was a grouping of tents beside a wooden watchtower. An unmanned watchtower. *Everyone's gone to watch.*

Grint took his first step onto the slope when Rent's voice boomed out. "Go no further." It sounded like steel pulled from the blacksmith's forge, hissing in cool water.

Grint stood soaked, shivering, bloody, and tired. What was he going to do against a god? Throw a firejack at him? Rent waited with six of his shadows, all lined across the dunes. "Just, just let me do this."

"You think one life will cancel out all those who have fallen by your side? By your hand?"

"No," Grint admitted. "But maybe it's a start." Hobbe's words to him. They weren't that different after all.

Rent raised his hand as if he were about to pick a piece of fruit from a tree. "You don't want me," Grint continued. "There's a woman on top of the cliff. The one I fought. She'll serve you. She wants to serve you."

"Silence," Rent said. "There are forces at work here that would oppose me if I deterred your path." A smile spread as he bowed his head. Hobbe said something similar. Coming here would cause complications. Rent wasn't Hobbe. Would he invite the opposition? The god watched Grint, eyeing him in a way he never had before.

As he remained silent, Grint took a hesitant step back. Then another. Grint ran up the slope. Rent's words reached out to him as a whisper, "No more games, child. Save the girl or don't, I do not care. But when you're done, you are mine."

Whatever force forestalled the God of Murder wasn't a friend. Grint asked himself the question he often did, "What have I gotten myself into?"

Effulg shone over the island while crimson Nacinth began its intersection. A red tint lit the edge of Effulg, blood from the Stabbing. Arcs of lightning snapped at the sky in an ever-increasing pace. Grint reached the crest of the slope on his hands and knees, careful to stay low as he peeked over the lip. A jagged crater dominated the center of the island, with four concentric ledges ringing it at lower intervals. Crumbling stone buildings sat on the upper ring. Plain architecture built to serve a purpose, not for beauty. Each sat at a point of the compass. No doubt the original inhabitants of the island felt the crater held power. Maybe it did. Maybe that's why the count chose it.

Streams of green fire emanated from the buildings, crackling as they converged on a central point. Necromantic magic, drawn from spirits and deals with demonic forces. The air throbbed, moaning in its vain attempt to crush the unnatural magic. Below the fire, soldiers stood in formation. Wisps of white energy flowed from their backs, rising to the buildings. The count was using his own army to power the ritual. Three hundred, maybe four, all willing to die for his goal. The third ring sat empty, save for a single wooden tower with a plank of wood stretched out, floating on its own. At the end of the plank, directing the streams of emerald flame stood a man in purple robes.

"Danghier," Grint whispered.

The floor of the crater churned with a mass of minor demons. Diminutive creatures with red skin and black horns. Grint's run-ins with the creatures taught him they held little in the way of intelligence. More appeared every moment, pouring through an archway portal activated by the necromantic fire. Hundreds of the little creatures spilled out, rushing toward... Well, Grint wasn't sure what this was. The demons massed at the center, shoving and climbing over one another in their effort to climb two thick pillars. The way they writhed reminded Grint of the corpse abomination. The pillars came together in the shape of a torso, and floating where the center of the chest would soon be, was Lark.

Grint climbed over the lip of the crater and slid down the partial slope on his back. If he stopped the channeling, perhaps he could force the portal shut. How he would do that was anyone's guess, but the lack of a plan never stopped him before. A ten-foot drop waited at the end of the slope. Grint's knees nearly buckled as he jumped down. Moving like a ghost, he crouched in the shadows whenever he could. No one patrolled. No one watched.

The upper ring ran a quarter mile around. Great stones littered the ground, some as large as cottages. Grint had explored many abandoned ruins in his unending quest for riches, but few showed this level of decay. It must have been pre-Zorn, thousands of years old. The complex glyphs carved in the wall confirmed it. Grint had never seen their like.

The ancient ruins provided ample cover for him to get close to the first of the holds. Three robed necromancers sat outside, resting in silence. Their faces sagged, all color drained from their flesh. Each nodded their gratitude as a young page brought water. The magic required for the ritual was killing them too. The count was going all in on his Cheat Me hand. A horn blew within the structure and the page vanished through the darkened doorway. The necromancers stood, shaking and unsteady as they shuffled after the young man. The emerald magic flickered and vanished, then reappeared in the span of a breath. Three different necromancers stumbled outside, collapsing against the wall. *So, they're working in shifts.*

Grint ran the totals. *Six necrolocks per building times four.* Subtlety wouldn't last beyond the first. Once this fire went out, the other groups would be on guard. "Unless they think there was an accident," Grint said trying to convince himself. Rummaging through his bag, he pulled out the wrapped cluster of firejacks. "Four left. Four buildings. It could work."

Nacinth delved deeper into Efflug, the Stabbing wasn't giving him time for careful planning. It needed to happen when they were all together and for that he had to wait for their change. Seconds turned into minutes. Nacinth inched ever on. Grint bounced on his toes, eager to attack. If they didn't move soon, he'd have to... The horn blew and the page came to fetch the three. *Finally.* Grint took the first firejack and threw it in the doorway. As it detonated, he dove behind a curved stone and covered his head. The night inhaled, sucking the air from his chest. Stones shattered as green fire flew everywhere, raining magic that sizzled through the rock. Then came the screams. Grint poked his head over the wall and laughed. The wreckage teetered and slid into the soldiers below, crushing two divisions.

"If I can do that three more times, I'll be dancing by morning."

Grint sprinted, his feet silent in the rough dirt pathways. The demon horde slowed - if only by a hair. The necromantic fires conjured by the remaining necromancers wasn't enough to keep the portal running at its fullest potential, but there were still too many demons coming out. Those in the center climbed on top of one another, screaming as they reached for Lark's feet. Nacinth marched on, unconcerned with the needs of the mortals below. *I can still get the other three buildings,* Grint lied to himself. The truth would crush him if he allowed it to.

"Who's this charffing mutt," a necromancer smoking a long pipe asked as Grint slid to a stop. The whole group at the next post had wandered further from the structure than the last, surprising him. No one raised an alarm. They stood, staring at one another.

"Runner from the third division. Supposed to deliver a message and make sure no one is using magic other than those up top." Grint gestured to the ruined hold.

"Third division?" the necromancer on the left asked.

"We don't use runners, do we? They send orbs?" That was the one on the right. Maybe. With their hoods up, they all sounded the same.

"What's your name?" Middle asked. Grint threw Black blade into the dark shadows of his hood then kicked Left in the groin. Before Right could scream, Grint slammed his forehand into their mouth. With the next firejack in hand, he threw it into the hold and shifted Right's body to take the full brunt of the blast. The hold blew apart, showering the ring in stone and ash. A red light soared high into the sky. Alarm horns blew. Long wails that disrupted the ritual. The hold didn't collapse like the first, forcing Grint to scramble through piles of stone. The doorway was blocked by debris, so he jumped onto a wooden crossbeam and slid through what used to be a second-story window. Cries from the not-yet-dead rose through the rubble. Necromancers longed for death, so let them have it.

Grint ran on, halfway done, just like The Stabbing. If he knew a spell to stop time, he would use it. Lark vanished beneath the swarm of demons who were now forming into arms. The lower half of the creature solidified, shaggy hair sprouting from the red flesh. Giant hooves appeared where feet should have been. It wasn't too late for Lark. She was still somewhere in that mass.

An orb of green fire hit the wall ahead of Grint, throwing him sideways. His antics had drawn Danghier's ire. Grint locked eyes with the count as he got back on his feet. *Do you recognize me? Do you remember me? I promise if you don't now, you will before tonight is through.* Grint gave the count a four-fingered gesture translating to a rude part of Krypsie's anatomy.

Soldiers no longer needed for the ritual climbed onto the top ring. Balls of green fire flew towards Grint, lobbed from necromancers stationed all around the crater. Bolts of magic zipped by in haphazard criss-crossing patterns.

"Focus on the portal, you idiots!" The count screamed for them to re-focus. Grint slugged a soldier, knocking him down, and kicked another in the face before they finished lifting themselves onto the ledge. If he could disrupt just one more of the holds, he could save that last firejack for the count.

Arrows cut through the night, raining everywhere. Grint slid under the arcing wave and screamed in frustration as one of the count's fireballs hit the ground by his feet, igniting his boot. He slapped at the fire, but it refused to go out. The shelf cracked and collapsed, taking Grint down with it. Riding the avalanche, he kept himself on top as the debris rolled through the archers. Hands reached up, begging Grint for help. Their screams cut short as the stones consumed them. Grint rolled onto the third ring stopping at the edge. A hundred angry demonlings snarled and clawed at his feet dangling over the side. At least his boot stopped burning.

Grint scrambled away from the horde with a petrified howl. *Charffing demons!* Destroying the holds was no longer an option. The Stabbing neared completion. Grint took one of the two remaining firejacks and threw it at the portal. *You never know till you try, as Seve used to say.* Destroying the portal could stop the flow of demons. The firejack flew toward its target and stopped. It hovered there then curved to the left. Had it bounced off an invisible barrier? It landed at the base of the tower, obliterating the supports and scores of demonlings massed around it. The tower fell forward, the floating plank crashing into a hundred pieces.

The demonlings were replaceable, more pushed through the viscous fires of the portal every second. He wouldn't try again. The last firejack was for the count. Grint looked for him in the rubble, but he'd escaped the blast and floated atop the growing monster.

"Kill him," The count screamed while the demonlings formed around him. Grint realized, with great horror, that the kry-damned count intended to be the head of this thing.

Soldiers jumped down from the second ring in surging waves. Grint tackled one, driving him back through a doorway carved in the stone. The heavy, wooden door slammed shut as they toppled through. A second soldier banged into it, throwing it open. Grint greeted him with Blackblade, throwing it in his chest before pulling him inside. Intending to use the body to block the doorway.

The first soldier punched him in the back of the head with a gauntleted fist, planting Grint's face into the stone wall. Instead of pressing the attack, he pulled at the body blocking the door. Grint recovered, horse-collaring him, and slamming his face into the dirt.

"What are you making out there?" Grint kept stepped on the back of his head.

"The instrument of your destruction," he laughed.

"Where is the demon lord?"

"What?" the soldier sounded genuinely confused. "The count was never summoning a Lord. He is the Lord! No demon can be above him!"

The soldier was a sycophant believing in the all-powerful Count Danghier, but that didn't mean he was lying. The door shuddered as more soldiers battered it. "How do I stop it?" The soldier opened his eyes in surprise and choked with laughter. Grint stomped his face until the soldier went limp.

Outside, they bashed against the door with relentless abandon, shaking dust loose from the ancient, stone walls. The madmen weren't content to come through; they wanted to take the whole place down. Grint searched for another way out. It was a small space, maybe ten feet by ten with only one exit. The stone sizzled and melted as green fire chewed its way through. A crack appeared and a small spark ricocheted, strobing each time it struck something. Grint dove onto the floor, but a second crack appeared and the fire that came through hit his leg. His leather pants burned, and he slapped at them, burning his fingers in vain.

"Spell scarves," he yelled, slapping a dead soldier on the cheek. Grint pulled one from the bag and doused the flame as the sigils glowed. An axe punctured the wooden door and then a sword. They were coming through. More green fire bounced around. Grint tried hiding under the soldiers, but once they ignited, he had to abandon that idea. Wrapping his face in a scarf, he steeled himself. The green fire kicked like a mule when it hit. He needed to get out of here.

Dying wouldn't save Lark. Wouldn't stop the ritual or Danghier. Dying wouldn't even get him out of the deal with Rent. The God of Murder would yank his spirit back dead or alive. It was last resort time. Grint dug into the bag and pulled out the wax wrapping of Nacinti. *Orrish drug magic? What am I doing?* The red powder was a close cousin to Calystro, but its effects were nastier. Nacinti, like the moon of Nacinth, was fire-based rage magic and as potent as it got. It didn't guarantee he'd get through the soldiers, but he wouldn't feel a thing while he tried.

Are you sure this is what you want to do? That was the old Grint. The one before Eleanor and Kambar and Lark. A Grint unencumbered by emotional connection.

"That's a stupid question," he answered and not because it was too late to turn back.

All Grint needed to do was get through the army, get inside that thing, pull Lark out, and get her to port herself away. No need to take him with her. The withdrawals from the Nacinti would kill him if his wounds didn't. He wished he had Jessua's necklace, some small piece of her in these last moments. Grint put the powder on the end of the blade and inhaled.

The effects were immediate. His blood boiled as liquid fire scoured his body clean of fatigue, injury, and pain. A red tint soaked his flesh followed by the loss of rational thought. Everything receded into his raging desire to accomplish one goal: get the girl.

The door tore apart like parchment. The first soldier through tried to run at the sight of Grint's burning eyes, but the throng of men at his back would not budge. Grint pushed against the surge, the bones of those caught between cracked and shattered. Screams of the dying filled the air as word traveled. Slowly, the pressure lessened. In the open the soldiers circled him, slashing in panicked strikes. Their blades cut the surface of his skin but could penetrate no deeper. Arrows broke against him, leaving the faintest of marks.

A man charged, sword overhead. Grint punched through his chest. It was a blur of carnage. They harried Grint on all sides, but he kept swinging, striking, tearing, and bludgeoning. At one point he picked a dead man up by the ankle and swung him around, taking down a dozen more. The crowd parted for a giant of a man, armored in gold, and carrying a warhammer of bone. He waved the hammer around, laughing as they cheered him on. Grint ran at him.

"Death is the gift lon..." the golden giant said as Grint slapped him across the face with a firejack. The man's head disappeared in a burning blast, and the resulting shockwave sent the rest of the soldiers flying. Grint stood his ground, looking down at the empty space where his right arm used to be. Now it ended above the elbow. It looked to him like someone else's injury, so he paid it no mind.

The way to the wrecked tower was clear. The creature's head had swallowed Danghier, and the Stabbing was moments from completion. Grint ran, his feet dancing on burning wood that collapsed behind him. As he reached the end of the tresses, he jumped into the writhing mass of demonlings. They reached for him, welcoming him into their embrace like a long, lost brother.

19

"There isn't a single person I would put before myself."

- Grint

This wasn't what he expected. Grint stood on a grassy plain that stretched far beyond the horizon. There were no mountains, no trees or dips and rises. Just an endless flat prairie like a millpond on a quiet morning. A breeze brushed across his face, swaying the grass. The sun shined overhead, but it felt neither warm nor cold. Effulg hung low on one horizon. And on the other? *That must have been what Nacinth looked like before it shattered.* Grint stared at the red moon, unbroken and dazzling in its beauty. Yet, something was off about this place. The color of the grass, the deep blue sky, the dirt beneath his boots. The color faded. Grint wouldn't have noticed it had he not first looked at the rich color of... Nacinth moved, its position now beside Effulg, and once more shattered.

"Grint? You came for me!" Lark jumped into his arms. She buried her face in his chest, struggling to wrap her tiny arms around him. Tears soaking through the thin fabric of his shirt. Grint embraced her back, fighting back his own tears.

"I'm sorry about throwing a rock at you," she said, her voice strained after a long cry.

Grint smiled, "I would have thrown a rock at me too. But I wasn't selling you to them."

"I know that," Lark nodded. "Now." She looked around. The sadness in that look would have burned the heart of the coldest man alive. "You shouldn't have come."

"Nothing in Terragard could have stopped me."

"You'll die here." It wasn't a prediction, but a certainty.

"We all die." Grint put a hand on her cheek, too cool to the touch, even though sweat glistened through her dark hair. Wild strands stuck against her forehead and temples. A sallow tone crept into her complexion, washing away her vibrancy the way it had the world around them. Grint traced a thumb across the deep rings under her eyes. They once looked at him so full of wonder. Now they were listless, tired. *Like the day I found her.*

"Besides, you still owe me a lot of money."

Lark's responded with a weak smile and cough. "They're draining me," she said in answer to the question Grint couldn't bring himself to ask. "They're draining you too." Lark grabbed his right hand and held it up. Flakes of skin broke off, floating away like ash.

"I thought I lost this arm," Grint smiled, trying to ignore the truth of the situation.

"You did," she whispered. "This place isn't real."

Grint put two fingers under her chin and lifted her face. "We're not done yet. Let's find a way out of here."

"There is no way out!" Lark pulled away, screaming. "This goes on forever, because we're inside that thing and it's feeding on us."

"Nothing goes on forever." *Buttered bollocks! When did I become so cheerful?*

"This does."

Grint turned in a slow circle, the horizon ever constant. *Maybe she's right?* "Lark? If you're the heart of this, can you control it?"

"No, I'm its food source," she replied. "The control is somewhere else."

"Do you know where? Can you feel it?" Danghier would be the control. He made himself the brain of a dennel-powered demon of gargantuan proportions. If she could find him, they could get out.

"Maybe," she shrugged. "It's like a string pulling on me."

"Follow the string." Lark fought the idea, but Grint put both hands on her shoulders and steadied her. "We've gotten out of worse, right?"

"I would have died if you let them drain all of my blood." It was the first smile in minutes.

"And I would have died if you didn't port us away from Papa Deego."

"I can't make my light here," she said.

"It's okay. Just close your eyes and point the way the string is pulling." Lark nodded, squinting harder as the moments dragged on. Grint looked at his hands, bits of shedding skin danced on the wind. A squeamish feeling overcame him. The haunting echo of Noseless begging for his spirit as Hobbe put him inside the sylph. The way the hound dissolved had too many similarities to this.

"It's there!" Lark said, pointing to her right. Grint scanned the horizon looking for any changes but seeing nothing. "Maybe I'm wrong?"

"No," Grint said. "Look." The smallest speck of purple, no bigger than a pebble hid within the grass.

"It's far," she said, kicking a half-buried stone.

Grint cocked a thumb at his back. "Get on." Lark giggled and clambered up, her feet kicking into his side as she struggled to adjust. This was all a fabrication of the mind, but she felt light on his back. And frail.

The pocket world offered no notions of time. The sun never budged from its midday zenith. Effulg, its constant companion, skulked low on the horizon. The only visible change came from Nacinth. The remnant moon flickered from a shard to unbroken and back again. They ran through the grass for what could have been centuries, never stopping to rest, never needing to eat. The speck grew larger. Lark said it looked like a tower when she could still speak. Her grip faded halfway there, and she almost fell. The last leg of the run he carried her in his arms.

The tower grew on the horizon, sprouting like a weed looking to strangle the world. Clouds swirled overhead, heavenly whirlpools showing a window to the world beyond. "The monster's eyes," Lark whispered. Or did she? Grint couldn't be sure she spoke.

The eyes shifted to Faighur; The mighty dragon dared to stand in the demon's path. Grint yelled at the skies, "Kry-damned fool! Why didn't you stay on the beach? I don't want you to die too!"

When they reached the base of the tower, Grint set Lark in the grass. She tried to lie down, rubbing at her eyes. "I'm tired," she whined.

Grint made her sit up. Fear took root in his chest. Afraid she might disappear if she fell asleep. "I know. Just try."

The black stone tower sat alone in the landscape. A castle turret made of smooth glass. Grint pressed his hand against it, drawn into its reflection of the dying world. The glass sank under the pressure of his palm, but never broke. In a slow trot, he searched the tower, finding no doors or ways inside. There weren't even windows to leap to. All his search revealed: The tower was thicker at the base than the top. Could he trust that? Everything in this place felt like an illusion. Grint gritted his teeth, setting himself to climb. *More heights,* he thought. The smooth surface sank beneath his fingers, providing decent handholds. Grint pulled, pushing his feet in. Hold by hold he climbed. *Don't look down,* Hobbe laughed.

At the summit he found Count Danghier floating, arms spread wide. The necromancer wasn't aware of Grint. He hung catatonic, his eyes rolled back and mouth hanging open. Great strings extended from each of his fingers and whipped in the wind as he jerked them. The demon reacted to his movements. *The Control.* One of the gossamer strands extended past Grint, who leapt up and held on. He imagined Blackblade in his hand, and there it was, but no matter how hard he slashed, the string would not cut.

"Danghier," Grint shouted as he inched his way along the string to its source. "Death is the gift long promised." The barbs in the Count's beards struck out, extending several feet in long whips. They tore into him, but he ignored the pain, reminding himself it wasn't real.

"Are you sure?" Was that the count? It sounded like his oily voice, but his mouth never moved. Grint climbed, trapping the barbs within his body. Excruciating pain screamed like white light and clouded his vision.

"You can never win here," the count said, and this time he was sure it was him.

Grint stabbed Blackblade wildly. On the third attempt, he felt it plunge into flesh. The pain faded, and his vision returned. Blackblade protruded from Danghier's throat. Shuddering, a hideous noise emanated from his mouth, followed by the violent spewing of blood and green fire. The seizure culminated as dust exploded, snowing over him in soft flakes. Grint cheered, but the victory would be short-lived. The dust reformed in a shockwave of energy that threw him from the tower.

Grint landed in the grass, stood, and dusted himself off. The fall should have killed him, but the benefits of this purgatory worked for all of them. Grint climbed again. Killed the count. Fell. Climbed, killed, and fell - over and over. Each time the count reappeared. Each time Grint felt emptier - a little more tired than the last. How many times? Grint lost count. Count. He hated puns, even unintentional ones.

"Stop," Lark said, her voice strangled. Grint pressed his fingers into the tower, getting ready to climb. "Please stop."

Lark lay in the grass, having ignored Grint's request to sit. Could he blame her? How long had he left her there while he fought the count? Fought the count. As if it was ever a fight. Grint stumbled to her side, brushing the hair away from her pale skin. She smiled at him, her lips cracked and eyes fluttering. Grint sat and pulled her head into his lap. As he ran his fingers through her hair, the strands came out in great clumps. Grint looked away. Through the heavenly eyes, he watched Faighur fight. The demon battered his friend. Behind them, the night sky burned with streaks of green fire. It looked like quite a fight.

"I need to stop him," Grint wheezed, too tired to move. "I can stop him."

"You can't," Lark said, her eyes closed. "You can't destroy the mind here, it's too powerful. But I think I know another way."

"I'm open to suggestions." Grint wanted to lie down and close his eyes too. He pulled off his coat. The sun didn't give off any warmth, but he could pretend.

Lark pulled the knife from him. It didn't take much effort on her part. Blackblade looked dark in her tiny hands.

"I tried that, remember? He just keeps coming back."

"Not him," she said as she tapped the blade against her chest.

"No." Even shaking his head took effort. "No!" Lark nodded and tapped her chest again. Grint eased her head from his lap and stood. It cost him everything to do, but he if he stayed with her, he knew he'd relent. The selfish side of his mind whispered. It wanted him to do it. *Keep on living!* Lark didn't move, save for the shallow rise of her chest. Grint trembled as he paced. *When did we become so weak?* The flecks of skin poured off now. How much more did he have? *I'm not a hero.*

His right knee buckled as the joint dissolved. Grint collapsed beside Lark. Her eyes struggled open. "I don't want you to die here."

"Neither of us is dying. I still have to get you back to Thiel."

Lark tried to laugh, but it sounded more like a death rattle. "You know there's no Thiel."

"We have to hang on. Faighur will kill this thing and pull us out." Grint's waved a hand toward the clouds, but the gesture flopped sideways.

"We can't, and he won't," her voice took on a ferocity he never heard before. "Danghier will defeat him, and I'll watch you die. I'll watch as you turn to dust while I remain here, immobile for eternity, staring at a sky full of horrors." She sounded much older. Was it her parent? The part of her dennel blood the god existed in?

"I can't do what you're asking," Grint protested. He thought of his fever dream in the cave. He'd stabbed her in the heart, and it broke the visions.

"I used to dream about you. Chained in the basement. While dying a slow death. I knew one day you would come and rescue me. It made me happy when I woke up to see you. At first, I thought it was just another dream." She went silent, tears streaming from her eyes. "I'm sorry I enchanted you."

"You didn't," through tears of his own.

"At first, I did. Mostly I didn't. It's time."

Grint got on the one knee he had left and lifted the knife over his head. Blackblade shook, so he held it with both hands. It reminded him of that time - in an age gone by - when he contemplated doing this beside a river outside the Terrastags. The memory made him weep and drop his arms. "I can't. I'm supposed to save you!"

"Please," she begged. "Don't leave me like this. I can't move anymore."

"Lark..."

"Kill me," she screamed. Her voice echoed, strong and mighty. Grint found the strength to plunge the knife into her chest. As the world turned white, he found the strength to smile.

*****

Faighur walked the upper ring of the crater. Choosing his steps and avoiding the bodies amid an endless sea of demons and necromancers. Nacinth had passed through Effulg, marking the end of the Stabbing for another cycle. In the final moments of the ritual, the towering demon drew on immense power and prepared its killing blow. Defenseless and beaten, the skinling accepted his fate. And then... Well, then it exploded. The rain of death after the blast burned an indelible, chilling image into his memory that the skinling would carry the rest of his days.

Fashioning a long stick, Faighur found it useful for shoving bodies aside in his search for Grint. The outcome of this evening carnage was undoubtedly the thief's work. Faighur had reached the summit of the crater just as Grint leapt into the mass of demons. Whatever horrors he experienced on this island, he imagined they paled compared with Grint's trapped inside that thing's innards.

Faighur continued the search, even after the sun rose. There seemed little hope his friend survived, but he would not let him spend eternity in this abattoir. He would find his spirit and bring it back to the Red Goat Inn. Grint would hate that, but perhaps love it too.

Along the beach, not far from where Grint left him, Faighur found the first sign of life. A half-naked man sat in the surf. Some madness had befallen the poor soul as he sewed a demonling leg onto the vacant stump where his right arm used to be.

"Grint?" Faighur asked, his tone soft. The man lifted his head, and his tongue lolled under a deluge of spit and blood. What could you say when magic obliterated your lower jaw? *Merciful gods,* Faighur thought. At least it was not Grint.

"Danghier! Where is he?" Calabassus Rent appeared in a rush of darkness and foul wind, and grabbed the count's throat, lifting him above the waves. Danghier could give no answer even if he wanted. Realizing this, Rent alternated between drowning the dying man and strangling him. It was a macabre scene that Faighur wanted no part of.

In the rocky hills on the eastern end of the island, tucked in a small crevice, Faighur discovered the young girl. Only eight or nine by his guess. Carefully, he picked her up and cleaned the blood from her face with water from a skin. It was a wonder, but she still clung to life. Was this the child Grint sought? It gave him hope he may yet find his friend.

"Give her," Rent commanded, standing on a tall rock, flanked by his shadows.

"What is she to you?" Faighur asked, holding her close.

"How dare you question me?" Rent's shadows drew blades of dark ether. Faighur put the girl down and shifted. The massive dragon body poised to protect the child. Rent laughed.

"A skinling dragon? Real dragons hold no challenge for me, what do you imagine you will do?"

Faighur knew he was right. The battle against the demon left him beaten and tired. Even without that, there wasn't a scenario where he could present a challenge to the god. Neither was he prepared to let the God of Murder take the girl. Not after everything Grint sacrificed. It would be a dishonor.

"Move. Or I will move you." Rent's expression expressed a wish for conflict.

- ***Enough, Calabassus Rent, God of Murder.*** -

The ocean roiled. Angry waves crashed against the beach creating fountains of sea spray a mile high. A woman of significant stature rose from the depths, a mile offshore. Lobster-shell armor adorned a body draped in nets. A metal helm rested on her head, but the curved tusks extending in odd directions were a part of her and not an ornamental feature.

"Asper? What business is this of yours?" Rent's tone lost its bite, but he wasn't backing down.

- ***The child is dennel. I am making it my business.*** - The God of Oceans never moved her mouth. The voice echoed in the crash of the waves.

Rent looked at the girl with renewed interest. "Is she now? That's what the fuss is over? A dennel? Is she yours then, Asper?"

- ***No. I warned you to stay away. It is not a warning I shall repeat.*** -

"Who are you to warn me? I am the God of Murder, little fish." Rent's shadows postured with their blades but made no move towards the water.

A wave like no other Faighur ever witnessed rose behind Asper. It grew until it scraped the stars. Such a thing would swallow the island, the land beyond, perhaps the entire world.

- ***What is a thing like murder? Woman killing man. Man killing man. Such meaningless conflicts when held in contrast to the power of the sea.*** -

Rent vanished without another word, and when he did, the wave diminished. When it finally reached shore, it lapped harmlessly against the sand, filling the indentations made by Faighur's feet. Back in human form, Faighur turned toward the goddess.

- ***There is a willen at the Red Goat Inn. He will know where the girl is to go.*** -

"My friend?" Faighur yelled as Asper sank into the brine. She paused with just her eyes above the water.

- ***You will not find any meaningful part of him here.*** -

Faighur wept. When his grief had no further voice, he left. The girl continued to sleep, so he cradled her in his arm and carried her as they flew west. He did not look back at the island but vowed one day he'd return and scorch its existence from the world. The grief threatened to return.

The girl woke by the time they arrived at the inn. At first, the sight of a dragon terrified her, but she calmed once Faighur turned into a man. Her mood changed again when Tin Boots greeted them. Giggling with excitement, she bowled the willen over with a hug. Faighur smiled at the pair, pleased to see his friend. Hobbe had mentioned the willen lived but gave no further details.

"After the skeletons, the tribe decided I wasn't such good luck anymore. Oh well, what's given goes away soon enough. As the big boss always says." Tin Boots drank from a skin of fire rum as they stood beside the old barn. Faighur licked his lips, waiting for a taste.

"I should... I need to tell Alanna and..." Faighur struggled through the words.

"She knows.They all know," Tin Boots said as he handed Faighur the rum with a look of sadness shared between them like the rum.

"I should still..."

"Best if you don't," Tin Boots frowned at the shadows milling around the inn's door. "Not right now. Rent arrived just before you, apoplectic with rage about being cheated. Besides, we have to get this little one to Gorgolath."

The shadows watched them as they waited for their master. That would have been Grint's fate had he survived. "Perhaps you're right."

The first two nights of their journey were quiet. The trio sat around the campfire, pushing food across their plates rather than eating. They were islands in an ocean, each unto themselves, no one speaking or judging when someone broke into tears. And the tears came, sometimes from just one of them, sometimes from all three.

On the third night, they told stories about Grint. Tin Boots, ever the gifted narrator, regaled Lark with yarns to make her smile. "Grint once stole a bottle of whiskey from the God of Bargains." Faighur knew the story well but relived it through the wondrous expressions the girl gave. "The god visited the inn to trade with Blue Fingered Hobbe. A notorious cheater, Maguire was looking to trade a bag of pitted pearls and cracked diamonds for... Well, I don't remember what. While the gods argued, Grint popped out a second-floor window and picked the lock on Maguire's wagon."

"Something everyone thought impossible," Faighur added.

"Not for Grint," Lark smiled.

"No, not for Grint," Tin Boots agreed. "After sifting through piles of assorted junk, he found a slender, black glass bottle and snatched it. We all camped in the barn and got drunk. Hobbe was furious when he found us stumbling around, but later on, when he thought they were alone, he congratulated Grint."

"Always his favorite," Faighur said before breaking into tears.

The stories continued when the tears allowed. Faighur spoke of a time when Grint bought himself a pirate ship, which he ran aground two days later. Lark laughed at that, water shooting from her nose. Before the night ended, she told them of their journey from the Terrastags. The next night, she asked about Jessua. The pair of thieves grew quiet, exchanged glances, and in solemn voices told her about the Girl in White and Poor Dead Tebbs.

When they grew tired of flying, they stole horses from an unguarded tavern. The horses belonged to a trio of thief-catchers who chased them with stubborn doggedness until they abandoned the horses and flew off once more. The bags of silver the thief-catchers had left in the saddlebags went with them.

Twelve days after the Stabbing, they arrived on the sloping plains beside the Gaerus River. The floating island known as Gorgolath drifted in the breeze over the roaring waters. Massive stalactites hung below the island, forming into a singular point. Swirling white clouds obscured the magicians' castle, a conjuration of the weather meant to dissuade intruders.

"It's obnoxious. Who can get up there to disturb them?" Tin Boots said after Lark asked him.

"Milk-sotted Magicai," Lark said, and the thieves laughed.

"They're coming," Tin Boots pointed at four robed men stepping from a breach of light.

"Try not to call them milk-sotted to their faces. I suspect they will get angry," Faighur gave her a wink.

"Do I have to go with them? I'd rather be a thief."

"This life... It isn't what you think," Tin Boots patted her on the shoulder.

"And it isn't what he would have wanted for you." Faighur often felt clueless about Grint's motivations. They changed on a whim or as opportunity dictated, but he felt confident in this one.

"I think you're wrong," she said, a dangerous twinkle in her eye. "He would have thought it good fun."

"You may be right," Faighur smiled.

"Goodbye, Thundering Toad," Tin Boots used her willen name as he kissed her on the cheek.

Lark walked toward the waiting Magicai, but halfway there she stopped and ran back. "I forgot. Last night I had a dream. I saw Grint. He was older and on a farm with a young woman and a jester, and a magician. But also, Jessua was with him. I think he was happy."

"A good dream," Faighur fought against the lump in his throat. "I hope you have many more." *I hope in that place my friend finds what he could not here.*

The three hugged. Lark returned to the Magicai, but this time didn't look back. The tremble in her shoulders told them why. Taking her in their embrace, the Magicai disappeared in a dazzling flash of light. The thieves found it hard to leave and loitered on the slope without speaking. They sat in the tall grass along the river, watching the floating island shift direction, beginning a slow trek south. As day turned to dusk, Gorgolath vanished over the far horizon, speeding against the wind. That was that.

"What now?" Tin Boots asked.

"I would like a dragon's hoard," Faighur said. "I have never had one."

"Can we run the dragon slayer scam you and Grint perfected?"

"No," the skinling said without explanation.

"What? Why charffing not?" The answer must have bothered the willen. He rarely used profanity the way Grint had.

"No one would believe a willen could slay a dragon."

"Give me back my bloody wooden mask and I'll slay you right here. Incant you right into the ground!"

Faighur listened to Tin Boots as they walked, but it was Lark's dream that stuck with him. He hoped that night he might dream of his friend too. See him happy and reunited with Jessua. His friend Grint. The hero.

20

"No good story ends with a dead hero."

- Grave of a dead hero

The crashing waves soothed his aching head as the sun warmed skin that hadn't felt its kiss in a long time. It was a beautiful way to wake up. Sand contoured his back and cradled him in a mother's embrace. After the past few weeks, this was better than he could have imagined. Better than willen healing or the herbs Alanna... When a cold tongue licked his face, Grint waved his arms and sat up.

A fat dog, brown and white with great jowls, ran around him. After each circle it stopped to breathe, wiggle its bum, and lick Grint's face. "Hey now," he said, trying to avoid the latest round of kisses. The dog settled as Grint scratched him. "What's your name, huh?" The bulldog lifted a paw and put it on Grint's right arm. All thoughts of names escaped his grasp.

Nearest he could recall he'd lost the arm. It had disintegrated in a plume of red mist when he slapped a golden soldier with a firejack. *And I inhaled Nacinti.* Grint stood, and the dog rolled onto its back and stretched. Tested his arms and legs to make sure everything worked, he pulled up the thick, brown shirt he wore to look at his stomach. "No scars. No withdrawals from the Nacinti." All in all, quite confusing.

Grint found himself on a beach he couldn't remember coming to. White sand shifted beneath his boots. Behind him, the dunes swept up in thirty-foot swells. Dried grass and cattails crowned ridge. The beach curved north for a half a mile where it ended in a forest of green trees. The southern stretch looked similar, except for a broken stone jetty, thick with barnacles reaching past the surf. An island sat a hundred feet offshore. It was a small thing of sand and rock with a single palm tree hanging over the water. A monkey sat in its shade, watching him with disinterest. The bulldog caught sight of it and barked, darting back as the waves crashed in. Beads of sweat formed under his clothes, and he remembered that the clothes he wore were meant for winter, not the summer's heat.

"Going to call you Newman," Grint said. Newman appreciated the name and jumped on Grint to lick his face. "Alright, boy. No one needs to act like a Baltrudian."

The memories leading up to now were cloudy, disjointed. He'd been in Cattachat. That was where he lost the arm he'd gotten back, and this was not Cattachat. The northern shorelines of Cattachat, Taryn, and Baltrude were harsh places. Lots of stone and little in the way of trees. He recalled an island, but not the monkey's island. Something larger, full of death and green fire. Had there been a yellow field of grass? That made little sense, but he couldn't shake the image. Or the tall, black tower. And the girl dying in the grass.

"Lark?" he said, craning his head around. "Lark!" Grint ran up the beach shouting her name. Memories crashed in like waves, leaving the pain of his choices behind. *Kill me*, she had said. "Lark!" *Kill me.* Kry-damn idiot he was; He did. Grint fell to his knees in the sand and cried out, screaming in rage at the sky. Newman waddled over and laid with his belly in the sand, resting his head on his paws. Grint punched the sand until his energy faded and waved the dog over. Newman leaned against him, licking the tears from his cheeks. This time, Grint let him.

When he settled, he decided to climb the dunes and look west. Nothing but wetlands filled with long-legged white birds and herds of deer. An alligator floated along, waiting for a chance to feed. Thick forests obscured the horizon beyond with little to show in the way of landmarks. *Is this Golganna? Somewhere further south, like The Keeps?* There had been a white light at the end. Did Lark send him here? Did she send them both?

"Lark?" the white birds took wing, and the deer scattered, but there was no sign of the girl.

Newman ran around the beach, digging and barking at something in the sand. Grint slid down the dune, feeling ill, imagining Lark buried there. The bulldog bit onto something and pulled, grinning happily as Grint ran up. "Let me see," he said, and Newman deposited it at his feet. The hilt was one he had become comfortable with, but the blade of the large knife had become twisted and scorched. Blackblade was a ruin of its former self.

"I liked this knife," he said and then shouted, "Lark!" at the monkey.

"She's not here," Hobbe answered. Grint spun around, brandishing the wrecked knife like a fool. "You planning to scratch me to death?"

Hobbe looked happy to see him, the way someone does when they haven't seen you in a long time. Grint lowered the knife, thinking to put it in his belt, but tossed it aside. Newman ran after it and brought it back. Grint waved him away, so he laid down and gnawed on the hilt.

"It's good to see you, boy."

"Where's Lark?"

"Safe. Alive. She's been with the Magicai. Is a Magicai. The youngest student who ever achieved the rank of Wizen." The waves crashed as Grint processed that information. *She has been with... rank of Wizen...*

"There's a lot I don't know about the Magicai," Grint said, piecing it together. "Doesn't it take decades to become a Wizen?"

Hobbe squinted and averted his eyes. "Maybe we should sit down." Two chairs appeared in the sand. Grint sat, unsure where the thief master was taking this. Hobbe pulled a large beef sandwich from under his chair, the juices running through the meat soaked into the cuts of bread. "I expect you're hungry." Grint felt ravenous and took the sandwich as his stomach rumbled. Not wanting to miss out, Newman left the knife and settled his head in Grint's lap, waiting for a taste.

"As you know, gods play games." Hobbe laughed at the look Grint gave him. "Not the ones you've come to, uh, love from me. Or Rent. There are gods, powerful gods, who get bored every century or two and use the world as their gameboard. Daemar, Asper, Lorelai. Krypholos used to join in before he got funny."

"This was... This was a game?" The last half of the sandwich dropped from his hands and into Newman's mouth.

"Parts," Hobbe admitted. "I'll be honest, I don't know everything they were up to, but it led to that island and whether or not they could start a dark age."

"And you sat back and let it happen?"

"Open your eyes," Hobbe snapped. "When you fell in their path, I did what I could. I put you in the pocket of a god they wouldn't cross. It wasn't perfect, and it caused you grief, but I had hoped it would stop them from meddling with you."

"How far back does this go? Rent chased me for a year before Eleanor."

"Long before that." Hobbe pulled out another sandwich and a mug of amber ale from his reserves at the inn. Grint wanted to take it, but something pulled at him, making him feel cold.

"You keep saying these things like they're ancient history," Grint said. "It went back years. Lark became a Wizen. I left her a few hours ago. What aren't you telling me?"

"You didn't just leave her." Hobbe squirmed in his chair and offered the ale again. Grint took it and drank. Something told him he would need it. "When it ended, it ended bloody. The necromancers died, and Lark lived. But you were... well, she sent you to a place none of us knew existed." Grint spit out the ale.

"Took a fair bit of time to figure that out, but I sifted through the wreckage of the island until I did. Asper helped a bit. I think she felt bad. I traded a bauble here and a promise there. Used leverage where I had to. Finally, Daemar took me to her brother, Fenter who made me a device to retrieve you and put you back together."

"Was I dead?" Grint felt the world tilting.

"Not dead. Not alive. The dennel magic transported you to a limbo outside of time."

"How long, Hobbe?"

"It took me seventeen years to make this moment happen," Hobbe admitted with tears in his eyes. Grint sprang from the chair and ran to the water. He fell on his hands and knees and vomited that tasty sandwich. Newman barked at him, distressed at his sickness and salty about the wasted food.

"Seventeen years?" Grint trembled as he stood. "Seventeen?" Hobbe patted him on the shoulder. "Lark grew up. Does she know I'm alive?"

Hobbe shook his head. "No one outside of me and the other I mentioned. And Rent. I told him. He won't bother you again."

"How did you manage that? More leverage?"

"The sylph you boys stole had a spirit inside he wanted more than you."

"And what of Faighur? Tin Boots?" Hobbe gave him a sympathetic look. Grint choked on the burgeoning lump in his throat. It's what you did when someone gut punched you.

"Tin Boots was about ten years ago. Thief-catchers from an upstart group called the Brine Batch."

Tin, you kry-damn fool, why did you get back into the life?

"Faighur lost himself in the dragon-side. The dragon king killed him over territory."

"The others? Bakka? Veselli? Mappy? Chambers?" Grint had lost a lifetime in just seventeen years. It seemed so small and yet stretched like an ocean of time.

"Brotherhood Knights, Ropes, salt witches."

"I'm the last."

"If you're thinking you won the Last Man Wager you all made; Mappy claimed it a few years back." Hobbe laughed, a soft sad sound from a father who'd lost all his children. Grint couldn't help but feel the first spark of pity and love for the god he had in years... Decades. "Come back to the inn, Alanna will cover you with kisses." Grint smiled at the offer, but the horizon called.

"I think I need to find my feet," he said. Hobbe nodded. He understood.

"If you need anything, you know where we are." Hobbe started walking away but then turned and flipped a gold coin. Grint snatched it from the air and looked down at it. "It's from the winners. For services rendered, they said. Throw it in the ocean if you want or give it to the monkey, but if you're open to suggestions, there's a town about half a day through the forest with a tavern full of bad gamblers. Oh, and the bulldog is from me. Been training him for you. Figured you could use a friend. He'll follow you to the ends of the world."

"Hobbe?" The god cocked his head, waiting for the questions. "Who made Lark?"

"She didn't join in the whole mess, but it was Myralee." Goddess of Hope. That made Lark a little sister to Zorn.

"And the game? What did they win?" Hobbe shrugged in response. Some things even he didn't know.

The God of Thieves vanished, leaving Grint and Newman to find their way. Good to his word, there was a town through the woods. They reached it by the time the sun was setting, and walking was a tiring business. Grint went straight to the inn. The placard out front had a dog's tail holding a mug with the name Wag the Grog. Newman growled at it, earning a scratch. "Good dog. Puns are bad."

Like most rural inns, the common area doubled as a tavern. The server, a dark boy with a quizzical look came by with a tray full of mugs. Grint availed himself of one. "Hey now," the boy squawked. Grint drained the mug and put it back on the tray.

"Send another grog over to the card table. And get me a room with bath privileges. I haven't bathed in seventeen years."

"That all costs coin, mister."

"Grog now, bath later. I'll have the coin by the time the bill is due." The far table had a game of cards in full tilt. Cheat Me. Grint laughed at the poetry of it. An empty chair called his name, and he pulled it over from the neighboring table.

"Table is full," a mean-looking man with a thin mustache said. Grint took out the gold galleon and rolled it across the top of his hand. All eight players eyed it with great anticipation.

"Jaymes, I think we can allow one more," a beautiful young woman with chocolate skin said. She'd be trouble. Just the kind Grint loved. Newman laid down beneath his chair and started snoring.

When the cards fell, and the dice rang out, Grint smiled. It wouldn't take long to fill his pockets. He could go most anywhere from here, ride north into the hedge kingdoms or hire a boat south and find a job in Rhysin. *No,* he though. First, he'd pay Lord Ballastrine a visit. Beat him black and blue and drain his blood into a kry-damned urn. And if a privy was close by... Well, the possibilities were endless.

"What's funny?" the woman asked.

"Nothing. Just finding I enjoy poetry." Grint picked up his cards, two howling dogs, and tossed the gold coin into the pot. "Let's gamble!"

GRINT WILL RETURN

IN

ALL THE GOLD

What's worth more to a thief? Gold or friendship?

Notorious thief, Grint is only too happy to work alone. Partners and friends require trust, and that only leads to a knife in the back.

Nazarra is an accomplished fighter and commander of the Royal Guard, but has lost sense of who she is, burdened by the weight of protecting her sister's crown.

Chell is a defeated warchief, sent from his lands in search of an atonement that will return him to his former glory.

At the center of it all is a sea of gold so vast as to inspire legends. When Grint stumbles across the glittering hoard beneath a manor he's robbing, his simple snatch-and-grab job turns into a heist for the ages.

But plans don't always go as intended. What is set in motion will unearth a dastardly plot to unseat the queen, revealing betrayals and introducing new friends. When their three paths come crashing together, it will threaten to tear asunder the very foundations of the city and change each of their worlds forever.

What's worth more than all the gold? Duty? Atonement? Friendship?

ABOUT THE AUTHOR: D.S. TIERNEY BY GRINT

So how does this work? I just tell you? Okay.

D.S.Tierney is the scribe who first wrote about me in 2012 when I robbed the *Seventh Tower* along The Papality's pilgrimage trail. There was a demon involved. And a Rope. Bad business. You can read about it on the *Aphelion* webzine. I have no charffing clue what a webzine is, but there you go.

I think he was a bard before that, writing mummer shows and performing in them. Yeah, kind of like a jester without the monarchy nonsense involved.

There's also the podcast about Terragard. It's called ***Terragard Tales.*** Stories from around the world. None about me yet. I guess I'll have to steal more stuff to get a story on there!

He lives in Boston, MA but also has a web address: www.dstierney.com

Web address? Webzine? Is he a spider? Gross. Okay, that's good? Great, time for an ale. No. No, I didn't pickpocket you. I will not empty my pockets. Let's not be hasty. No need to call a Brotherhood Knight into the room...

NEWMAN TIERNEY

I always wanted a bulldog.

We got Newman as a puppy; Around the same time I created Terragard. I remember him watching as I painted the first map on my corkboard. Back then he liked to bite feet. Made for interesting writing sessions!

Newms liked to lay on a little blue bed in my old office, watching me write. That's where he was when I penned *Seventh Tower* - my first story featuring Grint. And there when I wrote *Salt Run.*

His place by my side never wavered as I struggled through the first draft of this book. He knew when I needed a break and would make me put the laptop down so he could crawl in my lap. By my side. Newman was there when I finished *Dark Ages* and when I started *Terragard Tales.* Sometimes he liked to come down and talk while I recorded. I got annoyed at the time. Stupid.

We lost Newman shortly before this publication. It broke our hearts. Shattered them.

In every other draft, the dog at the end was named Yap. I changed it to Newman and made him a bulldog. Maybe that's a selfish author thing to do. I don't care. I'd give anything to have him back. But I can't. So I gave him to Grint. I know they'll watch out for one another. Until we meet again.

Connect with

D.S. TIERNEY'S
WORLD OF TERRAGARD™

www.DSTIERNEY.com

World.of.Terragard

/worldofterragard

@dstierney1

World of Terragard

@d.s.tierney

/terragard

D.S. Tierney

YOUR ADVENTURES IN TERRAGARD DON'T END HERE!

Terragard Tales tells new stories full of exciting action, intrigue, and magic! Each story features new characters, monsters, locations and journeys spanning the world of Terragard and its history.

The Terragard Tales Audiodrama Podcast is available everywhere podcasts are found.

iTunes - Google Play - Stitcher - Spotify - Amazon
www.dstierney.com/podcast

Season 1: The Lunar Sundering - Available Now!

Season 2: Gods & Monsters - Available Now!

Season 3: The Longest Tale - Coming Soon!

Made in the USA
Monee, IL
25 May 2024